THE ADVENTURES OF ÜBERGIRL

- BOOK #1 -

MY DAD IS A MAD SCIENTIST

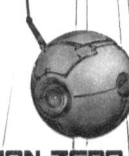

DIVISION ZERO PRESS
WWW.MATTHEWCOXBOOKS.COM/WORDPRESS

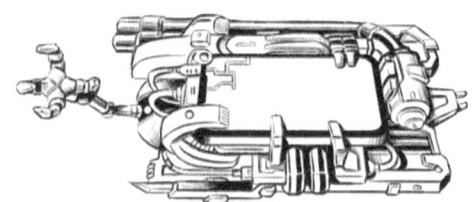

My Dad is a Mad Scientist
The Adventures of Übergirl
Book One

Cover and interior art by: Ricky Gunawan

ISBN (ebook): 978-1-950738-02-1

ISBN (paperback): 978-1-950738-03-8

CONTENTS

CHAPTER ONE

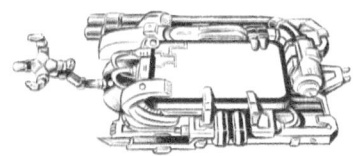

Nobody.

At least, if anyone ever bothered to ask Kelly Donovan who she was, she'd have said nobody. If someone asked Alexis Stephens, California's most perfect fifth-grader, who Kelly was, she'd likely have answered with 'turd,' 'four-eyes,' or 'noodle-butt.'

Kelly's parents had accused her on multiple occasions of being kinda smart. It certainly didn't help her social standing at school that she'd skipped forward and wound up the smallest kid in fifth grade at only nine years old.

This, of course, made her somewhat of a target for Alexis and her little group of popular girls.

Kelly stopped a few steps away from the doors at the end of the hall, clutching her backpack strap tight in both hands. Other kids streamed around her on both sides, eager to get out of school and enjoy the rest of the day. She stared down past her denim skirt at the red-and-white striped tights covering her noodly legs. New purple sneakers—her favorite color—made her feet look too big on her body. Dad got the bright idea to buy slightly-too-large shoes so they'd last longer. Just another thing for Alexis and her friends to tease her about.

A boy bumped her by accident, muttered an apology, and hurried out the door.

She wanted to leave school and enjoy the rest of her afternoon, too, but this moment represented one of the two biggest pain points of her day: arriving at school and leaving it. Alexis and her friends occasionally messed with her during lunch, but not a day passed where they didn't do *something* after school. On good days, she only had to duck a box of chocolate milk or something slimy flying at her. Dad suggested trying to ignore them and they'd stop, but that hadn't worked.

Sighing, Kelly slung her backpack off her shoulder and opened it, tucking the comic book she'd been carrying inside. She just *knew* Alexis and the others would be waiting for her at the bottom of the steps. Bad enough they would torment her, but she didn't want them ripping up *Star Prince #17*. Dad still hadn't told her mother how much that one cost due to it being rare. Honestly, she should have left it at home. Not like she could ask Alexis to leave it alone because of its value. That would only make the girl deliberately *try* to mess it up.

She zipped the backpack, slung it over her right shoulder, and sighed again.

"Might as well get it over with."

Head bowed, face hidden behind her fluffy red hair, Kelly Donovan—aka Nobody—trudged out the doors of John Q. Petersen Middle School and went down the stairs. The school district had recently decided to move fifth grade into the middle school due to space limitations. She had hoped being in 'big kid school' would've given Alexis something else to worry about other than bothering her. Alas... about all that really changed was having to run a gauntlet between different classrooms every period instead of staying in the same room all day long, more opportunities for Alexis—or her group—to mess with her.

A line of school buses waited off to the right near the huge sidewalk. Kids ran back and forth heading to buses or parents waiting in the pick-up lane. Some headed off on foot if they lived close enough, like Kelly. Her house sat two blocks over six blocks up from the school, a short walk. A shorter walk if she took the direct route which involved three backyards and a tree swing.

The instant her new purple sneaker hit the sidewalk at the bottom of the steps, someone moved in front of her. Kelly didn't have to look up to know who got in her way. The black ballet flats on the perfectly-suntanned feet may as well have been a name tag.

"Hi, Alexis," said Kelly, still looking down.

Four hands, two per bicep, grabbed Kelly from either side.

"Hi, Brittany. Hi, Colleen."

A third pair of hands from behind administered the expected wedgie.

"Hi, Rachel," muttered Kelly, once she stopped cringing.

"Where do you think you're going?" asked Alexis Stephens.

"Just home. I don't have as many friends as you."

"Correction. You don't have *any* friends." Alexis giggled, as did the other three girls. "Aww. That's so sad."

"Maybe you should go back a grade with kids your own age," said Brittany Chang, presently holding her left arm.

"Naw." Colleen Brandt shook her by the right arm. "Smarty McSmartpants is too good for that."

Kelly continued staring at her sneakers.

"Aww, she's sad," sing-songed Brittany.

"Gonna cry now?" Colleen squeezed her bicep as if testing it. "I think her arms are even skinnier. I've seen spaghetti bigger than this."

"Please leave me alone." Kelly tried to twist away from the two girls holding her, but they wouldn't let go.

The girls laughed.

Alexis plucked Kelly's glasses off, making anything more than five feet away turn into a blur. "Wow, Donovan. These are thicker than Mike Hopkins."

"Give them back!" She tried to grab for her glasses, but couldn't reach with Colleen holding her right arm. "And Mike's not stupid. He's just lazy."

"Aww." Alexis leaned back, waving the glasses over her as if teasing a dog with a treat.

Fortunately, she got bored with that fairly soon when Kelly didn't try to grab them. Smirking, Alexis tossed them at her chest. Kelly managed to catch them before they fell.

Her backpack unzipped. "What'cha got here, noodle-butt?" Rachel McMeadows, Alexis' best friend, reached into her bag.

"Stop. That's my stuff!" Kelly put her glasses on and struggled in earnest, grunting, but having two girls bigger than her holding her arms kept her right where Alexis wanted her.

"Hmm. Math. Spelling… *Booo-ring.*" Rachel tossed textbooks aside one by one into the grass.

"Stop! Please leave me alone." Kelly squirmed. She almost broke her self-imposed rule and screamed for help, but that would only make the girls tease her worse. It's what they wanted: for her to break down and start yelling for a teacher like the little kid they all thought she was. If she caved in and did that, they'd know they could break her and they'd only give it to her worse. She clenched her jaw and kept on fighting, though couldn't get away from the larger eleven-year-olds.

"Ooh, what do we have here?" Rachel pulled *Star Prince #17* out of her backpack. "Eww. A comic book? Oh. My. *Gawd.* You are *such* a nerd, Donovan."

Colleen giggled. "It's probably for her *boyfriend*. Girls don't read comic books."

Alexis glanced off to the side, surprisingly not saying anything or even smiling.

"Noodle-butt with a boyfriend? Are you serious?" asked Brittany.

"Of course not," said Colleen. "Don't be ridiculous."

All four of them laughed.

Kelly struggled to twist around, reaching for the comic back. "No! Please don't. My dad will kill me if…" She bit her lip. If she dared finish that thought and speak the dreaded words 'anything happened to it,' the $300 comic would surely be destroyed.

"If what?" asked Rachel, flapping the comic. "It must be special. It's in a plastic bag."

Kelly struggled harder. "I put them *all* in plastic protectors. Please. Get off. Stop."

"Open it," said Brittany. "What's so special about it?"

"It's just a stupid comic book." Alexis rolled her eyes and tossed a lock of her perfect, straight blonde hair behind her ear. "Only nerds and losers read comic books." She looked off to the side, not making eye contact with anyone.

"Which is why Donovan has one, obviously." Colleen overacted a sigh.

Paper fluttered behind her.

Kelly strained to peer back, dreading what she'd see… but Rachel merely had the book open, looking at it.

"It's just pictures of stupid people in stupid outfits doing stupid things." Rachel shook her head. "Why would anyone want this junk?" She tossed the comic into the wet grass.

"No!" screamed Kelly, finally at the verge of crying. "Don't ruin it! It's rare and cost a lot of money! My dad's gonna kill me. That's *Star Prince #17!*"

Alexis sucked in a little bit of air.

"So stupid." Colleen laughed. "What kind of idiot would waste so much money on stupid cartoon books? I thought you were supposed to be like a brainiac or something, Donovan?"

"Rachel," said Brittany in a fake scolding tone. "You know better than to litter on school property."

"Oh! I'm so sorry!" Rachel ran over to grab the comic. Humming victoriously, she jogged toward the giant black garbage can near the front doors, containing the toxic aftermath of today's cafeteria science experiments.

"Stop! Rachel. Don't! Please! That's *Star Prince 17!* Only 5,000 were ever printed." She kicked and squirmed, fighting so fiercely Brittany and Colleen lifted her completely off the ground, feet pedaling at the air. This, of course, only made them laugh.

Rachel held the comic over the trash can with two fingers, glanced back at Kelly with an 'I win' smirk, and opened her fingers, allowing the comic to fall into the trash can. Almost as an afterthought, she tossed the empty plastic protector in after it.

Defeated, Kelly hung limp in her tormentor's grasp, and screamed.

"C'mon. Teachers are gonna hear the little turd yelling," said Colleen.

"Wait." Alexis held up one finger. "I have a better idea. She wants to take her book and go home. Let's help her go home. Right down The Hill."

Kelly shivered. The Hill ran along the entire left side of the school, a giant grass-covered slope that made for epic sleigh riding in the winter. Unfortunately, it also made for less-than-epic trash can rides once or twice a month for her.

"Ooh," chimed Brittany and Colleen together.

They started dragging her toward the garbage can. Kelly set her heels on the sidewalk, fighting as hard as she could to resist, but the girls simply picked her up off her feet again. Being small, super skinny, and two years younger certainly did not count as advantages.

The girls hauled her into the air and stuffed her headfirst into the trashcan, burying her in a stinky mess of orange juice, half-eaten spaghetti, mashed potatoes, and some green stuff she couldn't recognize. A splash of chocolate syrup hit her on the left cheek the same time she plunged face first into a mass of nacho cheese sauce.

She struggled to right herself, but slipped deeper into the can when the older girls dragged the giant plastic container of horror across the front of the school and tipped it over sideways. One of them kicked it squarely on the side, sending it rolling down the enormous grass hill. All manner of liquids, slimes, and solids soaked into her clothes as she spun over and over and over. Her—albeit minuscule—weight pressed into the side, turning rolling into progressively bigger bounding. She did her best not to scream. Opening her mouth would be... flavorful.

After the tenth bounce, Kelly flew out of the can in a spray of trash, but kept rolling for a little while more until she came to a sliding stop against the chain link fence surrounding the athletic field behind the school.

"Turd all the way to the fence!" shouted Brittany. "One thousand points!"

Kelly sat up and pulled her chocolate-syrup-soaked hair off her face. Chocolate milk had splashed all over her shirt. Mustard smeared her skirt and leggings all down her right side. A blob of spaghetti fell from her shoulder into the grass with a *splat*. Four girl-shaped blurs at the top of the hill patted each other in congratulations before walking off. Girl-shaped blurs meant that her glasses had disappeared somewhere between trashcan entry and fence contact. She peeled a half-eaten French fry off her forehead and tossed it aside.

Desperate, she scrambled around investigating various blurry objects until she finally found *Star Prince #17*, and held it a few inches in front of her face so she could see it. The precious book had been mildly crinkled and stained with spaghetti sauce, soda, and strawberry ice cream. She sank to sit in the grass, head bowed, and wept.

Stupid. Stupid. Stupid. Why did I bring this to school?

Having something to do for the three-quarters of math class she expected to be idle—due to finishing the test first—wasn't worth the disappointment that would be all over Dad's face when he saw it destroyed.

Already, in her imagination, he called her irresponsible for taking such an expensive comic to school. He'd be hurt that she'd been so careless with something like that, and probably would never trust her again with any real responsibility.

A glint in the grass not far from where she sat turned out to be her glasses. Those, at least, hadn't been broken—but they did have a coating of nacho cheese sauce. She cleaned them as best she could with her fingers, wiped her hand in the grass, and put them on.

The plastic lenses brought the mutilated comic into great and tragic detail.

She hung her head, and sighed. "I hate school."

A little more looking around later, she found the clear protector in the grass, completely pristine, not even one crease. In a complete fit of irony, she decided not to put the book in the plastic sleeve to keep the *plastic* clean.

No one remained in front of the school by the time she finished trudging back up the hill—only a lingering haze of bus exhaust. She collected her textbooks from the wet grass, stuffed them in her backpack, and dragged herself home, carrying *Star Prince #17* in her hand… to keep her books free of spaghetti sauce.

CHAPTER TWO

MOM, YOU AREN'T HELPING

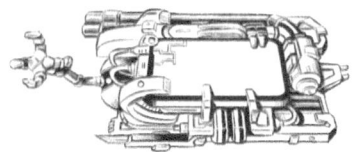

Much like the comic book characters Kelly loved, her mom had superpowers.

She had the uncanny ability to sense unfinished homework, un-picked-up clothes, un-brushed teeth, and last (and most annoying), she always sensed when her daughter wanted to be alone—so she could rush over to ask what was wrong. Or, like today, be standing right in the front hall as soon as Kelly walked inside.

"What happened, sweetie? You're late," said Mom in that overly sweet voice she always used whenever she sensed a problem. "Oh, my. You're a mess."

Kelly hid the comic behind her back. "I stepped on a banana peel."

Mom smirked. "You stay right there."

While her mother ran off to the kitchen, Kelly looked around for a quick hiding place. She stashed *Star Prince #17* in the umbrella can, moved Dad's giant black umbrella to hide it, then waited patiently for her mother to return with damp paper towels.

Mom's other major superpower involved the ability to sense the tiniest amount of dirt from across the house. She wiped at Kelly's face, hair, and arms, attacking the goopiest stains first. "Honestly, sweetie. How did you get chocolate sauce in your *hair*? There's nacho cheese all over your back." She gasped.

"The banana peel was right next to a trash can. I fell in it… and went rolling down the hill."

"Your new sneakers…"

"They're waterproof. Just need to be wiped."

Mom continued to fuss over her. "Sweetie, those other girls won't tease you forever. Once you're done with eighth grade, you'll probably never see them again."

"Eighth grade? That *is* forever." She flapped her arms. "I don't wanna keep going to school. Can't you just teach me here?"

"You know I work, hon. Besides, you need social interaction."

Kelly reached up with both hands, pulling her hair away from her face like a theater curtain opening. "No, Mom. I don't. I've had enough social interaction for a lifetime."

"Aww, sweetie. You've never been shy before."

"I'm not shy. I'm just allergic to trash cans."

Mom took the nacho-stained glasses off her and brought them to the kitchen sink for cleaning. "I don't understand why those girls bother you, sweetie. You're adorable. Certainly not even close to fat."

"Ugh. No, Mom. I'm a noodle." Kelly followed her to the kitchen and held her arms up. "I have pasta for arms and legs. They call me noodle-butt."

Mom rinsed the glasses clean, dried them, then slid them back on her. "That'll pass. I was the same way at your age."

"You are still skinny."

"Why thank you, sweetie." Mom patted her on the head. "I just don't understand why they tease you."

Kelly pointed at herself. "Because I'm a nerd, Mom. I'm nine years old in fifth grade. I like comic books and drawing and I *like* math. A kid who admits to liking math has their head shoved in a toilet while someone flushes it at least once a month. I don't play with dolls or care about makeup or fancy clothes. School is the ocean. Alexis is a shark, and I'm wearing a chum suit."

"Aww, it's not that bad. You're way too cute to be a nerd."

Kelly sighed at the floor.

"Give me that backpack so I can wipe it down. You go right upstairs and take a bath. Those clothes go *straight* to the hamper."

"Yes, Mom." Kelly shrugged the backpack off and handed it over before running down the hall to the foyer, snagging *Star Prince #17* from the umbrella pail, and dashing upstairs.

For the most part, Kelly Donovan behaved herself, did her work, obeyed her parents and—more or less—cleaned her room when told. She didn't lie often, but if Dad asked about the comic book, she'd probably come real close to fibbing for at least a little while. Change the subject, vague answers, or… something.

She sprinted to the bathroom, set the book on the sink, and proceeded to dab at it with a wad of toilet paper in a mostly futile attempt to soak up the spaghetti sauce and soda stains. The cover had taken the brunt of it—bad enough—but the soda had gotten to the edges, affecting every page. Seeing the true extent of the damage almost made her cry again, not for the loss of the object, but for how much it would hurt Dad to find out she'd been so dumb. He loved comic books, too. And giving her this one as a pre-birthday present— her tenth birthday wouldn't happen until next August—had been a weak excuse because he wanted to get it that badly for her. Years down the road, when she'd grown up, it could have become worth a lot of money.

And she'd destroyed any possible value it had. No collector would offer fifty cents for it now.

While doing her best to save the unsavable comic book, she daydreamed about throwing Alexis headfirst into a trash can. Even if Kelly had superpowers like Ms. Omni—Star Prince's girlfriend—she probably wouldn't do that. Alexis enjoyed making other people miserable. Kelly didn't.

She carried the wounded comic back to her bedroom, grabbed an old, battered protector sleeve to put it in, and hid it under her mattress. The still-clean protector it had come in, she put in her top left desk drawer. That sleeve had once held an important relic, now ruined due to her being dumb. She couldn't put a lesser comic in it, so it would be either a shrine to the fallen or a badge of shame depending on her mood at any particular moment.

With little more to do for the book, she grabbed a clean purple T-shirt and jean skirt from her dresser, then headed down the hall to the bathroom. As if having a priceless—well, expensive and irreplaceable—well, rare as heck and hard to replace—comic ruined wasn't bad enough, having to take a bath so early in the day felt like Alexis had followed her home and kept on laughing at her.

Still, she didn't enjoy being covered in the disgusting smell of school trash.

So, she dealt with taking a bath.

After cleaning up and changing, she trudged to her bedroom—hair wrapped up in a towel—and flopped on her bed, chin in her hands, feet up, reading *Star Prince #56*, the newest one.

"Doctor Fix's Mendy-ray could clean the crud outta issue seventeen and make it like new." She banged her head over and over again into her soft bed while muttering, "Dad's gonna kill me."

CHAPTER THREE

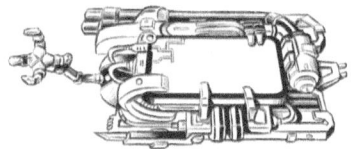

WEDGIES ARE FOR BEGINNERS

On normal days, Kelly didn't usually spend the *entire* day in her bedroom unless it rained.

She had homework to deal with, but not that much. Depending on the subject, her schoolwork ranged from 'not bad' to actually fun. Most of the other kids all complained about the 'vast amounts' of work heaped on them by cruel teachers. Kelly didn't think they gave out too much work. In fact, more often than not, she wanted the teachers to assign *more*… because she ran out.

Maybe that's why Alexis picks on me.

With a groan, she climbed off her bed, sat at her desk, and got started on her homework.

On normal days, she'd finish it in an hour or so, then either read for fun, use up some of her daily allotment of video game time—Mom limited her to one hour on school days—or go outside. They had a huge yard with a swing set, sadly no pool, but playing outside kinda sucked alone. Frisbees and soccer balls didn't work too well for a kid with no friends. She did, however, enjoy exploring other people's yards. Not snooping on anyone, merely treating her neighborhood as an adventure course: navigating fences, tables, trees, sheds, and so on while picturing herself as a superheroine making her way deep into a mastermind's lair.

Sometimes being a living noodle *did* help. She weighed so little, it didn't take much strength to pull herself up. She easily climbed fences and trees, or squeezed into narrow passages behind garden sheds. Most of her neighbors didn't mind, though the old couple at the end of the block complained to her parents, so she couldn't go in their yard anymore. Fortunately, Dad believed her about the ruined flowerbed. She really had no idea what happened to it. Neither did Mr. and Mrs. Stewart... so naturally, they blamed her.

Guilt over the destruction of the expensive comic took away any urge she had to do anything but hide in her room. Unfortunately, Mom could always read her moods. She had a way with people like that, always seeming to be able to tell how someone felt. Her father, also a giant comic geek, often joked that Mom abused her powers for evil purposes, having gone into sales rather than like counseling, therapy, or psychology to help people.

Her father's superpower would have to be time compression. Whenever he got into something he enjoyed, he could just sit there for hours and hours, losing track of time. This usually took the form of hobbies: painting miniatures, building model mecha, or something along those lines. He liked making stuff with his hands. Probably a side effect of his boring office job. It apparently provided plenty of money—which is why he still worked there— but his secondary superpower had to be weaponized feelings of inadequacy. Whenever he started complaining about other people at work getting promoted while he remained in whatever role he'd been in for the past eleven years, it made people leave the area. As superpowers went, not exactly a tier one.

Kelly couldn't help herself and finished her homework in fifty-two minutes. If she tried to stay hidden in her room all day and blamed a ton of homework, Mom would smell the lie. Kelly never took that long to finish her homework. If she sat in her room all day reading, Mom would still know something happened. If Kelly tried to act normal, Mom would *still* know she wanted to hide something.

That left only one choice: avoid contact at all costs.

She pulled on her socks and sneakers, then ran outside. Still too upset over *Star Prince #17*, she couldn't bring herself to pretend-infiltrate an enemy lair. Without imagining any laser trip mines or pressure plate traps or monsters, Kelly simply climbed a couple fences and hid in the narrow space behind Mr. Hollister's garden shed, arms wrapped around her legs, face hidden behind her huge floof of red hair.

Wasting a whole afternoon sulking didn't happen often, and when it did, it almost always traced back to Alexis Stephens. The last time Kelly had wanted to avoid everyone that bad had been a little over a year ago when Alexis had snuck up behind her in gym class and yanked her shorts down in front of everyone. To make matters worse, Ms. Farris, the gym teacher, hadn't been looking at the time and yelled at *Kelly* for not pulling her shorts back up faster. How the teacher hadn't noticed Alexis stepping on them, she couldn't explain.

Shame over being stupid enough to take such an expensive, delicate thing to school—straight into the danger zone—eventually gave way to her feeling dumb for just sitting there doing nothing for most of the afternoon.

She made her way home, slipped in the back door past Mom in the midst of cooking dinner, and flopped down in the living room at her MegaStation 4 to fire up the newest *Star Prince* game, *The Trials of Tabrin*, which had come out a couple months ago. She liked this one because it gave players the choice of using either Star Prince or Ms. Omni as the player character.

Before she started playing, she wrote down the time on the small dry-erase board Mom kept there to log video game hours. Her mother most likely decided to limit her screen activity so strictly because of Dad. In the years when her parents dated, he'd often waste entire weekends playing games. Mom had a thing about 'too much video game time.' She didn't want Kelly to develop the same obsessive-addictive thing her father had.

Unfortunately, Kelly *did* have it... just not for video games. She could lose herself in three activities: interesting schoolwork or science, reading (comics or books), and imagination. The third option most often took the form of running around outside pretending to be a superhero or a character from a movie, but sometimes involved daydreaming or drawing. When she sat down with a pencil and art pad, whole afternoons could disappear.

For some reason, Mom didn't mind her losing time with schoolwork, reading, or drawing—she just had a problem with video games.

Even her father teased her sometimes that *enjoying* schoolwork to the point she lost track of time while doing it meant she failed at being a child. Kids weren't supposed to *like* school. Even though he joked, Mom always yelled at him for 'sending the wrong message.'

Speaking of Dad, he came up from his basement workshop about half an hour after Kelly started playing, swooping into the living room to pluck her off the floor. She managed to hit the pause button before the controller fell out of her hands. He swung her in circles twice, then gave her a huge hug.

Her father stood quite tall, but skinny, with a long, pointy face and a contagious smile. She had no doubt why she had a body like a stick figure. Thanks, Dad. Her parents were younger than the other parents she'd sometimes seen at the school during teacher meetings. Mom had only turned thirty-one last July. With only two weeks separating their birthdays, they joked that once Kelly got old enough for birthdays not to be a big deal, they'd just have one celebration for both of them.

That, of course, made no sense.

How could birthdays *ever* not be a big deal?

"There's my little Fire Phoenix." Dad kissed her on top of the head. "Didn't see you when I got home from work. Burn down any enemy lairs today?"

"Jack, our daughter is not a pyromaniac," called Mom from the kitchen.

Kelly looked at his chest to avoid giving away her epic failure. "I was outside."

"Is something wrong, sweetie?" He leaned closer, peering into her eyes.

Crap! Darn! I have Silver Ion's stupid screen on my forehead. The fully robotic character from *Star Prince* couldn't talk. A small screen on his face scrolled text whenever he wanted to say something, and Kelly's forehead screen betrayed her.

"Alexis again," muttered Kelly.

Mom poked her head around the kitchen archway. "C'mon you two. Dinner time."

"Aww. Don't pay any attention to those girls." Dad carried her over to the table and set her in a chair before helping her mother move stuff to the table. "It's just a rite of passage for us."

"Us?" asked Kelly.

"Anyone who isn't like everyone else." He smiled.

He and Mom sat down at the same time.

"Alexis isn't like everyone else. She's perfect. Blue eyes, blonde, tall, graceful…"

"Smart?" asked Mom.

"Umm. Not really." Kelly stuck out her tongue. "She's not stupid. That's Colleen. Every time the wind blows, that girl hears a whistling sound."

Dad snickered.

Mom smirked.

"We are people of a certain… character." He scooped some lasagna on a plate for her, then let Mom take a portion first, then helped himself. "We often wind up as easy targets for those with issues of self-worth. Other kids used to call me Egon in school."

"Egon? What the heck does that mean?" asked Kelly.

"It means we are going to watch *Ghostbusters*." Dad held up a triumphant finger. "As it appears I have been remiss in your education."

She shrugged and picked at the lasagna.

"So, what happened?" asked Mom.

Kelly shifted her gaze to her mother. The woman's perfectly-shaped black bob of hair never had chocolate syrup in it. Her flawless makeup and movie-star face had never seen the inside of a toilet bowl. Mom never wound up shoved in a garbage can, either. She suspected her mother might have even been the Alexis Stephens of her middle school, or at least a hanger-on like Rachel McMeadows. More likely, Mom had been her generation's Gina Vasquez—a rare combination of looks, brains, and charm. Gina could easily have been Alexis, but lacked the desire to torment people. Sometimes, Kelly had heard the boys trying to decide which girl was prettiest between Gina or Alexis. Of course, no boy ever mentioned *her* name. But at nine, a year or more younger than everyone else, they all thought of her as 'the little kid.'

She did 'cute' in the sense of 'aww.' Not the sort of cute Alexis or Gina had that made boys forget how to talk if they got too close.

"Well?" asked Mom. "You're just sitting there staring into your food. What are you thinking about?"

"Can you homeschool me?"

"We don't have the time for that, sweetie." Mom patted her hand.

"Hmm." Dad. "Maybe we should talk to Principal Walsh again."

"Don't. I'll only get teased worse, and the school won't do anything."

"What happened?" asked Dad.

With a heavy sigh, Kelly explained about being thrown into a garbage can and rolled down The Hill. She didn't mention the comic, hoping her parents would read the awkwardness she felt at lying—by not saying anything—as being upset over the girls teasing her.

Her parents shook their heads.

"Those bullies will regret it eventually. They'll rue the day!" Dad thrust his arm up, then lost confidence, glancing at Kelly. "That's the phrase, right? Rue the day?"

"Umm." She shrugged. "Maybe. It's not a big deal. Ninety-nine percent of the kids I'm going to school with now, I'll never see again after I grow up. It's not a big deal. I don't care if anyone likes me or not because when I'm old like you guys it won't matter."

"Today's wedgie is a laugh over beers in twenty years, or something," said Dad.

"Jack, in case you didn't notice, we have a daughter. Wedgies are a *boy* thing." Mom sighed and stabbed her fork into the lasagna.

Kelly squirmed in her chair. Maybe her mother *hadn't* been a bully in school. She had no idea. Every period between classes became a gauntlet in the hallway. If she ran into Alexis or any of her crew, *something* would happen. Either they'd trip her, try to step on her heels to make her shoes come off, go for the wedgie if she didn't have a dress on, yank the zipper on her backpack so everything fell out... and so on. Most times the bell went off, Kelly felt like a soldier trying to make it through a minefield to the next classroom.

"Umm, girls *do* the wedgie thing, too, Mom. At least Alexis and her friends do."

Her mother shook her head. "Amateurs. Back in my day, the mean girls didn't rely on such primitive tactics. We had it way worse than the boys. A wedgie stops hurting after an hour, but a truly deep emotional cut is a work of art that lasts a lifetime."

"Good grief, Melinda." Dad blinked.

Mom smiled. "I'm just saying if Kelly decides to get a little revenge on the girls picking on her, there are far more elegant means available that befit a young lady of superior intelligence. Though, she is a little young yet. Girl bullies don't truly evolve into their final state of advanced wickedness until like fourteen."

"You're kinda scaring me, hon." He fake cowered away from her. "Did I marry the mean girl?"

Melinda Donovan examined her fingernails. "Oh, I never started anything. But I cut back."

Kelly couldn't picture her mother being cruel to anyone, but she did have a scary glint of satisfaction in her eyes.

"Why don't you try making a few friends? It's much more difficult for those girls to bother you if you're not alone." Mom smiled, back to her usual warm self.

"No one likes me." Kelly shrugged. "I don't care. I'm happy alone."

"Sweetie," said Mom, a few minutes later. "You can't spend your whole life alone in your room reading comic books and playing video games."

Dad looked over at Mom. "Why not? Oh, right. Stupid job thing. It is kind of addictive having food and a roof."

"I don't just play video games and read comic books, Mom." Kelly cut off a piece of lasagna with her fork. "I read books too."

"Mel," said Dad, "she's only nine. We don't have to hit her over the head with the reality bat yet."

Her mother rolled her eyes. "The two of you are stuck in a fantasy world."

Dad pursed his lips, nodding. "That's because this world is so boring."

"Will you take the trash out after dinner, hon?" asked Mom.

"Sure. I am the garbage whisperer, after all. Oh, I rolled all the way down and hit the fence today. Extra points."

"Aww, honey…" Dad reached across the table to pat her hand. "We really should talk to the principal."

Kelly kept her head down while she ate. Her parents briefly discussed what to do about the 'bullying problem.' She mostly ignored everything except her food until a voice from Mom's little television on the kitchen counter caught her attention with the word 'alien.'

"… observatory have picked up what they believe might be objects of unknown origin near Saturn. The objects in question were not observable a month ago, which leads some scientists to speculate that they are moving at incredible speeds."

"Oh, here come the aliens," said Mom, rolling her eyes.

"It's probably just a comet. Maybe a big one collided with Saturn's rings and scattered some stuff that made the instruments go crazy." Dad shrugged… then took more lasagna.

For a rail-thin guy, he sure could eat.

Kelly daydreamed about aliens invading Earth and zapping all the bullies with nacho cheese guns or energy beams that instantly tied shoelaces together while finishing her dinner. Her parents briefly discussed work. Mom made a big sale today, but her father suffered another unimportant day of doing the same old boring stuff he did every other day. The most exciting thing that happened for him was watching someone named Pritchard drop coffee in the break room.

Her desire to get out from under parental eyes beat her lack of appetite. Kelly finished off her dinner, set the plate in the dishwasher, then proceeded to change the bag in the kitchen trash can before hauling the full one out to the big can outside.

She went straight to her room afterward, flopped on her bed, and resumed reading. The ruined comic book under her mattress practically filled the room with a heartbeat, a loud, constant drum advertising her guilt. Kelly kept fidgeting on the bed, too consumed with worry that her father would find it and she'd get in trouble.

Eventually, she needed to use the bathroom, so she trudged down the hall. On the return to her bedroom, she paused inches from her door when Dad's voice speaking her name carried up from downstairs.

Kelly crept down a few steps and stuck her head through the banister posts. Her parents' shadows stretched into the hallway from the kitchen.

"… just think it's unhealthy for her," said Mom. "She needs to have friends. Even *you* had friends growing up."

"Ouch," said Dad, chuckling. "That's cold."

"Aww, Jack. That's not how I meant it. Anyone looking at you would know you're extremely intelligent. Until our daughter opens her mouth, she looks normal."

Kelly rolled her eyes and whispered, "Yeah, sure. Hubble telescope lenses on my face sure look normal."

"You're saying intelligence isn't normal?" asked Dad.

Mom chuckled. "Have you gone outside for anything other than work at any time in the past, oh, twenty years?"

"Good point."

"What I'm saying is, you were at the extreme end of nerd-dom, but you still had friends. I'm not saying she needs to get in with the popular crowd. A pack of fellow nerds is still friends. Kelly doesn't even *look* like a nerd. Maybe we should try to get her into TV commercials or something. She's certainly photogenic enough. That would boost her confidence."

"We keep assuming she's socially awkward," said Dad. "Maybe she just doesn't have time for the foolishness of lesser mortals."

I am *socially awkward.* Kelly started to frown, but couldn't help cracking a tiny smile at the lesser mortals thing.

"Look, let's give her a little time. Maybe she only needs to run into a kid on the same wavelength. If we force her to hang out with other kids she doesn't really like, that could make things worse."

Kelly gave a thumbs-up. "Go, Dad."

"All right." Mom sighed. "I'm just worried about her. She seems extra miserable today. I can't help but think there's something she hasn't told us."

Eep!

"Hmm. Maybe. Oh, hon… what exactly did you mean about deep cuts?"

"Heh. I had a bit of a problem with this girl in high school. Carrie-Anne Simons. Thought she was queen of the school and felt threatened by me for some reason."

"Well, you were the prettiest girl in the entire class."

The soft sound of a kiss made Kelly cringe and stick her tongue out.

"She started a rumor that cost me my boyfriend at the time. So, I planted some seeds here and there. Pretty easy to tell who had secret crushes on who and set things up to look like things happened that didn't. Carrie-Anne and all five of her friends broke up with their boyfriends in the same week, all the girls blaming each other. I don't think any of them are on speaking terms to this day."

"Wow. You killed five relationships and made a pack of best friends hate each other for the rest of their lives?" Dad whistled. "Remind me not to get on your bad side."

"Like I said. Wedgies are small time." Mom waved dismissively.

"Crap," whispered Kelly. "My mother is scary!"

She scrambled back to her room, flopped on her bed, and stared at the comic without reading it. Daydreams of somehow making Alexis, Colleen, Rachel, and Brittany all hate each other occupied her thoughts. But… she couldn't do that. Those girls had been friends ever since first grade. Making them hate each other over something that hadn't been their fault would be worse than stuffing them in a nasty garbage can.

"Kelly?" Mom leaned in. "You didn't put the MegaStation away. And, it's bedtime."

"Sorry, Mom." She hopped off the bed. "I'll get it now."

Mom patted her on the head when she ran by. The whiteboard didn't have an end-time filled in for her play today, since Dad interrupted it. She once tried to debate for the ability to transfer unused time into the next day, but her mother insisted on a 'use it or lose it' policy.

Kelly sat on the rug, unpaused the game, and started flying Ms. Omni back to the safe zone.

"I said put it away, not play it." Mom walked up to stand behind her arms folded.

"I still have like twenty minutes left, but I'm not actually playing it."

Mom tilted her head. "You're not? Sure looks like you're playing it. What are you doing then?"

"Dad made me pause in the middle of a mission. I'm just moving Ms. Omni back to a save crystal so I can turn the game off without losing where I was."

"All right."

Kelly directed the character over to one of the glowing blue spheres, saved the game, and shut the system down. After putting the controller back in the cabinet under the TV, she hurried upstairs.

While changing into her nightgown, she paused to sigh at herself in the mirror on her closet door. Embarrassingly skinny. *I look like one of those floppy noodle men at the car place.* Even though Alexis hadn't yanked down her underpants, the gym shorts fiasco had started a recurring nightmare of finding herself randomly naked at school. Every time Kelly saw her reflection, she just pictured the whole class laughing at her for being freakishly thin, almost like a cartoon character. In her nightmare, even the gym teacher laughed at her. She hated looking at herself—and slammed her closet door to hide the mirror.

Sad, but too angry to cry, Kelly slipped into her nightgown and stormed off to the bathroom to brush her teeth and use the toilet one last time before bed. Soon, she crawled under her purple-and-white comforter and stared at the ceiling, also purple, flecked with hundreds of glow in the dark star stickers—Dad's idea. But she liked them.

Tonight, however, she didn't.

They made her think of Dad.

And how sad he'd be when he found *Star Prince #17.*

Because, of course he'd find it.

Eventually.

The longer it took him to find it, the worse it would be when he did. Not only would he be upset with her for being careless with it, he'd be hurt she didn't tell him about it. She would have to confess. Having the evidence directly under her beneath the mattress felt like a sign waving back and forth over her head with 'guilty' written on it. Mom already suspected she hadn't told them something.

Okay. Okay. I'll confess. Tomorrow.

Her parents walked into her room. Both smiled, kissed her good night, and wished her pleasant dreams. She couldn't even look at Dad. They exchanged a glance that proved they knew *something* was wrong. For whatever reason, neither one pressed her on it. They probably decided to give her at least until tomorrow to come clean. Of course, her parents knew her too well.

Kelly Donovan also had a superpower: guilt.

Mom tucked Floppet, her favorite stuffed animal—a bright purple rabbit with oversized ears—into bed beside her and patted it on the head.

"Good night, sweetie." Mom kissed her on the head again, then followed Dad out into the hall.

For a while, Kelly lay there, tapping her foot on air under the blankets, staring at the glowing stars. Cuddling Floppet made her feel somewhat better. She eventually closed her eyes and imagined having Ms. Omni's powers, being able to cartoonishly beat up Alexis and her friends, stuff them all in matching garbage cans, and roll them down The Hill so hard they went *through* the fence onto the football field.

"Nah. That would make me just as bad as they are."

Kelly sighed.

Dad says I should ignore bullies, but how long is it gonna take them to realize I'm ignoring them?

CHAPTER FOUR

NINE MORE YEARS

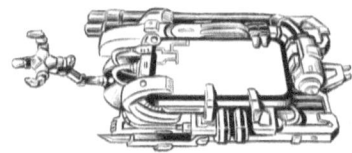

Kelly took her time walking to school the next morning.

She didn't want to be late and get in trouble, but if she cut it close, it reduced the chances of Alexis and company attacking her. Spending the entire school day with juice soaked into her clothes stank. At least if they got her on the way out, it didn't take her long to get home and clean up.

Head bowed, hiding from the world behind her hair, Kelly meandered the six blocks down, turned left at the corner, and walked the last two blocks to the school. The loudness up ahead from a few hundred kids still hanging out said she hadn't dawdled enough. But she couldn't stop here, not in sight of the school. Just standing there alone on the sidewalk would get her picked on even worse.

She couldn't let them see that they bothered her.

"Hey, Donovan! Think fast!" shouted Brittany.

Kelly peered up a split second before a basketball smashed into her face hard enough to knock her on her butt and send her glasses flying. Laughter—from far more than Alexis and her three friends—came from everywhere. Stunned, Kelly sat there staring at the blurry world, trying to figure out what just happened.

A slender girl in a pink skirt, white top, and white ballet flats stepped into her view. "Gonna cry now?" asked Alexis.

"Umm, no," replied Kelly in a dazed voice. She looked around, grabbing at dark spots on the sidewalk in hopes of finding her glasses. Miraculously, neither Alexis nor her friends stopped her from picking them up. After putting them on, she peered up at the four girls towering over her. "Oh. Hi."

"She's not crying," said Colleen.

Brittany shot her a look. "Thanks for pointing that out. I hadn't noticed."

"Go on. Cry," said Alexis.

"Nah." Kelly rubbed the sore spot on her nose where the basketball crushed her glasses into it. "It didn't hurt." Rarely, she *could* lie and not feel guilty.

Alexis grabbed Kelly by the collar of her purple dress and dragged her from sitting on the sidewalk to standing on tiptoe. "How 'bout if I break your face?"

She didn't struggle, hanging limp from the girl's grip. "Go ahead if it makes you happy. I guess your life is pretty bad if picking on me makes you feel better."

Colleen folded her arms, her long black hair swaying as she shook her head. "She's trying some of that psycho stuff on you."

"The word is psychology," said Kelly.

Colleen growled. "I think it's garbage time for smarty pants."

Kelly glanced down at herself. "I don't have pants today. This is a dress."

"Trash can time." Alexis smiled. "What do you think about that, Noodle-butt?"

"Can we reschedule this bullying session to after school? If I'm covered in slime all day, the teachers will notice and you might get in trouble."

"We're not gonna get in trouble." Alexis carried her down the sidewalk toward the big can. "Because you're gonna tell them you're a clumsy idiot and fell in."

"You got so much hair you can't see where you're going!" Brittany giggled.

Kelly watched the big can coming closer and closer. Still, she didn't struggle. No point in it. She would end up going down The Hill either way. Not fighting only meant she wouldn't be tired by the time she crashed into the fence. At least, this early in the day, there wouldn't be *too* much stuff in the can. It only became truly horrible after lunch.

Mr. Potts, a seventh-grade teacher, happened to walk out the front doors mere seconds before the girls upended Kelly into the garbage can. He paused, looking at them. "Is there a problem here?"

Alexis let go, jerking her hands back as if she'd grabbed a boiling pot, then patting Kelly's dress down to smooth it. "No, Mr. Potts. She tripped. We were just helping her up."

"Miss Donovan?" asked the teacher.

"It's okay." Kelly stared down at her purple sneakers.

"Hmm." Mr. Potts looked at the older girls with a suspicious smirk. "Indeed. All right. Get on inside. Bell's about to ring."

As soon as he walked off to the left to chase the kids hanging out on the grass into the building, Alexis pushed Kelly against the wall and pointed at her face. "You know what happens to snitches."

"I didn't say anything, did I?" asked Kelly in a bored voice. "If I was gonna tell on you, I would've done it right here."

The tall blonde gave her a 'that's right' nod, then led her clique past the doors.

Kelly dusted herself off. *Great. Nine more years of this until I'm free.*

A small green car rushed up to the sidewalk out front. Mike Hopkins, another eleven-year-old in her class, jumped out the passenger side door while his mother continuously yelled at him for not getting out of bed on time and making her drive him here so he wouldn't be late. If Kelly personified the nobody and Alexis personified perfection, Mike Hopkins would be the personification of average. Shaggy brown hair he couldn't be bothered to comb framed a face neither particularly handsome nor weird looking. His clothes, baggy and bland khaki-beige were the kind of thing no one would remember if they tried to describe him an hour after seeing him.

He jogged up the sidewalk, muttered, "Hey, Kell," as he passed, and dashed inside.

Mrs. Hopkins yelled at him for leaving the door open while struggling to reach it from within the car.

Kelly laughed at that, then ran inside and rushed down the mostly-empty hall to Mr. Reynolds' room. As a general rule, she loved school—except for social studies, which felt more like a history class. She didn't exactly dislike it, but it bored her to death. Admittedly, it made no sense since she loved reading stories and comic books. The only real difference between them and history was that one really happened. Maybe the boredom came from dealing with the teacher's dreadful monotone voice first thing in the morning. At least she had second period with Mrs. Webb to look forward to. She loved math.

Upon taking her desk, she pulled her text and notebook out from her bag… and found herself doodling Ms. Omni within five minutes. She had to do something to avoid falling asleep as the slightly heavyset teacher droned on and on about the American Revolution.

"Miss Donovan?" called Mr. Reynolds. "This is social studies, not art class. Please pay attention."

"Sorry, Mr. Reynolds." Kelly set her pen down, sat up straight, and tried to pay attention.

As soon as he turned back to the presentation, a spitball stuck in her hair. She ignored it, sighing out her nose.

Nine more years… and I'll never see her again.

CHAPTER FIVE

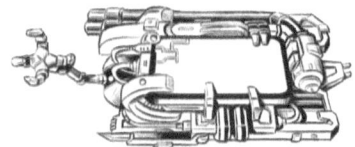

Lunch period presented the third most risky time of the school day.

Kelly had gotten into the habit of selecting lunch items like sandwiches or hamburgers that she could carry outside right away while the rest of the kids ate at the cafeteria tables. That protected her from various missiles and other projectile attacks while eating. She sat on one of the metal benches by the small playground area behind the school, a spot where the teachers assigned to monitor the lunch period often congregated as it kept them in the shade.

Even Alexis wouldn't mess with her—usually—directly in front of teachers. None of the kids bothered with any of the playground equipment anymore, not since third grade. Mostly, they hung out in groups to talk or ran back and forth playing tag. Some of the boys occasionally played a form of soccer involving a tennis ball, but no one touched the seesaws, monkey bars, or swings. It surprised her that the middle school even had them.

Naturally, Alexis and her friends taunted her about being a little kid at the playground, but she didn't let that bother her. Mostly because she didn't *use* the playground, merely sat near it. For once, her total non-reaction to teasing actually worked. They'd stopped picking on her for that.

As usual, Kelly kept her head down and ate. By the time the other kids finished their meals inside and flooded the area between the school building and the football field, she'd be done with her food and able to keep her full attention on her surroundings.

After eating, she sat with her hands in her lap, scuffing her shoe back and forth over the blacktop. She didn't make the same mistake again. No comic books came to school with her, nor would they ever again. Having nothing to do but wait for the period to end, she merely existed.

Soon, the din of other kids broke the calm. Two teachers took up their usual position near the door. Some of the boys ran off to kick the tennis ball around, while most of the others arranged themselves in their usual friend clusters. She spotted Alexis, Brittany, Rachel, and Colleen off to the side, keeping their distance.

Rachel could've been Alexis' twin, except for having light brown hair instead of blonde. Both wore the same outfit of white tops, pink skirts, and black ballet flats. Rachel always tried to do whatever Alexis did, including dress alike.

Do they call each other in the morning to plan that?

Brittany Chang's neon green shirt and matching jeans could be seen from outer space. That girl had a lot of nerve for teasing Kelly about skinny. Colleen's pink sweater covered in sparkly red hearts almost looked cute, until she remembered who wore it.

Weird that they're all the way over there. The four of them standing at almost the farthest point away from her within the area kids could go during lunch worried her. Even if they didn't have the nerve to actively harass her right in front of teachers, they usually stood close enough to keep making faces or throw stuff whenever the teachers weren't watching.

A scuff came from the left, close. Kelly jumped and whirled toward the noise, locking stares with another girl in her class, Paige Warren. She, too, was on the small side but not as short as Kelly. Then again, at ten, Paige *belonged* in fifth grade. The girl hadn't skipped a year. Not much came to mind about her in the first few seconds of recognition. Kelly didn't pay too much attention to her classmates at all, but this girl had stealth technology woven into her T-shirt and denim skirt or something. She practically didn't even exist in the class as far as anyone knew.

Kelly broke eye contact first, looking down—at the girl's pink flip flops and purple-painted toenails. The last time she'd worn flops to school, someone had stolen them out from under her desk right in the middle of class. She'd spent the rest of the day barefoot. Not that she minded *that* much, but it got her yelled at in every class.

"Hey," said Paige.

"Hi."

"Is it okay if I sit here?"

Kelly cringed mentally at having to deal with someone invading her personal sanctuary… but her parents *did* want her to have friends. Prior to Alexis making it her mission in life to torment Kelly, she never would have considered herself shy, merely feeling content with her own company. However, this girl approached her. That didn't count as Kelly going out of her way to change things.

"Okay. You're Paige, right?"

"Yeah." She sat. "Kelly, right?"

"Yeah." Moment of awkward silence. "I like your nails."

Paige raised one foot. "Thanks. Purple's my favorite color."

"Mine, too." Kelly smiled.

"Really? That's cool. I thought redheads liked green."

"Where'd that come from?"

Paige shrugged. "Dunno. Just what I thought."

"So, umm… why did you wanna sit here?"

"You always sit alone. I always sit alone. People think I'm weird."

Kelly glanced at her. The girl appeared relatively average in most respects. Dark brown hair, hazel eyes, on the pale side. Neither too thin nor too thick. Clothes neither stylish nor old. "Why would they think you're weird?"

"I don't know. Maybe because I had an Amazing Anna lunch box in first grade."

Kelly smiled. "Those comics are okay. She's powerful and all, but I hate that she keeps getting kidnapped and needs to be saved."

"Most of the time she saves herself. And don't forget Flying Fox and Sparrow… Sparrow always ends up getting into trouble and Flying Fox has to save him."

Kelly tapped a finger to her chin. "That's true, I guess."

"Guess you like comics."

"Yeah." Kelly grinned.

"I saw what happened yesterday with number seventeen. Sorry."

Mood destroyed. Kelly stared down. "Thanks."

"Your parents should complain to the school and demand Rachel's parents pay for it."

Yeah, right. I'd have to tell Dad first. "Maybe."

Paige swung her legs back and forth, snapping her flops. "Did you ever wonder why bad guys always use these complicated things to kill the heroes instead of just, umm, killing them?"

"Probably because if they just killed them, the story would end."

"Oh. Good point. But that's the writers, not the characters."

"Besides, they don't kill characters in normal comics. Only the dark ones." Kelly pulled her hair off her face. "Yeah. But the complicated death machine stuff is like part of it. Comics aren't supposed to be too serious."

"My brother has some serious ones. He won't let me read them because he thinks they'll give me nightmares."

"Neil Wright's *Ebon Wraith* series?" asked Kelly.

Paige gasped. "You've read them?"

She slouched, chin on her fist, smirking. "No. Dad won't let me read that one either. And, technically, those are graphic novels. The cover art looked cool, but he said I have to wait for like fourteen before he'll let me read them."

"It must be *really* cool if they won't let us see it."

"That's what I'm thinking. But, it probably is really scary and dark if my dad won't let me read it. He's pretty laid back about comics."

"Wow." Paige blinked. "Ben said people die in it. Wraith kills bad guys."

Kelly blinked. "People aren't supposed to die in comics."

"Didn't you say they're graphic novels, not comics?"

"Ooh. Right." She cringed… and asked Paige if she read normal books too. That set off a long conversation.

… which ground to a halt when Alexis and her crew walked up to stand in front of them.

Kelly braced for impact. *So much for Mom's idea about having friends will make them leave me alone.*

"Who is this again?" asked Alexis, gesturing at Paige.

"Umm, Patty I think," said Colleen.

"Priscilla?" Brittany scratched her head.

"Penelope." Rachel scrunched up her nose, pretending to think.

"Oh, look, it's a Bimbie doll four-pack," said Paige. "Two even have matching costumes. How cute."

Rachel's face went red.

Kelly *almost* laughed but managed to keep a straight face.

"You should stay away from this loser, Paige," said Alexis. "You wouldn't want to get on my bad side."

Paige leaned back, both eyebrows up. "Wait… you *have* a good side?"

Brittany gasped. Rachel gawked.

Colleen looked at Alexis as if framing her for a photograph. "She does!"

"Watch it." Alexis pointed at Paige. "You hang around the runt and you're socially dead."

"Umm. I'm already socially dead. You didn't even know my name, remember. Why do you think I care anyway? *You* probably have nightmares worrying there might be someone in school who doesn't think you're awesome. I don't care what people think."

"Forget this loser," said Colleen. "She thinks she's *sooo* smart."

Kelly pointed at Colleen's spring water bottle. "You shouldn't drink too much of that. It contains dihydrogen monoxide, which can kill you."

"Eep!" Colleen dropped the bottle.

Paige laughed.

Rachel glanced worriedly at the abandoned spring water.

Alexis and Brittany both stared at Colleen in disbelief.

"Don't be an idiot, Coll. That's just nerd words for water." Alexis picked up the bottle and handed it to her. "She's only trying to make you look stupid."

Colleen swiped it back and glared, despite blushing. "I knew that. Water can't kill anyone!"

"What do you call drowning?" muttered Kelly.

For a second, Colleen appeared about ready to jump on her... but hesitated due to the teachers watching them. She seethed, glaring.

Paige jumped to her feet and grabbed Kelly's hand. "Come on. Don't listen to them. It's pretty sad they have nothing better to do than tease you. Go pick on Gina Vasquez if you're that brave. Only a real wimp would pick on the tiniest girl in the whole school."

"Gee, thanks," muttered Kelly.

Alexis glowered, but only stood there making faces as Paige dragged Kelly off the bench beside the playground and pulled her out onto the grassy field. They stopped at the narrow sidewalk crossing from the middle school to the music building that served as the left boundary of the lunch area, pretty much as far away from the doors back into the school as they were allowed to go until school ended for the day.

"Ugh. I hate people like that." Paige rested her hands on her hips. "Why do you just stay quiet and take it?"

"Look at me." Kelly held her arms out to either side. "If I make them mad, they will end me."

"Nice with the dihydrogen monoxide." She giggled. "You totally scared her."

"Yeah, but outsmarting her is even more unsportsmanlike than Alexis beating me up."

Paige sat on the grass and patted the ground beside her. "Enough about them. So what was the last book you read?"

"*The Waif of Westminster* series."

"Haven't read them. What kind of book is it?"

Kelly sat on the grass and rambled about the series starring a twelve-year-old orphan named Elise Thomas in Victorian London who gets stuck living with her mother's half-sister. The woman didn't really want Elise but put up with taking care of her to avoid social shaming. The girl basically existed as a ghost in the giant house since no one really paid attention to her. She overheard various things which led to her solving mysteries in and around the manor grounds, once even stopping an assassination plot against the King of England. Of course, the story fictionalized the names of the royalty and other famous people, not referring to anyone real.

"Sounds cool," said Paige.

"I guess you're right. Elise does get captured a lot by the bad guys, but she always manages to escape or outsmart them."

They talked for the rest of the lunch period. Turned out, Paige was into comics even more than Kelly, but hadn't much tried novels. She also really adored the *Wolfdark* comics, which Kelly hadn't read. They involved vampires and werewolves, specifically a werewolf with additional superpowers.

"Except for *Star Prince*, I mostly read comics with female main heroes... there aren't that many."

Paige rolled her eyes. "I know, right. But, you should try *Wolfdark*."

"You should read *Waif*." Kelly grinned.

"How 'bout we swap? You bring in the first book of that and I'll bring in the first issue of *Wolfdark* and we can borrow."

"Umm. I would, but Alexis will ruin it." Kelly looked down. "I don't wanna bring any comics to school anymore."

"Oh yeah. You should totally tell on her for that. Three hundred dollars? She'd get in a bunch of trouble. Like I said, the cops might even make her parents pay for it."

Kelly fussed at the grass by her knees. "That's exactly why I haven't said anything. I don't want to know what they'll do to me if I get them in trouble."

"They'll never stop bothering you until you do something about it."

"Yeah, but—"

The bell rang.

Paige stood. "Umm, what bus do you take?"

"I don't. I walk."

"Wow. Really?" Paige grinned. "Me too! Don't gotta bring books to school. You could come over if you want. Or I could go to your house."

"Umm. Okay." Kelly got up. "That sounds cool."

"Donovan, Warren," shouted Mrs. Zahn from across the field. "Hurry it up."

Kelly ran for the door. When Paige caught up and ran beside her, she grinned.

Maybe having a friend might not be so bad after all.

CHAPTER SIX

HANGING OUT

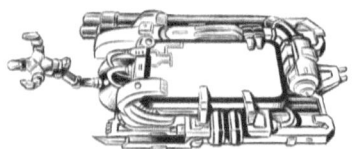

A side from Rachel McMeadows tripping her in the hall between science and English class, the rest of the school day breezed by. She spent more time thinking about having a friend than worrying what Alexis or the others might do to her next. Unfortunately, Paige hadn't said anything about *when* she wanted to come over.

In fact, Kelly wound up in such a happy mood by the end of classes that she didn't even hesitate before walking out of the building along with the stream of other kids. She raced down the steps... but didn't reach the sidewalk.

For an instant, floating in the air confused her.

Then she noticed Alexis had grabbed her by the backpack from behind.

Dread exploded. Out of sheer panic, she tried to run, but only flailed her legs in the air. Alexis burst out laughing as she carried her to the left, away from the crowd of kids all rushing to buses or waiting parents. Blind fear faded enough that she hung limp like a scruffed kitten, but couldn't help trembling. Something seemed unusually wrong. Alexis looked furious.

Rachel, Colleen, and Brittany fell in step behind her.

Once around the corner of the building out of sight from adults, Alexis dropped Kelly on her feet and shoved her against the wall.

"Nice carrying handle," said Brittany. "What kind of dork wears a backpack with both straps on?"

"This kind of dork." Colleen tried to slap her, but she ducked.

"Ooh," said Rachel.

Colleen snarled, pushed her against the bricks, and slapped her on the cheek. "Turd!"

Pain stung her face, but Kelly refused to cry. Of course, she didn't try to hit back either.

"You're dead meat, Noodle-butt." Alexis grabbed a fistful of her hair and yanked.

That came closer to causing tears.

"I didn't do anything," said Kelly, almost sounding like she didn't whimper. She cringed at the pain in her head from the hair pull. Maybe Paige would be looking for her and find them before she got her butt kicked too badly. But... all her favorite characters always wound up being trapped somewhere, and they—most of the time—escaped on their own. "Get off me."

Alexis threw Kelly to the ground by her hair, dropped to sit on top of her, and punched her a few times. Kelly grunted, doing her best to shield her face, still refusing to scream or cry.

"You got us all in trouble!" Brittany kicked at the ground, throwing dirt at Kelly's face.

After a few more punches, Alexis stopped sitting on her and pulled her upright again. "You're gonna get it this time, Turd. We got detention tomorrow."

"I didn't tell on you. You were gonna throw me in the trash can. Mr. Potts *saw* you."

Alexis grabbed the collar of her purple dress in both hands. "I don't believe you."

"You think I'm stupid, but telling on Alexis is more stupider," said Colleen.

"More stupider?" asked Kelly. "If you're going to threaten me, at least use proper English."

Colleen slapped her. Pain bloomed across Kelly's face, stinging her cheek as well as her eyes.

"Aww. Look. She's starting to cry." Alexis smiled.

While true, hearing the taunt gave Kelly the strength to get angry instead. Her eyes watered, but no tears fell. "If you guys got detention for almost throwing me in a garbage can, you better get out of here before anyone sees you hitting me."

"We already have detention," said Alexis. "We're gonna give you a couple bruises to go along with it."

The other three girls dropped their book bags and punched their fists into their other hands, grinning at her.

Kelly lunged at Alexis; the unexpected offensive move caught the girl off guard and she fell over backward, landing on her butt. With no one holding onto her anymore, Kelly bolted to the right, but Brittany caught her by the backpack again, throwing her to the ground by it so hard, she slipped right out of the straps. Rachel and Colleen jumped on top of her, pinning her arms to the ground. Brittany tossed the backpack against the wall, smiling at Kelly's defenseless face and chest.

"Wait…" Alexis stood and dusted herself off. "I don't want to get this outfit dirty. It's new. Tomorrow, I'm gonna wear something old so I can kick your butt across the school. Right now, I have a better idea."

The other three looked up at her.

Kelly struggled, nowhere near strong enough to lift two eleven-year-olds kneeling on top of her.

"Rache," said Alexis. "Need to borrow your bag. Throw your stuff in mine."

"Okay.

Brittany moved in to hold Kelly down as Rachel jumped away and hurried off.

Alexis walked around them in a circle, smiling. "You are going to learn that no one, and I mean *no one* gets me in trouble."

"I didn't even *do* anything," said Kelly. "You tried to throw me in the garbage right in front of a teacher. How stupid *are* you?"

Alexis scowled.

Rachel ran over with a huge, pink floppy book bag. "What are you thinking?"

"Stuff Noodle-butt inside it."

Rachel laughed. "Awesome."

Kelly put up a valiant struggle, but couldn't overpower three larger girls wrestling her into the bag. Laughing, Alexis yanked the zipper closed. Kelly punched and kicked at the flexible prison holding her, not that it cared. Rachel's giant book bag smelled like perfume and stale paper. The canvas-like fabric didn't have much shape, so when someone picked it up, her weight caused the sides to squeeze in on her, mushing her knees against her face. Whoever walked behind the bag carrier kicked her in the butt every few steps, but not hard enough to be more than annoying.

Being stuffed in a book bag ranked with some of the worst things they had done to her, but she preferred it to an actual beating. She didn't scream or start shouting for a teacher, figuring that exactly what the girls wanted her to do. As soon as she acted like a little baby, they'd get the satisfaction they wanted, and it would only encourage them to keep doing it.

Of course, Dad's idea of ignoring them hadn't been working too well.

She bumped against someone's back for a few minutes before the squeak of a gate rang out. The girls carried her for a little while longer, then dropped her on the ground. Kelly attacked where she thought the zipper was, reaching up to scratch at the heavy fabric.

"Grab that," said Alexis.

"What are you doing?" asked Brittany. "Oh. I see. Epic!"

"Aren't we gonna get in trouble for this? No one's going to believe she hung herself on the goal post," said Rachel.

"Turd knows better than to tell anyone anything, right Turd?" Alexis shook the bag. "Here, loop that through and toss it up over the post."

Something rattled outside.

"Guys, please don't do this." Kelly kicked at the bag.

"Aww, guys, please don't do this," singsonged Brittany.

The girls laughed.

A hollow metal clatter like a cable banging a flagpole came from somewhere above. The book bag straps tightened, hauling her up off the ground, twisting side to side. Colleen and Brittany grunted together each time the bag lurched upward a little ways. The girls' constant laughter gradually moved downward until it came from below her rather than above.

"That's good. Tie it off there," said Alexis.

Kelly squirmed, trying to move so her right knee stopped jabbing her in the shoulder.

Someone grabbed the bag and spun it. The girls slapped her repeatedly on the butt, which stuck out at a rather exploitable angle due to her being squished into a tight ball on her back, nearly upside down. Kelly tried pushing with her feet to defend herself, but could barely move. Colleen and Brittany kept slapping her harder and harder until the inescapable stinging became too much for her to take and she finally yowled in pain.

"Ow! Stop hitting me! Please!" screamed Kelly.

"Okay, okay… Enough," said Alexis. "Lay off."

"What's wrong with you?" asked Colleen, slapping her again. "It's just Turd."

"Just… stop. That's good for now."

"Like, what's your problem?" asked Rachel. "Why do *you* look upset?"

"Forget it," said Alexis in a commanding tone. "We made the little girl cry. Stop hitting her." She grabbed the bag, leaning close. "You just hang out here for a while and think about how much you're sorry for getting us in trouble. *Maybe* I won't come to school tomorrow in old jeans so I can kick your butt."

The tight bag made it difficult for Kelly to breathe. "Let me out! Please. I'm scared. I'm sorry you got in trouble, but I didn't tell on you. I swear!"

"Are the Piranhas playing today?" asked Brittany.

"How should I know?" replied Colleen. "Like I care about football."

"Your brother's on the team, isn't he?" Alexis laughed. "How can you not know?"

"Pff. Like I pay attention to what he does."

"Umm, aren't you on the cheer squad?" asked Brittany.

"Yeah. There's no cheering today."

"If there's no cheering, that means there's no game," said Alexis, sounding pained.

Kelly bit her lip to stop herself from making a comment about Colleen's intelligence. She didn't want to go through another round of Spin-N-Slap. She waited, confident that the girls only hung her from the goalpost to scare her and they'd let her out soon. Shame burned across her face with blush since she'd caved in and screamed for help, but at least she stopped herself from sniveling out loud despite being terrified. Ms. Omni wouldn't cry if the bad guys trapped her somewhere.

A discussion of cheer practice and game days among the four girls faded off into the distance.

"Guys?" asked Kelly.

The girls' laughter eventually fell away to silence.

"Guys?" yelled Kelly. "Hey! Don't leave me here! Did you seriously leave me here?"

No one answered.

They're messing with me. They pretended to walk away and they're gonna laugh if I scream and cry.

Grumbling, Kelly glared over her knees at the pastel pink fabric inches in front of her face.

"I'm not scared. Ha ha. Hang out. I get it. You can let me down now."

Minutes passed. Shouts from other kids or adults occasionally broke the stillness, but they all sounded far away, at least in front of the school. She swayed in silence for a while, waiting for Alexis and her friends to get bored and stop acting like they weren't right there.

Eventually, Kelly started to suspect the girls really had been mean enough to leave her hung up on the goalpost alone. She strained to push her legs out, but couldn't. So, she squirmed about while reaching in search of the zipper. With all her weight dangling from the handles, the bag had distorted into a raindrop shape, the zippers bunched up in a dense wad of canvas at the top.

No! I wanna go home! I don't wanna hang here all day!

She struggled to stretch out lengthwise, forcing the bag to expand enough to reveal the zippers, but her hanging weight kept too much compression on the top for her to budge them. Based on what she'd heard earlier, she figured the girls had strung a cable of some kind through the handles, thrown them up over the horizontal bar of the goalpost, and probably tied the other end to the base. That meant she probably dangled about ten feet off the ground. Wait, no. She couldn't be that high up or they wouldn't have been able to slap her.

Hoping that jostling the bag hard enough might cause it to drop to the ground, Kelly spent a while rocking side to side as hard as she could. Even if the cable didn't come untied, someone seeing a bag swinging itself would hopefully come to investigate.

She ran out of steam and lay there, struggling to breathe with the bag compressing her into a ball. That scared her more than a drop. The possibility that she could *die* entered her mind. It didn't seem likely the girls who put here there even considered that. How often had they been stuffed in book bags and hung from goalposts? They wouldn't know how bad it squeezed, how difficult it made breathing. Not to mention, how much air did she have left? Then again, the book bag wasn't airtight.

Despite being late September, she found herself sweating like the middle of August.

"Help!" yelled Kelly, finally caving in after what felt like an hour. "Please! Help! Someone let me out of here!"

If Alexis and the others remained there to relish this moment of victory, they did a remarkable job of staying quiet. *No, they wouldn't still be here. Not one of those four have the patience to wait over an hour for a payoff, even one as good as me screaming for help like a little kid.*

She kept looking for a way out, eventually locating a grommet in the side of the bag not quite big enough for a pen to escape. While the tiny air vent didn't offer a way out, it did give her somewhat of a view. Sure enough, she hung from the horizontal bar of one of the goalposts on the school's football field in an empty stadium. No one up the hill at the school could see her from here, if anyone even remained at this hour.

Still being at school so late after last bell made her angry and sad. Alexis and her idiot friends stole the day from her. She had homework to do, games to play, books to read. She didn't want to waste the entire afternoon trapped in a stupid book bag. Worse, she hadn't even *done* anything to deserve retaliation.

Furious, she kicked and scratched at the bag for another few minutes until she collapsed, exhausted, and no closer to being out.

What would Ms. Omni do if Greenfang put her in a crystal prison over a lava pit? Kelly pictured herself as Ms. Omni, trapped helpless in an orb of Pyraxian diamond, the toughest material in the known universe. Ms. Omni didn't need to be rescued. She would… use her laser beam eyes to cut the chain through the diamond, because diamond didn't stop lasers. And the diamond ball would protect her from the lava until it softened enough she could super strength her way out.

Alas, no matter how hard Kelly stared up at the cable she pictured tied through the book bag handles, no laser beams came from her eyes.

She hung there, more angry than scared for a while. The Petersen Piranhas didn't have a game tonight, which meant people wouldn't go to the stadium. But there still had to be someone, a janitor or something checking around, right? Her parents might not be home from work yet, so they wouldn't necessarily know anything happened to her.

A few more attempts to scream for help didn't do any good.

Kelly grunted, resigned to hanging there until someone found her.

I can't believe they really did this. If I tell on them, they might get suspended.

"Heeeeeelp!" screamed Kelly, kicking at the bag. "Let me out!"

She listened, but the only reply came from the gentle tapping of a metal cable against the goalpost.

Being trapped in a pink book bag did have at least one upside: the bullies couldn't see her crying.

CHAPTER SEVEN

REBORN

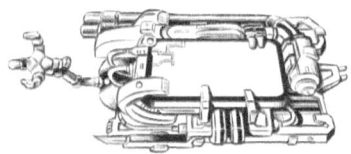

Hours passed.

Kelly hung from the goal post, the inescapable canvas bag trapping her squished into a fetal position. She stopped crying soon after the girls left, too worried about breathing to have time for fear. Every so often, she shouted for help, but so far, no one had been there to hear. The world outside her bag had become eerily still, not a single voice or sign of life breaking the silence for a long time, merely the occasional whoosh of a car driving by in front of the school. A growl from her stomach said she should be eating dinner about now. Her parents *had* to know she didn't come home from school.

Mom and Dad would probably be frantically looking for her, scared out of their minds.

Had Alexis, Brittany, Rachel, and Colleen seriously gone home and proceeded with their day like nothing happened? How could they be so cruel to leave her here like that? Worse, she *really* had to go to the bathroom. Any minute now, she'd stop being able to hold it and wet herself. Someone had to find her soon, right? She wouldn't like spend all night hanging there until morning, would she?

In between moments of shivering dread, Kelly grew angry enough that she decided to tell on Alexis this time. Leaving her trapped in a bag all day went too far, especially when she felt like she'd suffocate at any minute. Also, she had Rachel's book bag as proof. No way could she deny involvement. If that girl got in trouble, she'd turn on the others. Despite her trying to be Alexis' twin, McMeadows still wouldn't take the punishment all alone.

To distract herself from how bad she had to pee, Kelly ran through various daydreams, replacing supervillains in her mind with the four bullies, as the League of Honor caught them for their crimes. She hated ending up the helpless girl that needed to be saved, but she *was* only nine. Even Mr. Awesome had trouble with a four-on-one fight when the bad guys all had Tier One powers.

A distant man screamed.

Hopeful, she squirmed to line her eye up with the grommet hole. The sun had begun to set. Seeing it so close to dark out set off another fit of kicking and punching at the bag. She *had* been there all day! The whole afternoon wasted. *If she ever got out of the bag, she'd have to go straight to sleep.* For the first time in her life, she wouldn't complete her homework before bedtime.

No, she definitely wouldn't keep quiet this time. The teachers couldn't be mad at her for not doing homework after what Alexis and her friends did. Maybe they'd even get kicked out of school for this. Could they get in trouble with the police even?

She bit her lip, not wanting it to go that far. As mean as Alexis had been to her, she didn't want her to get kicked out of school *or* go to jail. Did the cops even put eleven-year-olds in jail?

Another scream came from somewhere far away. She'd only ever heard adults scream like that in horror movies.

Kelly resumed peering out the grommet, but other than a fast-darkening football field and empty school building, didn't see anyone. *Oh, no! I'm out after dark. I'm gonna get grounded, too.* She scowled. *Stop being stupid. I can't get out of this bag myself. Someone's going to find me and Mom and Dad will know it's not my fault. They've called the police by now. Cops will find me soon.*

Car tires screeched somewhere not too far away.

"Help!" shouted Kelly. "Can anyone hear me?"

"What the heck is that?" yelled a man, his voice faint, probably from the street in front of the school.

A moment of kicking and trying to rip the bag by stretching didn't work. Again, she peered out the hole, and gasped.

The entire football field glowed with red light as if a huge colored spotlight hung in the air above it.

"Umm…"

She scrunched lower in the bag, trying to peer upward via the tiny hole. After a bit of wriggling, she caught a flash of bright light. More squirming lined her vision up with the source of the glow: a massive red crystal shard the size of a small skyscraper... falling straight toward the football field.

Kelly screamed and flew into a panicked frenzy, kicking, clawing, even *biting* at the bag, doing everything she could to escape. Other people may have been screaming, but she couldn't hear much over her own shrieking. The metal cable clattered against the hollow goalpost as she swung the bag harder and harder.

Roaring came from the sky, growing louder.

"Daddy!" screamed Kelly. "Mom! Help!"

Red light from outside shone through the canvas, so bright it hurt her eyes.

She thrashed at the bag, beyond terrified. A brief rip came from somewhere. She kept fighting, but the bag didn't feel any weaker.

The roaring became so loud she couldn't hear herself screaming.

A deafening explosion engulfed her in a maelstrom of intense crimson light. Pain like Band-Aids continuously being ripped off too fast washed over her everything, only five times worse. She tried to scream again, but couldn't hear herself. Amid the chaos of blinding red, she couldn't even see her hand in front of her face—or feel anything but burning.

Until she blacked out.

Kelly opened her eyes, absolutely certain she'd had a nightmare.

Alexis and her goons couldn't possibly have been cruel enough to leave her trapped in a book bag all day. She had to be home in bed. Except, the stars above her looked quite real and not at all like the cartoony glow-in-the-dark ones on her bedroom ceiling. Of course she couldn't possibly have been trapped in a book bag for hours. If that were true, she'd have to go to the bathroom *really* bad, but she didn't.

It had also gotten rather chilly.

A strong source of red light stood somewhere out of her field of view, past her feet. She appeared to be lying flat on the ground, outside. Tingles of not quite pain crawled over her skin and the stink of burned stuff hung heavy in the air. She reached up to pull her hair off her face.

The warped remains of a mostly-melted goal post hovered over her, like a novelty candle left out in the sun too long. Thin steel cable wrapped around its base had turned black. A scrap of plastic coating still clung to the short bit of cable at the back of the goalpost away from the field.

"Whoa..."

Kelly sat up. The football field had also turned as black as charcoal. Still feeling dizzy and not quite all there, she turned her attention forward, and nearly fainted.

A massive red crystal jutted up from the ground twentyish yards away from her, almost as wide as the entire field and at least ten stories tall. It appeared to have fallen from the sky and stuck into the earth like a knife, quite likely with as much crystal below ground as above if not more. The odd object gave off a constant thrumming energy that resonated inside her body.

After sitting there for a few seconds trying to comprehend the sheer ridiculousness of finding a skyscraper-sized crystal stuck in the field of the John Q. Petersen Middle School Piranha's Football Team, curiosity got the better of her. She scrambled to her feet and approached the crystal. Something felt wrong as she walked, like her sneakers had filled with dusty grit.

A rim of raised dirt created a hill surrounding the base of the giant crystal. Kelly walked up to the side, reaching out to touch the strange object without understanding why she wanted to. Maybe she had to feel it to believe her eyes.

She pressed her hand against the perfectly smooth crystal, finding it somewhat warm. Gloopy bubbling noises came from the ground. Kelly peered down past her toes at the edge of a chunk of earth pushed upward by the sinking crystal. A narrow moat of bubbling magma surrounded the crystal, but didn't appear to be damaging it.

"That's lava. I think... It's only warm though. Shouldn't lava be hot?"

Her gaze shifted a few inches back to her *bare* foot, then up her leg to her bare everything else. She blinked, and looked up at the crystal... and her reflection. All her clothes had disappeared, even her glasses, though a smear of purple-and-clear plastic stuck to her cheek.

She picked at it until it peeled off her skin, then held it up to look. The plastic appeared to have melted and re-solidified, and also happened to be the same shade of purple as her glasses' frames.

"No, I have to be dreaming. I can see just fine and..." She felt at her eyes, confirming she did not wear any glasses at the moment. "I shouldn't be able to see without my glasses."

Kelly glanced down at herself again.

"Oh. I'm naked at school. I've had this nightmare before. I'm definitely dreaming."

No trace of the book bag she'd been trapped in remained anywhere. Most of the metal bleacher seats had also melted, drooped like strands of licorice left out in the sun. The school building's wall had also turned black, but all the way at the top of The Hill, it didn't seem to be damaged, merely charred.

She raised and lowered her toes in the dirt, still refusing to believe she did anything but dream. Alexis and the others had left her trapped in a book bag, and she'd fallen asleep while fantasizing about a superhero escape. Giant red crystals falling from the sky sounded like something from *Star Prince*. That didn't happen for real.

And even more unbelievable, she stood naked outside at school.

No way could that be real. She'd totally be freaking out, not just standing there like 'no big deal.'

Living her absolute worst fear proved this a nightmare.

Any second now, hundreds of kids and teachers would show up and all start laughing at her scrawniness.

But, being able to see more than a few feet without glasses had never been in any of her dreams before. She shook her head.

"No. Nope. No way. This isn't real."

A small scrap of pink canvas fell out of her hair, charred at the edges. Kelly watched it flutter to the ground, squatted, and picked it up. A piece of Rachel's book bag, burned to a crisp.

"Hah. Yeah right. If something happened hot enough to burn the book bag, melt the goal posts, and *char the school 200 yards away*, I would be dead."

She stood, dropping the canvas scrap, and put her hand on the crystal again, which remained soothing and warm, like a nice mug of hot chocolate.

"Total nightmare."

An odd sense of power thrumming in the crystal resonated inside her, almost like the vibration of an idling car engine.

Glorp.

A bubble of lava popped in the moat, throwing several chunks into the air. One potato-sized blob hit her in the chest. She screamed—but stopped herself, remembering she only dreamed. The lava, about as hot as Mom's leather car seats in June, made her gasp and squirm, but it didn't burn her. She watched in awe as it slid down over her stomach, leaving a thin trail of paper thin stone flakes. Confused, she grasped the clay-like blob and plucked it off herself, holding it up. Glowing lava squeezed between her fingers, throwing off smoke and fumes.

"So weird."

She dropped it back in the moat, brushed herself off, and rested her hands on her hips.

"Great. I have a superhero dream and I don't even give myself a costume. What is wrong with me? Okay. Time to wake up. I hate this stupid nightmare."

She slapped herself.

Nothing changed.

"Umm."

She slapped herself harder.

"Oh, *please* don't tell me I really am at school with no clothes on."

Another slap didn't change anything, but it did make her stumble backward down the raised ground.

"This is so totally messed up."

She hurried over to the remains of the goalpost. No sign whatsoever of the book bag remained. One lump kinda resembled the sole of her brand new sneaker. Kelly grabbed the warped goalpost, tugging at it. When it bent easily, she shook her head. Steel shouldn't bend like modeling clay.

"This is so unreal. Weirdest dream ever." She looked down at her lack of clothes again. "There is no way I would be this calm if I wasn't dreaming. Heh." She laughed. "If I really am at school naked and someone sees me, I would be so embarrassed I'd crawl under my bed and never come out again. I am dreaming, right? Right?"

She folded her arms and glanced around. Even as far away as she could see, nothing appeared the least bit blurry. Here and there, the distant voices of men and women faded in and out, talking about 'strange red crystals' or 'NASA and aliens.' One woman even used the word 'bombardment.' Someone said 'first contact.' Try as she might, she couldn't lock in and focus on any one person.

"Umm. Okay. When someone is dreaming, and they know they're dreaming, they can wake up if they want to."

She'd read that online soon after she started having the no-clothes-in-class nightmare. Usually, it went something like she'd be in social studies or science class like any other day, then all of a sudden, she'd realize her clothes had disappeared. No one would notice right away and keep acting as if everything was normal—until the teacher called on her to answer a question. Then, everyone would look at her and burst out laughing and making fun of her.

Sometimes, she could make the 'I know it's a dream, I wanna wake up now' thing work and avoid the humiliation. But not always.

And, it appeared that her present dream belonged in the 'not always' category.

"Grr. This makes no sense. How am I even still alive? Look at all this burning!" She grabbed a fistful of her red fluff and held it up. "Not even my hair is damaged. What possible sense does it make that everything burned off me but my hair is just fine?"

She fumed for a moment, then examined herself again.

Still no clothes.

"I'm not even burned. Like, at all. And I can see without my glasses on."

A police car shot by the school at high speed, lights and siren blaring.

Kelly gasped, staring up the hill.

"Umm. Holy crap! What if I really am naked at school!?" She bit her lip, fidgeting nervously. "I really, like, ought to stop standing around with nothing on."

Part of her wanted to crawl under the bleachers and hide. But, if she did that, someone would still eventually catch her and laugh. Streaking all the way home did *not* seem like a good idea either… until she remembered she had a gym uniform in her locker. The more she started to think she might *not* be dreaming, the harder she blushed.

Kelly ran across the football field to the gate in the chain link fence surrounding it, then sprinted up The Hill toward the school. Fortunately, since it had become dark, no one would see her. She zoomed to the school's back door beside where she usually ate lunch, pulled the doors open, and hurried inside.

The patter of her bare feet echoed in the empty school as she ran through the cafeteria, down the hall to the central atrium, and into the east wing. It didn't occur to her until she stopped in front of her locker that she didn't feel the least bit tired after all that running.

"Of course. I'm dreaming. People don't get tired in dreams. And the doors should have been locked. But I'm still not taking the chance." She grabbed her padlock and dialed in the combination. "If my gym uniform is here and I can put it on… that's going to prove that this isn't a nightmare. The whole point of having a nightmare is for those buttheads to all laugh and make fun of me."

She eased the locker open. Her school T-shirt and gym shorts hung on the hook where she expected them to be.

Her stomach did a backflip. "I-I'm not dreaming…"

She hurriedly pulled on her gym uniform, then stared at herself for a good long minute to make sure she actually felt the touch of fabric at her skin.

"Umm. This is not good. If I'm not dreaming, there's an enormous crystal stabbed into the football field. What the heck?"

She pushed her locker closed, secured the lock, and padded back down the hall to the door she came in from, since she expected the front doors would be locked this late at night. When she reached the cafeteria exit, she stopped short with a gasp.

The door had peeled away from the frame like a sticker half-removed from its backing, curled. She crept closer, noting small grooves in the steel about the same size as her fingers. After a moment of staring at it in shock, she grasped the metal and squeezed. It squished under her hand like a sponge, but didn't spring back when she let go.

Kelly stared past The Hill at the huge, glowing crystal against the dark indigo sky. "Wow… something really… *weird* is going on."

Despite the total strangeness, she didn't want to think about anything else but going home as fast as possible. After the scare of being stuck in a book bag, she *really* wanted her parents.

CHAPTER EIGHT

THE ARRIVAL

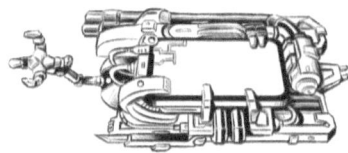

Her purple backpack still sat on the ground beside the school where Brittany Chang threw it.

Kelly cringed and eased herself forward to step barefoot on the gravel at the base of the wall. The sharp rocks didn't hurt at all. She blinked, added her second foot, and walked back and forth a few times over a bumpy, but not-painful surface. Weird as that felt, she had bigger worries to deal with.

She picked up her bag and hurried back to the sidewalk, heading for the front of the school, staring down at her feet. Despite the gravel not bothering her, walking barefoot on the coarse sidewalk still felt as normal as ever. So, her soles hadn't gone numb. She rounded the corner toward the front entrance and took the stairs down to the lot by where all the buses normally waited. Eerie flickering red light on the ground made her look up.

… and gasp.

Dozens of reddish trails marked the sky in every direction, traced by hundreds of objects falling from space. The smoke pillars flickered in places as though something inside them continued to burn. One such trail led up from the tip of the giant crystal jammed into the football field behind her, disappearing into the heavens.

A glint of gunmetal blue way overhead also looked out of place. She stared at that spot, watching clouds drift past the underside of a titanic round…

spaceship. Not only did it hover quite high up since it floated above the clouds, it also appeared to be far larger than the biggest object ever created by humans—with the possible exception of how big a butthead Alexis Stephens was.

Kelly twisted to look back at the glowing crystal shard towering over her school. A flicker of memory flashed and faded: hanging helpless, pain like all her skin had been peeled off, then flat on her back with everything in sight of her scorched to nothingness. She gulped. This didn't appear to be a bad dream. She really had been trapped at school all day long in a bag.

Her worst nightmare—stuck at school with no clothes on—really happened.

At least it had happened *well* after hours when no one had been there to make fun of her. Maybe her parents would be so happy to see her home again that they wouldn't ask why she'd changed into her gym uniform, or what happened to her sneakers.

"Well, being trapped in a bag all day got me out of telling Dad about *Star Prince #17*." She managed a weak smile. "There's a spaceship over San Francisco the size of New Jersey. Who cares about a rare comic book?"

She walked down the street, heading home the 'long' way since bare feet and gym shorts didn't go well with climbing fences and walls. Even if she had stepped on gravel without hurting herself, she didn't care much about anything but getting home so her parents didn't both explode from worry.

The occasional car roared by. Small groups of people emerged from side streets, running about in a state of panic. She paused to watch them, but no one appeared to notice her even though a nine-year-old walking on her own at this hour ought to have been strange. Of course, she had never been outside after dark before, except to take the garbage to the can. Maybe people didn't think it weird for a kid her age to be walking home from school at whatever-o'clock.

Two blocks away from the school, she turned right at the corner, crossed the street straight ahead, and left to the opposite side, then headed up the road she lived on. Screams still came from random people too far away to see, though they no longer shouted in panic, mostly things like 'holy crap did you see that?' or 'what the crap is happening.'

And many of them used words Kelly hadn't yet become old enough to think, much less repeat.

Her house appeared normal. Lights on. No police car in the driveway. Her parents didn't appear to be pacing the living room in a state of panic. She padded up onto the porch, fished her house keys out of the side pocket on her backpack, and unlocked the front door. It might have been risky or wrong for her parents to allow a nine-year-old to spend a few hours home alone each day from the time she left school until Mom returned from work. However, between her intelligence and almost obsessive need to be 'good,' they started trusting her early. They'd programmed the house phone with the number for Mr. Audsley next door in case of emergency, as well as the grandparents—though none of the grands lived closer than a one hour ride.

And of course, Kelly knew all about calling 911 if something bad happened.

She pulled the door open and stepped inside, walking into the living room, looking around. "Mom? Dad?"

The door swung closed behind her.

"Mom? Dad? Are you here?"

Her mother, still in a skirt suit from work, breezed down the hall from the kitchen. "Oh, hi, sweetie. Did you have fun at school today?"

"Umm. Not exactly." Kelly blinked in confusion at her. "Mom, what time is it?"

"Oh, it's almost ten."

"Don't you think that's a bit odd?"

Her mother scrunched her eyebrows. "Ten is an even number. What's odd?"

"Mom. I'm *just* getting home from school now."

"Really? What were you doing there so long?"

Kelly glanced off to the side. "Oh, just hanging out."

"That's nice, dear."

She tossed her backpack on the sofa and walked up to her mother. "Are you feeling okay?"

"Fine, dear. Why? You seem confused. Bit worried too. Did something happen?"

"Did something happen?" Kelly stared open-mouthed. "Have you looked outside?"

"Yes. Large red crystals falling from the clouds. Spaceships. That sort of thing." Mom took Kelly by the hand and walked her down the hall to the kitchen. "It's been all over the news. Some crazy weather we're having, isn't it? This is kind of ridiculous for hail. Are you hungry? Dinner's almost ready."

Kelly's stomach grumbled. "Almost? At ten? Why aren't you upset that I'm coming home so late? Didn't you guys notice?"

"Notice what, dear?" asked Mom while tending to pots.

Whoa. What is happening? Why is she so spacey?

"Umm, only that I came home from school at *ten o'clock at night!*"

"There's no need to shout." Mom smiled back at her, then resumed poking her tongs at the contents of a pot. "It's understandable, dear. Things are a bit strange with the world at the moment."

Something still didn't make sense. "Mom, why are you still in your work clothes? Did *you* just get home, too?"

"Sort of. I somewhat remember your father and I driving in circles for some reason." She tapped the tongs on the pot. "Darned if I can remember why. The news said some extraterrestrials showed up, but they're friendly and we don't need to panic."

Kelly sat on her usual chair, swinging her feet back and forth. "Don't panic… yeah right."

CHAPTER NINE

VEGETABLES

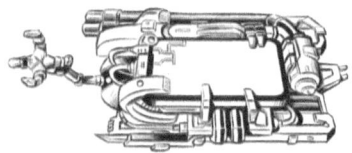

In complete disbelief, Kelly sat there watching her mother prepare dinner at ten o'clock at night, while still wearing her work clothes, after her daughter had been missing all day. It felt almost like everyone skipped four hours forward. Except for the time, this could have been 6:00 p.m. Meaning, it felt like Mom walked in the door from her job twenty minutes ago and started on dinner.

But that still didn't explain why her mother hadn't been freaking the heck out that Kelly had been missing all day.

And aliens? Did Mom say something about aliens showing up like it's no big deal? Like she told me Grandma's coming to visit?

Dad hurried in the patio door from the backyard, grinning broadly. "Oh, hi, hon. How was school?"

"Awful."

He tilted his head at her. "You've never said 'awful' before when I've asked you that."

"Yes, well, I've never been stuffed in a book bag and left hanging from a goal post all day, either."

"Oh, yes. I can see where that would have a negative effect on your enjoyment of the day. How does that relate to you wearing your gym clothes? What happened to your sneakers?"

"Finally!" Kelly grinned. "Someone noticed. Mom's on Planet Tweak right now."

"Oh, she's coping with things in her own way." Dad walked over and picked Kelly up into a hug, patting her on the back. "Are you all right, hon? Hmm. Your hair smells like burnt plastic."

She clung to him, nearly crying from joy at being home. It had started to feel like she'd spend the rest of her life in that bag. But… the whole crystal thing kind of pushed that aside as not a big deal. "I'm a little freaked out."

"Understandable. Tell me what happened." He sat in his chair at the table, holding her in his lap.

She recounted the story of being attacked by Alexis after school, beat up a little, then stuffed in the bag and left there. "I couldn't get out and no one heard me screaming."

"That's horrible." Mom clucked her tongue. "I'm going to send a strongly-worded letter to the principal… and call Mrs. Stephens first thing in the morning."

"Oh. I understand. You changed because you soiled yourself." Dad squeezed her. "Poor kid. Do you need to go clean up before dinner?"

"No, Dad. I didn't soil myself." *At least, I don't remember if I did. That fire or whatever hurt really bad.*

"Who let you down from there?" asked Dad.

"No one. A ginormous crystal landed in the field. Everything burned… including the bag. That's how I got out." She held her foot up, wiggling her toes at him. "And it burned my sneakers off."

"Just your sneakers? That is most peculiar." He rubbed his chin.

"No… it burned everything else, too." Kelly blushed, hard.

He examined her hair. "But your…"

"Yes, I know. I don't understand. Oh. Do you notice something else different about me?" She stared at him.

"Hmm. You're pale."

"She's always pale," said Mom. "She gets that from my side of the family."

"Nope." Kelly shook her head. "Try again."

"Umm." Dad looked at her for a long moment. "I… your eyes are blue?"

"Nope. They've always been blue."

"Your eyes shrank?"

"Getting warmer."

Dad snapped his fingers. "You took your glasses off!'

"Not exactly. They melted straight off my face."

"Oh, dear," said Mom in a not-at-home sort of voice. "That must have been quite warm."

"Mom, please stop doing that. You're scaring me."

"Give your mother a chance to cope. Aliens showing up for the first time in human history is a major event. It will take her time to adjust."

"You're not scared?"

Dad grinned. "Nope. It's given me so many *wonderful* ideas. I can't wait to get started."

"Started on what?"

"My wonderful ideas."

Mom carried plates over to the table.

"And that means?" Kelly slipped off his lap and took her seat.

"It means I can't wait to get started on my wonderful ideas." He beamed.

"Right." Kelly leaned back so Mom could slide a plate of food in front of her.

Steak, a lump of mashed potatoes flowing with butter, and a small pile of broccoli that didn't smell at all right. In fact, it smelled quite repulsive. Looking at it made Kelly want to jump back from the table... but she didn't.

"Umm, Mom, I think this broccoli expired... in 1857."

"It looks fine to me, sweetie." Her mother sank into her chair, flashed a plastic smile, and picked up her fork.

"Did you replace Mom with a robot or something? She's never this... this... bland." Kelly cut a piece off her steak. "It's like we're in an old sitcom with TV Mom."

"Nope. She's just in shock. Lot of people are." Dad loaded a hunk of steak up with mashed potatoes and ate them together. "Mmm. Wonderful."

Kelly stared in disbelief as her parents got into a quick discussion about the food being good. It had been a long time since she saw her parents completely happy. Dad always had a chip on his shoulder about his job, and Mom... well, her mother usually came home from work in a good mood—especially if she got a sale, but at the moment, she seemed *absent*. Like no real personality existed inside her anymore. Both parents happy at dinner had about the same odds of occurring as Alexis hugging her at school. No better time existed for the bomb she had to drop.

"Umm, Dad?"

He looked over at her. "Yes?"

She took a deep breath, held it for a bit, then let it out her nose. "I did something stupid."

"That's unlike you. What do you think you did?"

"I had a math test yesterday. I knew I'd finish it early, so I brought *Star Prince #17* to school to read after I finished the test."

"Oh. The teacher took it away from you, didn't he? No problem. I'll call the school."

"No, Dad. Worse. Alexis and her friends beat me up after school and threw me in the garbage can. Rachel found the comic book in my backpack and threw it in the garbage, too. It's all stained and ruined." She started to cry. "I'm sorry. You were so happy when you gave it to me… and I ruined it because I'm stupid."

"Aww, Kell." He got up and walked around the table to take a knee beside her. "It's only a comic book. What matters to me the most is that you told the truth and didn't try to pretend nothing happened. Sure, I'm disappointed that a rare number seventeen was damaged, but I'm more upset those kids pick on you." He hugged her. "And I'm proud of you for telling me."

She pulled back her tears, almost managing to smile. "Really?"

"Yep." He smiled, patted her on the head, then stood. "Now, go on. Eat your dinner."

"Okay."

Kelly, feeling like a weight the size of that spaceship had been taken off of her shoulders, attacked her dinner—except for the foul-smelling broccoli. Her parents both ate theirs, not even hesitating. Watching them eat it almost made her throw up, so she turned her head.

"Sweetie," said Mom. "We've talked about this. Eat your vegetables."

"It smells bad."

"You always say it smells bad. They're good for you."

"Please let me skip it tonight? They smell *really* bad."

Mom shook her head. "Kelly, if I let you talk me out of eating vegetables once, it's going to become twice, then three times, then you'll stop eating them completely. It's for your own good. When you're all grown up and on your own, you can eat however much or little veggies as you like. But as long as I'm responsible for keeping you healthy, you need to get all your vitamins. Now go on."

She stared a plea at Dad.

"Listen to your mother, hon."

Kelly hung her head and stabbed her fork into a piece of broccoli. The closer it got to her face, the more she wanted to throw up. It stank like boiled cat box fermented in sour milk. She couldn't get it within an inch of her mouth before she put it down.

"Oh, please don't put us through this again. Do I need to play the airplane game?" asked Mom.

"I'm not three." Kelly sighed.

"Eat your broccoli."

"Fine." She closed her eyes and stuffed her face with the horrible broccoli, gulping it all down so fast she barely chewed or tasted it.

"There. Was that so bad?" asked Mom in a sugary tone.

Kelly looked at the four copies of her dinner plate swirling in circles in front of her eyes. Her stomach cramped up as though she'd swallowed a bag of needles. She grabbed her gut, curling up on the chair and groaning.

"Oh, little drama queen." Mom leaned on the table. "It's only broccoli. Only broccoli. Broccoli. Broc-c-c-c-oli." Her mother's repeating voice echoed off to silence.

"Mohhm—" She erupted with a deep, resonant belch that shook the windows. "I don't feel so goo—" She burped again even louder. Something upstairs fell over.

Her parents' hair wilted visibly in the air blast that came out of her throat, which nearly knocked Mom and her chair over backward.

Dad's right eye twitched. "It's quite past time to change the cat litter."

"We don't have a cat, dear."

"Did that smell come out of our daughter?" Dad gagged.

Mom cringed. "I believe it did."

Kelly's body stopped listening to her. She face-planted the plate, then collapsed out of her chair like a limp silicone doll, spilling onto the floor on her back. The ceiling blurred and twisted in a disorienting smear while the alien space fleet got into a pan-galactic war inside her stomach.

"Hon, are you all right?" asked Dad, sounding miles away.

She tried to answer, but as soon as she opened her mouth, she belched for sixteen seconds straight, tinting the ceiling green and setting off two car alarms outside.

Mom fainted.

"That's a little pungent." Dad got out of his chair and opened the window over the sink.

Kelly curled up in a ball, holding her stomach. It hurt so bad she cried.

"Hmm." Dad took a knee beside her, waving his cell phone back and forth over her like something out of a science fiction movie. "That's quite unexpected. Most interesting."

Mom moaned and sat up. "What on earth is that smell? It stinks so bad I'm dizzy."

"It appears that our daughter is having a bad reaction to the broccoli." He tapped his phone screen.

"She always has a bad reaction to broccoli."

"Yes, Mel, but has she ever burped and knocked you out before? Hmm?" Dad smiled at her.

Mom peered up at the greenish ceiling. "No… That's a first."

Kelly screamed past clenched teeth at a flare of pain inside her stomach. "Dad! Help! It hurts so bad! Make it stop. Please!"

Her father scooped her up off the floor. "It's all right. There's nothing we can really do but wait. You'll be fine. Just sleep it off."

Kelly groaned. The motion of him standing up and turning with her made her seasick in an instant. She heaved a few times, but couldn't throw up. In a blink, she found herself in bed, not remembering how she got there. Her father sat next to her, running a hand over her head in a repetitive, soothing gesture.

She sweat from everywhere, feverish, shaking, feeling like death warmed over. The edges of her vision turned black, creeping inward, cutting off her sight to two tiny dots… which disappeared. Blind, she lost the ability to feel any sense of direction, as though she floated in nothingness.

I knew it… vegetables are gonna kill me.

CHAPTER TEN

NOTHING AN E-TABLET WON'T FIX

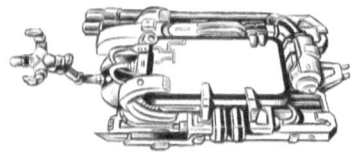

Kelly woke in her bed, feeling normal.

Mostly normal anyway. Her stomach ached a little. She sat up and flew into a panic, wondering why her alarm hadn't gone off or her mother didn't wake her up for school. She flung off her gym uniform and got halfway dressed before she froze, one leg in her jeans, hopping up and down on the other foot, staring at her clock.

Saturday: 9:48 a.m.

"Oh… whew." She leaned her head back and exhaled in relief. Not late for school. No big deal that she hadn't done her homework last night.

Her stomach gurgled.

Nature called… collect.

Kelly ran to the bathroom in such a hurry to get on the toilet that it almost seemed like she literally flew off the ground at the doorway, spun about in midair, and came down sitting. Her gut churned. Her stomach started to hurt. Something *bad* was about to happen. She braced herself against the walls, near to the point of screaming from the pain in her belly.

Boom.

She landed on her chest in the hallway, jeans around one leg, stunned.

"What the hell was that?" yelled Mom downstairs.

"I dunno," called Dad from the back yard. "Sounded like someone farted into a microphone hooked up to an arena concert sound system. Shook the whole freakin' house."

Kelly blushed. She picked herself up off the floor and started to go back into the bathroom—but froze in horror. The toilet lay in a ruin of small pieces. A narrow stream of water sprayed upward from the thin pipe sticking out of the floor. Fortunately, it appeared that only gas had come out of her. The only disgusting part of cleanup would be touching toilet water. However, all the pain and sickness had gone away. She felt amazing.

Crimson faced, she pulled her jeans into place then walked downstairs.

Mom sat at the kitchen table with her laptop and a large cup of coffee. "Morning, sweetie."

"Umm. Mom? I just blew up the toilet."

"Oh, don't worry dear," said Mom. "Your father does that all the time."

"Umm. No, Mom. I mean literally. It exploded. Pieces. And there's like water spraying."

Mom blinked at her.

"Seriously."

Mom stood and went upstairs, Kelly following. Her mother stopped in the bathroom door, took in the devastation, then shut the water valve off before calmly calling the plumber to bring a new toilet. Evidently, an exploding toilet didn't strike her as odd at all.

"I'm not in trouble?" asked Kelly.

"Why would you be? Did you do that on purpose?" Mom retrieved the mop from the hall closet.

She shook her head, standing there in silence while her mother cleaned up the water.

"Do you feel better? You were pretty sick last night."

Kelly rubbed her stomach, which growled. "Umm. Yeah. I feel okay now."

"Good." Mom dumped the bucket into the sink, then hugged her. "Come on. I'll fix you some breakfast. How about waffles?"

"Awesome!" Kelly grinned and followed her mother to the kitchen.

FOR AS LONG AS SHE LIVED, IF DAD NEVER UTTERED THE WORDS 'FARTED OVER AN arena sound system' again, she'd be happy. Once he found out what happened, he'd laughed for fifteen minutes straight. As it stood, for the next, oh, twenty years, any mention of gaseous malfeasance would make her blush —even if she had nothing to do with it. She absolutely refused to acknowledge a noise like that came out of her. Touching lava with her bare hand and having it feel like warm modeling clay would apparently be only the first of many weird things.

Broccoli, it seemed, did horrible, horrible things to her.

She'd always hated it. Now at least, she had a good reason to avoid eating it ever again. Unless, of course, her mother had simply bought a really —*seriously*—bad batch of the stuff.

The waffles came out super yummy though.

After breakfast, she headed up to her bedroom. Since she didn't have a cell phone—Mom refused to give a nine-year-old a cell phone—and didn't know Paige's number, she contented herself to read the next *Waif* novel. Every few pages, she stared past the e-reader at her bare feet sticking out from her jeans. It had been a long time since she'd painted her toenails. She hadn't bothered after the flip-flop theft incident. Why spend the time if no one would ever see them? But seeing her new friend wearing toenail polish tempted her to break out the polish. Well, her hopefully new friend. She still didn't know for sure if she'd see the girl again.

Hammering, sawing, and strange whirring drifted in from the backyard.

"What the…?"

Kelly set the e-reader on her bed, slid to the floor, and crept to the window to peer outside.

A square hole about the size of a big elevator shaft had appeared in the center of the yard. It hadn't been there yesterday and already plunged deep enough that she couldn't see the bottom from her second-story bedroom window.

Dad stood near the edge holding a chrome e-tablet, wearing a long white labcoat, and seeming infinitely pleased with himself. He kinda reminded her of one of those guys at construction sites who stands there doing nothing, watching other people work all day.

"Okay, this is getting really super strange."

She headed into the hall, jogged downstairs, and crossed the house to the kitchen, going out via the sliding glass doors to the yard. Cold, dew-coated grass tickled her feet as she padded over to her father. Various whirrs, bangs, buzzes, and rattles echoed up from the big hole.

"Careful hon, don't fall in." Dad smiled. "Oh, here. I have something for you."

"What is this?" Kelly looked up from the hole to her father, who handed her a silver Frisbee with blinking lights on the top, kind of a tiny UFO.

"Which are you referring to, sweetie?"

She examined the Frisbee. "Umm. Let's start with this."

"It's a Frisbee."

"Obviously."

"Try throwing it."

She shrugged and gave it a toss. It flew in a nice, even glide to the other side of the yard. A bright blue light lit up around the rim... and it sailed right back to her. Despite her shock, she caught it instinctively.

"It's a self-returning Frisbee." Her father grinned, infinitely proud of himself.

"Uhh, Dad? This is basically making fun of me for having no friends." Kelly blinked. "Wait. This is a self-returning Frisbee."

"That's what I said."

She threw it again... and it flew back to her.

"What the crap, Dad? Stuff like this doesn't exist." She turned the item over in her hands, awestruck at all the glowing bits. "Whoa... it really flies back."

"Yep. I made it for you."

"Great. The girl with no friends gets to play Frisbee with herself." She threw and caught it again. "Umm. Thanks, Dad."

"One of many wonderful ideas I have." He clasped the lapels of his lab coat and rocked back on his heels.

If she didn't know better, she'd have said his face got a little taller and a little pointier. "What's with the big hole? Where did that come from?"

"I made that, too."

Kelly blinked and leaned out over the edge to look down. The bottom had to be six stories deep, with a metal floor and a doorway already leading to some manner of chamber. All the construction noises came from inside.

"Careful, not so close there, kiddo. The top hasn't been properly reinforced yet." He tapped at the e-tablet screen.

Multiple robot voices chorused, "Command accepted," from below.

The dirt beneath her feet crumbled. Kelly slipped off the edge, but hung in midair, her heels only a few inches below the top of the shaft.

"Amazing. You're flying." Dad raised his e-tablet as if to take a picture of her with a ridiculously oversized smartphone. His actual cell phone appeared to be a small rectangle attached to the middle of the back panel.

"No, I'm 'not falling.' This isn't flying."

"Think about going up," said Dad.

Kelly peered down past her toes at the elevator shaft she *should* be falling into and dying. *I touched lava and didn't burn. I ripped the doors off the school. No darn way...* She thought about gliding upward, and did.

Dad poked a button on his e-tablet. The floor of the shaft rose up like an elevator, stopping even with the ground. He stepped on it and went down to the bottom. "Come on down here, hon."

Kelly flew around in a circle, only a little faster than she could've walked. "Holy crap. I'm actually flying."

"Sweetie," called Dad. "Come on down."

She angled toward the shaft and floated in feet first, sinking at a relatively slow glide until stopping near the bottom high enough off the floor to be eye-level with Dad. "This is awesome! Am I dreaming?"

"No, hon."

"Seriously? I'm not sleeping in the bag still hanging on the goal post at school?"

"Nope."

Kelly folded her arms. "Can you prove it? Tell me something I wouldn't have any way to know myself so I couldn't possibly dream it."

"Hmm. Anything I can think of off the top of my head, you're not old enough to hear. Oh, here's one. Every time your mother and I went on a date before we got married, she always ordered a frozen margarita."

"She usually gets them when we go out to eat now. That doesn't prove anything."

"Did you know she got them before?"

"Well, no... but it's logical to think that if she likes them now, she would've liked them before."

Dad chuckled. "Okay. What about last night? That broccoli hurt you. Wouldn't that amount of pain have made you wake up?"

She scrunched her toes at the memory of feeling *so* sick. "Yeah. Probably. But, this is so unbelievable. I'm flying."

"That you are."

"And you've built a..." She peered left past the doorway into a large room filled with bizarre technological equipment and a small army of robots still whizzing back and forth building the place. Flying orbs with four extendable arms worked near the ceiling while humanoid ones only a little larger than Kelly hurriedly extended another hallway into the earth. A veritable stream of boxes-with-legs carried dirt out of the tunnel and dumped it into one of the big machines, which spat out an almost-continuous supply of shiny metal. "Lair. You're building a lair."

Dad grabbed her out of the air into a hug, swinging her around and around. "Oh, this is beyond wonderful. Aren't you thrilled?"

"To be honest? I'm freaking out just a little bit."

He beamed, hugging her tight. "You're flying! You got it too! I couldn't be happier."

"Got what too?"

"*It!*" said Dad, with extreme gravitas.

"Umm." She furrowed her brows. "It?"

"Yes." He wagged a finger in the air. "Those aliens. Whatever they did. The crystals they dropped all over the planet. They've changed people. Some have changed like us. Some... in other ways."

"Other ways?"

Dad let go of her and tapped his fingertips together, cringing. "Umm. Don't worry about that for now."

She raised an eyebrow.

"Anyway. I have so many ideas!" He walked deeper into the room, gesturing at everything. "I'm building a lair. McManus has seen the last of old Jack Donovan, that's for sure. No more nine-to-five for this man. No sir-ee. You're still little yet, so I don't want to involve you in any of the plans. Be a child. Have fun. Don't worry about anything. The world has become a wonderful place."

"Dad, are you feeling all right?"

He thrust his arms out to the sides and spun around on tiptoe. "I feel wonderful! I haven't been this happy in years."

"Sure… Why is Mom acting like she's been replaced by aliens? Did they take her?"

"No. She's in shock. Trust me, that's really your mother. Remember, aliens just showed up, dropped giant crystals on the planet, and some people now have superpowers." He made a pinchy gesture. "That's a bit much for her to process all at once. You might not want to hit her with a truth bomb just yet."

"Truth bomb?"

"Yes. Don't show her that you have powers right away. It might be the last straw. She's struggling to cope with things." He again fussed at the e-tablet and a small army of child-sized robots raced out of one hallway and attacked the wall, beginning construction on another passage.

Kelly floated over to him. "And she's letting you build a lair in the backyard? She wouldn't even let us have a swimming pool."

"Shall we say, I am taking advantage of her momentary separation from reality. Soon, there will be a tool shed above the elevator access, so this will be all concealed and normal looking from the outside. What your mother doesn't know, won't hurt her."

"Dad, isn't that lying?"

"Not at all." He grinned. "If she asks, I'll tell her it's here. You know what they say, better to ask for forgiveness than permission."

"And what if she doesn't forgive you?"

"She will. This isn't a swimming pool. She objected to a pool, not a vast underground lair filled with the very latest in technology." He raised his arm in a sweeping gesture while gazing off into the distance. "Just think of all we could do!"

"I am, Dad, and that's kinda why I'm freakin' out here. This isn't the same as sitting in the basement building model robot mechs all Saturday long."

"Hah! No. I'm going to make one of them for real, eventually. I have the plans already."

Kelly spun around, looking over all the machinery, blinking lights, *actual robots*, and other things. "Where did you get all this stuff?"

"I made it."

"From where?" She flailed her arms. "How can you afford it?"

"Who said I bought anything?" He wagged his eyebrows and held up the e-tablet. "Started with my phone, and I just kept tinkering."

"How did you... do that? I mean, like, did you just pull alien technology out of thin air?"

He examined his e-tablet. "Honestly... I don't remember. I just sort of found myself looking at the phone and thinking it could be so much better. So, I added on to it. Not really sure where stuff came from."

She facepalmed. "Dad, I'm the nine-year-old here. I'm the one who's supposed to be living in a world of imagination."

A ball robot shot by so fast and close that Kelly ended up spinning like a top. With a snarl, she caught herself and stopped in an instant.

"Oh, good control. Nice braking."

"Dad!"

"So, I bet now that you have powers, you can put those bullies in their place, right?"

"Umm." She blinked. "I never even thought about that. I mean, like not for real. I daydreamed about it before, but didn't actually have powers then. But... powers? Who has powers?"

"You do. I do, all the lucky ones do!" He cheered, then used the e-tablet to command more robots over to the machine making metal plates, which they carried into the newest hallway.

"I'm not even sure what I can do, other than apparently fly and touch lava."

He rubbed his chin.

"Dad, did your face get pointier?"

"It's possible." He tapped at his e-tablet. Various robots swung around and ran in different directions. "Aha. Wonderful!"

She furrowed her eyebrows at him. "You're not helping."

He laughed. "Give me some time, dear. Once I have the lair fully operational, we'll do some testing and see what you can do."

"Yeah, sure."

"Should I make a titanium toilet bowl?"

Kelly blushed scarlet. "Dad!"

He snickered.

She pointed at him. "We shall *never* speak of that again. Never."

"Okay." He raised one hand as if swearing in court. "I promise."

Whew.

"At least until you bring your first boyfriend over."

"Dad!" screamed Kelly. "No!"

He raised both hands in surrender. "Okay, okay. Fine."

"Ooh. Boys! Why do you find farts funny?"

"Now that question might exceed my computational ability." He winked. "However, I don't merely find farts humorous. Now, ones that destroy toil—"

"DAAAAAAAD!" screamed Kelly.

He cackled.

Fire practically wafted from her face, her cheeks had become so hot. "I'm going to go read."

"Sure, hon."

Kelly gazed around the lair—which seemed noticeably bigger and loaded with even more tech than it had even five minutes before—and flew up out of the shaft.

"So, so weird… says the flying girl."

CHAPTER ELEVEN

INERTIA

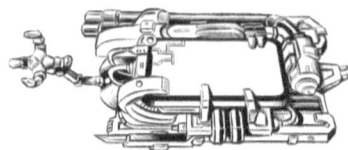

O ther than the constant noise of construction coming from the backyard and Mom's total indifference to it, the remainder of Saturday went by in a relatively normal manner except for the voice of cable news downstairs on the television talking about visitors from another planet calling themselves the Nolmek. These aliens had evidently sent emissaries to all major world governments to offer assistance and establish diplomatic relations with the people of Earth.

Kelly had paused in her reading long enough to listen from the top of the stairs to the news anchor relaying the message that the crystal bombardment had not been an attack, but the aliens' effort to save the planet. According to the Nolmek, the Earth's magnetic field had developed a dangerous instability which would have caused it to entirely collapse over the next six or seven years. When it ultimately failed, the planet would have no magnetic field at all and suffer the devastating effects of unshielded cosmic radiation that would burn all life to ashes.

So nothing major.

Somehow, these crystals would prevent the decay of the magnetic field for another million years or so. Certain unintended side effects (superpowers, mutations, and 'unknown effects on animal life'), the aliens claimed accidental and unexpected.

She shrugged and returned to her room to read.

When the plumber showed up with a new toilet at roughly one that afternoon, Mom offered up a smooth-as-silk explanation that her husband had been trying to kill a spider with a sledgehammer, missed, and smashed the toilet. Hearing her mother lie so easily—and well—felt wrong, but for this one time, she'd forgive her. She would never show her face in public ever again if anyone found out she'd destroyed a toilet.

Saturday, being a weekend—that is to say, *not* a school night—had the added perk of an increase in allowed video game time to three hours. Kelly decided to take advantage of that around two after the plumber left. She played *Star Prince: Trials of Tabrin* straight until dinnertime. Like Dad, she had a tendency to become absorbed in a fun activity and lose track of time. Video games didn't usually do that to her, but… *Star Prince*.

Suspiciously, Mom didn't walk in when she had five minutes remaining of her three hours and tell her to stop playing.

Her mother cooked again, as she and Dad traded stove duty a week at a time. Starting tomorrow, he would be doing all the cooking for one week. She made meatloaf with sides of mac-n-cheese and green beans. The beans *looked* okay, but they smelled like the school's garbage can plus dead bird.

Once again, Kelly ignored the veggies.

"Sweetie, veggies," said Mom.

"Please, no," whimpered Kelly in an uncharacteristically timid voice. "The broccoli made me super sick. Like, I'm seriously not lying."

Mom shifted her jaw side to side.

"Melinda." Dad made an explosion sound effect. "Do you want to replace the toilet again?"

"Ugh." Kelly folded her arms on the table and hid her burning red face. "Really?"

"It's fine, hon. Let her skip the veggies for now."

Kelly sat up, still blushing.

Mom and Dad exchanged a knowing look.

"All right," said Mom.

Annoyed at her father once again bringing up 'the event that shall never again be talked about,' Kelly returned to the MegaStation after dinner intending to further exceed her time limit as a direct retaliation for being embarrassed. Mom didn't nag her at all about having spent nearly five hours at the game. When she hit the six-hour mark, she voluntarily stopped, not wanting to push things that far. Superpowers were one thing, but Mom not being the Queen of Time in regard to video games qualified as a legit miracle.

Wow. Guess the alien crystals really have warped reality.

Kelly went up to her room to read comics until bedtime. Whenever she saw a character using a power, she pointed her arm at the window and tried to activate the same power. Alas, nothing more happened than any other time she pretended.

She attempted to fly again, floating up off her bed in the same position—right foot resting atop her left knee—and settled back down.

Okay, so I can fly. I think I have super strength. I might be tough if lava can't burn me. What else can I do?

"I mean, flying is wicked awesome already. How much more do I need?"

At 8:57 p.m., Mom poked her head in. "Almost bedtime, sweetie."

Kelly looked up, surprised at the normality. "Yes, Mom."

She set the comic aside and got ready for bed. Fortunately, her relationship with toilets hadn't become permanently ruined. In the absence of toxic vegetables, everything worked as it should.

Yeah, had to be the broccoli. Hmm. Mashed potatoes didn't smell bad. Potatoes are a vegetable, even if I do like them. Is it only green ones?

Mom waited to tuck her in bed, once again placing Floppet by her side and kissing her on the forehead. Dad rushed into her room, slightly charred, smoke peeling up from his hair, with an expression as if he'd been hit with a strong shock.

A loud *zap* and flash happened when he tried to kiss her on the head; he flew back as if punched in the face by a giant robot, landing on the floor halfway into the hall. Kelly felt nothing more unusual than a gentle kiss. However, the air smelled like ozone.

"Dad?" She sat up. "Are you okay?"

Mom blinked at him. "Jack, what on Earth are you doing now?"

"Little bit of a latent charge from the gravitronic phase-actuated matter relocation field." Dad stared at the ceiling, lightning bolts repeatedly crawling up his shocked-spiky hair.

Kelly blinked. "Umm. What?"

"The teleporter needs some work." Dad grabbed the wall and pulled himself upright. "It's not ready yet."

"Are you serious?" Kelly blinked.

"No, I am Jack Donovan." Dad winked, waved, and ran out.

"What is wrong with that man?" muttered Mom.

Kelly held her hands up. "Don't ask me. *You* married him."

Mom laughed. "Go to sleep, hon."

"Night, Mom."

"Night dear."

"Goodnight, sweetie," crackled Dad's voice from the alarm clock.

Kelly and Mom both stared at it.

"My alarm clock just spoke," muttered Kelly.

"Now *that* is unsettling." Mom shut the light off.

"Yeah, only a little." Kelly snuggled into bed and closed her eyes.

KELLY FOUND HERSELF AWAKE IN THE MIDDLE OF THE NIGHT, STARING AT HER glowing-star-covered ceiling.

Nothing hurt, felt weird, or seemed wrong. However, the construction noises coming from her window hadn't stopped. She tried to ignore the racket and fall back asleep for a while, but the constant hammering amounted to Chinese water torture.

The alarm clock showed 11:58 p.m.

"Ugh, Dad, the neighbors are going to call the police."

Kelly slipped out of bed and went over to the window. An ordinary-looking brown and green tool shed stood over the shaft. Large for a garden shed, but still nothing too suspicious… other than being right in the middle of the yard.

She opened her window and leaned halfway out. "Dad?" After a minute of nothing, she repeated, "Dad" louder.

Still no response.

Grinning to herself, she pushed the window up more, brought her right leg up to step on the windowsill, curling her toes over the end.

"This is cool."

Kelly jumped out the window and flew to land beside the shed. "Okay. I just flew out my window. I really have superpowers." She pumped her fist with a whispery "Yes!" and bounced on her toes. "This is totally worth being trapped in a book bag all day. I'm not even mad at them."

The shed *looked* like one of the prefab ones from a chain home improvement store, but it felt like metal. At first, it appeared to be locked with no way to open, but she spotted a cleverly disguised palm-print-reader under an outdoor power outlet beside the door at the height of a doorbell. The front face of the outlet lifted up, revealing a shiny silver panel.

Kelly rested her hand on it.

A happy sounding chirp sounded, and the door opened with a faint hiss and blast of cool air. She stepped into an ordinary garden shed, complete with tools, gas cans, and a lawnmower. Everything appeared new, never used.

"Wow. Dad's going all out. Secret lair city."

The door closed.

A camper's lantern hung on a wall peg high to the left projected a purple scanning laser over her.

"Identity confirmed. Access granted," said a pleasant female voice that sounded like Mom.

Kelly, and a large square section of the floor beneath her, shot straight down six stories in almost an instant with a loud *shoomp!* noise. The elevator dropped so fast that her nightgown briefly flapped up over her head.

She blinked at the opening to the large lair chamber she remembered seeing earlier that afternoon. Dad didn't appear to be anywhere in sight, at least from here. She padded in over smooth mirror-like floor, gazing around in amazement at a scene straight out of one of her favorite superhero movies. Most of the technology in here defied explanation. Lights flashed, dials flickered, quivering tubes carried who-knows-what back and forth from cabinet to cabinet. He'd added four other hallways, building out into what appeared to be a massive underground complex.

"Dad?" yelled Kelly.

One of the humanoid robots ran over to her. Except for having a head, two arms, and two legs, it didn't look at all like a person, essentially a bunch of geometric shapes stacked on top of each other.

"Your father is not here," said the robot in a robotic voice.

"Where is he?"

"In the house."

"Can you guys build a little quieter until morning? Maybe even take a break? I can't sleep... and the neighbors might call the cops for the noise."

"Processing request. Command accepted. We shall reserve high-volume activities until morning."

"Thanks."

"Gratitude," said the robot before whirling around and tottering off down the hall it came from.

Kelly shook her head, yawned, and walked back into the elevator. "Okay... how do I make it go up."

As soon as she said the word 'up,' the floor shot upward with a *shoomp!*

Somehow, in defiance of physics, she didn't launch off the floor and hit the roof when it stopped.

"Weird."

She exited the 'tool shed' and started to glide back up toward her bedroom window, but froze in midair at a loud *bang* from about two blocks behind and to the left. Curious, she flew higher and accelerated toward the area where the noise came from. When she went high enough to see over houses, a car accident became obvious in the street. An older sports car sat in the middle of the road, its front end crumpled inward as though it had hit a telephone pole, only the wreckage partially embraced a boy instead of a tree.

"Ack!"

Careful to hold her nightgown from blooming up, she rushed over and landed on the road by the boy—who she recognized as Mike Hopkins from school. Despite it being past midnight, he still wore day clothes, dark T-shirt, jeans, sneakers, not pajamas. He scowled at nothing in particular, making a sour face like he'd had a fight with his parents.

"Mike?" asked Kelly.

"What?" He didn't look up.

"You got hit by a car! Are you okay?"

"Yeah. Donnie's a butthead."

Kelly glanced at the guy in the driver's seat, about eighteen or nineteen, unconscious and bleeding from the face. Alive, but quite clearly out cold. "Holy crap! Did you do that on purpose?"

"No." Mike, hands still in his pockets, shrugged. "He could'a drove around me. Didn't."

She walked over. "You have to get out of the road."

"Why?"

"Because a car hit you."

He finally looked up at her. "So?"

"Grr." She put a hand on the car and pushed it back, then wrapped her arms around Mike, intending to lift and carry him to the sidewalk.

Much to her surprise, he didn't pop right up. She struggled, emitting a gasp of surprise when the pavement cracked beneath her bare feet. The effort to lift the eleven-year-old felt roughly normal, as though pre-superpower Kelly Donovan had attempted to pick up a boy that size. Well, perhaps she had *more* success at it considering he did leave the ground. Grunting and gasping, she lugged him over to the sidewalk and set him on his feet, nearly out of breath by the time she put him down.

"Wow… you're heavy." She took a step back.

Mike gawked at her. "Whoa! How the heck did you do that?"

"Huh?"

"Nothing has been able to move me yet. Not even my mom when she tries to drag me out of bed in the morning to go to school. But that was before. Now, I mean *nothing* can move me when I don't wanna go anywhere… except you."

"Never underestimate a redhead with a mission." Kelly folded her arms and held her chin high.

"Uhh, yeah, sure. Seriously, what happened?"

"We got superpowers."

"No duh. Donnie just ran me over with his Mustang and it didn't even hurt. Am I dreaming?"

"I thought so, too, but now I don't think so. This really happened."

Mike blinked. "You're outside in your PJs."

"It is midnight. You should be in bed."

"You're even smaller than me. You should be in bed, too."

"I know, but… I couldn't sleep. Heard the crash and wanted to see what happened."

Mike scratched his head. "Should probably call the police or something and report this. Not gonna tell him what he hit if this is really happening."

"Umm. I guess. Or just say it's an accident. Did you want to hurt him?"

"No. I didn't even see him until he hit me."

Kelly shrugged. "There you go. Accident."

"I don't know if I should tell anyone I have powers. You know, like a secret identity. Hey, what do you think I should use for a name."

"How should I know?"

"Do you have a name yet?"

"Just Kelly."

He ran a hand up over his head, briefly pulling his hair off his eyes. "You can't use your real name if you have powers."

"Why not? Madeline Starbright does."

"That's made up. And besides, no one really has the name Starbright. I'm thinking about Inertia or TMO. Which one do you think is better?"

"TMO sounds like TMI."

"It's for The Immovable Object."

"Wouldn't that be TIO?" She raised an eyebrow.

Mike shrugged. "Yeah, but that's like Spanish for uncle."

"Use Inertia. The other one makes no sense and it's too easy to make fun of, TMI."

"Good point. Thanks."

A siren arose in the distance.

"Umm. I should go home." Kelly waved.

"Okay. See ya."

She leapt into the air, rising in a graceful turn until she faced toward her house, then zoomed straight to her window, climbed inside, and crawled back under her blankets, gazing up at a purple ceiling decorated with glow-in-the-dark stars.

The banging and noise from the lair had ceased. Some light whirring continued.

"Ahh. Much better." Kelly closed her eyes and smiled.

CHAPTER TWELVE

SMALL VICTORY

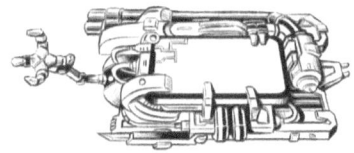

Monday morning—after a surprisingly unremarkable Sunday at home with the parents—Kelly walked her usual route to school, cutting across backyards. Today, however, she went over fences by flying low and close, so anyone watching from a distance would think she climbed.

A trip to the mall yesterday resulted in replacement sneakers of the same type she lost. Mom didn't even appear upset that they'd been utterly destroyed after only two weeks. Perhaps it annoyed her, but any irritation Mom felt would've been directed at the girls who trapped Kelly in a book bag. Not like she lost her sneakers to being reckless. Still, she felt rebellious today and decided to finish off her jeans and babydoll top outfit with flip-flops—after painting her toenails bright purple. Might as well take advantage of California September before she *had* to wear sneakers or freeze.

Then again, something told her she could probably wear a bikini in Antarctica now and not feel cold. Heck, she could probably *go* to Antarctica now… on her own.

She leapt the last fence, which put her on the same street as the school one block closer than where she normally turned. For the first time in years, she strolled down the sidewalk toward the school building with her head held high.

The giant crystal still towered over the building. For that matter, she thought it pretty stupid that they hadn't closed school on account of 'massive alien crystal.' One-quarter inch of snow would shut things down but a ten-billion-ton alien rock didn't? Bleh.

Principal Walsh had, however, put up nice, informative signs all over the front entrance.

Until further notice, the John Q. Petersen Middle School Sports Field is closed. All Piranhas home games have been rescheduled to away.

"Wow. Thanks. Never would have guessed a skyscraper-sized crystal might get in the way of a football game." Kelly rolled her eyes.

She made a right turn onto the sidewalk approaching the stairs.

As soon as she reached the top, Brittany called, "Hey, Turd, think fast!"

Since she hadn't been walking with her gaze on the ground as usual, she spotted the basketball coming for her face. The girls were only six feet away, but the basketball—in fact the entire world—appeared to be moving in slow motion. Kelly, however, didn't. She raised her left arm, making a fist.

The basketball bounced off her knuckles, ricocheting back at Brittany and nailing her right in the face. Her expression didn't even change until the ball hit her, knocking her back two steps. The throw didn't have any more force than what the girl had put into it herself, as Kelly had only blocked. She figured it all happened in a second or two, no different than if Brittany had spiked the ball into the side of the school building as hard as she could and caught the return in the chin.

"Hi, Brittany," said Kelly.

A bunch of other kids in the area laughed, pointing at her.

The girl snarled. "What did you do with my bag?"

"I don't know where it went. I left it there."

"Nice flip-flops," said Alexis. "It would be a real shame if anyone steals them."

"Yeah." Kelly folded her arms. "It would be a real shame if anyone stole them. 'Cause, like seriously? Who does stuff like that? Four-year-olds?"

Colleen leaned into her face. "Nice jeans, Noodle-butt. Your mom get them at the thrift store?"

"What's a thrift store?" asked Kelly.

"It's the place where all the poor people get used stuff." Colleen scoffed.

"Oh, wow. Really? Never heard of those. How do *you* know so much about them?"

Rachel's face turned red. She clamped a hand over her mouth—to keep from laughing.

Colleen gasped. "You little…"

"Today's the day." Alexis, for the first time ever wearing a flannel shirt and jeans in public, walked up in front of her. "I'm dressed for a butt kicking."

"Why do you want someone to kick your butt?" Kelly scratched her head.

"You wouldn't hit a kid with glasses, would you?" asked Brittany in a mocking voice.

"Hey, where's her glasses?" Colleen pointed. "Turd got contacts."

"Are you guys done?" asked Kelly. "Really. This is getting old."

Alexis snarled. "You got a big mouth, don't you?"

"Nah. It's kinda small." Kelly poked two fingers into her cheeks. "Like the rest of me."

Brittany picked up the basketball. She tried to act casual, but Kelly saw the sneak throw from the side coming a mile away. The instant the girl threw it, the world slowed down. She blocked with a fist again, but added a tiny bit of a punch this time.

The basketball walloped Brittany in the gut, knocking her over. She let out a noise like someone had kicked a goose. Alexis narrowed her eyes. More students watching erupted in laughter, making fun of Brittany for being a doofus.

"You little…" Brittany lunged to her feet and charged, raising a fist.

Kelly stood there.

Brittany smashed her fist into Kelly's cheek, but the hit didn't move her at all. The girl may as well have punched a stone statue. She stumbled to the side clutching her hand to her chest and screaming. Alexis gave her a weird look, but said nothing before walking over to check on Brittany.

Kelly eyed the big garbage can. It *did* have enough room for all four girls.

"Nah," she muttered to herself, and strolled into the school, smiling.

CHAPTER THIRTEEN
THE CHIN OF EPIC POINTINESS

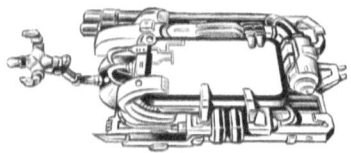

K elly arrived home from school Wednesday afternoon feeling weird.

Not weird because she could fly, had become ridiculously strong, or had been exposed to toxic green vegetables. No, she felt weird due to Alexis and her friends more or less totally avoiding her for most of Monday and all day Tuesday as well as today.

Monday afternoon, Colleen had tried to swipe her flip-flops out from under her desk in math class, but every time she tried, Kelly noticed and stepped on her flops, pinning them to the floor so the other girl couldn't take them. Brittany showed up for third period with her hand in a cast, the punch having broken her wrist.

Ever since the other three saw that, they'd been avoiding her. No one had summoned Kelly to the office about it, so she assumed the girls had lied about how the injury happened. She didn't expect to get in any real trouble over it considering she had only stood there and taken the punch. But... as Mike brought up, maybe it would be a good idea to keep her abilities quiet. At least, for as long as possible.

The TV news had been doing stories on other people going public with super powers all across the globe. It didn't seem like many people had been lucky enough to develop abilities, and the ones who'd gone public varied considerably in potency and usefulness. One man in Brazil could evidently brew coffee by staring at a pot of water and coffee grinds—but couldn't boil water, heat soup, or even make tea. His power only worked with coffee.

Locally, however, a few people with notable abilities had revealed themselves. A black guy in a white-and-black suit with a star logo on the chest, calling himself The Phoenix, announced he had formed a team under the name Aegis with two others. A woman with brown skin and snow white hair who went by Mindfreeze, and a big pale guy using the identity Igor the Red.

The news anchors still snickered when speaking of 'superheroes', but with each passing day, the humor faded a little more. Kelly couldn't help but be thrilled that her comic book daydreams had essentially happened for real, but she did think it strange that aliens from another planet somehow did something to Earth that started giving people superpowers. Had they been watching television for a while and thought it would be cool? How would aliens even *know* that the idea of superheroes even existed?

So far, the Nolmek claimed to be benevolent and said that they came here only because they sensed the potential of humans and wanted to save them from extinction when the magnetic field of Earth fell apart. Having read tons of comics and watched every movie with aliens involved (that her parents let her see), something about their constant reassurances of peace and goodwill didn't sit right. They sounded *too* friendly. *Too* nice. The whole world adored them, mostly due to the rapid spread of small technologies to make life easier, more fun, and cooler. Also, in the few short days since their arrival, they had—according to the news—made great strides in providing water to drought-stricken areas and alleviated famine in parts of the globe with food shortages.

And despite all that, the thing that made Kelly feel the weirdest had been going to school for two whole days without an Alexis Stephens problem.

That, and having a friend. Paige caught up with her at lunch on Monday, and they had been hanging out—not in book bags—all the time since then. In fact, Paige followed her in the door on Wednesday when she returned home from school.

They vegged out in the living room for a while playing video games and talking about comic books, novels, and all the crazy things going on in the world. Paige went into full fangirl mode over Phoenix and Mindfreeze. She had been trying to talk her parents into taking her out to the hills where the Aegis had begun building a stronghold.

"Oh, man. I'm so jealous," said Paige. "I wish I had powers, too. That would be amazing!"

"Yeah," said Kelly, with an odd little smile.

"What about you?"

"Oh, totally. I'd love to have powers. I've only been a comic geek my whole life." She floated up off the couch.

Paige stared at her for three seconds, then squealed. "Oh Emm Gee! Are you serious?"

"No, I'm Kelly."

"Oh, *gawd*. That's such a dad joke."

She landed. "Yeah. I heard it from my dad."

Paige tackled her. "Holy crap you were floating."

"Flying."

"Ooo!"

Kelly grimaced. "You're not jealous?"

"Of course not. Well, I am jealous a little but not envious."

"Huh?"

"That means I wish I had powers, too, but I don't like resent you because you have some."

"Cool." Kelly looked down. "It really would bother me if you did. Like, I'd almost want to give them up if it meant you'd hate me."

"Don't be stupid. Powers are *ah-may-zing*. And only a total butt-breath would get mad over something like that. Besides, you've only known me for three days. Nowhere near long enough to get all emo and give up your powers like Madame Daystar."

"Oh, I hated that story arc. She was *so* stupid." Kelly shook her fists in the air.

"Totally stupid. Like who gives up her powers for a stupid man to love her, then he turns out to be lying all along. I wanted to choke Simko and Ryan. They shouldn't be allowed to write comic stories anymore."

"Yeah seriously."

Mom walked in. "Hey, Swee—who is that?"

"Hi, Mom. It's—"

Her mother rushed around the couch and picked Paige up as if examining a big doll. "Hmm. This appears to be another small human."

"That's Paige."

Paige waved. "Hi, Mrs. Donovan."

Mom glanced at her. "Is she housebroken?"

"Mom!" Kelly laughed. "She's not a pet. She's my friend."

"Does not compute." She set Paige on the couch again. "You have a friend?"

Kelly stuck out her tongue. "Gee, thanks, Mom."

Her mother laughed. "I'm just teasing. You two seem like a good pair. I'm really happy you've found a friend."

"More like she found me." Kelly flashed a cheesy smile.

Mom waved and headed upstairs to change.

"Don't feel bad. Mine's the same way." Paige rolled her eyes. "Last night after you went home, she freaked the heck out that I finally had a friend."

"My father made me a Frisbee that comes back if I throw it. So I can play Frisbee alone."

"Aww, that's so sad."

They both laughed.

"Kelly, c'mon down here a sec please," said Dad's voice from the TV.

"Whoa. Your MegaStation is talking." Paige pointed.

"That's my father. I think he's hacked everything electronic in the house. Hey, come on. Check this out."

Kelly got up and jogged to the kitchen, not bothering to step into her flip-flops. They headed out into the yard, Paige trailing after her over to the shed.

"Umm. Your dad lives in a tool shed? Weird."

"Not weird. Super! And he doesn't *live* in it. He works here now."

She pulled open the front of the electric outlet and touched the hand scanner.

"Ooh!" Paige squeezed her from behind. "Is that real?"

The shed opened.

"It's real."

"It's a shed." Paige gazed around, touching a few tools.

Three seconds after the door closed, the elevator floor descended at a relatively normal speed.

Dad waited for them by the opening. His e-tablet appeared... bigger, almost the size of a cafeteria tray, with numerous sub-modules and even a small robotic arm at the top. It had become... mega-tablet.

Kelly ran over and hugged him.

"Hey, sweetie."

"What's up, Dad?"

"Oh, hello there." He waved at Paige. "Who is this? Do I need to erase her memory of this place?

Paige, evidently oblivious to the question, gawked at the excessive display of technology surrounding them.

"That's my friend, Paige."

"You have a friend?"

"Don't say it like that."

Dad chuckled. "No, I am merely confirming. Does she have powers?"

"No. She's my normal human friend who doesn't have any special gifts or abilities but provides an invaluable sense of warmth to the storyline and helps out in clutch situations despite being totally normal."

"Yes, that makes sense." Dad nodded.

"Either that or when I finally develop an arch-nemesis, it'll be Paige's job to get kidnapped and used to make me do something I don't want to do." Kelly stuck out her tongue. "I hope we're not living one of *those* stories."

Paige continued gazing around.

Dad rubbed his—oddly pointier—chin. "It depends entirely on what's going on. Do you think we're living inside some kind of scenario the aliens have forced on us?"

"Umm. Not sure. I don't think so." She blinked at his face. His entire head appeared even taller, somewhere between a real person and an animated character.

"Well, if we're not inside a simulation or being somehow controlled and manipulated, your predictions for your friend are nothing to worry about. We're not living inside a fictional world." Dad gazed off into the fourth dimension. "Or are we?"

"Oh, stop that." Kelly laughed.

"Holy cats," blurted Paige. "You have a serious secret base. Awesome!"

"So, the lair is completed." Dad beamed. "Follow me. This is the main antechamber, presently housing some of the machines that make the helper robots as well as my matter converter." He led the girls down a long hall with silver walls and blue raindrop-shaped lamps in pairs every fifteen feet. "Down here is my research area and lab. Testing facilities on the left." He pointed at several rooms with tables, machines with robotic arms, and a few chambers that appeared armored enough to survive giant explosions... perhaps for testing powers or devices.

"Wow," said Kelly. "I'm still wondering where you got all this stuff."

"I made it." Dad grinned, and whisked back down the hallway.

Kelly and Paige ran to keep up.

He stopped in the main room again, going to the right down a passage leading directly away from the entrance. "This is the living quarters. Bedrooms, bathrooms, a pool, a small dining facility, observation area—virtual of course—and a stairway up to my control center."

Stunned at the vastness of it all, Kelly could only stand there gawking like Paige.

Dad hurried back to the main room and went left. "Down here, we have the important stuff. Reactor, air processing, storage area, more fabrication devices, and the escape rocket."

"Escape rocket?" asked Kelly and Paige at the same time.

"Of course." Dad clapped. "Every La—erm, secret base, needs to have an escape rocket. Okay, tour's done. Now, if you'll come with me, I want to try a few things."

He hurried off to the right.

Kelly shrugged and followed.

"Kel?" asked Paige.

"Yeah."

"Are you cold?"

"No, why?"

"Well, I'm kinda cold in here. The floor's metal, and you left your shoes in the house."

"Oh. Nope. I'm okay. You know that big crystal that landed at school?"

"Yeah."

"It's got lava all around it. I picked some up and it didn't burn me."

"Wow! How did you get back there? They closed it off and there's like cops all the time."

"I, umm, was there when the thing landed."

Paige's eyes bugged. "Are you serious? Is that why you got powers? Crap you could've been killed! What were you doing at the school at night?"

"Long story. I'll tell you as soon as we're done in here."

"Okay."

They walked into the 'testing area.'

Dad poked a few buttons on his mega-tablet. One of the flying robo-spheres with four tube arms started to fly toward him, but emitted a crackling spark and burst into flames.

"Drat!" yelled Dad. "I've been having some glitches."

The orb flipped over and zoomed straight at Paige like a missile... but abruptly jammed on the brakes, creeping along in slow motion just like the basketball. Sensing imminent disaster, Kelly jumped in its path. The out-of-control robot crashed into her less painfully than a pillow, exploding with a loud *boom* and a faint puff of warmth that felt kinda nice.

When the smoke cleared, Kelly looked down at herself and gasped. Her babydoll top had half-burned away, riddled with holes as big as oranges. Same for her jeans. Most of her front had charred black.

Paige started screaming, then realized nothing would hit her. She gulped and stared at Kelly. "Whoa."

"Amazing," whispered Dad. "And no, that was totally *not* what I wanted to do. I'm still working the kinks out of some of these machines. Kinda winging everything here."

"My clothes!" shouted Kelly.

Dad rubbed his chin. "Hmm. We'll need to work something out for that." He walked over. "Ehh, they're not that bad."

"They're ruined!"

"The jeans are fine. Your mother used to cut holes that big in hers on purpose when she was a teenager."

"I am not Mom. Nor am I a teenager." She tapped her bare foot, making a soft clapping noise. "Will you please get me a new top like this? It's cute."

"Of course." Dad held up the mega-tablet and hit a button.

A small robotic arm extended from the back—and blasted Kelly in the face with a flamethrower.

Paige screamed and dove flat to the ground.

Kelly started to shriek, but upon realizing it hurt only about as bad as standing in the path of a hair dryer—albeit a hair dryer soaked in kerosene—merely frowned. "Dad, stop. That stinks."

The flamethrower fizzled out and retracted back into the mega-tablet. "Amazing. Not a single hair damaged. Let me scan your hand?"

"Umm… your dad just shot you with a flamethrower," said Paige from the floor. "That's not normal."

Kelly extended her arm. "Nothing's normal anymore. It didn't hurt."

He held the mega-tablet over it. Green laser light drew a grid on the back of her hand for a few seconds while the pad beeped… then another robotic arm sprang out and stabbed her with a knife—which bent.

"Ow!" Kelly shook her hand out. "Dad!"

"What the heck!" Paige jumped to her feet. "Dude…"

He turned the mega-tablet over, examining the small blade. "Tungsten carbide… and it bent. Didn't penetrate at all. Very interesting."

"Argh! Stop sticking me with knives!"

Paige blinked. "Things you never thought you would say to your Dad for 400."

Her father pulled a large handgun out of his labcoat pocket.

"No!" Kelly swatted it out of his hand, launching the weapon across the room. It shattered on impact with the wall. "Do not shoot me!"

"… And amazingly strong." He typed on the touchscreen. "We need to do many more tests."

"Dad! My clothes are ruined!"

"No they aren't. Just a few holes."

Kelly growled.

"Okay, okay. A few *large* holes. I'm working on your clothing situation. I already have some wonderful ideas."

"I need to change."

"All right, sweetie. Thanks for putting up with my curiosity. I would like to check a few more things out."

"Does it have to be right now?" She gestured at Paige. "I have a friend over."

"Hi, Mr. Donovan." Paige smiled and waved. "Please don't light me on fire. I'm a norm."

Dad glanced at her, at Paige, and back to her. "Oh. Yes. All right. It can wait." He smiled. "Go have fun with your friend."

"Thanks." Kelly stormed down the hall to the elevator, picking at the smoking remains of one of her favorite tops. "Unbelievable."

Paige scurried to catch up and fell in step beside her. "Dude, your dad is kinda weird. I think he's like a mad scientist or something."

"Nah." Kelly shook her head. "Mad scientists are bad guys. He's something else. Eccentric inventor?"

"I dunno." Paige peered over her shoulder at him, whispering, "Aren't you at least a little upset he blasted you in the face with a flamethrower?"

"Other than nuking my top, not really. Dad wouldn't do anything he thinks would hurt me."

Paige stopped looking at him and jogged to catch up. "He keeps calling this place a lair. Only bad guys have 'lairs.'"

"That doesn't mean anything. He reads even more comic books than we do."

"Well duh, he's like old," whispered Paige.

"I can hear you," said Dad's voice from the ceiling.

Kelly and Paige cringed.

"Sorry, Dad." Kelly rapidly poked the elevator button, trying to make it hurry up.

CHAPTER FOURTEEN

LEGiT

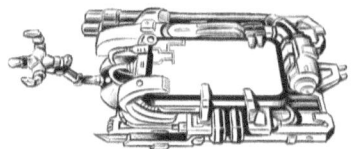

W hile Paige waited in the living room, Kelly ran up to her bedroom and changed into a T-shirt she wouldn't particularly miss and an intact pair of jeans. She couldn't bring herself to throw the remains of the babydoll top out despite it being closer to a fishing net than an article of clothing. *After* Dad replaced it, she'd surrender the smoldering remains to the trash. Grandma Becker—mother's side—gave it to her last month for her ninth birthday, and she adored that woman.

She liked Dad's parents, too, but the Donovans were kinda weird. For example, Grandpa Donovan had a specific necktie for every day of the year including a special February twenty-ninth leap-year tie—the bright lime green one with yellow smiley-faces that had blinking LED eyes—and if he couldn't find the right one for the particular date, he'd obsessively search for it, doing nothing else until he found it, or went to bed. Grandma Donovan, while reasonably nice, wasn't what one would call 'warm and loving.' She constantly spoke to Kelly like she addressed an adult who also had double PhDs. Whenever the woman cooked or baked, she would use scientific instruments to measure out ingredients to the microgram. Once, she'd dumped an entire bowl of cake mix out and started over because Kelly had added vanilla extract to it the 'normal human' way with an ordinary teaspoon. That is to say, an inexact quantity.

Once dressed, Kelly went downstairs and they played the cooperative mode of a slightly older game, *Star Prince Ascension*. Paige had no problem using the prince himself so Kelly could control Ms. Omni, who could only be used as a second-player.

Roughly fifteen minutes into the game, she had to move a car off a secret door to go underground.

"Hey," asked Paige. "Can you like do that for real?"

"Umm. I dunno. I pushed a car the other night."

"Wanna see if you can?" Paige grinned.

Kelly gave her side eye. "You're starting to sound like my dad."

"Aww." Paige laughed. "I'm not that… eccentric."

Laughing, Kelly hit pause. "Okay. C'mon."

They ran outside.

"Hey, you left your flip-flops inside again," said Paige in a mock worried tone. "You might step on something and cut yourself."

Kelly grinned all the way across the street and stood innocently in front of Mrs. Gregory's little grey car while looking around to see if anyone happened to be watching her. Since the coast looked clear, she crouched, grasped the bumper, and tried to lift.

Size made it unwieldy, but the front end came up off the ground, feeling as if she attempted to relocate a somewhat uncooperative beanbag chair.

"Wow," whispered Paige. "You're lifting a car."

"Just the front end of one. It doesn't feel heavy at all. Like a giant model made out of foam." Kelly set the car down, not wanting to break it. "It's weird though. When I like hugged my dad, that felt normal, too. I don't think he's super tough, but if I used as much strength to hug him as I did lifting this car, he would've popped."

"People don't *pop* in comics. No one dies. The Planet punches normal-sized guys all the time and they should really explode. The guy's fist is the size of a house."

Kelly glanced over at her. "Okay, you're talking about *Galaxy Enders*, right? Not real life?"

"You don't know The Planet?"

Arms folded, Kelly frowned. "Of course I know *Enders*. I'm making a joke that reality has gotten weird."

"Oh." Paige grinned. "Right. Hey, here." She stooped, grabbed a rock, and handed it to her. "Can you make this into a diamond?"

"This isn't carbon." Kelly took the ordinary egg-sized stone. "It's not gonna turn into a diamond under pressure."

"Darn."

"However…" Kelly gripped the rock and squeezed until it burst into dust and fragments. "I think I can cancel that gym membership."

"Oooh." Paige stared adoringly at the powder dripping through Kelly's fingers.

"Let me try something?"

"Okay."

Kelly hugged Paige, squeezing her as tight and normal as any other hug. It felt as if she used more force to do that than she'd exerted lifting the car. "Wow. That doesn't make a lot of sense."

"What?"

On the walk back to the house, Kelly described how lifting the car felt as though it took less effort than the strength she hugged with. They went inside to the living room, where Kelly broke out the video game system.

Paige sat on the rug and picked up the controller. "Your powers probably self-limit based on the situation. It would totally suck if you squished your parents and friends by accident."

"Umm. Yeah… It totally would." She stretched out on the floor, resting her head on the sofa cushion behind her, and resumed the video game. "Do you think my powers would know it if I, like, got into a fight with Alexis? If I punched her, would she 'pop,' or would it know I only wanted to give her a black eye at like normal people strength?"

"You're gonna fight Alexis?" Paige gasped.

"No. Just an example. Like if some bad guy is doing something and I get into a fight, I don't want to hurt anyone on accident. How will I know how hard to hit something?"

"Kell. You fly and just lifted a car off the ground. I think logic has gone straight out the window here."

Kelly laughed. "Maybe."

"Oh, why does your dad's face look weird?"

"What do you mean?'

"He's like, really tall and thin. And his chin is pointy. His whole head is like skinny, almost like a cartoon character. Are the aliens changing the world into a cartoon?"

"Umm." Kelly examined her hands. "I still look normal. So do you. So does everyone… except Dad. And he's not really *that* bad."

"Anyway, wow. You're like a legit superhero now, huh. That's awesome!"

"Yeah. You're really not jealous at all?"

"No silly. I get to be the plucky sidekick who gets to stay safe and watch all the cool stuff from just close enough to be part of it… sorta."

"Hah."

"There are other people developing powers, too. I heard some are even turning into creatures."

Kelly looked over at her. "Creatures?"

"Yeah, like, umm, werewolves? Half-spiders. Trolls even. And this one guy in Texas, his head sank into his neck and he has a face on his chest." Paige traced a line across her stomach. "He's got a big mouth on his whole belly now."

"Eww. That's completely gross."

"Yeah. The world's going crazy. I don't trust those aliens. They are being too friendly. No one drives ten million miles across the known universe to jump-start a planet they've never visited before."

Kelly laughed. "You're right. I don't trust them either. They are being *too* helpful and haven't asked for anything."

"Well, I mean, what *could* we give them? They have *so* much more advanced technology. Maybe it's like a rich person walking down the street and seeing a homeless guy, so he gives him money. To the aliens, humans are technologically poor. Maybe it's no big deal for them. But, the skinny ones do really freak me out."

"Huh? Skinny ones? You've seen them?"

Paige shook her head. "Not up close. Only on TV. There are two kinds of Nolmek. The small ones look like snakes with arms and like sorta-human heads, only they're weird. Oh, and they have red skin. The other kind aren't snakes. They look more like us, but really thick. Like wrestlers. Their skin's dark orange and they have these little horns all over their faces and their teeth are black and yellow. Disgusting."

"Hmm. Weird. Do you think it's like men and women?"

"I don't know. The ones on TV all looked like men."

Kelly shrugged. "They're not humans. They might not even have males and females. Or the difference might not be visible. Like, could you tell a male or female frog?"

"True. But the Nolmek are really scary."

"What they look like doesn't mean anything. What are they doing?"

"Acting too friendly."

"Besides that."

"Umm." Paige scratched her nose on her forearm so she didn't have to let go of the controller. "Hanging out with like world leaders and stuff. They built a machine that purifies seawater for cities in the desert, getting rid of drought. I also heard on the TV that the Nolmek announced that they would *not* help any country currently participating in wars of any kind. So, they've managed to stop a lot of conflict."

Kelly whistled. "Wow. But you know as soon as some places get alien tech, they're just going to go right back to being buttheads."

"True. Well, that's what superheroes are for, right?"

"I dunno. I'd rather be like Fennec. She just protects normal people where she lives."

"Yeah, but Fennec's fourteen. She's old. And her powers are kinda lame. Runs fast, can climb walls, turn into a were-fox."

"She's super agile and she can hear a pen scratching on paper at like a mile away," said Kelly.

"Oh, *that* will come in handy." Paige rolled her eyes while making Star Prince blow up a henchman's little flying sled thing.

"Butt." Kelly poked her. "I don't mean literally hearing pens scratching. She could hear bad guys talking or doing stuff from far away."

The front door opened. Mom walked in and smiled at the girls. "Hi, sweetie. Hi again, Paige."

"Hi, Mom."

"Hi, Mrs. Donovan."

Mom stood there for a moment with this odd smile, then walked over, sat between them on the floor, and pulled both girls into her lap with an arm around their chests, squeezing them in a hug while rocking side to side.

Kelly held the controller up, still trying to play. "Oof. Mom?"

Paige grunted. "Mrs. Donovan? I need air."

She continued rocking the girls side to side, her chin atop their heads.

"Mom, we're not shelter kittens. What are you doing?"

Paige gurgled. "She's mutated into Boa-Mom. Trying to hunt us via suffocation."

"She's been a little strange ever since the crystals fell." Kelly guided Ms. Omni into the air, flying over a skyscraper.

"Oh, sweetie. I'm just *so* happy to see that you have a friend and that you two are so close already."

"Of course we're close, Mom. You're crushing us together."

Paige emitted a wheezy laugh, then looked over at Kelly with this expression like she would jump in front of a train if she asked. Total adoration. Even worse than the way Rachel McMeadows stared at Alexis.

"Umm... Paige, knock it off. That's creepy."

"I love having a friend. I've been lonely for a long time, too."

Kelly glanced at her. "Yeah. It's nice having a friend."

Paige's desperately adoring stare went way into awkward territory. If not for Mom holding them more or less immobile, the girl might have koala-hugged Kelly.

"Pay? Are you feeling okay?"

The girl blinked, shaking her head slightly as if snapping out of a daydream. "Yeah, why?"

"You're way too good at that."

"At what? The game?"

Mom kissed Kelly atop the head, then relaxed her hug, allowing both girls to slip off her lap to sit on the floor again. "I'm absolutely thrilled for you two. Every girl needs at least one true friend."

"Umm, sure. Thanks." Kelly paused the game, watching her mother head upstairs to change out of her work clothes. "Okay. Mom's still not quite back from Crazytown."

"What happened to her?"

"Ugh. I dunno. Dad thinks she's not coping with the change to the world too well. She's been kinda upset that I didn't have any friends before, so she's probably just overreacting to me having a friend over."

Paige shrugged. "I'm glad I decided to finally try talking to you." She took Kelly's hand, smiling. "It's nice to have a friend."

"Dude. You're still being creepy."

"What?" Paige grinned. "I just, like, am totally happy right now. Meeting you was the best thing that ever happened to me."

Kelly looked her friend up and down. Other than an intense expression of 'I like being around you' the girl appeared normal. True, she had only known Paige for a few days, but something seemed off about her. Still, not *so* strange that she felt it worth talking about.

They resumed playing the game. Paige leaned against her like a clingy little sister or a super loyal golden retriever.

Okay. This is messed up. I mean, she's an awesome friend but, what the heck?

Maybe a half hour later, Paige shifted her weight, cling-leaning somewhat less. Soon after that, she sat up, cross-legged. "So do you think the aliens are evil?"

"No idea. Are you feeling okay?"

"Yeah. Why?" Paige glanced at her, no longer overly adoring.

"No reason. And I don't know about the aliens. They have to want something. No one is that altruistic."

Paige nodded. "Yeah. They kinda give me the creeps."

"But they aren't human."

"No kidding. They're aliens."

"Right. But I mean, *humans* would never be that altruistic. Most of us never do stuff unless we're getting something out of it. Maybe the aliens really *are* that nice."

Paige smirked at her.

Kelly laughed. "Yeah, I know. We gotta keep our eyes open."

CHAPTER FIFTEEN

BENEVOLENT PROTECTORS

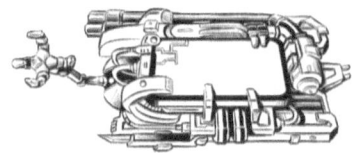

W hen Paige left to go home shortly before dinner, something strange happened.

A wave of sadness hit Kelly while she watched her friend walk down the street. The emotion seemed totally inappropriate for Paige merely going home, more like she'd left to move halfway around the world and they'd never see each other again. She sank to sit on the floor by the front door and burst into tears at being all alone again, sobbing fairly hard for a few minutes until the oddity of it struck her.

She's only going home. I'll see her tomorrow. Why am I crying?

Still, she couldn't stop. Like her friend had died or something. She hated being apart from her and wanted to keep hanging out.

Mom looked over from her seat on the sofa. "Sweetie? What's wrong?"

"Paige had to leave," said Kelly in a teary voice.

"Aww…" Mom hurried over and picked Kelly up like a three-year-old. "It's all right, sweetie. You'll see her tomorrow."

Having her mother hold her like that—even though she felt way too old for it—comforted her much more than expected. She pushed aside her sadness, taken by a sudden, strong need to cling to her mother. Mom returned to the couch with Kelly in her lap.

Over the next few minutes, sorrow as if she'd permanently lost her best friend gave way to an overwhelming need for mommy, then to feeling completely foolish and embarrassed at all of it. Soon after she returned to a normal emotional state, Mom kissed her on the head and set her seated on the cushion next to her.

"There. All better?"

"Umm. Yeah. That was really strange."

Mom stood. "I'm going to see what's taking your father so long in the kitchen."

"Okay."

Her mother got up and went down the hall. "Jack? What on Earth are you —aaaah!" Mom screamed.

Kelly flew straight up off the couch and zoomed down the hall, landing beside her mother.

A huge floating metal sphere hovered at the stove, its eight tubular robotic arms busily preparing food. Two stirred pots, one tweaked dials on the oven, three had already started washing the mixing bowls it must have used earlier.

"Jack?" asked Mom. "What the heck is in our kitchen?"

"Hello, dear." Dad's voice came from the robot. "It's merely an extension of my arms. I'm controlling it via my new inductive capacitance neuro-interface helmet. It feels like I've got an extra pair of eyes and eight more arms. Admittedly, it's taking a bit of getting used to."

"Where the heck are you?" Mom crept into the kitchen, gawking at the three-foot-diameter silver ball.

"In the lair, working on a project."

"Jack… this is well beyond your obsession with painting those little figurines and model robots. You've been down there every minute you haven't been at work. What's going on?"

"That's not technically accurate, hon. I haven't been going to work."

"What?" yelled Mom.

"I quit. I don't need the job anymore."

Mom swooned into a chair, hand to her forehead. "What are you doing? How are we going to pay for the house? Kelly will need to go to college."

"It's handled, hon. Check the account."

"I-I don't know if I can deal with this anymore." Mom pulled out her phone, fiddled with it for a few seconds, and screamed again.

"Told you," said Dad from the robot.

"Mom?" asked Kelly.

"That's… That's… seven zeroes?" Mom appeared on the verge of fainting.

"Precisely. Sold a few designs and prototypes to various companies."

Mom dropped her phone on the table and buried her face in her hands. "We have a bank account with seven zeroes."

The robo-cook whirled about and thrust three plates out, almost up Mom's nose. "And dinner's ready."

"Gah!" Mom jumped back from the robotic arms, then sat there staring at the pasta dish, shivering. "Jack, we need to talk. Are you going to eat dinner by remote, too?"

"Of course not." Dad's chuckle came from the robot. "I'll be up in a moment."

"Go wash your hands, hon." Mom patted her on the head.

Kelly flew—literally—to the downstairs bathroom.

When she returned to the kitchen, the big robot had landed in the corner and retracted all of its tube arms into itself. Small gripper claws sticking out all over the sphere made it resemble an old-fashioned ocean mine. Dad walked in via the patio door, pressing a button on a silver wristwatch that made his labcoat-and-khakis outfit change in a flash to the T-shirt and jeans he usually wore around the house.

"Whoa," said Kelly. "Neat."

The chicken-and-pasta dish tasted like something that had come out of a restaurant. He somehow managed to remark that he had made the pasta from scratch without sounding like he bragged. To Kelly's great delight, he also informed her she didn't have to help with the dishes, since the octo-bot would load the dishwasher and then clean the kitchen in automatic mode.

After they ate, Dad returned to his lair while Mom—still in a daze—sat on the couch to watch TV. Kelly didn't dare complain about not being able to get to the MegaStation while her mother used the screen for actual TV. She'd already played well more than the hour of video games she normally got on a school day, almost as if Mom had entirely stopped caring about tracking her usage time.

Kelly headed up to her room and attacked her homework. She still found it fun to do, and lost herself in it the same way she did whenever doing something she enjoyed. Midway through her math assignment, the ground rumbled. She'd experienced plenty of earthquakes in her nine years, and this one ranked low on the scary scale, the kind of earthquake the boys at school would blame on Mrs. Benson tripping in the hallway. The poor woman was… unsmall, but one of the sweetest teachers in the school. It always bothered her to hear kids make fun of the kindergarten teacher for her weight. Perhaps next time it happened, Kelly would finally be brave enough to say something.

Somehow, she had a feeling the 'earthquake' happened as a result of Dad.

With a sigh, she shook her head and resumed working on math.

Once she ran out of assignments to do, she headed downstairs in search of a drink, pausing in the living room at the sight of a weird creature on the screen. The snake-like alien fit Paige's earlier description of the skinny Nolmek aliens. Dark red skin, all-black eyes, and a tiny mouth, little more than a dark line, made them almost seem cute. It didn't have hair—or ears—and a jaw too small for the head above it. Though the serpentine alien didn't appear obviously male or female, something about it made her want to call it male. He wore a somewhat gaudy gold-trimmed orange cloak and also appeared to be a member of the Noodle Arms Club. Though, the Nolmek even had Kelly beat. Her arms, though thin, still had *some* shape.

"Scientists are estimating that two to five percent of the population of the globe may have developed unusual abilities, mutations, or experienced 'other unknown effects' since our benefactors have arrived on Earth," said the anchorman. "They assure us that this power flux is an unavoidable but benign side effect of their work restoring the planet's magnetic field, which, I remind you, was on course to entirely collapse and eradicate all life within five years." He smiled. "No one likes a mass-extinction event."

"No, they absolutely don't, Marty," said the woman next to him. "Intense cosmic radiation is a total downer for weekend plans."

Kelly blinked. "Is that guy for real? He just made a joke about the end of all life?"

"Everything feels so surreal lately," said Mom. "Aliens… superpowers… who would've ever imagined?"

"Not me." Kelly smiled. "But it is kinda cool."

The image of the Nolmek in the smaller window above the anchor changed to a thick-chested creature with no discernable neck and dark red-orange skin that appeared to have a somewhat alligator-like quality. Not exactly scales, but tough and leathery. Though the creature generally possessed an overall human shape, its facial features resembled a toad. A broad, flat face and large, red eyes with vertical-slit pupils added to the reptilian appearance. Dozens of tiny horns sprouted above its eyes, along cheek ridges, jawline, and even cresting the tops of its ears. If it had scales, it would have reminded Kelly of the Draconids from the *Star Prince* series, a race of aliens that could shapeshift into dragons. In that fictional world, they had visited Earth centuries ago and started the legends of dragons, but spent most of their time in their smaller, humanoid forms.

The big Nolmek also had the most disastrously gross teeth she'd ever seen. Paige was right. They'd give dentists nightmares. Mostly black with yellow and green spots, they looked as if they decayed straight out of its mouth fast enough to witness them melting. Worse, the teeth didn't at all resemble human ones, curved to points like thick, stubby cat claws that didn't really line up properly with each other.

"Ick," said Kelly. "Their teeth are nasty."

"Hopefully their society doesn't value kissing much." Mom laughed.

"Eww. Mom. Seriously?"

"The Nolmek ambassadors are meeting with the United Nations at the end of the week to lay out their plans to help bring humanity into the next age of technological advancement. Our benevolent protectors predict they will eradicate poverty, famine, and most diseases within four years. We should all be grateful for their help."

"Absolutely, Marty," said the co-anchor, a woman a bit older than Mom with over-styled blonde hair. "I can't begin to express how happy I am that the Nolmek decided to help us."

"Wow." Kelly leaned on the back of the sofa. "That's not creepy sounding at all. Are they real people or robots?"

"I can't tell, sweetie. But these two have been on this news station for as long as I can remember, so I don't think they're robots."

Kelly narrowed her eyes. *Unless the aliens replaced them—or replaced their brains.*

CHAPTER SIXTEEN

SHOOMP!

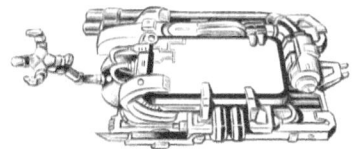

Once again, Kelly spent a day at school not feeling right.

Alexis Stephens had stayed well away from her. The girl didn't even look at her from across the field behind the school at lunch. Or, maybe, Kelly simply hadn't noticed. She'd been too busy sitting next to Paige at a table inside eating like a normal student before going outside. No one paid much attention at all to her. It seemed that without the catalyst of Alexis picking on her, no one else wanted to either... not that other kids really messed with her that much to begin with.

The giant crystal remained stuck in the football field, still shining bright. All the cops who'd been guarding the field to keep people out had disappeared—but Army soldiers replaced them. That seemed silly since *so* many of those crystals had landed everywhere. The Army didn't have enough people to keep everyone away from *all* of them. Did they worry that someone might attack the crystals or steal bits of them? Could be they didn't want curious kids getting too close and falling into the lava moat around it.

Sadly, Paige had gymnastics after school so couldn't hang out right away. Again, for no valid reason, being separated from her friend made the walk home from school an emotional gauntlet. Her thinking mind knew she shouldn't feel so upset over a two-hour delay, but the rest of her wanted to cry at her friend abandoning her forever.

Kelly clung to the idea of her extreme sadness making no sense as a tool to keep her from breaking down in tears on the trudge home. By the time she reached the house, the gloomy spell had passed. While she no longer wanted to cry at being separated from her bestie, she worried about these unexplainable emotional spikes. Sure, she had made it to the ripe old age of nine without any real friends. Having one now, even a sudden, close friendship with a girl that she had a lot of common interests with, should *not* make her all weepy over not being able to spend every single minute of the day hanging out with her.

Something else had to be going on.

Sure, she *wanted* to hang out with Paige all the time, but distractions like school, sleep, gymnastics class, or whatever else parents dragged them off to would happen—and should in no way result in a storm of tears.

"Grr."

It also worried her that everything green in the school cafeteria smelled like castoff from a nuclear reactor that also processed used diapers. Even being within three feet of green vegetables made her dizzy. Fortunately, the lunch ladies didn't challenge her claim of being allergic.

By the time she reached her bedroom, kicked off her sneakers, and sat at her desk to do homework, she'd become angry at not understanding *why* every time she and Paige couldn't be together it felt like she'd never see her again. She couldn't be *that* much of a wimp.

Grumbling, she hunkered down and started on her homework.

"Kell?" asked Dad from her computer, loud enough to make her brain vibrate in her skull.

"Gah!" Kelly jumped back out of her chair, floating in the middle of her room, holding her ears. "Dad! Holy crap. Too loud!"

A painful microphone squeal hurt like a knife slicing her brain for a few seconds, but it rapidly dropped in volume to normal. "How's this?"

"My ears are bleeding."

"Actually or are you being sarcastic?"

Kelly looked at her hand. No blood. "Sarcasm I guess."

"Are you busy?"

"Doing homework. Only got about a half hour of it today. Teachers are getting lazy."

"I should invent a brain scanner to figure out what's going on in that head of yours. Children aren't supposed to *enjoy* homework. It's supposed to be a punishment."

"For what?"

"Having the audacity not to be an adult,' said Dad.

Kelly laughed.

"C'mon down here. I have a surprise for you."

"Does it involve knives, fire, or guns?"

"Possibly, but I promise you nothing will hurt."

She sighed.

"Please?"

"Okay. Fine. Be right there."

Kelly changed into an old pink dress she wouldn't miss. She didn't really like pink stuff, but Grandma Becker adored her in it, so she tolerated pinkification in short stints whenever visiting Mom's family. Dad sometimes joked about German people being robotic, but Mom's parents couldn't be sweeter or more loving. So much so that she didn't even complain about pink —or frilled socks.

Speaking of socks, she skipped those and shoes, not wanting her father to incinerate any more of her wardrobe. Whatever he wanted to test on her would undoubtedly cause destruction. Being a superhero would definitely be expensive in the clothing department.

She again leapt out her window and flew to the tool shed. As soon as the door closed, the floor fell out from under her with a loud *shoomp!* The platform went to the bottom so fast, her dress blinded her again. Six-stories in under a second.

"Eep!" yelled Kelly. "What's wrong with this elevator?"

Dad appeared in the large foyer at the end of the little corridor leading to the elevator shaft. "What do you mean?"

"Yesterday, it went up and down like a normal elevator. Today, it tried to steal my dress."

"Oh. That's because of your friend. I figured you would be upset with me if she exploded like an over-ripe tomato."

Kelly gawked.

"The elevator platform can detect the physical resistance of people riding it and automatically adjusts its speed for maximum efficiency and safety, up to the limits of its hardware. You can tolerate moving at 800 miles an hour and stopping in an instant. She can't."

"Rrrright." Kelly put her hands on her hips and padded up to him.

"Aww. You look adorable. I didn't think you liked pink."

"I don't, but I had a feeling you are going to incinerate me again. If you burn this off me, I'll only be upset at you for embarrassing the heck out of me, not for destroying it."

He chuckled. "C'mon, kiddo."

She sighed, shaking her head, and walked down the hallway, following him past the test chambers to a room containing several large machines. He guided her over to one and pointed at an open-faced cylindrical chamber attached to the side.

"Hop up in there, sweetie."

"What is this going to do to me?"

"This isn't a test. I promise."

"Okay." She stepped up on the raised platform and turned to face him. "So what is it?"

"Just stand there calm, arms at your sides, and relax."

He pulled his mega-tablet out of seeming nowhere, and poked a few buttons on the screen. She couldn't tell for sure, but it might have become a bit thicker... with more stuff on it.

The clear cylinder rotated closed. Bright white light filled the air, so intense she couldn't see anything. For an instant, it felt like all her clothes had disappeared, but when the light faded in a few seconds, she found herself wearing an outfit that took purple from a simple color to a life statement. The main part felt like a soft one-piece swimsuit in a rich shade of violet with a short, light-purple pleated skirt. Her silvery mesh belt had a bronze buckle. High-tech looking sneaker-boots, the same shade of dark purple as the skirt— their cushiony soles pale lilac—had appeared on her feet, and silver metal bracers covered her forearms from her wrists halfway to her elbows. They had no seams or any apparent way to remove them, molded perfectly to the size and shape of her arms. Something also stuck to her face, mostly around her eyes.

She held her right arm up, using the bracer's mirrored surface to check her reflection. A purple mask covered the upper part of her face, somewhat butterfly-shaped with two points going up, two downward.

The cylinder opened with a squeak.

Dad snapped a picture of her with his mega-tablet. "You look amazing! I hope you like it."

She hopped down from the platform inside the cylinder, her hair bouncing. "Umm. It's really purple."

"That *is* your favorite color, right?"

"Yeah."

A blast of flamethrower came from the mega-tablet.

Kelly yelped in surprise and crossed her arms to shield her face. "Dad! You just made it! Don't dest—" She gawked at the sight of the outfit ignoring the fire as easily as her hair disregarded it. "It's not burning."

"Precisely." He walked across the room to a giant tank of water, something like one of those carnival 'dunk the idiot' booths, only it didn't have a bench or a dunking mechanism. "Hon, would you stick a finger in this water and tell me if it's hot, cold, or neither?"

Kelly walked over, floated up off her feet to reach the top, and poked a finger in. "Umm. Neither."

"Would you go under and see how long you can hold your breath?"

"Dad. It will take forever to dry my hair."

"I have a flamethrower."

"Okay, fine."

She flew up, lowered herself in to her neck, took a huge breath, then dropped underwater, arms folded, standing on the bottom of the tank making puffy cheeks. Dad paced back and forth on the other side of the clear barrier for a while. After a few minutes, Kelly raised both eyebrows, impressed with herself for not feeling like she needed to breathe.

Eventually, he tapped on the glass and pointed up.

Kelly floated out of the tank, and let out the breath she'd been holding.

"Impressive." Dad whistled.

"How long?"

"Twenty minutes and you didn't show the slightest signs of distress about air. I calculate that you can probably hold your breath for a few hours, but I'm not going to ask you prove that one out. How's the suit?"

She looked down. It had dried instantly. "Dry."

"Any damage?"

Kelly tugged at it in spots, peered under the skirt, then shrugged. "Nope. Looks fine. Why?"

"Because that's not water. You just spent twenty minutes holding your breath in a tank of sixteen-molar nitric acid. That's why I wanted you to test with a finger first, just to make sure it wouldn't hurt you." He pulled a one-inch metal bearing out of his pocket, held it up so she could see it, then tossed it into the tank. Within seconds of it the hitting the bottom, the sphere began to dissolve fast enough to see it shrinking.

She stared in mute silence for a few seconds at the disintegrating ball bearing. "Umm, Dad. Where did you get a giant tank of acid?"

"Why does that matter?"

"Because it's a giant tank of acid!" yelled Kelly, gesturing at it. "That's not normal! Normal people don't have giant tanks full of acid."

"I don't think either one of us qualify as normal anymore." He grinned. "We are extraordinary."

"Right." She fussed at the bracers. "How do I open these?"

"You don't. They're one solid piece. Anti-theft technology. No one can steal them if they can't take them off you."

She stared at him. "So I'm stuck in them forever? You do realize I'm only nine and am going to grow up, right? They won't even fit me in a few months."

"Taken care of. The suit will adjust." He tapped his finger on her left arm bracer, making a metallic *plink, plink* sound. And, as you've seen, it's pretty close to indestructible. On you, the suit will survive extremes that would destroy ordinary materials."

Blush tinged her cheeks at remembering her escape from the book bag.

Okay. Big plus there. Not going to get stranded somewhere with nothing on. Being a superhero is explodey. She smoothed her hands down the front. "What is it made out of?"

"Super stuff. A highly complex molecular structure. I invented it."

"Okay, but what is it?"

Dad pursed his lips. "I'm not entirely sure. Just got an idea and ran with it. Fed the parameters into the fabricator, and presto." He put a hand on her shoulder and guided her over to another station with two baseball-sized metal spheres on posts. "Be a dear and grab those orbs at the same time."

Shaking her head, she reached out and rested her hands on them.

Bang.

A brilliant electrical flash filled the air with light and her mouth with a taste like she licked pennies. She vaguely noticed a massive lightning bolt fly from her nose right before she ended up sliding on her back across the room, almost hitting the wall on the other side, fifty feet away.

Kelly lay there on the floor, smoking.

Dad walked over and peered down at her. "Did that hurt?"

"Tingled a little, but no... not really." She held her hands up so she could look at them. No red marks or burns, though she still couldn't taste anything but metal.

"Hmm. Your body temperature spiked up to almost six hundred. Suit appears to have withstood it quite well. The mask didn't even come off."

"Are you testing me or the costume?"

"Yes." He smiled.

Again, Kelly used her bracer as a mirror to examine her face mask. "What's holding it on? There's no strap. Did you glue this to my face? If my eyebrows come off with it, I'm going to be upset."

"No. It's held on by an ionic intention field."

"What? You're babbling nonsense, Dad."

"Try to take it off."

Kelly reached up to grasp the facemask. It popped off easily, feeling more or less as though she had a bit of plastic wrap stuck around her eyes with static cling. "No way would this have stayed on when you shock-blasted me across the room." She glanced at him. "And by the way, Dad, *normal* people do not shock-blast their children across the room."

"I think we've already established there is an abundant lack of normal in this household."

She folded her arms and huffed.

"It didn't hurt, did it?"

"No, but that's beside the point." Kelly attempted to put the mask on, and it stuck to her again. "This is too weird."

Dad approached, grabbed the mask by its upper corners, and tugged. She stumbled after him as if he tried to drag her forward by her skull—at least until she wanted to stop. He continued trying to rip the mask off her, but neither it—nor Kelly—moved.

"This is too weird."

He stopped pulling on it and smiled. "If you want it to stay on, it will. If you want it to come off, it will. Ionic intention field."

"What about the rest of the suit? What if I like, you know, have to go to the bathroom? Is it, like, stuck to me?"

"No, it's stretchy if you want it to be. Would you mind following me over there a sec? Few more experiments, please?"

"So this thing is indestructible?" She ran a hand down her front, feeling the soft fabric.

"The properties of this material depend mostly on the super wearing it. *You* are particularly tough and resilient, so the fabric is as well. If a normal person were to wear it, it wouldn't be any tougher than an ordinary bit of clothing. Someone who had powers that… say allowed them to grow into a giant, the suit would expand with them."

"Oh. That's neat."

"Come on then, sweetie. A few more tests."

Grumbling, she plodded after him over to a machine that looked like it belonged in a gym: a metal frame supported a horizontal bar connected to weights. It also had an entirely excessive amount of blinking lights that didn't seem to have any real purpose.

"Push up on that bar. Strength test."

Kelly peered at the bar over her head. "I can't even reach it. Did you forget I'm tiny?"

"Oh. Sorry." He hit a few buttons on the mega-tablet and the bar crept downward with a faint whirring.

She squatted and positioned herself with the bar across her shoulders, grabbed it, and pushed up, not noticing any resistance. "Is this plastic?"

"No." He tapped more buttons. "Try again."

She squatted and pushed up again. It felt somewhat heavier.

"Again, please… wow."

This went on several times in a row before her boots dented the metal floor when she lifted the bar—which also bent. It hadn't exactly become *heavy*, but she noticed some weight.

"Incredible," muttered Dad.

Kelly walked out from under the weight machine. "Dad, what exactly are—?"

She screamed when a metal tentacle seized her by the head, lifting her into the air and throwing her across the room. Kelly caught herself in midair to avoid hitting the ground or wall, and stared confusedly at a pair of robotic tween girls—with more than a passing resemblance to Alexis Stephens. The one on the right retracted the metal tentacle into its mouth. The other one fired laser eyes into Kelly's chest, but they merely created a warm spot.

"Seriously?" She looked down at where the beams hit her, looked back up, and huffed.

The fake Alexii both charged at her, sprouting claws.

Kelly ducked the handful of razors, swung her hips to the right to avoid the second robot thrusting its claws at her gut, then popped up and kicked Alexis #2 in the face, blasting its mechanical head apart into flying circuit boards and metal scraps. A small door at the middle of Alexis #1's chest opened, exposing the front end of a gun. Bullets pelted Kelly all over the face and chest in a machine gun rain of dry spitballs.

Alexis #3 came out of nowhere from behind, wrapping its tongue tentacle around Kelly, pinning her arms to her sides—for all of one second. She forced her arms apart, breaking the tentacle into several pieces, then grabbed the fragment of sparking metal snake sticking out of the robot's mouth, using it to swing Alexis #3 into the other fake Alexis, smashing both robots into twitching piles of scrap metal.

Dad giggled with glee. Actually *giggled*.

"Umm… Where did all this stuff come from?"

"I made it." He stood in a triumphant pose, clutching the mega-tablet like a clipboard.

"How did you go from painting four-inch-tall plastic fake robots to building real ones?"

"Not that difficult. Just a matter of putting my mind to it." He smiled, tapping at the mega-tablet's screen. "You are off the charts, young lady. Absolutely fabulous."

"Ugh." She hung her head, and wound up staring at her belt buckle. Specifically, the initials 'GS' emblazoned on the bronze.

"Umm… Dad?"

"Yes, sweetie?"

She looked up at him. "Why does the belt buckle have 'GS' on it?"

"Oh. That's your supervillain identity. You're Ginger Snap."

Kelly screamed in anguish.

He blinked. "Something wrong?"

"No, Dad. No way. Not happening. That is *so* lame. Ginger Snap? Are you serious? Oh, real hilarious. Girl with red hair. Ginger Snap. Har har."

He grinned, walked over, and patted her on the head. "You'll get used to it. Besides, it *is* intentionally bad. Lame puns are just another form of supervillainy. Another way for you to cause pain to our enemies. Now, go stick it to those bullies, sweetie."

"I am *not* Ginger Snap. I can't use that name. It's… it's… *too cute!*"

"But you are cute. Cute and evil." Dad picked her up, turned… and the room changed in a flash to the main foyer. He set her down on the elevator platform. "It's perfect. And it's *supposed* to be painful."

Shoomp!

Kelly found herself in the tool shed. "Argh! I am not evil. I don't even stay up late reading comics with a flashlight. The worst thing I ever did was cheat Mom's video game limit." She sighed, and lifted her foot to start walking out.

Shoomp!

Lair again.

Disoriented at the rapid descent, Kelly waved her arms and blinked.

"I forgot to give you something." Dad handed her a thin silver bracelet with a—naturally, purple—gem on the top. "Here."

Kelly examined it. "I assume this is something more than a simple piece of jewelry?"

"Correct! It is the ZOOM. The Zippy Outfit Oscillation Module."

"Zippy?" She raised an eyebrow.

He offered a weak smile. "Needed a Z word to make the acronym work. Anyway, you push the gem and it swaps whatever you're wearing for your super costume. Push it again, and your super costume trades places with whatever you have on. Basically, it contains one outfit at a time. Whenever you push the gem, it swaps whatever clothes are inside it for whatever you have on. While you could use it to change instantly into your gym uniform at school, my intention for it was to allow you to always have your super costume with you."

"Oh. Neat." Kelly clipped the thin bracelet on in front of the bracer on her left arm, then pushed the gem.

A blast of lavender light surrounded her for an instant. Her super costume disappeared, leaving her naked—except for the bracelet.

She stared at herself, progressively reddening in the face for two seconds before shrieking and mashing the gem again. The super costume reappeared. "*Dad!*" screamed Kelly. "What the heck! What happened to my clothes?"

"Umm. It appears the Fabricator-2000 may have cannibalized their materials while generating your costume. The ZOOM bracelet always swaps whatever is inside it with what you have on. Since it had nothing inside it, you ended up wearing nothing. You'll need to push the gem to store the super costume, then put something else on. I suggest you go up to your bedroom first."

Still blushing, and unable to look him in the eye, she stared down. "*May* have eaten my clothes? What else did it do that you didn't expect?"

"Nothing!" Dad poked a finger at the tablet.

Shoomp!

Tool shed.

She sighed, shaking her head. "Being a superhero is definitely going to be rough on my wardrobe. At least this suit won't burn."

Shoomp!

Lair.

"Argh! Dad! Stop it. You're gonna make me throw up."

"Oh, I almost forgot. Here." He reached into his labcoat and pulled out a flat metal box, which he handed to her.

Curious, Kelly accepted it, noticed a latch, and opened it—to see *Star Prince #17*, once again pristine and in a protective plastic comic book cover. She gasped. Thrilled became freaked out and back to thrilled. "You found it! How did you find it? You were in my room?"

"Scanners. And, technically, one of my robots retrieved it for me. I know how upset you were over what happened, so I made the Paper Purifier 3000."

She slowly lifted her gaze off the comic to stare up at him. "Did you have 2,999 failed experiments before you got one to work?"

"No. I usually get things right the first time."

Something exploded deep in the lair and an alarm went off with flashing red lights and a klaxon.

Dad flashed a cheesy smile. "Mostly."

"So, umm… why does the Fabricator have a 2000? Why is it the Paper Purifier *Three-Thousand* and not the Paper Purifier?"

"Because." He leaned back with a commanding smile. "It sounds more impressive!"

Shoomp!

Tool shed.

"Gah! You're gonna make me sick!" Kelly floated up off the floor just in case he forgot something else… and sighed.

Thousands of issues from dozens of different comics flashed across her memory. Her father had an almost cartoonishly tall, thin, pointy-chinned head. He spent all his time wearing a labcoat and running around a giant underground lair while making various machines he could no more explain *how* he made them than why. He owned a massive vat of dangerous acid. And he seemed to have an affinity for robots that exploded… and he called her evil.

Oh, crap. Kelly slouched. *My dad really* is *a mad scientist.*

CHAPTER SEVENTEEN

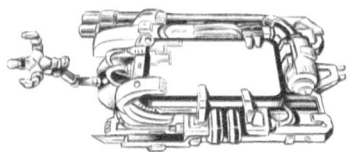

NOT EXACTLY FRIENDS

T he ZOOM bracelet glimmered in the sunlight. Kelly fidgeted it around her wrist while sitting at her desk in math class Friday morning. She tilted it back and forth, making a reflected spot of light dance on the wall. Not even Mrs. Webb, probably her favorite teacher, could lift her mood today.

Her father was a mad scientist.

He'd gone villain.

Though, nothing about him appeared particularly evil. Unfortunately, it would only be a matter of time before he did something like unleashing a massive robot army in a doomed bid to take over the world. Or perhaps he'd start small, and merely set out for California domination instead of world domination. *Wait. This* is *Dad after all. He's going to settle for taking over San Francisco.*

He also seemed to believe Kelly was a supervillain as well. She couldn't think of a single thing she'd done that would have given him that idea. It had to be simply that he'd gone villain, so he expected his daughter would as well.

But nothing could've been further from the truth.

No way could she do bad stuff. Even in fighting games on the MegaStation, she never used the 'bad guy' characters. Despite there being no real-world consequences for it, she couldn't follow the 'evil' route in video games because it made her feel bad to be mean to people—even fake video game people and fighting games with only the most basic attempt at a storyline.

Trying to figure out how in the heck she would cope with having her dad go supervillain kept her up most of the night. More so than the stupid elevator, that made her sick to her stomach. Okay, to be fair, his wanting to call her Ginger Snap made her the sickest of anything.

Maybe I shouldn't let him keep measuring my powers. When he finds out I'm not going villain, he's gonna use that data against me. The notion that her father would be disappointed in her for *not* being evil created a paradox in her head that reduced almost everything the teachers said to meaningless trombone noises.

At least she adored math, so she found herself able to pay attention for one class.

All the thrill she'd felt at having powers had evaporated overnight. Her dad couldn't be a bad guy, he just *couldn't!* Head down, she trudged along with her classmates out into the hall. Kids went in different directions based on their next class period. Despite the change of going to separate rooms for each class as a middle-schooler, at only fifth grade, the group of kids still mostly stayed together except for a few students in remedial math or English. Nothing like the eighth graders who all had different schedules and a new class group every period.

Although she walked in her old, usual way with her head down, no one deliberately bumped into her. No one grabbed at her backpack, pushed her, threw stuff at her, or even called her Squirt, Turd, Noodle-butt, or laughed when someone else did. Colleen had even been behind her in social studies first period and never once tried to steal her flip-flops. Of course, most of the class *had* been asleep.

Odd that Mr. Reynolds hadn't yelled at anyone for it.

Halfway down the hall to fourth period English, Kelly cringed at the all-too-familiar grating sound of Alexis' voice chirping, "Oh, look who it is."

She lifted her head, prepared to tell the blonde princess to go throw herself into a garbage can, but found herself alone. The taunt hadn't been aimed at her. Kelly looked around, honing in on the bright yellow hair of her nemesis—or former nemesis apparently. The girl leaned on the lockers by Donna Hernandez, another girl in their class.

Where Kelly had been young and small, Donna stood almost as tall as an adult already and had some extra weight, a quiet voice, and a shy personality. In short, she made another easy victim for Alexis. She'd probably chosen Kelly as her first target because no matter how angry she got, her minuscule size would've made any sudden rage laughable. Donna, on the other hand, could break Alexis in half if she ever became truly angry. But… for a big girl, she almost never spoke over a whisper.

Watching Alexis and her friends tease such a nice kid went past Kelly's ability to merely keep walking. She turned so fast she almost lost a flip-flop, and marched over to them.

"Alexis."

"Oh, look who it is," said Colleen, sneering at her.

The other three girls—especially Brittany—all leaned back, eyes widening in fear.

"Why are you bothering Donna? She's like the nicest kid in the whole school."

Donna blinked, staring at Kelly with a 'wait… what?' expression. Tears brimmed in her eyes but didn't fall.

Alexis fidgeted, taking another step back.

"You did something really mean to me, but… I'm over it." Kelly did her best 'tiny girl looming' lean toward them. "But, if you keep teasing Donna, all four of you are gonna go down The Hill, and I guarantee you, my throw will hit the fence."

"Get out of my face, Turd," said Colleen.

Alexis made a quick hissing noise at Colleen, as if she tried to call a cat.

"Make me."

Colleen grabbed Kelly's shoulders and tried to shove her over backward, but pushed herself away, shoes sliding on the floor. She blinked, going from angry to confused in an instant. "Umm. What?"

"Just go to class and leave people alone, okay?" Kelly smiled up at Donna, then hurried down the hall to English.

KELLY SPENT THE REST OF THE SCHOOL DAY THINKING ABOUT ALEXIS…

Except for lunch when she hung out with Paige and had a long talk about mad scientists. They stood on the merry-go-round in the playground, Kelly propelling it at a gentle spin by means of her ability to fly. No one appeared to notice that neither one of them ever put a foot to the ground to push it.

Her friend did agree that almost all supers who fell into the 'mad scientist' category ended up being evil. The few who couldn't be labeled 'evil' advanced to the 'dangerously misguided' bucket. The even fewer not considered evil nor dangerously misguided wound up in the 'ineffectually hapless' category, making crazy, purposeless contraptions more for comic relief than anything. Dad created a high-quality costume for her, a giant lair, and he'd repaired *Star Prince #17*. None of that sounded purposeless or silly.

And he'd also directly admitted to being a supervillain.

Paige worried only briefly, but repeated assurances from Kelly that she would never go villain calmed her. At that, her friend offered to let her live in her bedroom if she ever ran away from home.

"Thanks. But, my mom... she's a norm. I can't leave my family, and I can't leave her alone with Supervillain Dad."

Paige nodded. "I understand. Just saying. Offer's there if you want it."

"Do you remember getting super clingy and weird the other day?"

"Yeah. No idea why I did that. I mean, we're like best friends and all, but I have no idea why I felt like life had no meaning whatsoever without you."

"You've been reading too many love stories."

Paige laughed. "Not like that."

"So, umm... what do you think I should do about my dad?"

"I don't know yet. Probably best to wait and watch what he does. Maybe he'll be one of those mad scientists who just stays underground brooding all the time, waiting to get revenge on everyone who ever wronged him, but never actually does anything."

Kelly's eyes widened. "Oh, crap."

"What?"

"That's it! Dad... he *always* complained about being a nobody at work. No one ever recognized him, never got promoted. He spent the last eleven years feeling like no one appreciated him. No wonder he went villain."

"Did anyone do something really bad to him? Bad childhood?"

"No. Well, not really. I mean, Grandma and Grandpa Donovan are... weird. But they're not mean. I don't think anything really bad happened to him. Just, more like he drowned in mediocrity."

"Oh, then he's probably not going to be *too* evil." Paige smiled. "More like the kind of evil that mixes Scootles, N&Ns, and Royce's Bits in the same bowl."

Kelly gasped. "That's super evil. Dad's not that bad."

"Chocolate covered Brussels sprouts?"

"Ugh." Kelly's stomach grumbled at the mere idea of it. "No way. That's still too evil."

The bell rang.

"Can you come over after school?" asked Kelly.

"Not 'til later. Gymnastics tonight. I can hang out for a little bit after dinner."

"Okay, cool." She grinned, stopped the merry-go-round from spinning, and hopped off.

AN IDEA CREPT INTO KELLY'S MIND EARLY IN LAST PERIOD, COMPUTER CLASS.

After lunch, she'd returned to thinking about Alexis, wondering if the girl might be like the middle-school version of a supervillain. Paige's question about Dad possibly having a childhood trauma made her think of something the school counselor said in one of his anti-bullying presentations. He thought bullies picked on other kids because they had unhappy home situations… and she remembered Alexis' odd reaction when the other girls had been hitting her. She had almost seemed sorry or ashamed for making Kelly scream and beg not to be hit.

Concern got the better of her, and once the bell rang, Kelly stashed her backpack in her locker despite having homework. She raced out the door with the rest of the kids, but ducked around the side of the school where Alexis and the girls had taken her the day they stuffed her in the bag. Once in a spot where no one could see her, she pushed the gem on her bracelet. Her new, replacement babydoll top, jeans, and flip-flops changed with an instant flash of light to her super costume. She took a second to admire the lack of a cape— Dad was, after all, practical. And, considering her long, fluffy hair, she kinda already had a cape.

Kelly flew straight up over the school and scanned the crowd of kids going to buses for the familiar blonde head of her arch-nemesis. It surprised her to discover the tops of school buses were white. She hovered about the same height as the tip of the crystal that remained stuck in the football field, which still had a ring of molten lava surrounding it. The rock not cooling had to mean something, but she didn't know exactly what.

Alexis emerged from the school and made her way to a bus with a big #83 on the roof.

A few minutes after the time she would have already arrived home from walking, bus #83 pulled away from the curb and drove off. Kelly flew higher, following the bus as it drove across San Francisco. Eventually, it stopped going straight without making any stops and proceeded to weave among streets, letting kids out here and there. Kelly shadowed the bus from the air until she spotted Alexis stepping out the door onto the sidewalk at a stop.

The girl who had bullied her so mercilessly for the past two years didn't even look like the same person anymore. She walked with her head down, a sad frown on her lips, exactly how Kelly must have looked every day at school prior to the crystal falling.

All the anger and resentment she'd ever felt for the girl flipped over into guilt.

Well… most of it.

Keeping high and out of sight, Kelly followed her ex-bully a few blocks to an ordinary-looking suburban house. A man and a woman inside shouted at each other about his not having a job for too long. He barked back at her, mostly calling her names. Soon after Alexis went in the front door, Kelly dropped onto her feet and crept up to peer in the living room window.

A blonde woman in her early forties with past-her-prime movie star good looks and a healing black eye paced about, yelling at a man sitting in a recliner watching television. She wanted him to get a job. He claimed to be working on it and ordered her out of the way of the TV screen. Alexis went into the kitchen, returning a moment later to sit on the couch, where she opened the wrapper of a snack bar.

The parents shouted at each other a little more before the woman shifted her attention onto Alexis and yelled at her about a modeling competition coming up that weekend, telling her she shouldn't be eating that because she had to be perfect and win because it's her future at stake.

Alexis nibbled on the bar. "Mom, it's just granola. I'm hungry."

"That's 120 calories you don't need. Do you want to get fat? That's always how it starts. You're hungry, so it's only a granola bar, then 120 calories becomes 240, then 500, then you're too fat to compete. I mean look at you. You're only barely at competition weight as it is."

"I'm not fat," said Alexis.

"Well, you're not far from it."

Kelly blinked. In no possible meaning of the word 'fat' did any of it apply to Alexis Stephens. The girl looked like a living Bimbie doll—if those dolls had human proportions.

"Whatever. It's just one bar. If you didn't pack me such tiny salads for lunch, I wouldn't be hungry when I got home."

"Don't 'whatever' me, young lady!" screamed Mrs. Stephens.

Alexis defiantly chomped a bite of the granola bar at her.

A man stood from a recliner.

Mrs. Stephens moved in front of him. "Jim. No. It's okay. Don't."

The man walked toward Alexis like a zombie fixated on brains, pushing Mrs. Stephens out of the way without using his hands.

"Jim!" yelled Mrs. Stephens.

"This is why she doesn't respect you," said the man… right before slapping her.

Mrs. Stephens collapsed to the rug holding her face.

Alexis scrambled in reverse over the sofa back. Her father ran around the end, corralling her in the corner next to a hall leading deeper into the house. Alexis cowered, eyes wide in fear, looking as terrified as Kelly felt whenever the girls came after her.

"Don't you dare disrespect your mother, missy," said Mr. Stephens, raising his hand.

Kelly dove through the screen window, zipping across the living room. She put herself between them in time to catch the slap meant for Alexis. Mr. Stephens' hand crashed into her face with about the same power as a thrown pillow. However, the hit made a *crack* like a small gunshot.

Alexis screamed and sank to sit on the floor, expecting the slap, still not aware Kelly had gotten in the way.

Mr. Stephens stood there for a few seconds with his hand on her face, his expression a combination of confusion and pain. He removed his hand, glanced at it, then her. "The hell are you supposed to be?"

No way would she ever answer that question with 'Ginger Snap.' Nope. Not happening. On the spot, she briefly thought about her beloved Grandma Becker's habit of sometimes absentmindedly not using English.

"I'm Übergirl!"

"What the heck does that even mean and what are you doing in my house? Are you one of Alex's little friends playing dress up?" He shook his head at her 'silly' outfit… then noticed he addressed a small girl at eye level—and her boots didn't touch the rug. He went from glaring at her to blinking in confusion.

"Wha?" asked Alexis. "Who…"

"I'm a superhero. And I stop evil." She pointed at him. "If you want to hit something, you need to go to the gym. Alexis and Mrs. Stephens aren't punching bags."

"Mouth on you for a little thing. Get on outta my house before I call the police."

"That's a good idea. I'll tell them how I watched you hit Mrs. Stephens and try to hit your daughter. They'll like that. Oh, you also hit me."

Mr. Stephens looked at his hand. Rage bloomed in his face and he swung at her again.

Kelly simply folded her arms and took the slap. It made a lot of noise, even louder than the last one, but didn't hurt.

He grabbed his hand and grunted in pain. "What the heck?"

She glided closer, grabbed his shirt in both hands, and pulled him a few inches off his feet. "Did I stutter? You are obviously a bad father, the kind the counselor at school talked about. Alexis has some issues, but she doesn't deserve to be slapped by her own dad. If you don't leave her—and Mrs. Stephens—alone, I'm gonna drop you right into jail, and I might not bother landing first."

He gurgled, his shirt squeezing around his throat. Legs pedaling at the air, he grabbed at her, but couldn't pull her hands away from his collar. His shirt started to rip.

Kelly eyed the recliner, estimated distance, trajectory, and angle… then threw him *just* hard enough to land him in the chair without causing any pain.

"Jim, did I just see a little girl throw you across the room?" asked Mrs. Stephens, still on the floor.

"The world's gone crazy," whispered Mr. Stephens.

Kelly landed, walked over to the recliner, and put her boot on the footrest. She shoved it closed, forcing him to sit upright. "If you need to punch girls to feel big and strong again, let me know and I'll come over. You can hit me instead of your family."

"Insolent little…"

She tapped her foot, hands on her hips. "Go on. Punch me. Or are you scared of a kid?"

"Dad," said Alexis in a whispery voice. "Don't."

Mr. Stephens squeezed his right hand, evidently sore from the slap. He looked at her with a 2+2=13 sort of expression.

"Good." Kelly nodded. "You're *supposed* to not want to hit girls. Especially small ones. Stop being a butthead." She pivoted and walked over to Alexis, who still sat on the floor in the corner. "You okay?"

"Yeah." Alexis blushed, scowled, and got up. She seemed about to say something, but trudged off down the hall without a word.

Kelly followed her to a bedroom crammed with overly girly stuff—loads of pink and white.

"Why are you in my room, Noodle-butt?" asked Alexis in as non-aggressive a tone as she'd ever heard come out of the girl.

"Umm… I'm Übergirl."

Alexis sat on the edge of the bed, head down, face hidden behind a wall of blonde. "Your hair is kinda distinctive… and that little mask doesn't cover much. And your voice is the same."

"Oh." Kelly set her fists on her hips. "I won't tell your friends."

"Really?" She peered up through her hair. "You're not gonna make me like the laughingstock of the whole school? I'm such a cliché. Perfect life on the outside but it's really a nightmare."

Kelly sat on the bed next to her, boots dangling. "No. That's private and personal. Unless he's really hurting you, I won't tell anyone… especially your friends."

"Nah. He just slaps us. Nothing real bad. Yells a lot. Mom's actually worse. She never hits me, but she's always on me about modeling and calories. I don't even remember the last time I had a meal that I enjoyed."

"You are *not* fat."

"I guess you're the expert on being too skinny."

Kelly laughed. "Yeah. That's from my dad's genes. Can't help it."

"I'm always hungry. I always feel like I'm fat. Every time I want to eat something, Mom's voice tells me I'm a whale and I look the other way."

"Alexis… you're like super pretty. You don't have to make fun of anyone at school. Okay, your parents stink, but everyone else is jealous of you."

"So? Maybe they think I'm pretty, but they don't hate going home every day. My mom was a model a long time ago. She misses it and she's trying to, I dunno, relive it by forcing me to do it."

"You don't wanna do it?"

"It's okay, but I don't *love* it like she did. I'd give it up. If I could, I'd be as ugly as Donna Hernandez if my parents loved me."

Kelly grasped Alexis' cheek and pulled her face to look her in the eye. "Donna's not ugly. She's normal. Okay, maybe a little bigger than normal, but she's not ugly. You are *ridiculously* pretty. That doesn't mean normal is ugly."

"Sorry."

"Don't say sorry to me, apologize to Donna tomorrow."

"Sorry... for being a turd to you for so long. I... wanted to stop them from hitting you. The way you screamed at them sounded just like me and Dad. I couldn't speak. My voice would've cracked, and then they would've teased me for being upset."

"I was really scared in that bag. Couldn't breathe much. When you guys left me there, I thought I'd never get out. But, I forgive you."

"Really? That was pretty seriously uncool of us to do to you. I thought someone would find you in like an hour."

"Yeah. I should probably thank you. If you guys didn't leave me there, I wouldn't have superpowers."

"What?" Alexis looked up with a gasp.

"That crystal landed like right in front of me. I think I got a super huge dose of whatever energy they have. That's why I'm so strong."

Alexis slipped off the bed to all fours, retching. She managed not to vomit, but kept shivering.

"Umm? Is my breath that bad?"

"No... you were right next to a crystal? They said on the news that a lot of people who were near the crystals when they hit died. Burned alive in seconds. We—I—almost killed you."

"You didn't know a giant alien crystal was going to land on the field."

Alexis shifted to sit on the floor. "Still freaking me out to think you could've died."

"Well. I didn't."

"Hey..." Alexis reached under the bed and pulled out an electronic tablet. She fiddled with it for a second, and held it up, revealing an e-comic. "*Foxbat and Sparrow.*"

Kelly's jaw dropped. "*You* read comics?"

"Yeah. Not as much as you, though."

"What happened to only nerds and losers read comics?"

Alexis blushed a little. "I was including myself in that when I said it. I know I'm a loser. Being pretty doesn't automatically make someone not a loser. As much of a bitch as I've been to you, loser's the only word for it. Guess I'm a nerd, too."

"Nah. Nerds get much better grades."

"Hah!" Alexis laughed.

"So, umm. Truce?" Kelly offered a hand.

Alexis shook it. "Truce. This doesn't mean we're like best buds now or anything, but we're cool."

"Yeah. I still kinda flinch whenever I see you coming."

"You have superpowers."

"I know. Being super-powered doesn't automatically make someone brave. You scared me to death for two years. Just seeing you made me want to run away. But I didn't, 'cause I thought you'd tease me worse if I did. That's gonna take some time to get over."

"Wow…" Alexis stared down at the rug. "I'm so sorry. I know how you feel. My dad does the same thing. Every time I see him, I just cringe inside."

"If he hits you again, tell me. Please."

"Please don't hurt him."

Kelly grinned. "I won't hurt him. Just scare him. Eventually, he'll learn not to hit you."

"Okay. You're really not gonna say a word about my crappy parents at school?"

"Nope. I promise." She stood. "Okay. I think my work here is done."

"Thanks."

Kelly struck a superhero pose, then walked back out to the living room where Mr. and Mrs. Stephens engaged in an argument of rapid whispers. She sounded appalled that he'd slapped Kelly, a child he had no relation to, and worried the cops would arrest him for it. He appeared somewhat out of it, like he didn't quite believe any of the past twenty minutes had happened.

They both stared at her in silence as she crossed the room and let herself out the front door.

CHAPTER EIGHTEEN

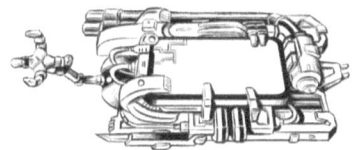

The following Tuesday morning, Kelly sprang out of bed when her alarm went off, got dressed, and headed downstairs for breakfast.

One of Dad's 'smart' robots, a four-armed floating ball, had taken over all cooking duty, and set a reasonable portion of pancakes in front of her soon after she sat at the table. Mom walked in a few minutes later. She flicked on the little TV beside the microwave, then poured herself a mug of coffee before sitting at the table.

Her mother had been less than happy at Kelly's story last Friday when she'd told her about going to Alexis' house. The 'super powers' cat had gotten out of the bag already regarding Mom, so she heard the full story—except for the Übergirl part. She would eventually tell Dad about that, but didn't want to hurt his feelings yet, both for rejecting the horrible GS name and going hero. Her mother hadn't made *too* big a deal over the Alexis situation other than to grumble about how some people shouldn't be allowed to have kids if they didn't want to love them properly.

The field reporter on the TV stood in front of a gleaming white-and-gold building surrounded by natural hills and trees, clearly nowhere near downtown. "Thanks, Marty. This is Andrew Cole coming to you live from a little ways east of the Calaveras Reservoir where The Aegis have completed construction of the first facility of its kind in California. As you know, we have our very own group of honest-to-goodness superheroes." He chuckled. "It sure does seem like life has become a comic book thanks to our wonderful, benevolent alien friends. It's difficult to imagine how humanity would have been able to continue without the assistance of such a kind, caring, compassionate, and generous people as the Nolmek. We are truly lucky to have been chosen to benefit from their munificence."

Kelly raised an eyebrow at the screen. "Does it sound like he's kissing butt?"

"Yes. Far too much." Mom shook her head.

Andrew Cole continued praising the Nolmek for giving humans leaps ahead in medical technology, green energy, electronics, and so on, going so far as to suggest humanity may finally have flying cars within ten years.

"... and in national news, authorities are still attempting to determine if a super-powered individual in Fort Lauderdale who calls himself Florida Man is, in fact, a hero or a super villain," said Marty.

"Oh?" asked the woman. "Isn't it obvious?"

"Not exactly, Karen." Marty smiled at the camera, appearing to fight the need to laugh. "Apparently, Florida Man arrived on the scene of a bank robbery. And, while the robbery was ultimately foiled, fourteen individuals— mostly bystanders—required medical treatment for alligator bites."

"My, that does seem unfortunate." Karen, the co-anchor, shook her head. "But I'm sure our benevolent protectors will help him."

"No doubt." Marty turned slightly red in the face. "I just hope they got all those alligators out of the bank."

Alligator bites? What the heck. She stared at the screen in disbelief.

Kelly and her mother tuned out the television and chatted mostly about her schoolwork over breakfast. It stank that Dad didn't eat with them, but he had apparently thrown himself completely into some project and lost track of time —days even. Though, he dragged himself up out of the lair for dinner at least.

She hugged her mother, set the plate in the dishwasher, and ran out the door, heading for school.

With the threat of Alexis or her friends bothering her ever again gone, school had changed from a place of fear to something she looked forward to. Kelly freely admitted it made her weird to like school so much and—mostly except for social studies—enjoy her time there. More and more, Mr. Reynolds' class had gotten into the habit of entirely sleeping through the period, except during tests. Somehow, despite Kelly being pretty much the only kid awake, no one failed the last test. In fact, the whole class got As.

Kelly darted off her porch, down the walkway to the sidewalk, and cut left. Two blocks later, she turned onto the street that led to the school, six more blocks away. A loud screech of tires came from behind her, followed by a deep *boom*.

She whirled to look back.

A large armored van skidded across the parking lot of the corner SF-Mart a few blocks behind her, a big man in a blue bodysuit perched on its roof. Another man in a red-and-white costume with a long, flowing cape and metallic gold gloves strolled along after it in no great hurry, whistling. The van crashed into the wall of the convenience store, flinging the big guy off. He hit the wall upside down above the van, denting the bricks.

"Ouch."

The blue man peeled off the wall and fell flat, face-down on the roof with a *clank*.

"Open says me!" called the man in red. He raised his arms toward the van, projecting a stream of nearly-white fire from each glove at the rear doors.

Men inside the van screamed.

"Uh, oh." Kelly mashed her hand onto the gem atop her bracelet. Her clothes (and backpack) traded places with her super costume in an instant.

She flew down the street, ramming into the guy cooking the armored van with enough force to throw him to the ground and send him rolling.

"Gaaaaah!" screamed the man as he tumbled into the side of a parked truck.

"Knock, knock," called the big guy in blue while bashing his fists into the rear doors of the armored car, leaving knuckle marks in the charred metal.

"Stop that!" shouted Kelly.

"Someone call the cops!" screamed a woman near the store entrance.

"What the heck would cops do?" replied a young guy in an SF-Mart apron.

"Go away little flea," said the blue man while continuing to pummel the doors.

The red man stood, pointing at her. "Get out of here, kid. Don't make me have to resort to violence on a child. Where are your parents?"

"Mom's at work and Dad's... well, Dad's busy." She walked over to the big guy, grabbed the back of his belt, and tossed him away from the armored car.

He went headfirst into a dumpster with a tremendous *boom*, crushing the side in.

"I am Übergirl, and I'm here to stop you from stealing! Stealing is bad. That means you shouldn't do it."

"Droll. I warned you, but you shall now taste the might of Doctor Blaze's flame gloves!" The man in red shot two streams of whitish fire at her.

Surprisingly, it felt quite warm. Almost painful even. Almost.

After a six-second blast, he stopped, blinking at her standing there unscathed, surrounded in heat blur.

"Oh, I'm sorry," said Kelly. "Was that supposed to do something?"

Dr. Blaze gestured at her, sunlight glinting from his golden gloves. "Myo, would you mind? This little brat needs a spanking."

The blue guy, who had already run back to the armored car, decided to stop punching the doors and pick up the whole van. Kelly turned to face him the same instant he swung the vehicle sideways like a mallet, smashing her against the convenience store wall.

Bricks burst like foam blocks behind her back. She grunted, reminded of how it felt to have Brittany and Colleen sitting on top of her. Kelly braced her hands against the armored car and shoved it aside.

Dr. Blaze and Myo both gawked as she emerged from behind the truck, dusting brick powder off her arms.

Myo growled and lunged at her. She ducked his first punch but walked into his second.

Parking lot became convenience store in an instant. Cough syrup, pretzels, and Demon Puppy snack cakes fell on top of her from the shelf she'd crushed. She blinked at an Übergirl-sized hole in the brick wall. Several people inside the convenience store gasped when she sat up.

"The kid's okay!" yelled a woman.

Growling, Kelly launched herself into flight, cruising fists-first out the same hole and flying into Myo's back. She stopped dead on impact, Myo zooming off as fast as she'd been flying. He crashed into the armored car's rear doors with a dull *clank*, his impact warping them enough that they popped open.

Myo stumbled about to face her, sporting a bloody nose and a small cut over his left eye.

Dr. Blaze covered her in fire again.

Kelly zipped up to him, grabbing his wrists and mashing his hands together a few times until the fire streams stopped and the gloves cracked open, spewing sparks instead of flames. "If you keep being mean, I'm gonna have to take those toys away from you."

She dragged him across the parking lot, tying him to a telephone pole with his cape. Four men in uniforms hopped out of the van, two with combat rifles, and took up a guard position by the back doors—though they didn't seem too confident.

Myo grabbed her from behind. Kelly grumbled, her tiny arms gradually forcing his giant bear hug wider until she could spin to face him. He grabbed at her, but she caught him in a super-powered game of mercy, her little hands vanishing in his enormous mitts. He tried to force her down, but she held firm. If not for being so much shorter, she might have overpowered him. To break the stalemate, she kicked his right leg out from under him. When he fell on his chest, she grabbed him by both middle fingers and swung him around, up over her head, and straight down onto the paving, cracking it. She walloped him over the other way, back and forth six times until he stopped putting up any noticeable resistance.

Dr. Blaze kicked and struggled, slight ripping noises coming from his cape.

"This is ridiculous! The Great Doctor Blaze does not admit defeat to a mere child!"

"I'm not a *mere* child. I am Übergirl!"

Myo appeared delirious, but not seriously injured.

Kelly dragged him across the lot and threw him into the armored van. He hit the inner wall hard enough to push the van forward a few feet. She zipped over to grab Dr. Blaze from the pole.

"You will not defeat me!" shouted Dr. Blaze… before erupting in a fireball.

Kelly flinched her face away, still holding him despite standing completely within roaring fire. "Are you done?"

"Foolish child!" Dr. Blaze started to laugh maniacally, but after a few seconds, noticing Kelly didn't appear to care much about the fire, stopped laughing. "Burn! Why aren't you burning?"

"Stop being mean!"

She smashed him into the ground, but the pavement didn't crack under him as it had with Myo. The *slap* he made on contact sounded much the same as a non-super person throwing another non-super person to the ground.

Hmm. He's probably no tougher than a norm.

Kelly hauled him over to the armored car and threw him in before slamming the doors and punching them at the center, crimping them closed. "There."

"Umm," said the nearest guard. "The money and coins are still in there. I think you just helped them."

"No. they're stuck in there. What else should I have done with them? The blue guy's pretty strong."

"My name is Myo," moaned a weak voice from the van, "The Blue Guy lives in Detroit."

"Myo," said Dr. Blaze. "Shut up."

"Sorry, boss."

A small army of police cars rolled into the parking lot. Two or three officers started to point guns at her, until the armored car guards waved them off.

"She stopped the thieves." One of the security guys holding a combat rifle gestured at the armored car. "The two who attacked us are inside."

Fourteen cops approached, cautiously. A fortyish officer with salt-and-pepper hair looked down at her, blinking in disbelief. "Who are you?"

She puffed out her chest. "I'm Übergirl."

The cop pointed at her belt. "Why does your buckle say GS if you're Übergirl?"

Kelly slouched. "Ugh. Don't ask. Please."

"Yeah, that doesn't make any sense," moaned Myo from inside the van.

"Be quiet," said Dr. Blaze.

"I'll break open the door and we get outta here, boss?"

"Do you forget that *you* are bulletproof, my dear friend. *I* am not."

Kelly glanced over her shoulder at the armored car. "Do they know we can hear them?"

"Not a bad job, kid." The cop smiled. "This is a little over our pay grade. Fortunately, the benevolent protectors are helping us deal with criminals we can't handle. They've constructed a special facility to process people who abuse their powers."

Oh, no... Dad... "Umm. 'process?'"

"Aww, just process in terms of paperwork and holding. It's a big fancy prison." The cop squinted at the sky. "Can't handle the 'special' ones in the normal facilities."

A thirtysomething guy in a black-and-white bodysuit flew out of the sky and landed nearby. His mask fully enclosed his head except for the lower half of his dark brown face. As soon as he landed, a white-haired woman in an equally skin-tight bodysuit appeared in a flash of light next to him. Her costume started off dark midnight blue at the shoulder, lightening to white at the knees with a hundred different shades of blue in between. She didn't wear a mask, and looked to be in her early twenties. She had a darker complexion as well, though much less so than the man. Eyes made entirely of cobalt blue light widened when she noticed Kelly, giving off an unmistakable sense of 'aww!'

"What happened here?" asked the man.

"Whoa..." Kelly blinked at them. "You're Phoenix and Mindfreeze."

"Correct, little one." The man smiled at her, then gestured at the armored car. "Is this your handiwork?"

"Not entirely. The two bad guys who tried to rob it are inside. I put them there." She set her fists on her hips and puffed out her chest. "I'm Übergirl."

Phoenix pointed. "Why does your belt say GS?"

Kelly blushed. "Umm... my dad wanted me to go by Ginger Snap. You know, red hair."

"Aww." Mindfreeze covered her mouth. "That's adorable."

"Totally adorable," said Dr. Blaze sarcastically, his voice echoing inside the truck.

"Actually, it kinda is," replied Myo.

"Myo? Please stop speaking," muttered Dr. Blaze.

"While we appreciate your efforts here, shouldn't you be in school at this hour?" asked Phoenix.

"Yeah. I was on my way to school, but I heard the crash. Dr. Blaze was burning the van, trying to make it so hot the guys inside came out. I didn't want him to hurt anyone."

"That's quite heroic of you." Mindfreeze took a knee to eye level. "We can handle it from here. You should get back to school."

"Okay. Wow. It's awesome to finally meet you." Kelly grinned.

Phoenix patted her on the head. "Hmm. The little one is fluffy. This hair must be a superpower."

She laughed, waved, and flew off, heading for school.

Yikes. The aliens have a super-prison. That's… well good, but not good. I don't want Dad to end up there. Oh, please be a not-really-evil mad scientist. Please.

CHAPTER NINETEEN

POWERS

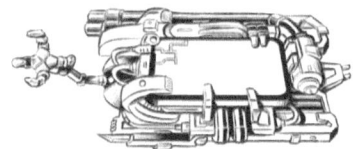

A fter finishing her lunch, Kelly decided to hit the girls' room before going outside.

Alexis came out of nowhere and barged into the stall with her, shutting the door. For an instant, Kelly froze, paralyzed in fear. The last time Alexis rushed her in a bathroom stall, she'd ended up having her head dunked in the toilet for repeated flushing.

But, the tall blonde girl looked… broken.

Kelly's fear evaporated to worry. "What's wrong?"

"Did you do something to my parents?" whispered Alexis.

"No?"

"Are you asking me? What happened to them?" Alexis fidgeted her hands together. "It's really messed up."

Kelly's fear lessened; she stopped leaning away. "Why are you whispering?"

"Because we're talking about stuff I don't want anyone to know about. And I don't want anyone to see us talking. What did you do to my parents?"

"I didn't do anything. Just told your dad to leave you alone the one time when you were right there. Why? What happened?"

Alexis raked a hand up through her hair. "I… don't know how to deal with this."

"Oh, no. Please… tell me what happened? Are they hurt?"

"No. They're not hurt. They're acting weird."

Kelly chuckled. "Parents acting weird. Isn't that what parents do? Act weird? Mine have been totally bonkers ever since the crystals came down."

"No, this is past weird into crazy. Ever since Monday, they've both been totally different people. They're like super affectionate now. Mom keeps wanting to cuddle me like I'm two. Dad's even really looking for a job. He and Mom still argue, but as soon as I walk in, it's like they turn into the perfect parents from a TV show. It's *so* messed up."

"Umm." Kelly shrugged. "I have no idea what happened. Are they doing bad stuff? Hurting anyone?"

"No, not really. I just don't know how to deal with this. My mom hasn't been sweet since I was like seven. Ever since the modeling stuff started, she's been more like my manager than my mother… and it only got worse and worse. Now she's treating me like I'm made out of glass."

"If they're not hurting you, why not just go with it?"

"I'm trying. But I'm afraid it's gonna stop. And, maybe Mom's gone a bit *too* far the other direction, but I'll take that over being screamed at all the time."

"Yeah. I would, too."

"Sure, but you're a little kid."

Kelly laughed.

"Umm. Okay. Sorry. I just thought you might have used a superpower on them or something."

"I can't do anything like change someone's attitude. I'm kinda like Ms. Omni. Strong, tough, fast, can fly. But I don't have ice beams or psi powers. And I can't summon intra-dimensional beings."

Alexis grabbed some toilet paper to dab tears from her eyes. "Yeah. Omni's a bit overpowered. They gave her too many different abilities and there's no real explanation for why. Nothing links them together. It's like the writers keep putting her in these impossible situations and she needed to pull some new ability out of her butt to escape. Like how many times can one character suddenly realize they can do something they never even tried before?"

Kelly laughed. "Yeah, seriously."

"Okay. Umm. If you didn't zap my parents then, I guess I'll just try to deal with it… and—" She froze as the doors opened, other girls walking in.

Kelly floated up, sitting cross-legged in midair so no one saw two pairs of legs in one stall.

Alexis tilted her head in confusion.

Kelly pointed down at her feet, then held up two fingers.

Nodding, Alexis turned and sat on the toilet fully dressed, pretending to be using that stall.

They waited in awkward silence until the other three girls left.

"Good thinking," whispered Alexis. "Being together in the same stall, especially the two of us, would've been hard to explain."

"You could've just said you were gonna give me another swirly."

Alexis cringed. "I'm really sorry about that. So disgusting. I don't know why I let Colleen talk me into that idea. She got it from her brother. He and his friends did it to some boy they don't like."

"My mom said a swirly was definitely 'boy bullying.' But, maybe we should get out of here before someone else walks in. If someone catches us, you can just say you were picking on me again so they don't start teasing you."

"Wow. Are you for real?"

"What?"

"You're like way too nice. Why are you so nice?"

Kelly shrugged. "I dunno. Guess it's just who I am."

Alexis made an almost-guilty face at her. She turned her back, opened the stall door to peer out, then rushed off upon not seeing anyone out in the bathroom.

With a sigh, Kelly locked the door. "Can't a girl pee in peace anymore?"

Strangely, she didn't see Paige anywhere during the rest of lunch period.

Her friend reappeared in gym class after lunch. She hadn't yet gotten used to having gym every day instead of twice a week, another new thing that came with being a 'big kid in middle school.' Also, the kids had the option to shower after if they wanted to—assuming they could finish and change in ten minutes. The idea of being anywhere near a locker room with showers terrified Kelly at first, but since Alexis no longer made it her mission in life to target her, she no longer dreaded being pranked in there. A few kids occasionally still chuckled whenever they saw her in gym shorts, remembering the dreaded de-pantsing incident.

They broke up into teams for volleyball—except for Brittany who still had a cast on her hand and sat the period out on the bleachers making sour faces at her. Kelly wanted to ask Paige about her lunch period disappearance, but they wound up on opposite teams... so she just played, and didn't even use her powers to cheat. Well mostly. She took advantage of them twice: she sped herself up to step past Colleen Brandt when the girl tried to trip her, and again when the girl attempted to crash into her and knock her over. That time, Kelly dodged. Colleen tried to ram empty air and wound up flinging herself to the floor.

This, of course, got everyone laughing at Colleen for being such a dork that she tripped over her own feet.

The locker room, formerly the single most terrifying place in the world, still represented prime opportunity for the most embarrassing pranks imaginable. Becoming Übergirl made gym class trivial from a physical exertion standpoint. She didn't even come close to working up a sweat. That, awesomely, meant avoiding the showers wouldn't leave her spending the rest of the day feeling funky.

As usual, squeals of a few classmates snapping each other with towels echoed from the shower area. None of them sounded mean spirited, just friends horsing about. Kelly contented herself to change out of her gym clothes and wait for Paige outside the locker room.

"Hey," said Kelly, when her friend appeared. "Didn't see you at lunch?"

"Sorry. I"—she looked around, then whispered—"snuck down to the field to check out the crystal."

"Oh. How did you get past the soldiers?"

"Easy. Just snuck in. They're so bored they're not even really watching."

"Anything going on there?"

"Nope. Just a big boring red thing stuck in the ground." She sighed, disappointed.

Kelly put an arm across her shoulders. "You licked it trying to get powers, didn't you?"

Paige blushed.

"It's not the world's most epic cherry popsicle."

"Yeah. It tasted like glass."

Kelly laughed. "You really did lick it?"

"A little." Paige clasped her hands behind her back and whistled innocently. "I might have spent most of lunch trying to hug it."

"Umm. Wasn't it super-hot?"

"The lava was, yeah, but the crystal is only *really* hot." Paige showed off a red mark on her hand. "Like soup that just came off the stove. That's why I said *trying* to hug it."

"Aww, I'm sorry it didn't do anything." Kelly squeezed her in a one-armed hug.

"It's okay. I had to try, right? Guess people can't just walk up to them and go super or everyone would be."

"Hmm. I wonder if that's why they put soldiers there? To keep people away from them so that doesn't happen?"

Paige shrugged. "Maybe. C'mon, we're gonna be late for music."

"Is it music or art today? I can't remember."

"Umm. Tuesday. Music."

"Life was so much easier when we just stayed in the same classroom."

Paige laughed.

WEDNESDAY NIGHT, PAIGE'S PARENTS FINALLY ALLOWED HER TO SLEEP OVER.

Of course, they both stopped by to meet the Donovans. Mr. and Mrs. Warren kept giving Dad odd looks even though he'd met them in normal clothes—not the labcoat. Kelly didn't think he'd become any more... unusual in appearance, but she'd adjusted to him. The Warrens' initial unease faded fast, and by the time they left fifteen minutes later, Paige's parents both acted as if they'd known Kelly's parents for years.

The girls went straight to pajama mode, Kelly in a nightgown, Paige in her Captain Stupendous PJ pants and Wobbles the Cat top. True, that comic was aimed at younger kids, but it had a secret following among older readers, even adults. According to Dad, it contained quite a few jokes aimed at adults that kids totally missed, but he wouldn't explain any of them.

Mom provided popcorn for movie night and hovered over the girls.

After a half hour of her mother standing behind the couch watching them watch a movie, Kelly peered up. "Mom?"

"Yes?"

"Why are you standing there?"

"It's just so wonderful to see you finally having a friend and doing friend things. I'm really happy. Your father and I were so worried you might be alone all through high school."

Kelly blushed. "Umm. Thanks, Mom."

"I'm thrilled you have a friend."

"Me, too, Mom." Kelly forced a 'please stop' smile.

Her mother got the hint, patted her on the head and walked down the hall. "If you need me, I'll be in the computer room."

"Okay."

"You have a friend, even if she's just a dumb norm without any powers," said Paige.

"That doesn't matter. You know I don't care about that. Last month, I was a total nobody. I don't feel better than anyone."

"I'm not jealous of you. Just... I wish I could do *something*. Even a stupid power like that kid Inertia. Ooh, he can stay put. Yay." Paige grinned. "But it's still something."

"People don't need to have superpowers to be heroes. Look at you."

"I didn't do anything."

Kelly let out a big breath. "This is going to sound like totally sappy, but you really helped me. I had been so sure I'd never make any friends that I didn't even try to find one. If you hadn't come over to talk to me that day, I'd still have no friends. Whenever my parents mentioned being alone, I'd always say it didn't bother me. But it did. I just didn't know it."

"You're right. That was super sappy."

"Sorry."

Paige looked over at her. "I don't mind. I was lonely, too. No one ever paid any attention to me at all, like I didn't even exist. At least you got picked on. They just ignored me."

"I would rather have been ignored." Kelly smirked.

"Grass is greener."

"Yeah." She smiled. "But there's no grass inside a giant garbage can. Trust me. Ignored is better."

Paige sat cross-legged on the sofa and shifted to face her. "It's cool that you got really sweet powers."

"They're okay. Not like I can make ice beams or teleport or do anything flashy."

"But you are stronger than that Myo guy. And really tough. He hit you over the head with an armored car and you laughed at it."

"More slapped me into a wall with one. If he clobbered me over the head with it, I'd have probably gone into the ground like a nail since I'm so skinny."

Paige laughed herself to tears.

Kelly made goofy faces at her until she stopped laughing.

Her friend's grin faded to a serious, worried look. "Wow, you're really lucky."

"I guess."

"No, I mean… I saw on the news that other people who were close to crystals when they landed got burned alive."

"Eep!" Kelly shivered, biting her lip. Admitting Alexis already told her that would open the door to explaining what she was doing at her bully's house. A small lie to protect the other girl's privacy didn't seem too horrible. She'd do the same for Paige's secrets. "Really?"

"They didn't feel much."

"That does not make me feel better."

Paige cringed. "Not what I mean. The goalpost melted. The whole stadium is blackened. Bleachers melted. Do you have any idea how hot the blast it gave off when it landed was?"

"Not exactly. I know it hurt like heck." She briefly explained how it felt like she'd fallen into a deep fryer for a second, but she fainted. When she woke up, it had all stopped.

"Wow. You had to have absorbed a lot of power from being so close to it when it landed. I wonder if you have any powers you haven't discovered yet. What's on the list so far?"

"Umm. Flight. Strong, tough, and sometimes everything slows down around me. Like when Brittany tried to hit me with a basketball, time just crept along. Same with the robot that almost crashed into you."

"Super reflexes." Paige nodded. "You're moving so fast, everyone else seems to stop."

"Yeah."

"Any energy beams, mind powers, transformations, matter control?"

"No. Been trying."

"Telekinesis?" Paige picked up a popcorn kernel. "Try to lift this out of my hand."

Kelly snatched it with her fingers and ate it.

"Dork! Use your mind!"

"I did use my brain. I am smart enough to know that telekinesis doesn't work for me, so I moved it with my hand."

Paige rolled her eyes. "Seriously. Try mental powers."

'Popcorn experiment take two' proved she did not possess the ability to move objects by thought power alone.

"Aww." Paige handed her the kernel. "Okay, so no telekinesis. What other superpowers might you have? Hmm."

"Staying up past bedtime on a school night is not one of them," said Mom from the doorway.

"The movie's got like eight minutes left. Can we please finish it?" Kelly put on 'pleading grin.'

"You're not even watching it now. You're just talking."

"You haven't learned the fine art of watching a movie while doing other things?" asked Paige.

Mom chuckled. "Okay, fine. But once those credits roll, you two are going to sleep."

"Deal." Kelly leaned against Paige and paid attention to the last bit of the movie.

... completely lost as to what had been going on.

CHAPTER TWENTY

CEREAL AND MINIONS

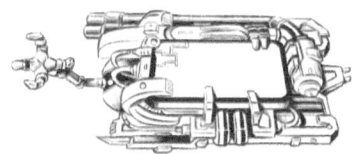

Saturday morning, Kelly awoke to the gentle tones of silence.

No alarm. No incessant construction noise. No sense of imminent interdimensional doom.

Smiling, Kelly got out of bed, made a quick trip to the bathroom, then got dressed in a purple sweatshirt and jeans before heading downstairs. She stopped short at the bottom of the steps, staring at something that shouldn't be in the living room.

Two somethings.

Rather, two some*ones*.

A pair of large men sat on the couch with muscles so big that they probably had to hire smaller people to scratch for them if the middle of their chest itched. Both wore identical black tank tops and off-white military style pants, the ones with the silly number of pockets. The man on the left had short blonde hair and a ruddy complexion, the other bald and shiny, a bit on the pale side.

Both stared intently at the television, more specifically, *Kobold and the Rulers of the Universe*, a kid's cartoon. They also both ate cereal from bowls that looked like teacups in their massive hands.

"Umm, hi," said Kelly, creeping closer. "Who are you?"

"I am Zorthax," said the bald man in a grand voice.

"I'm Bob," said the other guy in an average voice.

Both ate a spoonful of cereal at the same time.

Kelly slapped herself in the forehead. "Great. Dad has minions."

Zorthax raised a finger. "We prefer the term 'henchmen.' The term minion implies a high degree of subservient willingness to do anything the boss commands."

"But we have that." Bob blinked at him. "We do whatever he asks."

Zorthax glanced at him. "Would you jump into lava if the boss asked you to?"

"No."

"Then you aren't a minion."

Kelly shrugged, went to the kitchen to fix herself a bowl of Cosmix – with meteor marshmallows, and returned to the living room. She sat on the floor in front of the minions, watching cartoons.

Hearing two grown (and huge) men gasp at scenes meant to be scary to kids struck Kelly as a bit surreal, but she didn't question it as, being nine, the same scenes made her jump. *Kobold* took place in a medieval world where the small, green, goblin-like main character and his fellow adventurers (the 'Rulers of the Universe') went on various adventures. Many parents complained about it for being 'too scary' for kids under twelve. Naturally, this resulted in almost every kid under twelve wanting to watch it.

On today's episode, Kobold and his friends entered an underground crypt, fought walking skeletons, and ultimately confronted the undead mummy king. The art style didn't gross her out too much, but the show *loved* its jump scares. When the mummy king first popped on screen, Zorthax twitched so hard he dropped his (fortunately empty) cereal bowl.

Kelly drank the last of the milk in her bowl, lowered it, and whistled silently in her head. *I'm watching Saturday morning cartoons with Dad's minions.* She examined her toes. *Time for new polish… later.*

When the episode ended, the men stood at the same time.

"We must leave now," said Bob.

"There is work to do." Zorthax took Kelly's bowl. "I'll clean that for you."

"Thanks. Umm. What are you working on?"

"We are to help The Brain Trust with his plan." Bob smiled.

"The… Brain Trust?" Kelly tilted her head. "What the heck is that?"

"Your, umm, father," said both men at the same time.

She glanced between them. *Why do they keep doing that? Did Dad hire them or make them?* "Okay. What's his plan?"

"We're not supposed to talk about it." Zorthax shook his head. "It's secret."

"I'm his daughter. Does that count?"

The men exchanged a glance.

"I suppose that means you are part of the team." Bob grinned. "The Brain Trust has perfected a serum."

"A perfect serum." Zorthax stacked the three bowls.

"We are going to add it to the city's water supply." Bob clapped.

Uh oh. This isn't going to be good, is it? Nothing good is ever added to a city water supply. Especially by minions. Kelly tried to keep as innocent a face as possible. "What's it do?"

"It's a mind-control serum. The Brain Trust will soon have mental control over everyone in the city who isn't supered-up." Bob pointed at the TV. "*Quest Hour* is coming on. Can we watch it?"

"Later, Bob. We have work to do. The Brain Trust needs us."

Horrified, Kelly stood there with a forced smile as the minions walked out to the backyard. As soon as they disappeared into the shed, she paced. "Holy crap. Yikes. No. My father isn't going to mind control San Francisco. This is not happening. No way. This can't really be true."

She fidgeted at her ZOOM bracelet.

"I have to do something."

CHAPTER TWENTY-ONE

DAD'S GONE TO CRAZYTOWN

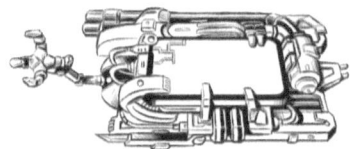

E very mad scientist's lair had at least two things in common: an emergency escape tunnel that could be exploited to sneak *into* the lair, and ventilation ducts that could also be exploited to sneak into the lair. Based on her memory of the tour Dad gave her, Kelly soon discovered the location of the rocket escape pod's exit port—right under the Williams' garage down the street.

Their neighbors would be mildly surprised (and probably quite upset) if Dad ever used the escape system since their garage would end up in low-Earth orbit. Unfortunately, she couldn't figure out a way to get in, as he'd buried the giant door a few feet underground. Or, to be more accurate, he'd dug up from below and stopped a few feet beneath the surface.

Dad, also being a comic fan, probably knew all about heroes exploiting the escape tunnel.

On the other hand, he still didn't know she wouldn't be going supervillain. For now, she *could* simply walk right in the front door. Being smart (indeed quite smart for her age) she knew her father would figure it out eventually. But, how would he react? She couldn't imagine Dad ever trying to hurt her. The worst thing he might do is try to imprison her somehow and make a machine that would turn her evil so they could do supervillain stuff together. Hopefully, enough of her father remained inside that man's head, not changed by whatever the aliens did, that he would be unable to twist the essence of his daughter's very personality that much.

Turning Kelly Donovan evil would be like feeding a few hundred baby white bunny rabbits into a wood chipper.

At least, she hoped he felt that way.

Kelly slapped herself in the head a few times for thinking of throwing baby rabbits into a wood chipper. She flew to the fake tool shed and went down into the lair. Another problem… she had a time limit.

Paige planned to come over in like an hour, and Mom would be taking them to her gym. The girls could go swimming at the indoor pool while Mom did her thing in the fitness center. *No big deal. I have one hour to stop Dad from becoming an actual criminal and mind-controlling the whole city.*

She cracked her knuckles.

"No problem."

Kelly jumped a few inches into the air and glided straight across the entry foyer to the hallway that went to the control room. The minions' voices, as well as Dad's, came from the left hall, probably in the room with the extra Fabricator-2000 machines, which he no doubt had used to produce the mind-control serum.

At the end of the hall, she glided up the stairs to the control room… and stopped in front of a laser fence in the doorway at the top. She gathered her floof of hair tight to her chest, sucked in her gut (not that she had one) and shimmied sideways between two of the laser bars. For once, being so darn noodly worked in her favor.

Evidently, becoming a mad scientist had affected Dad's brain in more ways than simply giving him the ability to invent such amazing devices. He had succumbed to the mad scientist flaw of overconfidence. Several large monitor screens displayed maps and diagrams detailing his plan, codename: MICE. Underneath the title, he'd written 'mental influence control elixir' along with several jokes about making mice of the people.

"Ugh. Dad jokes are his most deadly invention." Kelly bonked her head on the table.

She floated up to one of the big screens, reading his diagrams and notes, but most of it went over her head. That made her wonder if this stuff would make sense to anyone, even a real scientist. From what she could follow between all the mad-science gibberish, the serum, once added to the water supply, would render norms who consumed it susceptible to a signal that he would broadcast from another device he had called the CAT, for Control Antenna Terminal.

Kelly slapped herself in the forehead and dragged her hand down her face. "Ugh. Seriously, Dad? MICE and CAT?"

Once exposed to the serum, using the CAT would send command signals to affected norms, turning them into mindless servants until they finished carrying out whatever he wanted them to do, then they'd forget everything that happened between receiving the control signal and finishing their task. The system could selectively target any affected person one at a time, groups, or the entire city. Exposure to the serum made a person vulnerable to CAT for 'an undetermined time between six months and five years.'

Kelly bit her finger. "No. No. No. No. No. No. Dad. You can't do this."

She paced. On one hand, Dad. Her father, giver of life to the red-haired child spawn. Fellow comic nerd. Shoulder to cry on when needed. Provider of the purple bike. Remover of spiders… and not a bad cook.

On the other hand… mind controlling every non-super in San Francisco.

She kept pacing.

"I can't just turn on him. I can't tell Phoenix about this. Cops won't help. Mom won't understand. She *just* got back to normal. If she finds out Dad went bad, she'll freak out again and turn into a space cadet. I have to save him. Let's try subtle first."

She gathered her hair, shimmied sideways past the laser bars, then flew down the hall to the foyer, curved left, and rocketed along that hallway following the sound of voices until she spotted Dad and the minions standing by a pushcart loaded with huge fifty-gallon drums of glowing yellow slime.

"Hey, sweetie." Dad hugged her. "What are you doing down here? It's Saturday. Go play and have fun or something."

"Oh, I am. Mom's gonna take me and Paige to her gym so we can go swimming in like twenty minutes."

"That sounds fun. Try not to freak anyone out staying underwater too long or creating any whirlpools by flying fast in circles underwater, okay? The lifeguards will hate that."

"I won't." She walked up to the cart, gazing past her reflection on the clear drum at the glowing goop. "What did you make? Nuclear lemon meringue?"

He laughed. "Just a little project. Work stuff. Nothing you need to worry about."

"It's glowing." She leaned closer to the tank, studying her reflection on the clear cylinder. "I'm curious."

"Sure you are. Your urge to learn was already a superpower before the aliens showed up. That's why you skipped first grade. Hmm. I wonder if it's too early to bring you in to help… Nah. You're only nine. Not yet."

"So what are you doing?" She smiled.

"I am excited to put the first phase of my master plan into action. This wonderful stuff"—he patted the drum—"is soon going to let me into the minds of everyone in San Francisco. With it, we'll be able to take control of whoever we need to at any given time for whatever other project I have."

"Wow. Really?" She clenched her fists, keeping a forced smile. "That's amazing! Umm, why do you even want to do that? I mean, you have these two awesome minions already."

"Henchmen," said Zorthax.

"Sorry, henchmen." Kelly bit her lip. "And look how big they are. Do you really need to turn a whole bunch of people into mind-controlled zombies?"

"It's only temporary, sweetie. I shall only enslave them for as long as it takes to do whatever I need done. No point being unnecessarily cruel."

She nodded, deciding *not* to point out that mind control itself counted as cruel. "What about those heroes. Don't you think that taking over San Francisco might, like, make them notice us? I don't wanna go to jail. I'm only nine. I still have to finish school."

"Don't worry." He patted her on the head. "There are two major reasons why that will never happen. One: you're not directly involved. Two: I am The Brain Trust." He pressed a button on the mega-tablet that activated a thunder-and-lightning hologram/sound, then bellowed his best 'supervillain mastermind' laugh. After, he straightened his labcoat and cleared his throat. "Now then…"

"Umm." She eyed the fading storm illusion. "Wow. Nice evil laugh."

"Thank you, sweetie. I've been practicing."

"What's the second reason?"

Dad wiped a fleck of dust off the mega-tablet. "You forget, I am The Brain Trust. The idiots are running around out there looking for cretins who do things like break into banks or steal armored cars. I doubt they are smart enough to even connect me to anything my MICE do. The serum is tasteless."

"Yeah, it is," muttered Kelly.

"You think the fluorescent yellow is tacky? Everything's cooler when it glows."

She tilted her hand back and forth. "Not as bad as the ties you always wear on Thanksgiving."

"Ouch." Dad grabbed his heart. "That hurt."

"You wear awful ties on purpose though." She grinned.

"I do." He tapped a few buttons on the mega-tablet, bouncing the way he usually did whenever a new mail order giant-mecha robot model kit showed up at the door. "You should run off and go have fun with your friend. I have work to do."

"What are you going to have the, umm, MICE do?"

"I'm not entirely sure yet other than the Prime Objective."

Kelly raised both eyebrows. "That sounds ominous."

Dad pointed to the right. "The first thing I am going to command my MICE —specifically Philip MacLeod on the city council—to do is to send a notice to the darn Morrison's next door about that infernal hedge. It's two inches onto our property line and drops seeds and berries all over our lawn."

"Did you seriously invent a mind control serum just so you could make the next door neighbor move that stupid hedge you have been fighting with him about for the past three years?"

"Not entirely." Dad leaned back, rubbing his chin. "But the hedge is high on the priority list."

"You've been rubbing your chin a lot."

"It's a fine chin. Don't you think?"

"Yeah. Very fine... and pointy."

"Indeed. It is The Brain Trust's signature look. You know what they say about men who have long chins."

She blinked. "Uhh, no, I don't."

He tapped his head. "They have very big brains. Now go have fun with your friends and leave me to my nefarious schemes."

Kelly started to mope away, having no idea what to do, but stopped. "Umm, Dad?"

"Yes, dear?"

"What do you think about the Nolmek? I don't trust them. Do they creep you out too? Like all the news reporters and even the cops keep calling them benevolent protectors."

"Sharp." He wagged his eyebrows at her. "As smart as I expected from someone who carries half of my DNA. Yes. I don't trust them either. Fairly certain they are up to no good, but they are insignificant compared to"—he triggered the holographic lightning and thunder again—"The Brain Trust!"

She stared at him in disbelief as he laughed maniacally over the thunder.

Dad has gone to Crazytown. A lump formed in her throat, but she couldn't cry in front of him. She couldn't accept that her father had changed so much. It had to be those darn aliens' fault. They did something to him. Sure, he'd been unhappy about his job and pretty much constantly feeling like everyone walked all over him, but mind-controlling the whole city? The Dad she knew would never do something like that.

"Insignificant," whispered Kelly.

"Exactly. Once San Francisco is mine, we'll move on to the rest of the state, then the country, then the world." He thunderstorm-laughed again.

"Dad. Seriously?"

"What?" He glanced at her, finger poised to press something on his mega-tablet. "Is the laugh too much?"

She made a pinchy gesture. "Just a bit."

"Oh. Well. It's a work in progress. Do you think it's the laugh itself or the thunder that makes it... extra?"

"It's more *you* doing the evil laugh, Dad. You love me and Mom too much to laugh like that."

"Aww, sweetie." He scooped her into a hug and swung her around once. "I still love you more than anything. That hasn't changed at all. But I'm—we—are no longer nobodies!"

"Maybe you should wait a bit on this plan? What about the heroes? You don't have any defenses here yet. If they do find you, they'll walk right in the door. And if those Alexis robots you made to test me out are all we have, we're in big trouble."

"Pff." He waved dismissively. "I've taken them into account already. They don't know about the plan. They don't even know I exist... yet. See, that's where mad scientists always go wrong: wanting everyone to know who they are. My plan is to sit back and run the show from down here. This is not an ego thing."

"That explains the laugh."

"Ooh, sassy," muttered Bob.

Zorthax gave him a high five (with a tickle).

"Well, that aside. There is also a shield set up over the MICE control node. Nobody will be able to interfere. Now..." He set her on her feet. "Go play with your friend at the pool. She should be here any minute."

"Okay."

Head down, Kelly trudged away. Motion caught her eye right before she reached the door. A hallway that hadn't been there yesterday led off to the left containing numerous clear-walled holding cells. Her father had apparently taken approximately twenty people prisoner and locked them in a legit dungeon.

Kelly glanced at him, talking to the minions, then hurried down that hallway.

A few of the prisoners standing behind the clear wall in the nearest cell looked mildly familiar. She scrunched her eyebrows trying to remember... then it hit her. She'd seen them at 'take your kid to work day.' Dad kidnapped people from his old job. Worse, none of them noticed her standing there, all gazing into space like... well, zombies. Fortunately, they didn't *look* like zombies.

Ugh. Dad. Bad.

She started fiddling with the code lock on the cell door.

"Sweetie..." Dad appeared next to her in a flash of teleportation sparkles, and shooed her away from the cell. "No playing with Daddy's research subjects. These aren't toys. If they get loose, I'll have to go out and find new ones. You don't want to waste Daddy's time, do you?"

"Umm, no," said Kelly to the floor.

"Good. When you're older, you can help me experiment on people. Now, off you go. Your friend is almost here."

He poked a button on the mega-tablet. Her surroundings changed in an instant to the elevator, which promptly shot upward with a *shoomp!*

"Ugh. This isn't happening. What am I gonna do? My dad's really a mad scientist."

CHAPTER TWENTY-TWO

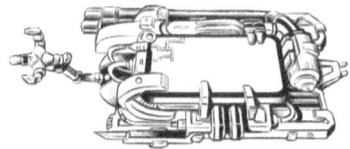

M om ran up to her as soon as she walked out of the tool shed.

Paige waved from the patio door, already in a dark blue-and-black two-piece swimsuit.

Kelly's supreme glumness and guilt evaporated. Out of nowhere, she felt so excited she could've jumped over the moon. Literally—assuming she could tolerate outer space, which remained untested.

"Go get changed, hon. You ready to go swimming?" Mom smiled at her.

"Yeah!" Kelly beamed. She flew up through her bedroom window, hit the ZOOM bracelet to trade the super costume for her normal clothes, then changed into her bathing suit before running downstairs.

Paige met her by the door. They ran outside and climbed into the back seat of Mom's car with plenty of room since going to an indoor pool removed the need for the huge bag of beach stuff. On the ride to the place, they talked about everything from comics to the *Waif* novels—which Paige had started reading and liked—to stuff about school. Kelly couldn't believe how excited she felt to go swimming with her best friend. She'd always adored swimming, a big part of the reason it made her so sad when Mom rejected the idea of getting a pool at home.

The fitness center pool did have a down side: she couldn't do anything *really* fun, like Paige's suggestion of flying around while towing her for waterskiing. Too many people would see them, and Kelly didn't want to ruin her secret identity. Once they got there, Mom left them in the care of the lifeguard with orders not to leave the pool area unless they came straight to her in the fitness center.

The girls had a blast at the pool, swimming, diving, and playing Frisbee in the water with a pack of random people who happened to bring one. Mom arrived at the pool after about an hour and sat in one of the lounge chairs, reading and sorta-watching them. Not quite two hours later, Mom made watch-tapping gestures (despite not wearing a watch) to tell them 'time to go.' As soon as the sadness of having to leave the pool hit her, a strange, nagging feeling that she shouldn't be having so much fun came out of nowhere. She *should* be worried about something. Or sad about something.

That idea needled at her as she climbed up out of the pool, walked over to stand by Mom's lounge chair, and toweled off. Water tamed even her mighty floof, turning her hair into a heavy carpet on her back. Though, having wet hair no longer felt like someone hung a concrete block on her head.

I can lift cars. Wet hair—even this *hair—is no big deal.*

Still, she did her best to squeeze the water out of it. A high-speed flight across the city would probably restore her hair to its usual fluffiness in minutes, but she couldn't exactly fly out of here without ruining her secret. Once the girls dried off as much as they could, they gathered their things and followed Mom out. While walking down the hall past the fitness center part of the place, Kelly scrunched her eyebrows trying to remember what felt wrong. By the time they got to So What If It's Only Thursday's for lunch, the bizarre cheerfulness finally cracked open.

Everything about Dad and his plans crashed down on her emotional state in the parking lot while she followed Mom to the door. She cringed at the sudden shift in mood, then became annoyed at herself for somehow allowing a play date with Paige to distract her from Dad's MICE plan. Sure, hanging out with her best (only) friend *was* amazing. It would've been far more amazing if she didn't have to worry about her dad doing something so bad—and having kidnapped people.

Did simply undoing what he did without getting him in trouble count as helping him?

But still. Seeing her best friend should not have caused such an instant, sudden shift in mood from wanting to crawl into a corner and cry to bouncing around like the best day of her life had arrived.

She kept up a straight face and normal attitude the whole time they got a table, ordered, and ate. At least having Paige there to keep her mind occupied helped. Talking about random stuff with her plus the rapidly shrinking hope that Dad would realize he planned to do something really bad and change his mind kept her calm.

When they eventually got home, Paige grabbed the bag she'd brought with her and went into the downstairs bathroom to change from her swimsuit to normal clothes. Kelly headed upstairs to do the same.

Soon, they met in Kelly's bedroom.

"Okay." Paige stared at her. "What's wrong?"

"Am I that obvious?"

"As soon as we got to the restaurant, you kept talking about so much random stuff so fast I knew something was up."

Kelly bowed her head, rubbed her face with both hands, and decided she couldn't deal with this alone. "It's bad."

"Spill."

They sat on the rug.

Kelly leaned close and whispered about the whole plan—so Mom wouldn't hear if she happened to go upstairs. She didn't need her mother to find out the truth about Dad and go back to being a space cadet.

"Wow. I'm sorry. That's totally bogus." Paige exhaled, then nodded. "Okay. You've got four basic options here: One, do nothing and let whatever happens, happen. Two, tell him you're not a supervillain and you can't let him do that, then stop him. Three, try to sneak around and stop him without him finding out who's doing it. Four, talk to the Aegis and ask them for help."

"You didn't say five, choose family over everything and help him."

"Because I know you too well. You wouldn't go evil, and besides, if you did, I couldn't hang out with you anymore. My parents would kill me if they caught me being friends with a bad guy."

Kelly almost laughed. "Right. Yeah. No way. He's my dad, but I can't help him be evil. I think the aliens might have done something to him."

"Well, yeah. They did something to the whole planet. Everyone with powers is because of the aliens."

"No, I mean… Why would aliens make people into superheroes? Maybe this is all a joke to them and they're forcing people to be characters. Like deciding who has to be good or bad and they forced Dad to play the mad scientist character?"

Paige scratched her shin. "Maybe, and I hate to say this, but I don't think so. We both think the aliens are up to no good, right?"

Kelly nodded.

"If that's true, why would they make super humans at all? They would be a threat to whatever bad thing the Nolmek are planning. The aliens would want to keep us as helpless as possible. I know it means that deep down, your dad had mad scientist in him somewhere. And, you didn't change at all, like personality wise."

"Yeah. I did a little bit. More confident." Kelly rested her chin on both hands, elbows on her knees. "I really should tell the truth and confess I'm not gonna go bad. Pretending to play along with him or avoiding it is kind of lying, and I hate constantly worrying if he knows. But, I'm also terrified of what he'll do if he finds out. I want my dad back."

"It'll be okay... somehow. Look, he hasn't done anything yet, right? Still working on his plan. Until he dumps that stuff in the water, he won't get in any trouble. So tell him you're a hero now and stop him before he does that."

"He's already kidnapped people, Pay. Like twenty of them. He's used them for experiments... probably how he made that serum. Kidnapping *one* person is a big crime. My dad is a criminal, Paige." She started crying. "He's really a criminal."

Paige scooted over and hugged her. "Don't cry. You're Übergirl. Even if your dad has to go to jail, he's still your dad, right? And if he's in jail, he can't hurt anyone so you don't have to worry about him."

"But then he won't be *here*!" She huffed. "I miss my dad."

"Can I say something without you hitting me?"

"I wouldn't hit you."

"Your dad hasn't really 'been here' lately. He's always down in the lair."

Kelly gazed up at the ceiling, her floofy hair draping off her shoulders. It hurt because the girl had a point. Dad had gone somewhere else. The Brain Trust lived under her house. "Ugh."

"Why don't you go talk to the Aegis? It might be better if you stay out of it entirely. Let them deal with him."

"Oh, yeah. Tattle on my dad. He'd never forgive me."

"I know tattling is one of those things that's both wrong and right at the same time. But, if someone did or is gonna do something *really* bad, we have to. If you saw someone going into a bank with a gun, you'd go get the cops, right?"

"No. I'd stop the guy."

Paige stuck out her tongue. "Before, I mean."

"Yeah. Yeah. You're right."

"No matter what he does, he's still your dad. You'll love him and he'll love you. But kidnapping and mind control is *super* wrong. We have to stop him."

Kelly gave a halfhearted nod, and her hair fell over her face.

"When's he going to do it?"

"A few days from now."

"Okay, so there's time. If I just go home for no reason, he's going to know something's up."

"He's going to know something's up when I tell on him."

"True, but if he finds out *before* you tell on him, he can stop you from telling on him. Then he does his mind control anyway."

"I feel like such a horrible daughter."

"This is for his own good."

Kelly let off a sad chuckle. "That's what he used to say when he grounded me."

"What did you ever do to get grounded? You are like the world's biggest goody."

"I wrote on the walls with a crayon when I was like two. I don't even remember it. And I used to fight with my mother over eating vegetables."

"Everyone does that. It only proves you're human." Paige tapped a finger to her chin. "Do you think Nolmek babies write on the walls of their spaceship?"

Kelly laughed.

"Okay. Time to commence 'Operation Act Normal.'"

"Fail."

"What?"

"Neither one of us is normal."

Paige raspberried her, then leaned close. "Let's play video games until I have to go home. After you have dinner, sneak out your window and go talk to the Aegis."

"How am I supposed to find them?"

"They have this big giant white fortress in the hills across the bay. Can't miss it."

"Just fly up and knock?"

"Sure. Tell them you're selling Explorer Girl Cookies or something."

Kelly sighed. "C'mon. Let's go play."

CHAPTER TWENTY-THREE

HELLO, DARKNESS YOU'RE NOT MY FRIEND

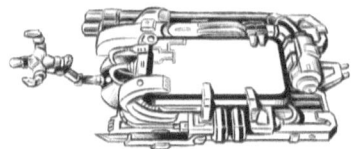

Acting normal and happy over dinner pushed the limits of Kelly's conscience.

She never claimed to be so perfect she couldn't lie—she merely stank at it. Also, her overdeveloped sense of guilt didn't help. Whenever she did bend the truth, it would gnaw at her and gnaw at her until she finally confessed. So far in her life, she had never been in a situation where she needed to tell a *big* lie. Nothing big and expensive had ever broken because she did something wrong. Never cheated on a test and had to claim she didn't. She'd never witnessed anyone break the law and had to lie about it.

Until now.

Dad had broken the law in a big way.

And there she sat across the table from him in her kitchen eating dinner like he didn't have twenty people locked up in the *lair* he'd built. In fact, Dad seemed happier than he had ever been in her memory. He talked with Mom about her day, complimented her for being perfect and beautiful, floated some idle plans for a vacation in the near future. Not one word about how much he disliked his job, how much John from accounting made more than him even though he'd only been there a year, no complaints about being underappreciated or overlooked.

Her father hadn't needed to become a mad scientist; he needed a new job.

Kelly couldn't even look at him. That person with the unusually tall, thin face and weapons-grade point on his chin wasn't Dad anymore. Something got into his head and made him into The Brain Trust. Her real father wouldn't be this happy and normal with twenty kidnap victims locked up in his basement.

At least Mom had stopped bothering to put green vegetables in front of her. Tonight had been chicken coated with Agitate and Incinerate mix with sides of alfredo pasta and peas, though none of the evil green orbs had wound up on her plate. Even from as far away as her parent's plates, they smelled foul, but not so bad the spicy flavored breading on the chicken stopped being awesome.

"What are your plans for the rest of the night," asked Mom. "There's something on I want to watch."

"Okay. I was gonna go up to my room, probably read a little."

Mom smiled. "All right, sweetie, as long as you aren't reading anything too scary for you."

"Nope. Just some comics. I'm finished with all the *Wraith* series. Might look for something else."

"Ahh. *Wraith* series. Sounds interesting." Dad wagged his eyebrows at her. "Little dark, for you, isn't that?"

"No. Oops. I mean *Waif*. Series. Duh. *Wraith* is the graphic novel I'm too little for. You know, 'cause I'm only nine and innocent and harmless." She flashed a big, cute smile. "Actually, from what I've heard about it, I don't think I want to read it anyway."

Dad winked. "All right. I'm up to my eyeballs."

"Aren't you always?" Mom put her hand on his. "Why don't you take a night off and spend it with me?"

"Well. There's no way I can turn down that suggestion." He stood, scooped Mom out of her chair, and carried her to the living room.

At the sound of them kissing, Kelly cringed. *Eww. Gross.*

She dodged the sphere-bot coming to collect the dishes and ran out the patio door so she could fly up to her bedroom window. That avoided her having to go past her parents being romantic in the living room. She landed inside, walked around loud enough to make noise, then opened a random comic book and read one line.

"There. Now I did a little reading. Not a lie."

The ZOOM bracelet zapped her into her super costume the instant she pressed the gem. Ready to go, but sick to death of the idea, she leapt out the window and flew up high, proceeding to travel east toward the bay while arguing with herself over the right-or-wrong of deciding between family or staying true to her sense of morality. She loved her parents too much to put into words, but she still wouldn't stand aside and let her father do horrible things if she could stop him. Two thoughts kept her from surrendering to her loyalty to him and turning back.

One: twenty people held captive. None of them deserved to be prisoners.

Two: The Brain Trust and Dad couldn't be the same person.

Übergirl had to stop The Brain Trust. Kelly had to save Dad.

A sudden, brilliant flash of white-blue light came from the ground near the northeast corner of San Francisco. She initially decided to ignore it, but when it happened again, and a blue-white beam shot into the air, curiosity—and the need to maybe help someone—overpowered her idea of going to the Aegis Citadel.

She dove toward the disturbance, accelerating much faster than she imagined possible. Feeling like a fighter jet, she held her arms tight to her sides and flew headfirst at the ground. The white beams came from a little north of the big skyscrapers near the coast. Kelly circled to the right, gliding out over the water before swinging back inland.

When she neared the coast, she spotted Mindfreeze in a small courtyard next to a large apartment building in the shadow of Coit Tower, throwing energy bolts at a hulking creature seemingly made entirely of darkness.

The monster towered over the young woman, easily ten feet tall with an upper body as wide as the front end of a pickup truck, its thick chest swollen in the form of bulging muscles. Long arms tipped in inky black claws hung nearly to the ground.

It lunged at Mindfreeze, swiping at her with claws the size of swords. She ducked once, then disappeared the second time the creature attacked, reappearing beside it and blasting it at close range with an energy beam that made it roar in pain.

Kelly had never seen a creature like that, but figured a being made of pure darkness trying to kill a hero would most likely be the bad guy. She pulled up into a vertical climb, went up until the city looked again like a little model, then dove, pouring on speed.

Mindfreeze teleported back and forth at short distances to avoid the creature's vicious attacks. It moved surprisingly fast for something that big, tearing slices in the street wherever it missed her. The creature spun, roaring when another energy bolt hit it in the back. Snarling, it faced Mindfreeze and opened its mouth, the whole head stretching and expanding wider. A torrent of black sludge sprayed forth, knocking Mindfreeze over and sticking her to the ground.

Black lightning flickered across the puddle. Her glowing eyes faltered.

The creature stepped closer, raising its claws, but Mindfreeze didn't teleport.

Kelly pushed herself to fly even faster, stretching her fists out in front of her… and flew straight down onto its head.

The crash felt as though a pre-superpower version of her had run full speed into the padded walls of the school gym. A loud *boom* accompanied the hit. It didn't exactly *hurt*, but she didn't enjoy the sensation. When the dust cleared, she found herself spread eagle on her chest atop a bubbling mass of tar... at the center of a four-foot crater in the road.

Whatever the monster had been, it appeared to have exploded into a puddle of liquid. Oddly, she didn't sink into it, floating like a leaf upon a cup of black paint. Correction: freezing cold black paint. Fortunately, the substance didn't stick to her or coat her in awfulness. It didn't even have a smell. She floated up out of the crater and landed at the edge.

Mindfreeze sat a few feet away, pulling snot-like strands of inky goop off herself.

"Hi. Are you okay?" asked Kelly.

"Kid? Where the heck did you come from?"

"Up." She pointed. "I was on my way to your citadel to ask for help and I saw yooooooooou—"

She realized something had hit her from behind only a split second before she crashed headfirst into the apartment building, stuck into the bricks like a dart up to the waist. Her head poked into a storage room while her butt remained dangerously vulnerable to the outside world. However, she didn't think the monster had any interest in paddling her until she cried. Nope. This thing probably wanted to keep chewing on her until something bad happened... like death.

A loud, demonic roar shook the air behind her.

"I think I made him angry."

She grunted, pushing her arms out from her chest. Bricks crumbled, loosening the tight tunnel in which she'd been planted. Kelly flew backward, zipping between the shadow monster's legs as it shredded the bricks around the hole with a flurry of claw swipes.

"Kid, get away from the nightvoid. It's extremely dangerous," shouted Mindfreeze while hitting the monster in the back with an energy bolt that knocked him against the wall.

The creature bounced off the bricks and spun toward Kelly. She popped up to eye-level with it and punched it in its not-nose, her fist sinking into its head to her bicep as if she'd mushed her arm into a gelatin mold. A second later, the creature peeled away from her and flew into the ground with enough force to again splatter into a puddle. She blinked, figuring she'd done that reflexes thing and time only appeared to run slow.

"Holy crap..." Mindfreeze gawked at her.

Slurps and squishing sounds came from the inky puddle as it gathered itself together, rising again into the shape of the nightvoid, which roared and grabbed Kelly by the right leg. It swung her into the building, bashing a trench through the bricks, then yanked her into the air and swung her at the ground.

Grunting, Kelly put the brakes on with flight before she crashed into the paving.

"Ow. Stop that." She huffed a brick chip out of her bangs.

Mindfreeze shot a bolt at the nightvoid that pierced its head from ear-to-ear and went into the building without damaging the stone. Sensing imminent disgusting, Kelly stomped the creature in the chest, launching it straight back. The mass of darkness sailed down Lombard Street, exploding into a shower of tar-like ooze about forty meters away.

"Did *that* kill it?" asked Kelly. 'Killing' inhuman monsters or robots didn't bother her.

"Yes." Mindfreeze walked up to her. "Are you okay?"

She looked herself over. "Fine. Just dusty. So what was that thing?"

"A nightvoid. They are creatures of animated darkness. We're not sure where they come from or why they are here. These beings have started appearing without warning and attacking anything or anyone near them. I have to say, child, I'm stunned."

"At?"

"The way that thing reacted when you punched it. You might be stronger than Igor the Red. But you're so small."

She held her head high, fists on her hips. "I'm Übergirl."

"That's twice now I've seen you. I hope you're not trying to be a hero already at your age."

"Umm. I'm not flying around looking for trouble, but it keeps finding me. Mostly, I just wanna be a kid and help people... but I have a big problem."

The remains of the nightvoid ignited in black fire, burning away to nothingness in a few seconds.

"That's one good thing about these guys. Cleanup is easy." Mindfreeze gestured at the crater. "Except for the road."

"Oops. Sorry. I didn't know that would happen."

"You said you wanted to find us? I'm afraid you're way too small to join. From what I've seen tonight, though, I'm sure you would be more than welcome once you're a little older. We can't really rely on a superhero with a bedtime."

"No. I didn't want to join... yet. I have a big problem."

"How can such a small girl have a big problem? Homework? Bully? Can't be a boy at your age." Mindfreeze smiled.

"My dad. He's..." She shivered, sick to her stomach. The next few seconds would be a total betrayal of her family. But... Dad kidnapped people, experimented on them, wanted to turn the whole city into mindless servants. Her father would never do that. The Brain Trust had taken her father away already. She had to get him back any way she could. "He's a mad scientist."

Mindfreeze raised an eyebrow. "What makes you say that?"

"He's making a mind control serum that he wants to put in the water supply. There's like a whole bunch of people in our basement that he's kidnapped for experiments. My dad isn't like that. The aliens did something to him. Turned him into a bad guy. He's not acting right. I wanna help him. I gotta stop his plan, but... he's still my father. I don't know what to do."

"Hmm. Will you come with me and explain this to the others?"

"Sure."

Mindfreeze took her hand.

"Don't we have to wait for the cops and tell them why there's a big hole in the road and that building?"

"Notice all the people watching us?"

Kelly gazed around at totally empty streets. "There's no one here."

"Right. They all saw the nightvoid and ran. Those creatures make norms run away in terror just by being here. Normally, I'd stay and wait for the authorities to show up, but your story sounds more urgent. The police know where to find us if they have questions."

"Okay." She smiled. "Let's go."

CHAPTER TWENTY-FOUR

THE AEGIS CITADEL

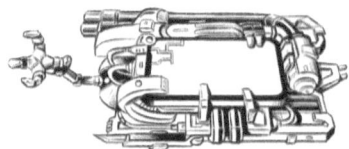

Mindfreeze emitted a quick blast of blue light and the city street changed in an instant to a giant room with two sectional couches in a sunken area facing the biggest television screen Kelly had ever seen. Behind the sofas, a long conference table shaped somewhat like an arrowhead took up the other half of the room by floor-to-ceiling windows that looked out over hilly woodlands.

A familiar black man with a sharp jaw in a dark sweater and military style pants reclined on the couch, sipping a diet soda while watching soccer. Beside him sat a big muscular guy with light brown hair and a red tank top. Another man bounced a basketball at the far corner of the room, shooting hoops with a net mounted to the wall. He appeared to be the youngest one in the room— except for Kelly—probably around eighteen or nineteen.

"Welcome back, Rowena... how'd it—who is that?" asked Phoenix.

"This is Übergirl." Mindfreeze, a.k.a. Rowena, walked her down the three steps to the sunken area in front of the sectional. "Hey Montez, got a sec?"

The man with the basketball blurred into a smear of color, appearing right next to them in an instant. "Aww. She's adorable."

Kelly couldn't help but grin back at his big smile. "Hi."

"Why are you just bringing random people into the lounge? We let our hair down in here. Secret identities and all?" asked Phoenix.

"Kevin… she's a little girl, a *powerful* super, and on our side."

"Well, since you're basically seeing us in our skivvies already… I'm Kevin Sinclair, also known as Phoenix. You've met Mindfreeze, Rowena Dominguez. This is Igor Kráceni, more famous as Igor the Red, and that's Ray Montez, or Bullet Man."

Kelly reached up and plucked her mask off. "Übergirl, but my real name is Kelly Donovan."

"Amazing." Mindfreeze swiped a finger at her forehead. "That nightvoid put her through a wall and that dinky little mask didn't come off. I'm on my fourteenth costume. Not a rip in hers."

"My dad made it." Kelly took a deep breath and let it out slow. "He's a mad scientist."

"Whoa, go back to that part about a nightvoid putting a child into a wall?" Kevin shifted his hand back and forth, generally pointing at them.

Mindfreeze explained the fight, how she'd spotted a nightvoid causing chaos and attacked it to pull it away from the city bus it had started peeling open like a sardine can. "I'd been fighting it for about ten minutes before it seemed to explode for no reason. Then I see this little kid crawl out of a crater. She'd hit the thing so hard it melted into a puddle." She told them the rest, ending with finally getting a solid hit with a PSI beam that penetrated the creature's armor and destroyed it… mostly because Kelly distracted it.

Igor sat up. "You, me, we wrestle the arms, yes?"

"No way, dude," said Ray. "Not at all fair. Her arm is only a little bigger than your thumb. You got an advantage in leverage and weight."

"Maybe later," said Kelly. "I have a big problem." She re-explained everything about her father, the kidnapped research subjects, and the plan. "He's got like a small base set up somewhere close to the San Andreas Lake. They're going to attack the pipe going north into San Francisco and dump the MICE agent into the water. There's a force field around it."

"Where are we talking about?" asked Igor.

"I saw his map. Do you have a map?"

Bullet Man flickered, then held out a tablet he didn't have before. "Here."

She opened the map program and pointed out the spot Dad's plans showed as the location for his outpost. "Right there. And, I'm a horrible daughter, aren't I?"

Phoenix rested his hands on her shoulders and looked into her eyes. "It's hard sometimes to be loyal to your family, especially when they do things you don't agree with. I can't even imagine a kid your age having to make a choice like this. But, the most difficult thing in the world is to stay true to yourself, what you believe in. If you're correct about your dad not being in his right mind, this is the best way to help him."

"Thanks." Kelly sniffled and wiped at her cheeks.

"Aww." Mindfreeze hugged her. "I'm sorry. We'll do everything we can to help your father."

"You believe girl?" asked Igor. "She has one heck of imagination."

Phoenix gestured at Mindfreeze. "It's extremely hard to lie to Rowena."

"Ahh, yes. I forget." Igor smacked his fists together. "Let us go and break—uhh." He flashed an apologetic smile at Kelly. "*Not* break this man's face."

She pressed a hand to her stomach, woozy with guilt.

"Are you okay?" asked Mindfreeze.

"No. I just tattled on my father. I feel awful. What if you guys can't break the alien control and turn him back into Dad? He could go to jail."

"Kelly." Phoenix stood beside her, hand at her back, and gestured at the giant windows. "All those people out there in San Francisco. Men. Women. Kids like you. Ever since this new reality landed on our heads, some of us have taken these unexpected changes and embraced them for the good of all. Others see opportunity to exploit those abilities. A handful just want an easy ride. The dangerous ones want power. And the worst of the lot want to hurt people. Your father, whatever's wrong inside his head, can't be allowed to poison all those millions of people."

"I know. That's why I'm here." Kelly put her mask back on. "But I still feel like I let him down for not joining him as a villain. Just like when I let the bullies ruin *Star Prince #17*."

"Whoa, you got a number seventeen?" blurted Ray. "Where the heck did you find that? And *ruined*. Aww man, what a shame."

"It was, but Dad made a machine that restored it."

Ray's eyebrows went up. "Hey, maybe we should cut the dude some slack on this mind control deal. He restored a SP number seventeen."

"Bullet, you are serious or joking?" asked Igor.

"I can't tell." Mindfreeze folded her arms.

"Little bit of both." Ray disappeared and reappeared next to Kelly. "Please tell me you put that thing in a vault."

"It's safe now."

"So, how much time do we have on this whole thing?" asked Phoenix.

"It's supposed to happen next Friday. He's still making more mind-control slime."

"All right, so we have some time to plan and conduct recon." Phoenix nodded at Mindfreeze, then smiled at Kelly. "Sit back and leave this to the professionals. If anything changes, you need help with anything, or just someone to talk to, you're welcome to come back anytime."

"Thanks. I can get the people out, but I might have to break doors. I don't know the codes."

"Perhaps it would be better for me to do it." Mindfreeze smiled. "Doors don't get in my way."

"Dad might have alarms and stuff down there now. I don't really know, but okay." Kelly gave them her address and explained the lair under the tool shed. The more she told them, the sicker she felt.

It *shouldn't* matter that heroes know where she lived, where her father's secret base was. Dad was too nice to be a bad guy. They had to fix it. She tried to tell herself that coming here hadn't been betraying him, but helping him.

Only, Kelly Donovan hadn't ever been very good at lying—even to herself.

But, stopping the mind control, helping the people he kidnapped, hopefully preventing Dad from doing worse things in the future... she knew she did the right thing.

CHAPTER TWENTY-FIVE
ANYTHING OVER TWENTY TONS GOES BACK

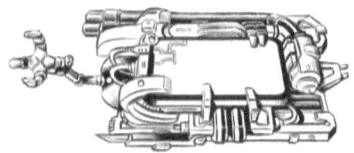

S unday morning, Kelly woke hugging Floppet with her face cemented to the pillow by a crust of dried tears.

Stopping Dr. Blaze and Myo from robbing the armored car had made her feel beyond awesome. But… doing the right thing evidently didn't always leave warm fuzzies deep in the bottom of her heart. Saying goodnight to her parents without breaking down and admitting she tattled had been the second most difficult thing she'd ever done. The first being the actual tattling to the Aegis.

Only, the tall-faced guy who kinda looked and kinda sounded like Dad who'd kissed her on the head last night couldn't really be her father. She had to believe that the aliens, or something like that, had gotten into his brain and forced him to 'play the bad guy.' That had to be it. People in movies who play the villains aren't *really* evil. They just put on a character for a while. She only had to figure out how to get her father to go back to being himself.

She peeled the stuck pillow off, wiped some serious eye crumbles away, and trudged to the bathroom, then downstairs still in her nightgown. Zorthax and Bob sat on the couch eating cereal while watching a really old movie with cowboys. Kelly fixed herself a bowl of cereal—flying up to reach the cabinets—then sat on the floor in front of her father's henchmen, half-watching the movie while eating her breakfast.

Not seeing Mom around worried her a little… but she and Dad spent the night together. Being Sunday, she wouldn't be at work. It didn't seem likely that he'd have taken her down to the lair. Mom seemed to know about the lair, but for whatever reason, acted as though they had an ordinary tool shed in the yard. Most surprisingly, she hadn't complained that Dad put a pool down there.

Trusting Kelly to be home alone for the three-ish hours between the end of school and one or both parents returning from work already stretched things. Mom would never leave her alone at her age except for unavoidable situations like having to work. On a Sunday? Something had to be wrong. Or, maybe, her parents hadn't gotten out of bed yet.

Kelly lifted each spoonful of Cosmix cereal to her mouth with the precision of a robot, her brain grinding thought asteroids down into smaller pebbles. She felt like she'd activated the timer on a bomb and lost track of it. How long would it take the Aegis to do something about Dad, and what would his reaction be? He'd probably know exactly who snitched on him. No one else would have had any way to know about the plans as he hadn't *done* anything yet.

The minions—sorry, henchmen—talked with her about *Kobold and the Rulers of the Universe* for a while. Apparently, Bob considered himself a big fan. He'd been watching the show since he'd been a small boy. He agreed with her that the character Witche (with a silent e) both had a silly name and existed more or less only to give Kobold a woman to save every other episode. According to her backstory, she had lots of power, but rarely used it. In a handful of episodes, she somewhat took over as being the main character, and those started an online petition for a spinoff series with her as the main. But, for whatever reason, the people making the show never did it.

"Yeah, I'd watch that," said Kelly with a half-interested voice, too worried about Dad.

"Absolutely. That would be an amazing show." Bob grinned.

"Bob," said Zorthax. "She's a little kid, not to mention a girl. She is the target audience for a show starring Witche as the main character. What's your excuse?"

"*Kobold* has surprisingly deep and mature layered storytelling that offers nuanced commentary on social injustice while appealing to a wide audience spanning all ages and cultural backgrounds," said Bob.

Kelly raised her eyebrows. "Umm… Wow."

"Bob…" Zorthax blinked. "Never speak again."

"Aww. Don't be mean. I agree with Bob."

Bob pointed at her. "See? She knows."

Zorthax threw his hands up, sighed, and stood. "Come on. We're late. The boss needs us."

"Okay." Bob stood, took Kelly's empty cereal bowl, and followed Zorthax out to the backyard by way of the kitchen, where he put the bowls in the dishwasher.

She leaned back against the couch, tapping her big toes together, no interest in the cowboy movie. Regret didn't help since she couldn't undo talking to the Aegis. After a few minutes of wanting to change her mind and go back in time, she realized she couldn't. Also, she *had* to do what she did. Dad kidnapped like twenty people. If he simply made the MICE serum without using it, she wouldn't have tattled, but hurting people was wrong.

I wonder if Mindfreeze rescued them yet.

The idea of going down to the lair to check the holding cells grew tempting. However, if Mindfreeze *did* save those people and Kelly went snooping there, Dad would certainly figure out she had something to do with it.

A car door closed out front with a *whump*. Small, rapid footsteps approached, and the doorbell rang.

Kelly got up and answered, finding Paige on the doorstep in her bathing suit, sunglasses, and painfully bright neon-green flip-flops. Her parents waved from their SUV in the driveway.

"Hey. We're going to the beach. Wanna come with us?"

Kelly clutched her toes at the rug. How could she go to the beach and have fun while Dad planned to mind control all of San Francisco? Or had kidnap victims in the basement? But, sitting in the house alone merely waiting for The Aegis to do something would make her crazy. She couldn't really do anything about anything unless she openly came out as a hero to her father. Waiting for other people to fix things *did* seem cowardly... but she *was* only nine and the bad guy in question *was* her father. Even normal cops couldn't be expected to arrest their own family, right? No shame in handing a job off to someone else because it carried too much emotional baggage.

"Yeah. I gotta ask permission first. Can you wait a minute?"

"Sure." Paige grinned.

Kelly ran upstairs to look for one or both parents, but couldn't find them. She went out the window to the tool shed to check the lair. The elevator dropped with a *shoomp!* that flipped her nightgown up over her head. Grumbling, she pushed it back into place and stormed into the lair.

"Dad?" called Kelly. "Where are you?"

No one answered.

To avoid any additional unwanted clothing repositioning, she hit the ZOOM bracelet to change into her super costume and flew around the lair in a high-speed search. Neither Dad nor his henchmen were anywhere in sight. Also, the holding cells had been cleaned out.

Whew. She saved them. I hope.

After going back outside, she flew into the house via her bedroom window, checked again, but didn't see Mom or Dad anywhere. She couldn't ask them for permission to go with Paige and her parents. But on the other hand, her parents had left her home alone. Going to the beach without permission felt like a less-bad thing to do than be home alone. Mom and Dad would want her in the company of responsible adults. Besides, they both knew she had superpowers, so it's not like they would worry about her.

So, she ZOOM-ed away her super costume, changed from her nightgown into her bathing suit, grabbed her sunglasses, towel, flip-flops, and canvas bag of beach stuff, then ran downstairs to write a note on the fridge whiteboard about where she'd be.

Paige waited by the front door, cheering when she saw Kelly in a bathing suit. "Awesome!"

"Yeah," said Kelly, not quite able to summon much enthusiasm. She scrunched her eyebrows, staring at her friend.

"Is something wrong with my suit?"

"No."

"Why are you staring at me like that?" Paige peered down at her stomach. "Seriously. What are you looking at? Is there a bug on me?"

Kelly stepped outside and pulled the door closed. "No bugs. This is gonna sound kinda weird, but when we went swimming at the pool, I was freaking out about something, but as soon as I saw you, I got like so super happy."

"I'm just that awesome." Paige grinned.

"Something weird is going on."

"Duh." Paige laughed, then pointed at the faint shape of the distant alien mega-ship floating far overhead. "Have you been paying attention?"

"Right." She followed her friend over to the Ichissan Trailseeker SUV and got in. "Hi, Mr. Warren. Hi Mrs. Warren."

"Hello, Kelly," said the parents roughly at the same time.

Mr. Warren, in the passenger seat, twisted to peer back at her. "Your parents gave you the okay?"

"They don't mind me going with you." Kelly hoped her cheesy smile didn't give her away. A guess didn't quite count the same as a lie, right? If she told the Warrens that her parents had both gone somewhere and left her alone at nine, they'd probably call the police. Or at least complain later.

"Okay." He faced forward.

"Melinda and Jack have our number," said Mrs. Warren. "If there's any issue, they'll call."

"Oh. That's a good point, Ann. I'll text him just to make sure it's okay." Mr. Warren pulled out his phone.

Kelly's heart almost stopped. She squeezed the seat cushion, holding her breath.

Mrs. Warren backed out of the driveway and headed down the road.

"All set. No problem." Mr. Warren put his phone away. "Your father says he's proud of you."

Kelly fake smiled. *Ugh. Dad thinks I lied. He knows I'm doing something without permission… and he's proud of me. He really has gone supervillain.*

Hope that the Aegis would be able to help turn The Brain Trust back into Dad kept her from breaking down in tears on the ride to the beach. She thought about issue 157 of *Powers League*. They slipped in a surprise plot reveal where the masked mastermind that Mr. Everything had been chasing for several issues up to that point was really his older brother who had turned true evil. The brother pretended to show remorse and exploited their family relationship to get the upper hand and almost killed Mr. Everything when he let his guard down.

That helped explain why she couldn't confront him, why she had to ask for help. How could she directly challenge her own father? Stopping the scheme he worked so hard on would probably hurt him as bad as if she had laughed and thrown *Star Prince #17* in the trash when he gave it to her. Okay, bad example—she'd never throw a rare comic like that in the trash. But still…

Paige distracted her by talking about seeing on TV that some of the giant crystals had been observed sinking deeper into the ground. They both already suspected that the huge red shards had something to do with the introduction of superpowers, and spent the rest of the ride discussing if crystals going deeper into the planet meant something bad, good, or neither.

Upon arriving at the beach, Paige's parents set up folding chairs on either side of an enormous umbrella. The girls stood patiently with their eyes closed and arms up while Mrs. Warren sprayed them down with sunscreen. Kelly doubted she needed it anymore, but to keep up appearances, she happily surrendered to the cool coconut-scented mist.

Soon, the girls knelt on the beach working on a sand castle version of the Fortress of Honor, the good guys' base from the *Powers League* series. No one but the most obsessive of fans would recognize the odd lumpy mound for anything but a mangled sandcastle, but it looked like the Fortress to Kelly. When they declared it finished, they headed into the water and swam for a while. Eventually, Mr. Warren called them out of the ocean for lunch. He took them up the beach to a booth where they ordered hot dogs with all the trimmings, carrying them back to the umbrella and towels to eat.

Hanging out with Paige on the beach would have been awesome, if not for everything Kelly had to worry about. A collision between that awesomeness and the dread of the Dad situation resulted in her feeling neither happy nor upset. She didn't say much while eating, once again lost to worrying about what would happen when the Aegis finally confronted her father. If by some chance, he *didn't* blame her, could she pretend to be uninvolved? Sooner or later, she'd have to confess to being a hero.

… and it bothered her that being a hero felt like something to be ashamed of.

After eating, they started back for the water. Mrs. Warren called after them not to swim since they just ate, but Paige said they only wanted to stand in the ocean and wouldn't be swimming. Neither of the parents came running after them, so they waded in up to their middles and stood there.

"Okay. What's going on?" asked Paige.

Finally out of parental earshot, Kelly spilled about going to the Aegis, her father's plan, how guilty she felt, that her parents had both vanished this morning… and even that Mindfreeze had saved the people her father had kidnapped. Assuming, of course, Dad hadn't gotten rid of them or put them to work helping with the MICE project. How much could two henchmen really do? Then again, Bob and Zorthax looked pretty strong.

"Do you think I'm being a chicken?"

Paige rubbed her chin. "A little, but I understand. My grandmother's a judge. If the person in court is related to her or someone she knows, she can't work on that case."

"Yeah, but that's a judge. Like, if a cop saw someone robbing a place and the robber was their best friend or sibling, would they call another cop to get involved and just watch?"

"I don't think so."

"Ugh." Kelly slapped her face into the water a few times. "I am being a chicken. I'm afraid to tell him I can't be a supervillain. Seriously, how messed up is that? My dad wants me to *break* the law and I just started middle school."

"Hmm. Have you tried talking to him? Tell him you're a hero. Maybe if he knew, he wouldn't expect you to do evil stuff. And, he wouldn't tell you what his plans are so you wouldn't have to feel guilty about what to do."

"You don't think he'd punish me?"

"For being a good guy?"

Kelly nodded. "Supervillains always try to do bad stuff to the heroes. I don't want my dad to be my enemy."

"He's still your father. Sometimes kids and parents don't agree. That doesn't mean they stop loving each other."

"Hmm. Maybe you're right."

Something blocked out the sun overhead.

The beach erupted in screaming.

Kelly gazed up at a colossal blue tentacle covered in pink suction cups as big as the kitchen table at home extending over their heads. She turned her head to the left, staring along the length of the bizarre appendage to where it connected to a giant octopus with four glowing green eyes. The tentacle's narrow end crashed down on the beach hard enough to dig a trench and knock people closest to it over.

Paige gurgled and cringed away. "Ugh. Don't look. We're not old enough to see that. It hit people."

"Umm. What? It hurt people?"

Paige shook her head rapidly. "No. They didn't feel anything."

"It *killed* people?" squeaked Kelly.

"I'm guessing. There's a lot of blood."

"But monsters aren't supposed to kill people!"

Shadow fell on them.

"We're not in a comic book, Kell. We're—"

Kelly dove into Paige, tackle-flying her out from under the tentacle before it crushed them. The octopus slapped the ocean where they'd been standing, throwing off a huge wave. Kelly dove underwater long enough to hit her ZOOM bracelet, summoning her costume where no one could witness the change from normal child to superhero.

She flew up out of the water, carrying Paige over to her panicking parents.

More screaming from the beach.

Paige's feet hadn't quite touched towel when a shadow racing over the beach caught Kelly's eye. She twisted to peer up at another tentacle careening downward toward a crowd of panicking beachgoers. She let go of her friend and zipped to intercept, flying under the tentacle—at a point where it had narrowed only to the diameter of a tanker trailer—catching it.

Tons of slimy octopus tentacle draped over her, only the last few feet of the narrow tip made contact with the sand, well away from any people.

"Bad octo!" yelled Kelly.

The creature's four glowing green eyes all widened at the same time. She threw the tentacle at it, slapping the octopus in the face—or as close as it had to a face—with its own limb. It rocked back in the water, shoving a ten-foot high wave out to sea. Kelly, against Paige's suggestion, peered to her right and down at the place the octopus had first hit.

Nine people appeared to have been hurt. All but two dragged themselves out of the trench in various stages of injured, most with at least a broken arm or leg, all of them bleeding. One man didn't move, though he still breathed. A girl Kelly's size struggled to get out from under him, suggesting he had jumped on top of her as a shield. The other unmoving person appeared to be a young lifeguard in a red one-piece bathing suit. Her sunglasses had shattered.

Fortunately, the sponginess of the giant octopus had prevented anyone from popping like water balloons.

A loud whooshing noise drew Kelly's gaze to the left—at a wall of suckers crashing into her. The octopus slapped her sideways, sending her flying into the ocean, skipping like a stone fired out of a cannon. She bounced six times off the water before catching herself and flying back into the air.

"What's wrong with you?" shouted Kelly.

As if it could both hear and understand her, the octopus let out an ear-splitting screech. It raised three tentacles at the same time, aiming for the still-fleeing crowd. Mr. Warren remained by their umbrella, calling out for her while Mrs. Warren and Paige ran away from the water along with the fleeing crowd.

Kelly zoomed as fast as she could make herself fly, grabbing the tip of the nearest tentacle and then dragging it around and around in a loop, twisting the three tentacles together, preventing the creature from walloping anyone else.

With a grunt, she chucked the tentacle bundle straight up, causing the octopus to roll onto its back. Another tentacle came out of nowhere and grabbed her, pulling her in toward the body where a hard beak the size of a one-car garage opened to bite her.

She pushed her arms out to the sides, unwinding the tentacle's grip on her, and slipped loose. Before the confused octo could react, she zoomed straight down and stomped on the top part of its beak, smashing it closed with a tremendously loud *clack* that echoed over the coastline. All four of its eyes crossed.

"Stop hurting people!"

The octopus screeched and whipped her with one of its tentacles.

One second, she hovered over the ocean. The next instant, she found herself embedded headfirst in the beach, only her feet sticking out.

Ugh. This guy is not *listening.*

By the time she'd fought her way free from being tent-spiked in sand, the octopus had crawled up out of the water, chasing fleeing people toward the parking area. Kelly backed out of the hole on all fours, looking up as the monster tossed a car into the city.

Like when Brittany threw a basketball at her face, time dragged down into slow motion.

Kelly stared up at the minivan tumbling through the air with two adults and three kids pressed against the windows from the force of it spinning. She shot upward from the beach, pulling a mushroom cloud of sand into the air behind her. The van sailed toward a row of expensive apartment high-rises across the highway from the beach, aiming to crash into it at like the twentieth story. Kelly flew up underneath it, pushing against the undercarriage, tilting, and steering the van to the side. They missed the silver-and-glass wall of the skyscraper by about six feet. The family in the van screamed continuously for the brief time it took her to carry it to the ground. At least being tiny, she didn't have any trouble crawling out from under it after setting it down on its tires.

The octopus continued to smash cars in the parking area, though at that point, everyone who hadn't already driven away had run off. Kelly zipped over and intercepted a tentacle before it could crush a nice convertible. Annoyed, she flew up to the right, dragging the entire octopus into the air. She went in a gradual circle, gaining speed while swinging the creature around and around like a hammer throw. The creature shrieked, blasting her with horrid, hot breath that stank of rotting fish.

She intended to chuck it out into the deep ocean once she got it spinning fast enough, but slimy tentacle and small hands had other ideas. Her grip failed, and the octopus soared across the highway and smacked into the same apartment high-rise the van nearly hit with a horrendous *splat* and the crunch of many broken windows. The whole building rocked from the impact, tilting back.

"Uh oh…" Kelly grimaced, wiping her hands on her chest. "Oops."

The costume Dad made appeared to be impervious to octopus slime, as the snot-like ooze dribbled away and fell.

Fearing the octopus would suffocate if left out of the water too long, she flew over to it, grabbed the nearest tentacle, and pulled it over her shoulder, once again hauling it into the air. This time, however, she didn't try to hammer-throw the monster. The tentacle she pulled on stretched a bit, but soon, the great beast peeled away from the building, tearing out windows that stuck to it, curtains, and some furniture. Large pieces of glass slipped away from the rising monster, falling to shatter in the parking lot below. A few people inside the apartments—now with *very* open windows—shouted, screamed, or simply stared in awe.

Kelly flew up high enough that the giant tentacles stopped dragging over the ground. She lugged the ridiculous octo out to a spot several miles off the coast. It hung limp, no longer flailing or putting up any fight. *Eep. I hope I didn't hurt it too much.*

"You need to stay out here in the ocean. The land is for people."

She dropped it, creating a big splash. The stunned creature sank beneath the waves, vanishing into the murk.

When she returned to land, she found Bullet Man and Phoenix standing on the highway, looking up at the apartment tower.

"So, they're saying a giant octopus did this?" asked Phoenix, scratching his head. "Are you serious?"

"That's what they said, yeah. A giant flying octopus. Leapt out of the water, smashed a few cars, then kamikaze charged the building, before flying home." Bullet Man, aka Ray Montez, shrugged. "That's what they said."

Kelly landed next to them. "Hi."

They looked at her.

"Übergirl?" asked Phoenix.

"Yep. A giant octopus attacked the beach. It crushed some people, so I tried to stop it."

Ray laughed, but stopped himself. "Octopus wasn't flying, was it?"

"I tried to throw it back into the water, but it slipped. It's slimy." She held her hands up, wiggling her fingers. "I lost my grip and it hit the building. I'm really sorry."

"Übergirl, you need to pay attention to what's going on around you. I realize you're eager to help people, and that's awesome... but if the heroes do more damage than the bad guys, everyone is going to start thinking of us as more trouble than we're worth."

She clasped her hands in front of herself and stared down. "Yes, sir. I'm sorry."

"Well, she's so small, no one even saw her. They think the octopus was flying on its own." Bullet Man grinned. He really seemed like he wanted to keep laughing, but held it in.

"How is nine people nearly dying and a few million dollars in property damage remotely funny?" asked Phoenix.

"Nah. I'm just picturing a crazy octopus flying out of the water, throwing itself into a building, and flying back out into the ocean on its own. Like that neighbor who's finally had enough of the noise next door. It's kinda funny."

Phoenix' overly serious expression finally cracked a grin.

"I don't want to lie. If I'm gonna get in trouble for breaking the building, I'll admit it." She kicked at the beach.

"That's what insurance is for." Bullet Man elbowed Phoenix in the side. "Besides, the Nolmek gave the city these construction robots that build stuff super fast. They'll probably have this whole tower fixed in a day."

"Umm. Have you guys done anything about the other problem?" asked Kelly.

Phoenix gazed up at the partially smashed building. "Row—I mean Mindfreeze was able to get the civilians out of that lair. We've currently got them at the Citadel, attempting to cure them of whatever agent they've been exposed to. It appears your father has built some kind of machine near the pipes that pick up water destined for San Francisco. It's cloaked, too. We wouldn't have seen it if we didn't know right where to look. However, we haven't yet been able to get in."

"We still have a few days, so we're not panicking yet." Bullet Man patted her on the shoulder. "Based on what you told us, even if we aren't able to get past that field, his plan won't be an *immediate* danger to anyone. If we can reverse engineer an antidote for the serum, it might not matter if people are exposed."

"Of course, our goal is to prevent that exposure. Things like this often have unintended side effects." Phoenix turned to face her. "You're still a little young for media coverage. Why don't you run off and we'll deal with the aftermath here? Unless you want the recognition. Not trying to step on your toes here." He smiled.

"It's okay. No, I don't wanna be famous. Just help people. Besides, Mr. Warren is going nuts looking for me."

She high-fived the two heroes, flew back into the ocean, and skimmed along underwater to the spot where they'd been swimming. After using the ZOOM bracelet to change back to her swimsuit, she popped her head above the water.

Mr. Warren *still* stood on the beach, in a state of near-panic, calling for her.

"I'm here!" shouted Kelly.

He spotted her after a few seconds and almost fainted.

She hurried out of the water and ran across the beach to him. "It's okay. I'm fine."

"Kelly! Where have you been? You scared us to death! What would we have told your parents if we couldn't find you?"

Ambulances and police arrived amid a wail of sirens.

She dug her toes into the beach. In order to keep a secret identity, she'd have to tell a certain degree of innocent lies. "I was hiding. Did you *see* the size of that monster? Sorry. I was too scared to move."

Mr. Warren looked her over. "Are you hurt?"

"No I, like totally freaked out. Paige and I ran to the beach and then I guess I just panicked and hid in a big hole someone dug."

"Whew… I am so glad to see you're okay. You didn't hear me yelling for you?"

"I did, but I couldn't move. Sorry for making you stay here where it's dangerous, but thank you for being so worried about me."

Kelly sat on the towels.

"What are you doing?"

"There's cops and stuff everywhere. We're not gonna be able to leave for a while."

"We can't stay on the beach." He crouched to take her hand, pulling her up. "What if that thing comes back?"

"I don't think he's gonna want to." She glanced over her shoulder at the ocean, and smiled.

CHAPTER TWENTY-SIX

CHiLL OUT

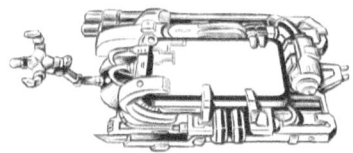

U pon returning home, the Warrens insisted on speaking to her parents.

However, neither Mom nor Dad were home. Mr. Warren texted Dad, and after trading a few messages, he announced Kelly would be staying with them until her parents became 'un-busy.' Neither Kelly nor Paige minded.

Mr. Warren sent Kelly upstairs to grab a change of clothes, then drove them the three blocks to their house. The girls took a quick shower to de-beach, Paige in the main bathroom upstairs, Kelly using a smaller shower in the basement.

Dried—except for hair—and changed out of their swimsuits, the girls flopped on the floor of Paige's bedroom, playing video games. The screen was only half the size of the one at Kelly's house, but the cool factor of it being *Paige's* TV in her bedroom made up for it.

"That was totally *awesome!*" shouted Paige after a few minutes of their superhero characters mashing each other's faces. "I can't believe you did that. Whoosh-whoosh-whoosh *splat!*"

"Yeah. It didn't kill anyone. Just hurt them a whole lot."

"That's good."

Kelly failed to block a combo from Paige's werewolf-like character that shredded her fire-hero. "Do you think there's something going on that's making things work like a comic book or did that happen because the octopus was so squishy and soft?"

"Probably the squishy. The news has been talking about people being killed by supervillains already. Well, maybe not 'supervillains,' just criminals who got superpowers and used them wrong."

"That's exactly what a supervillain is." She bowed her head. "Like my dad."

"I'm sorry. That totally stinks."

"Yeah. I'm pretty sure the aliens are affecting his mind. He's not a bad guy but he's acting like one. Almost like something is forcing him to be that character."

Paige scrunched her face in thought while making her werewolf chew on Kelly's character. "Hmm. We have been shooting stuff into space for a long time. Satellites, radio, television. Maybe the aliens found a comic book or movie and decided to make it real? What if they're really here for entertainment? Like, they tell us they're saving the Earth and being all nice, but to them, we're just like a TV show?"

"Maybe. I dunno." Kelly finally got the block to work, broke out of the combo and counterattacked.

Paige squealed as her character started getting its butt kicked, laughing too much to recover the defensive before she ran out of life bar. "Aww. Nice match."

"We could look at all the villains who have gone public and compare them to who they were pre-crystals. If we find enough 'normal, nice people' who started acting like bad guys, that could prove it's the aliens controlling them."

"Umm. Yeah, I guess. That sounds like a lot of work."

"Nothing is a lot of work for Übergirl!" said Kelly in a goofy tone while puffing out her chest.

Someone started screaming outside.

"Speaking of Übergirl..." Paige looked at her window. "Someone's calling you."

Kelly held her arm out. "You wanna push it?"

"Okay." Paige poked the gem on the ZOOM bracelet.

The T-shirt and jeans Kelly wore changed in a flash of light to her super costume.

"That is so neat."

Kelly held her arms out, wrists together, palms up. "It's the only way to take these bracers off. They're one solid piece. My dad is a dork."

The scream happened again.

"You better go look."

"Right."

Paige ran to the window and opened it for her.

"Be back as soon as I can. If your parents ask where I went, tell them I'm in the bathroom."

"Okay."

Kelly flew out the window and over the roof to the street, then floated up higher, looking for the source of the shouting. A blond boy ran around in the front yard four houses down the street from Paige's. She wouldn't have thought much of his sprinting in circles screaming, except for the blue light his hands gave off. The way the kid shouted, he sounded like he had fire ants all over him.

She glided over and landed in front of him. "Dude. Chill out."

The boy stared at her, shaking his glowing hands at her. From mid-forearm to fingertip, he'd become transparent, surrounded in an aura of light. "You don't understand! I just killed my parents."

"What!" gasped Kelly.

"The... the stove caught fire and, and..." He grabbed his face and burst into tears. Ice cubes fell to the grass.

"Umm." She hurried to the front door and looked inside.

Two adults, no doubt his parents, stood in the kitchen, both cringing as if afraid of the stove, encased in a thick column of ice that stretched from floor to ceiling and also covered the stove, sink, and half of the fridge.

She rushed into a punch that left a small dent in the ice. Something told her she hadn't used her full strength... probably because her subconscious knew that doing so would smash the whole ice column and hurt the people in it.

"Hey!" shouted Kelly. "Get in here!"

The crying, maybe twelve-year-old, boy trudged into the kitchen. His hands had gone back to normal. "I didn't mean to!"

"They're not dead."

He stared. "They're not?"

"No. Chill the heck out." She pointed. "You made that ice?"

"Yeah. Dad was cooking burgers and then it just like foom! Fire everywhere." He made a pushing gesture with both hands. "I jumped when I saw the flames and *that* happened."

"Didn't know you had powers?"

"Not until just now, no. What do we do? They're gonna suffocate." He ran over to the ice and grabbed it. "Mom? Dad? Are you awake?"

Neither of the adults moved.

"Maybe if you made the ice, you can un-make the ice?'

He looked at her, or at least would have if his blond hair didn't mostly cover his eyes. "Un-make?"

"Yeah. Do you read comics?"

"No. I like superhero movies though."

She scoffed. "Poser."

"What?"

"Forget it." Kelly grasped his shoulders, spun him to face the giant ice column, and pointed at it. "I don't know what the aliens did, but if this works anything like most heroes with ice control powers, you have *control* over ice. Not just making it. Concentrate on that ice and think about how much you want it to turn back into water, or go away."

The boy raised his hands in a weak attempt at a kung fu stance, pointing his palms forward, then made a series of faces. A few seconds later, his hands changed once more to transparent with light glowing from them, but nothing noticeable happened to the ice column.

"No rush or anything, but they're probably going to run out of air in less than another minute," said Kelly.

"No! Mom! Dad!" He grunted, his whole body shaking. Some parts of the outer column evaporated to fog.

"That's it. You're doing it. Just push harder."

He strained, face turning red.

She narrowed her eyes with an idea. She raised her hands, and clapped so hard it sounded like a gunshot.

The boy screamed in surprise—and all the ice poofed to fog.

As if they'd been frozen in time, the parents abruptly continued jumping back from the stove and yelling about fire. His mother slipped in a puddle. Kelly thrust her arm out to the side and caught the woman before she fell.

"Whoa," said the kid. "What the heck was that noise?"

"You froze them when the fire scared you. So I scared you." She mimed clapping her hands, but not hard enough to make a sound.

"Oh."

"Who are you?" asked the woman.

"I'm Übergirl." She smiled up at her.

"Are you one of Ryan's friends from school?"

"Mom... she's way too little. I don't hang out with *little* kids. What are you in like third grade?"

"Something like that," said Kelly. Admitting to being in fifth at her age would be a total giveaway. Then again, her costume didn't really do much to hide her identity, especially with the floof. "Looks like my work here is done."

"What happened?" asked the man.

"Your son has ice powers. Your hamburgers caught fire and he put them out." She patted the boy on the arm. "Little practice, you'll be fine. Just, you gotta stop panicking and chill out."

He laughed. "Chillout. That's gonna be my hero name."

Kelly whistled. "Great. Who doesn't love puns?"

She waved and let herself out. After a short flight back to Paige's house, she slipped in the window and poked the ZOOM bracelet to change. The explanation of what happened had her friend laughing so hard she cried, mostly at Kelly telling an ice-based hero to 'chill out.'

"I didn't do that on purpose!"

"You still said it. Own it."

Kelly stuck out her tongue. "Hey… that boy goes to our school. Do you think that crystal in the football field is still affecting people?"

"If it is, it's not affecting the right people." Paige fake-pouted.

"You licked it again, didn't you?"

"Not exactly."

Kelly raised an eyebrow. "Not… exactly?"

"I might have baked some cookies and offered them to the lava god."

"Wow. You wasted chocolate chips by dropping them in lava? Gah."

"No, I made oatmeal raisin."

Kelly rolled her eyes. "Well, no wonder the lava god didn't give you powers. You're lucky he didn't kill you for a false offering."

Paige laughed.

CHAPTER TWENTY-SEVEN

FLOPPET

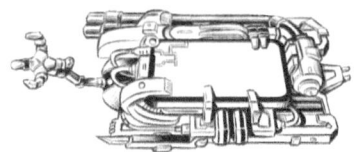

Mom arrived at the Warren's house a little after seven that night. Her parents had, via text, suggested Kelly have dinner there. Dad—again via text—apologized for the inconvenience and sent Mr. Warren $6,000 via MoneyFriend 'to cover any food she might eat.' Needless to say, the Warrens kept giving each other weird looks over dinner.

And no, Kelly did not eat six grand worth of food. She had a normal portion of chicken nuggets.

"How was your day, sweetie?" asked Mom as soon as they walked inside the house, in an oddly normal tone of voice—as though she hadn't been gone all day.

"Umm. Okay."

Mom smiled at her. "Did you have fun at the beach?"

"It was fine."

"Did you see the giant octopus or did that happen at a different beach?"

Kelly stared up at her with a 'really?' face. "I got a good close look at it."

"Hope you had fun playing with the giant octopus." Mom patted her on the head and went to the kitchen.

"Mom?" Kelly trailed after her. "Where were you all day?"

"Out."

"Out?"

"Yes. Out." Mom filled a glass of water from the fridge dispenser and drank it. "Sometimes adults go out to do things."

"But, you guys left me home alone all day. Isn't that like wrong? I'm nine."

"You're an exceptionally intelligent and mature nine-year-old." She drank half the glass in one long series of gulps, then refilled it. "With superpowers."

"If someone notices I'm here alone and they call the police, you guys could get in trouble. And you scared me. I worried about you."

"So, you could just lie about it. You're getting rather good at it."

Kelly bit her lip. "I would've asked permission, but you guys weren't here!"

Mom wagged her eyebrows and drank the glass most of the way empty again. "What do you want me to say, sweetie? I had stuff to do."

"Work?"

"Not really. More fun."

"You went out for fun?"

"Your father and I went out for fun. It had been far too long since we did so."

Kelly stared at her, feeling slapped. Did Mom just admit that her parents ditched her to go have fun? She wouldn't have cared if they expected she'd be with the Warrens all day first, but they just left without saying a word.

"Aww. Don't feel like that." Mom set the glass down and hugged her. "We both trusted you enough not to worry. You aren't an ordinary little girl anymore. If someone broke into the house, you would've given them one heck of a surprise. And if you burned the place down, it's not like you'd have been injured."

"That's not the point, Mom."

"Isn't it? The whole reason parents worry about leaving their kids home alone is that children are naturally prone to doing impulsive, reckless, dangerous things... and the little buggers tend to be stupid. Drinking poisonous cleaning products, sticking forks in electrical outlets, playing with matches. Fortunately, you've never been prone to mischief of that sort."

"Mom... I'm not stupid."

"And you're basically indestructible." She smiled. "So why should we worry something's going to happen to you?"

Uh oh. Mom's gone loopy again. Dad must have shown her the lair and she can't handle it.

"I guess."

"You guess? Tell me what you would possibly have to be afraid of being alone for a few hours in our house? Especially after you tossed a twenty-ton octopus around like a stuffed toy."

"Umm." She fidgeted. Bizarre as it sounded, her mother *did* have a point. "Okay, so I'm Üb—I mean super powerful, but I'm still a kid. I *missed* you guys. So what if I'm indestructible? I still have a kid brain." She hugged her mother. "Being alone is scary."

"Aww, sweetie." Mom patted her back.

Kelly, her face mushed against her mother's shirt, smiled, awash in love—for a few seconds. When the Aegis busted Dad, her mother would be crushed. Would she be angry at Kelly for her part in it, or simply sad that her father had broken the law in such a big way?

"Would you like to watch TV or something?"

"Okay."

Kelly spent the next hour or so curled up on the couch with Mom, watching the movie *Courage* from Pixel Studios, the one with the red-haired princess who didn't want to get married and had a big problem with a bear. Both Kelly and her mother cried at *that* scene. Like the princess, Kelly clamp-hugged her mother and sobbed in guilt.

"Shh. It's okay." Mom ran a hand over her hair in a soothing, repetitive gesture. "Just a movie."

In a couple days, stuff would happen that would forever change her family. Dad would either end up in prison or furious with her. Probably both. This moment of quiet affection with her mother might be the last one she ever had before their whole family fell apart—all because of those stupid crystals.

Superpowers should have been perfect and fun, but Kelly found herself wishing she never had them. She wanted the aliens to take the crystals back like they never happened. Even if that meant Alexis and her friends would once again torment her, she wanted her parents back. No more spacey, weird Mom; no more supervillain Dad. Just Mom and Dad, and an undersized comic-book geek girl who elevated the 100-meter garbage can bobsled to an Olympic event.

"Go on and get ready for bed, it's late."

"Yes, Mom."

Kelly slid off the couch and trudged upstairs. She'd never really been the sort of kid who ignored her parents whenever they told her to do something, though sometimes—like with bedtime—she'd pull the 'in a minute' thing until Mom or Dad added 'now.' 'Go to bed' got 'in a minute,' but 'Go to bed *now*' resulted in immediate compliance. Tonight, she listened without delay, as if doing so would somehow apologize for her role in ruining their family.

It remained unclear if Übergirl still needed to brush her teeth. If a twenty-ton octopus hammering her into the beach like a tent spike didn't even chip a nail, sugar probably wouldn't do anything to her mouth. However, out of habit, she brushed her teeth anyway… crying the whole time. If Dad walked into her room to kiss her goodnight, she would probably explode into a tearful confession and beg him to abort the MICE project and stop being a bad guy.

She wanted him to *not* show up as much as she felt heartbroken that he hadn't done so already.

A few minutes after she crawled under the covers, Mom walked in and sat on the edge of the bed. She picked Floppet up and nestled the stuffed rabbit under Kelly's arm before tucking her in snug.

"Is Dad coming?" whispered Kelly.

"Your father's going through a difficult time right now."

Kelly swished her feet back and forth under the blankets. *Ya think?*

"I'm worried about you, sweetie." Mom kissed her on the forehead.

"Me?" Kelly blinked.

"Remember we're a family. No matter what your dad's dealing with, he's still your father."

"I know, Mom. I'm worried about him, too. I love both you guys so much. Things are a big time weird now and I dunno how to deal."

"Well, just remember who your family is. That's the only thing that matters in this world." Mom brushed her hand over Kelly's hair a few times. "Your father loves you more than anything. And I love you, too. We'll always be there for you no matter how strange the world gets with those aliens around."

"Do you think they're going to leave when they fix the planet, or are they gonna stay forever?"

"Hmm. I'm not sure. We'll just have to wait and see." She gave Kelly's hand a squeeze, then made Floppet 'kiss' Kelly on the cheek while doing a high-pitched voice. "Good night, Kelly."

At any other moment in her life, that would've made her laugh. She did, at least, manage to smile.

Mom got up, smiled back at her, and crept out into the hall, easing her door closed.

No Dad.

He's not coming.

Part of her felt relieved that she didn't have to face him. A bigger part felt heartbroken that he didn't pop in to say goodnight. She crossed her fingers and hoped he only became so fixated on his plan that he couldn't pull himself away for anything, and *not* that he had discovered she tattled on him. No way could he have failed to notice his test subjects missing.

Worry that her father had become angry that someone stole his kidnap victims kept her wide awake. He couldn't suspect she'd done that since she didn't know the codes to the holding cells and nothing had been broken. She imagined Mindfreeze could teleport into the place, grab someone, and teleport out with them the same way she took Kelly to the Citadel. The woman wouldn't even have had to open the doors. Her only question was wondering if Dad installed security cameras in the lair or if he'd been so confident in believing it perfectly hidden that he wouldn't have bothered.

A creak from the window sounded an awful lot like the fake tool shed door opening.

Too anxious to sleep, and too curious to stay in bed, Kelly slipped out from under the covers and darted to her window, crouching low to peer over the windowsill. Bob and Zorthax hauled a phone-booth-sized shiny black box out from the shed, each holding up one end. They shuffled sideways before setting it on the grass about twenty feet away. Bob poked the side of the box, and it opened up, rapidly expanding into the shape of a small helicopter.

Kelly's mouth dropped open.

The two henchmen climbed into the apparently collapsible aircraft. Its rotors spun up, making quite a bit less noise than normal for a helicopter. Soon, the machine lifted off and flew into the distance. She started to open the window, intent on flying after them, but her alarm clock showed the time at 11:09, well past her bedtime for a school night. Today having been Sunday, she had to get up early tomorrow. If Mom or Dad caught her outside at that hour with school in the morning, she'd be grounded.

And, now, 'grounded' could have a quite literal meaning.

Would her parents punish her by telling her 'no flying for a week'?

Her suspicion that the henchmen went off to do something bad didn't give her permission to do something bad, too. Going outside this late at night would be like the most disobedient she'd ever been in her whole life. Besides, she had cereal with them a couple times. And Bob liked *Kobold*. Even agreed with her about *Witche* being under-used. How bad could those two really be?

She grumbled, but decided to behave herself and stay home.

After a quick trip to the bathroom, she crawled back into bed... and continued staring at the ceiling. Could Übergirl survive on no sleep for a night? She couldn't stop thinking about what her father might be up to. Worse, she couldn't stop dreading what would happen when the Aegis caught him doing something bad. They had found his water-poisoning place, force field and all, but failed to get inside it. Though Phoenix didn't say so specifically, it sounded like even Mindfreeze couldn't get past it with teleportation.

Mad scientists might be unpredictable and random, but Dad's inventions did seem to be high quality. Her costume, the collapsible helicopter, the lair, all those robots he made, even the Paper Purifier 3000, all of it *was* really cool. She wanted to be proud of him, but it annoyed her that he had to be a dork and pick the bad guy team.

Then again, he always did pick the bad guys whenever they played a board game. He even liked the Imperium in *Galactic Battles* instead of the rebels. And —most horrible of all—he actually liked pineapple on pizza, even laughing at the misery doing such a vicious thing caused other people. Like, he'd try to hide a hunk of pineapple on her pizza and cackle when she found it and nearly threw up.

Oh, crap. Maybe the aliens aren't *controlling him.*

Whirring arose outside.

Kelly slipped out of bed and crept over to her window. The suspiciously silent helicopter landed in the yard, its rotors slowing to a stop in mere seconds. She ducked down to kneel so only her eyes peered over the windowsill.

Bob and Zorthax got out. Bob stood by the nose waiting while Zorthax dragged an unconscious man in pajamas out from the middle section behind the two front seats and hefted him up over one shoulder. The poor man had a giant tranquilizer dart sticking out of his butt. Bob opened a panel on the side of the helicopter near the nose and pushed a button. The aircraft collapsed once again into a large, rectangular box. Zorthax carried the unconscious man into the shed with Bob following along behind, dragging the compact helicopter.

"Uh oh. That's not good." She looked again at the clock, 12:01 a.m. "Eep!"

Not only would she be grounded for going outside at this hour, she'd get grounded for being *awake* and out of bed. She'd never been awake at midnight before, not even the last two New Year's Eves when her parents gave her permission. Both times, she didn't even make it to 11:00 p.m., passing out on the sofa curled up with Mom, missing the ball drop.

"Dad's not going to kill that man. I can save him tomorrow after school. If I get grounded, I can't help anyone."

Worried that Mom might catch her spying on her father's henchmen, Kelly leapt back into bed, cuddled up with Floppet, and tried real hard to fall asleep.

CHAPTER TWENTY-EIGHT

FREE WILL AND OTHER MINOR INCONVENIENCES

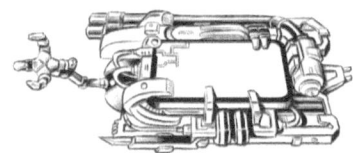

Monday morning, Kelly's alarm clock banged on her skull until she slid, kicking and screaming, into being awake. Evidently, Übergirl could still feel the effects of not going to bed on time. She peeled her eyes apart to reveal blurry Mom standing over her. Kelly opened her eyes a little wider and her mother came into focus with a big smile and excited expression as though she'd consumed an entire bottle of liquid happiness.

To Kelly, that meant cherry fruit punch.

To her parents, that meant coffee.

However, in this particular moment, Kelly meant actual liquid happiness, which she pictured as a sparkling pink potion.

"Good morning, sweetie," said Mom in a super-cheerful tone.

"Can I stay home from school today? I don't feel so good."

Mom put a hand on her forehead. "What's wrong?"

"I just don't feel good."

"Now, sweetie." Mom patted her head. "How is my brave little trooper who beat up an octopus the size of our house going to let a little tummy ache get her down?"

"Umm." Kelly stared at her feet poking up in the blanket.

"You're not still having problems with those bullies, are you?"

She shook her head. "No, Mom."

"You're a Tier One super, sweetie. You *can't* get sick." Mom gently peeled the blankets off her. "Come on, now. Get ready for school."

Busted. Kelly sat up, swung her legs over the edge, and scrunched her nose. "How do you know about hero tiers? And that's stuff from the comic books. It's not real."

"Oh, your father said it. He's probably just using terms he's familiar with so he can describe things. He always has been highly organized." Mom kissed her on the head. "Remember what we spoke about, dear. Your father loves you very much."

"I know." Kelly gazed down at the floor, guilt crushing her into a slouch.

She couldn't bring herself to say another word the whole time she got dressed in her blue Ms. Omni T-shirt and a jean skirt with flip-flops, ate breakfast, and wasted about ten minutes watching a cartoon on Mom's tablet until she had to leave for school. Dad not popping in at all worried and saddened her because when the Aegis arrested him, it would feel like this— not seeing him for a long time. She trudged to school with her head down, remembering all the happy times they'd shared. The idea that he might go away to prison made her toy with the idea of switching sides and trying to be a bad girl, but even the joy of doing stuff together with Dad didn't soothe her conscience about hurting people. She just couldn't be mean to anyone.

In the cafeteria before class, she found Paige and told her about the collapsing helicopter and the man's kidnapping. Also, she explained that as soon as she got home, she planned to go into the lair and check on him.

"I feel like I'm doing something bad because I didn't save that guy last night and I'm here at school right now instead of saving him." Kelly puffed at her hair, which partially covered her right eye.

"The only thing separating true heroes from the bad guys is that heroes respect the rules. You're a kid. You're not allowed out late at night and you can't skip school." Paige sipped from her juice. "Don't be upset. You're going as fast as you can, and besides, your father isn't going to hurt him. He obviously needs the man to do something."

Kelly glanced at her. "How do you know that?"

"They went out real late at night and kidnapped a specific guy. Has to mean your dad needs him somehow."

"Okay."

The bell rang.

Kelly got up and started walking toward her first period class, Social Studies with Mr. Reynolds, but Paige grabbed her arm—and slid along behind her for a few steps, being towed until Kelly noticed and stopped.

"What?"

"We're not going to the classroom today. We gotta go outside. Did you forget the field trip?" asked Paige.

"Oh... yeah, I did."

Mrs. Webb—her math teacher—and Mrs. Rivera—her science teacher—conspired to take two classes worth of kids to the Sci-Mazing World science museum today. Too caught up in worrying about the situation with Dad, she'd forgotten entirely about the trip. Her parents had signed the permission slip weeks ago, before the aliens showed up. Having her expectation for how the day would go abruptly changed annoyed her.

She'd planned to rush straight home after school and try to do something about the man she'd watched Bob and Zorthax carry into the shed last night, darted in the backside like an escaped bear from the zoo. Also, she would normally have loved going to a science center, but couldn't enjoy it with the guilt of knowing her father would go to jail soon. At least, he'd be going to jail unless he somehow managed to defeat the Aegis, and that didn't seem possible.

The girls headed down the hall in the opposite direction from their social studies class. Mrs. Rivera, a thin, fortyish woman, stood by four rows of kids already lining up by the buses that would take them to the museum. Kelly and Paige took their places as usual, leaving any further discussion about important stuff until later.

Mrs. Webb announced that the field trip would take most of the morning and include lunch at the museum. They would have only three classes upon returning, English, Social Studies, and probably art, which would bump the usual gym and computer classes that she had later in the day. Art, usually second-from-last, would be the final class today.

Kelly tried not to be too irritated at the field trip since it wouldn't make the day take longer.

They arrived at the Sci-Mazing Museum after a twenty-minute (mostly due to traffic) ride, gathered as a class on the big sidewalk in front of the place, and stood there waiting while the teachers sorted out the access passes and handed all the kids a plastic pouch to wear on a string around their necks to show they'd paid admission.

"All right, everyone," said Mrs. Webb. "You are all to stay with the group. No one is to go running off on their own. If, for some reason, one of you gets lost, go directly to the nearest museum worker—they have the bright yellow shirts—and show them your pass so they can get you back to the group."

Various murmurs of agreement came from the class.

A small car raced up to park behind the buses. Mike Hopkins hopped out with a sullen expression like he got in trouble. His mother walked him over to the class then apologized to the teachers for his being late. Apparently, she couldn't get him out of bed. Kelly covered her mouth to stop from snickering at hearing that, picturing the woman trying her hardest to drag the boy out of bed and him not going anywhere. Mrs. Webb got a devilish look in her eye and suggested she'd overlook his being marked late if Mrs. Hopkins stayed and helped chaperone.

She did.

The class made their way inside and proceeded to follow the colored trail that led between exhibits. Sci-Mazing had two halves. One for children, the other for adults and older kids in high school, kinda plain and boring by comparison—no rainbow path to follow or cartoon animals everywhere.

Kelly found the exhibits interesting enough to momentarily take her mind off Dad since they appealed to her nerdy side. A few other kids appeared to be having as much—well *more*—fun than her since they didn't have to worry about their fathers probably going to jail soon. Most of the class progressed among the various stations that demonstrated scientific concepts with looks of mild amusement, mild confusion, or enlightenment once something they'd learned about in class made sense at last.

On the other end, a few kids—like Colleen Brandt—stared at the exhibits with expressions of complete bafflement. Mrs. Rivera, the science teacher, spent most of her time trying to explain things to the low-performers while Mrs. Webb and Mrs. Hopkins focused on keeping all the kids in the same group, catching the wanderers, the stragglers, and the overly curious. After about twenty minutes of racing back and forth collecting stray kids, the look on the math teacher's face reminded Kelly of something Mom used to say about work—it made her want to crawl into a wine bottle.

This, of course, made no sense at all since a person couldn't fit inside a wine bottle.

As far as she knew, her mother had never successfully done that. But Mrs. Webb sure looked like she wanted to try.

The path changed colors based on the particular field of science each exhibit covered. Kelly smirked at purple—her absolute favorite color—being used for biology because the museum's biology exhibits mostly involved bugs or plants. Eww and kinda boring.

She decided to help the teachers out by keeping an eye out for stragglers who became so focused on playing with the exhibits that they didn't notice the class moving away. Mrs. Webb noticed her dragging Joey Lee back to the group before running to collect Susie Bleecker (who had a habit of spotting random things across the room and running to go check them out). Kelly expected to be yelled at for leaving the group, but the woman appeared to appreciate the assist. Sometimes, having a reputation as a teacher's pet helped.

Eventually, the colored path brought their group to the dinosaur chamber, an enormous, round room at the heart of the museum. A big archway on the opposite side led to the 'grown-up' wing, since the two halves both shared the dino room, which contained numerous dinosaur models, both skeletal and 'alive.' Interactive stations occupied booths along the outer wall, a few with virtual reality that took people 'back in time' to be among the dinosaurs. A gigantic brontosaurus model at the middle of the room allowed kids to enter via a door in its back leg and climb around inside it. Adults could *sorta* fit, but they wouldn't be comfortable in the tight passage.

Halfway between the two exits, a shorter corridor led out from the dino room with signs for bathrooms, vending machines, and security.

Given the size of the huge circular area, the teachers decided to let the class spread out as they wanted. Mrs. Webb stood by the archway leading to the kids' side of the museum while Mrs. Hopkins 'played goalie' at the other side in case anyone got curious to go check out the more advanced exhibits in the other section. Mrs. Rivera wandered the middle checking on the kids and answering questions as needed.

Kelly and Paige ran to the various dinosaurs, petting a robotic velociraptor, climbing into the brontosaurus, and exploring a prehistoric jungle in virtual reality.

While standing by a holographic model of a triceratops head that showed science's best guess at what their insides might have been like, Kelly spotted something strange out of the corner of her eye.

Two big guys in security guard uniforms escorted a nervous-looking couple in their early thirties into the small spur hallway. It didn't make much sense to her for ordinary adults who looked like pretty much any other parent of any other kid at school to get pulled away by museum security. She stared, watching them walk out of the dino room… and the guard on the left flickered.

Time seemed to pause.

Instead of a person wearing a security guard uniform, that man had become a Nolmek, one of the larger, two-legged kind with dark reddish-orange skin, little horn nubs everywhere, and a proper 'space alien' outfit. His huge three-fingered hand gripped the man's arm in a way that appeared a lot more like an abduction than a security issue.

Time resumed, the guard once again appearing human.

They've got like holograms to look like people. She narrowed her eyes. *Something is wrong here.*

Since the teachers wouldn't think it odd for any of the kids to head to the bathroom from the dinosaur room, Kelly ran over there. When she reached the hallway, she pulled her flip-flops off to be quiet and padded past the bathrooms to the security office, peeking past the doorjamb into the room.

A young woman in a security uniform and a man about Dad's age, also in a security guard uniform, sat at desks while staring into space… quite obviously hypnotized. The back wall of the security room swung open—a secret door—allowing the two fake security guards to bring the man and woman into a hidden corridor, turning left.

Worried that even barefoot she'd make noise, Kelly flew off the ground and launched herself across the room, diving past the rotating section of wall as it closed. To the right, dead end. To the left, the two security guards continued dragging the people along. Before they noticed her floating there, she darted into a hiding spot against the wall behind a big alien console, and peered around the edge.

The two Nolmek dropped their disguise at the end of the corridor.

"What's going on?" yelled the woman.

"Hey, you're not security." The man struggled to pull away from the big alien, but couldn't. "Why are you bringing us here? I thought you came to help us."

"Relax," said the Nolmek on the right, his voice deep and gurgling. A small silver device sitting atop his left ear flickered with blue lights as he spoke. "Follow us."

"Like we have any choice!" The woman tugged at her arm but also couldn't escape.

Kelly set her flip-flops on the floor and stepped into them, then pushed the gem on her ZOOM bracelet, switching to her Übergirl costume. *This stinks. Something is wrong here.*

Whatever material Dad made her boots out of, they didn't squeak on the metal floor as she hurried to follow the aliens and their captives. They turned left again where the corridor connected to a platform with a thin railing overlooking a lower level. Kelly stopped at the end, waited a second, then leaned past the corner to check out the room.

Thirty pods lined the circular walkway, only four of them empty. The rest all held unconscious people ranging in age from late teens to elderly. Thin wisps of orange lightning connected the top of each chamber to the head of the person in it, a continuous stream of energy.

"What the heck is this?" yelled the woman, still struggling to get her arm away from the Nolmek holding her.

"Why do they always ask?" The other Nolmek shook his head. "I'm tired of explaining this every time we put a human in the chamber. They're just going to forget it anyway. We should print out cards so we don't have to say it every time."

"Or we can just not say anything," replied the Nolmek holding the woman. He pushed a button on the wall that opened the chamber in front of him.

"No!" yelled the woman. "Don't do this!"

"What are you doing to us?" The man raised his legs, bracing his feet against the sides of the chamber to resist being shoved inside.

Kelly leapt into the air, flying up behind the Nolmek. She punched the one holding the man in the back of the head, knocking it face-first into the wall, then swung around with a kick at the other one. Her boot caught the alien in the jaw, knocking him back through the metal railing and sending him falling down into the sunken middle portion of the room.

A meaty *splat* came from below, as if she'd dropped a huge raw steak on the floor.

The people gawked at her in shock.

"What's going on?" asked the woman, recovering her composure first.

"I don't know. But I think it's bad." Kelly pointed. "You should get out of here."

"Who are you? What's a little girl doing here?" asked the man. "Did they kidnap you?"

"No. I'm Übergirl, and I saw the aliens taking you."

They exchanged a glance, appeared to decide simultaneously to stop asking questions, then ran to the exit.

Kelly landed and walked over to the hole in the railing, peering over.

The middle part of the room resembled a two-story deep soup pot, accessed by a small elevator from the walkway to her left. More chambers lined the walls down there, also full of humans. The pods up top would gradually rotate like a corkscrew on their way down to the bottom part of the room. The lowest tank, which contained a fortyish woman, stood beside a conveyor belt that led to a small double-door. An empty pod in front of that one had sunken halfway into a hole in the floor. She gazed around, imagining that all the chambers moved on a track in a constant, circular path, carrying people to the conveyor before returning empty to the top.

The Nolmek she'd kicked lay flat on his back on top of one of the snake-bodied aliens, who scrabbled at the smooth metal floor with his small arms, unable to pull himself out from under his much larger cousin. His high-pitched grunts of exertion and panic sounded male.

While the big Nolmek's clothing appeared to be light battle armor, the worm-like one wore something akin to a cape and a short-sleeved shirt. Kelly stepped off the edge and floated down to land in front of the creature. He lifted his large head to look at her, both his round, black eyes widening. Except for not having ears and being much wider at the top than the bottom, its head somewhat resembled that of a human's in overall shape. The alien's tiny mouth, a simple line barely an inch wide, shrank to almost a dot in an expression of surprise.

"What are you doing here?" asked Kelly.

"Oh, by Sardoxia, not another one," moaned the small Nolmek in a voice that made him sound like a bored rich guy.

"Another what?"

"Anomaly."

"A-nom-a-lee?" asked Kelly.

"An unexpected circumstance. You are wearing a ridiculous outfit as well as disregarding gravity, so you must be one of the humans who has been affected in strange ways."

She raised an eyebrow at its red cape with a high-backed collar. "*My* costume is ridiculous?"

The Nolmek hissed and lunged forward, its worm-body stretching. To Kelly's horror, its tiny mouth erupted open into a massive, gaping cavern filled with triangular shark teeth. It bit her on the shoulder, though she didn't feel much more than a gentle grasp. Several *snaps* made her cringe. A few teeth clattered to the floor. Two fat tears formed in the alien's eyes.

"That looked painful."

"It was," mumbled the Nolmek around a mouthful of Kelly.

"You shouldn't bite people then."

She plucked him off her shoulder and held him by a two-handed grip as high up on the serpent body as she could grab, beneath his head. He had body heat, roughly similar to the warmth of touching a human, though otherwise felt as if she held a rubber toy snake.

"Play nice. The big baddies went to sleep after I hit them only once."

Kelly took a step back and yanked the Nolmek out from under his bigger cousin. The alien's body tapered from about the thickness of the fire extinguishers at school to a thin point no bigger than an ordinary snake tail at the tip. If he could stand up pin straight while balanced on the tip of his tail, he'd be a little taller than Dad, but he made no effort to 'stand' while she held him.

"This is going to escalate to violence, isn't it?" asked the Nolmek. "That is what you humans do. Even the kittens."

"I don't want to hit you. Tell me what you're doing to people here?"

"Oh. Well, I could simply show you instead." Its all-black eyes flashed white. "Step into the chamber over there."

Kelly thought it would be a *wonderful* idea to do what the nice Nolmek said. She happily let go of him and hurried over to get in the clear-walled chamber. It closed around her, and she could hardly wait to see what happened next.

The Nolmek slithered over to a console. 'Standing,' it wound up being only a little taller than her, with most of its tail dragging behind it under its cloak. "You see, the problem with humans is that they have far too much free will. And they're stubborn. It is an unexpected complication that has greatly thrown off our initial calculations of how long this would take. But a delay is not a setback. Since you asked, and were so obliging and obedient, I may as well explain. This facility is one of many we are using to pre-condition humans. In fact, it is good that you arrived. You will provide us with valuable data. We have not yet processed a kitten. It did not seem purposeful yet."

"I'm not a kitten. I'm a person. Kittens are baby cats. Small humans are called children."

The Nolmek waved his hand dismissively. "I have no desire to learn more than one word from your language to refer to non-adults. You have far too many words. Every different species gets a different word for a juvenile specimen. Inefficient. Everything on this planet that is not an adult is a kitten. Now, where was I?"

"You were about to monologue about your great evil plan before doing something bad to me."

He snapped his tiny fingers and pointed one straight up. "Oh, yes. Thank you. This facility will remove that pesky stubbornness and sense of self-importance. When humans wake up from this procedure, they feel largely unchanged, but become docile and controllable with little capacity for individuality, easily influenced to any directive we desire." His teeny line-mouth curled into a smile.

"You have machines that turn people into Jaden Nieber fans?"

The Nolmek blinked. "What is that?"

Kelly rolled her eyes. "He's this boy who sings songs so basic a computer probably made them and everyone thinks he's like amazing, but I can't stand him."

"I don't understand," said the Nolmek.

"Seriously." She shook her head. "I don't either."

"That doesn't matter anyway." He held his hand over a button. "You will soon be ready for our future."

"What's the conveyor for?" She pointed at it.

"Our initial plan called for loading humans onto transport ships after initial processing. However, we also miscalculated the time it would take for them to absorb enough Naazlian energy to survive. For the time being, we are releasing them back into the wild, but that will change eventually. Now..." He eyed the button.

Her happiness at listening to the Nolmek abruptly stopped.

Hey. What am I doing in this pod? Oh, crap! The little goober mind-controlled me!

Kelly jumped up, braced her feet on the rear wall of the chamber, and kicked off, launching herself fists-first through the transparent cylinder, exploding it into a shower of shards. The Nolmek began to scream, but stopped when her uppercut made contact with the lower part of his head. Her punch launched the alien straight up.

He hit the ceiling with a squishy *splat*, and stuck, his eyes half-closed, arms stretched out to either side. A long, tubular black tongue hung from his mouth.

"Mind controlling people is bad! Don't do that again!"

The Nolmek didn't respond... but after a few seconds, his head peeled away from the ceiling, dangling. Its weight soon un-stuck the rest of the serpentine body and he fell. Kelly caught him, not wanting him to suffer too much injury. She placed him and the other Nolmek into an empty chamber, which she closed.

None of the controls on the consoles made any sense to her, all labeled with alien letters she couldn't read. Hopefully, the humans trapped in the pods here wouldn't be permanently changed since they hadn't finished the whole process. She approached the first occupied chamber, but before she broke it open, she noticed more voices from above. Bashing open all the pods would make noise. If this place had a ton of aliens, that might not be smart. Better to deal with them first so they didn't hurt the people trying to escape.

Kelly flew up out of the sunken area to the walkway she'd been on earlier. The voices came from another corridor leading off to the right. She hurried down the fairly long passageway and slipped into the back of a room that reminded her of a spaceship's bridge, where she hid behind a large computer-like box near the doorway

Two more serpentine Nolmek stood—as much as something with a snake body can stand—in front of a large screen on the front wall, which mostly displayed a map of Earth, but also had a smaller picture-in-picture window showing a sky-blue planet banded with white swirls. Three moons crept around it at various speeds from barely moving to slow.

"This has added an unacceptable delay," said the Nolmek on the left.

"But it is a necessary process. These humans have numerous unexpected traits that we had not been prepared for. Their average mental resilience is far higher than we anticipated. They are also… delicate. Far too fragile to be hastily transported to Vanthari 4."

Both aliens looked up at the blue planet and sighed longingly.

Kelly blinked, confused that they'd be speaking English, but didn't bother questioning that. Maybe they wore translators all the time since they pretended to be nice to humans and might need to talk to them on short notice.

Left Alien gestured at the big screen. "We could test with a small sample. The humans are not *that* delicate."

"They are, *Skrsssht*."

Kelly cringed at the static high-pitched noise. Evidently the aliens *did* have translator units, and those translator units couldn't process alien names into English.

"We tried taking a few there and they perished in mere hours, even with supplemental atmosphere," said Right Alien. "We must continue their exposure to the Naazlian crystals until their inherent biological structure has changed. The gravity alone on Vanthari 4 kills them in mere minutes. We need *all* humans to absorb enough energy from the crystals to become less brittle. Dead workers cannot extract ore."

"*Bzaczx,* some of them have already adapted well beyond parameters," replied Skrssht. "The anomalies. We could take those."

"Be reasonable. There are so few that it would be pointless to make the journey right now. A trip to Vanthari 4 takes us almost fourteen years. We must establish enough of a population of workers that we will not need to return here again. What is it the humans say? I detest the commute. Besides, these creatures reproduce at an alarming rate. If we were to take a sufficient quantity, say seventy to eighty percent of the humans on this planet, we would have an ample supply of mine workers forever."

"You do not think the Tribunal is correct? They fear humans will overrun us."

Bzaczx laughed. "Vanthari 4 is four hundred times the size of this planet. They would not overrun us. This species possesses the necessary features to be used as both ore extractors and constructors. They are quite versatile."

"Some of the things they create with no seeming purpose have a strange effect on my thought processes. I admire them," said Skrssht.

"Art, music, literature. I never imagined such a primitive species capable of it. It almost seems a shame to drain that creativity. But it is necessary for control. A revolt would be costly."

"Yes. Hmm. Do you think this 'creativity' is the cause of the anomalies? We brought the Naazlian crystals expecting their dimensional attenuation would have the effect of realigning humans to be more resilient, but some have begun exhibiting unpredictable side effects. Mutations, energy emissions, even mental powers similar to ours. This must have come from something deep within the psyche of this primitive species."

Kelly smirked. *Yeah… all the geeks, nerds, and superhero fans. I wonder if some people changed into other things?* She really wanted to ask these Nolmek about Dad, but the other red Nolmek mind-controlled her fairly easily, even if it didn't last long. Two of them at once might be able to keep her from breaking free. That would be bad. Worse, it didn't sound like the aliens deliberately put people into a 'superhero world.' The crystals gave off some kind of energy that the Nolmek knew would change humans, but the superpowers surprised them.

That means… Dad really did go evil.

Heartbreak would have to wait since like twenty people in the other room needed help. She leapt over the computer and rushed the Nolmek from behind, grabbing them and walloping their giant heads together with a wet *splat.* They both emitted faint squeaks and collapsed in a noodly heap. She grabbed the thinner ends of their tails, dragged them back down the hall to the processing room, and threw them in an empty chamber.

Next, she raced around as fast as she could move, time seeming to freeze. Each pod with a person in it, she smashed open, the broken chunks of plastic appearing to hang in midair due to her accelerated speed. One by one, she carried people out and lay them on the floor by the exit to the museum's security room. After she freed everyone, she smashed all the consoles in the lower room, all the chambers on the upper room, all the chambers up top, and everything in the command room—except for the main view screen. Destroying such an enormous TV seemed like a horrible waste, especially considering it only displayed information. The aliens couldn't use the screen to *do* anything.

She flew back to the exit, landed by the hidden door, and punted it down.

Both guards in the museum's security room still appeared to be mind-controlled, as they stared into space. Kelly carried all twenty-four people out of the concealed alien base and arranged them on the floor in the security room. Everyone remained unconscious, which got her thinking they might need more help than simply being pulled out of the pods. She walked up to the female security guard seated at her desk and whispered, "Call the Aegis for help," in her ear.

"Call the Aegis." The woman robotically picked up a phone, then appeared to realize she didn't know the number, and looked it up on the computer. Finally, she placed a call.

"Yes? This is Igor," said a deep voice.

Kelly swiped the phone from the woman. "Igor, it's Übergirl. I'm at the Sci-Mazing Museum. You guys need to get over here quick. Bring Mindfreeze. I found a secret alien base here. They're kidnapping people and putting them in machines. I got them out, but they still won't wake up. Also, I really need to get back to my class field trip or I'm gonna get in big trouble."

"I understand. We will be there soon. Thank you, child."

"Awesome. You guys rock."

She handed the phone back to the security guard and raced out into the hall at mega-speed, heading for the ladies' room. Mrs. Webb stood two steps in past the door, appearing frozen in reality due to Kelly moving so fast. She flew up over the stalls, dove down into one, and hit the ZOOM bracelet to change back into her normal clothing an instant before her feet hit the floor.

The instant her flip-flops touched down, Mrs. Webb yelled, "Kelly Donovan? Are you in here?"

"Yes, Mrs. Webb!" chirped Kelly. "Almost done!"

"Oh, okay. You've been in here a long time."

"Sorry. I get nervous in strange bathrooms. Takes longer."

Mrs. Webb let off a relieved chuckle. "All right. Hurry up. We're about to move on out of the dinosaur area."

Wow… I didn't even get busted.

KELLY HURRIED OUT OF THE BATHROOM, PASSING IGOR THE RED AND MINDFREEZE going the other way toward the security office. They both winked at her. She pretended to fangirl at seeing the heroes, standing there gawking until Mrs. Rivera and Mrs. Webb both called her over, at which point she trotted back into the class group beside Paige.

"What happened?" whispered her friend.

"Just went to the bathroom." Kelly gave her an 'I'll explain later' look. "It, umm, was real bad."

"Hah!" Tommy Anderson laughed. "I didn't think girls blew up toilets."

Kelly glanced at him. "Actually… no. Never mind. That's disgusting."

CHAPTER TWENTY-NINE

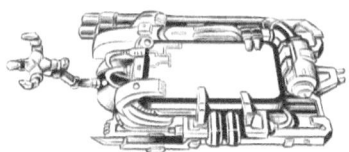

The field trip returned to school a little early, giving the kids a few minutes to hang out in Mr. Reynolds' classroom before Social Studies started. Some ran to the bathroom, others talked or pulled out their phones. Kelly tried to clue Paige in on what happened at the museum, but she couldn't hear whispering over the other kids.

"After we get home," said Kelly.

Paige nodded.

Mr. Reynolds began class when the electronic bell sounded. Unusually, the somewhat heavyset teacher who always taught from his chair got up and stood at the front of the room, pacing back and forth while lecturing. Within a minute, the entire class collapsed over their desks asleep… except for Kelly. Faintly visible ripples in the air came from Mr. Reynold's mouth while he lectured in the same boring monotonous voice he always used for class. Kelly gazed around at everyone drooling on their desks. She nudged Paige a few times, but the girl appeared about as limp as the man she'd seen the henchmen shoot with a tranq dart.

The teacher kept talking about the lesson, but gave Kelly that same wiggly eye he usually used on students he caught sleeping. He made a 'come here' gesture with one finger.

Am I seriously getting in trouble for being the only one awake?

She slipped out of her seat and walked up to the front of the room, flip-flops snapping loud over the totally silent class. "Yes, Mr. Reynolds?"

"You're not asleep."

"Aren't we supposed to *not* sleep in class?"

"I've made a slight change to my policy."

Students started waking up, groaning, yawning, and stretching.

Mr. Reynolds looked over Kelly's head and said two sentences about the Civil War. Everyone passed out with the clunks of multiple heads hitting desks at once. He peered down at her. "You have powers, don't you?"

She gasped. "So do you!"

"Well. I do know that students have considered my lectures a bit dry, but I'm not so bad that I can knock twenty ten-and-eleven year olds out in seconds."

"Maybe it doesn't work on me because I'm nine?"

"No. I've tested." He flashed a mischievous little smile. "I believe superheroes exist now. The aliens..."

"Yeah. So... you're Monotone?"

He bowed his head and groaned. "I had not come up with a name for myself yet, but I suppose that one fits... as much as it used to irk me."

"Well, Mr. Reynolds, you *do* speak in monotone, and now you actually *can* make people sleep. Umm." She peered back at the class. "Why are you knocking everyone out?"

"Because, dear child, my power has a happy side effect. Whatever I lecture about while using it, people remember perfectly even if they're sleeping. Did you notice the test scores? Everyone passed. Even Miss Brandt."

"Wow. That *is* a superpower." She laughed.

"Now, now, Miss Donovan. It's not nice to make fun of someone for struggling academically."

"Didn't you just do that by saying 'even Miss Brandt'?"

"I merely called attention to a D- student earning the first A she ever had in my class. It seems teaching really has become my calling. And I no longer need to confiscate cell phones, tell people to wake up, stop talking, pay attention, or give detention."

Again, the class started coming to.

He recited two lines of lecture and everyone passed out again. "Go on and take your seat and, well, learn the usual way."

"Yes, Mr. Reynolds."

She scurried back to her desk... and tried to stay awake. Even though she could resist his super-powered ability, his monotone voice *before* the alien crystals could knock her out if she didn't focus.

THE REST OF THE SCHOOL DAY DRAGGED ON, TAKING FOREVER TO END.

In fact, the whole day felt like an eternity, even for a place as cool as the Sci-Mazing Museum. Her need to go help that man caused time to crawl all day and prevented her from enjoying all the exhibits that would have otherwise fascinated her.

For Kelly, being eager to get out of school and go home didn't happen often. She found schoolwork and learning tremendously fun and engaging. The only reason she hadn't loved school had been the other children. If it could've been only her and the teachers, she'd have been thrilled. However, since no one bullied her anymore, school had become great—aside from worrying about her father and that man he abducted.

IN ART CLASS, MRS. SPINDEL HANDED OUT A LIST OF STUFF ALL THE STUDENTS needed to get for next week.

A new project required a bunch of supplies: charcoal pencils, graphite sticks, blender, something called a 'kneaded eraser,' and a whiteout pen. She shrugged, put it in her backpack, and proceeded to worry for the remainder of the day about how long she'd be grounded for saving the man her father kidnapped.

Paige had gymnastics right after school, which kinda worked out since Kelly didn't want her friend to get hurt if things with Dad got explodey. She'd have to confront him and tell the truth about not being able to go supervillain. Her friend's idea of how her mind may have shaped her powers gave her hope that her father might not completely freak out. Maybe it would be like before when they played fighting or sports video games: in competition with each other but not actually fighting. His being a villain and her being a hero could be like playing two different sides in a game. Except for the whole going to prison for a long time part.

If she confronted him and stopped him from mind controlling San Francisco, maybe the Aegis would let him off with a small punishment for the kidnappings.

With that hope in mind, she endured the sluggish classes, racing out the door as soon as the last bell rang.

KELLY DODGED AROUND THE STREAM OF KIDS SPILLING OUT THE DOORS, DASHED across the lawn in front of the building, and caught up with Paige on the sidewalk.

She fell in step beside her as they headed home. "The aliens are evil."

"Evil?" Paige's eyes widened. "Are you sure?"

"They wanna kidnap all of us and make humans into slaves on some big planet far away."

Paige whistled. "Yeah, that's pretty evil."

"Yeah."

"So, umm… why did they give some people superpowers if they want to do something like that? Wouldn't making heroes be stupid? Like, why give people the ability to potentially stop them?"

"They didn't want to." Kelly explained how the big crystals tapped into some other dimensional energy which the aliens thought would gradually make all humans tougher so they could survive on the other planet. "The Nolmek are like supers. I punched them as hard as I could and it just knocked them out."

"I don't think you punched them as hard as you could. For someone who threw around an octopus as big as a house, you'd crush anything the size of a person if you wanted to. Your power won't kill anyone. One, you're way too sweet and two, it probably came from the comics we read, and none of the heroes ever kill. If you'd been a *Wraith* fan, you'd be splattering people everywhere."

"Eww, no." Kelly shivered.

"So, I think your powers know what you wanna do—like knock them out —and you use just enough strength to do that. Otherwise, when you hugged normal people, you'd squish them."

She thought that over for a moment. It did kind of make sense. The aliens said something like humans made themselves change based on 'creativity.' Thus, if Kelly thought of superheroes as being noble and virtuous, refusing to kill, her power would be based on that kind of world. That made her feel a lot better about Dad, because he also read the 'nice' comics. He might be a supervillain, but he wouldn't be like the supervillains in the *Wraith* series who blew up buildings and killed hundreds of people with poison gas. Dad would do inconvenient and highly-annoying things to people… like make a machine that left every toilet seat in the world up in the middle of the night.

"I hope you're right." Kelly bit her lip.

"Why?"

She explained her hope about Dad.

"Yeah. I hope so, too. But that means other people who like the dark comics might be dangerous."

"What about other creatures than supers? Vampires? Zombies? Monsters?" Kelly cringed. "That could be scary."

"The news said some people have turned into monsters. And who would *ever* want to be a zombie?" Paige shook her head. "Everyone who's into zombies wants to run around shooting them, not turn into one. Who wants to be mindless?"

They looked at each other, said, "Jaden Nieber fans" at the same time—then giggled.

AFTER PAIGE VEERED OFF TO THE RIGHT WHERE HER ROUTE HOME DIFFERED, KELLY ran the rest of the way home. She bolted through the front door, tossing her backpack toward the stairs and planning on going straight across the house to the patio, back yard, and lair.

That man needed help.

Mom got up from the couch. "Hello, sweetie."

"Eep!" Kelly jumped, skidding to a stop and probably making a face like she'd been caught doing something wrong. "M-Mom? What are you doing home this early?"

"I've adjusted my schedule to work from home a bit during the week. It's not right for us to leave you home alone at your age."

"Oh." She studied her mother with a suspicious furrowing of her eyebrows. *A couple days ago, she said it's fine leaving me home alone because I have powers. What the heck is going on? Did Mom flake out again?* "That's, umm, cool."

The 'how was your day at school' conversation eventually led to mentioning the art supply list.

"Let me see it?" asked Mom.

Kelly fished it out of her backpack and handed the paper over.

"Oh. This stuff doesn't look terribly hard to find or expensive. Might as well pop out now and get it."

"Do we have to go right now?" asked Kelly.

"Did you have plans?"

She fidgeted. After her mother's little talk about 'supporting your father' last night, it didn't seem likely she would have a good reaction to being told he kidnapped someone. Or that Kelly wanted to go rescue the poor guy. She suspected her mother knew Dad had powers, and possibly that he'd gone evil. Why else would she have that tone when she said they needed to support him no matter what?

"Umm, just excited to start reading a comic Paige is letting me borrow."

"Well, that's hardly pressing. Come on. Let's deal with this now so it doesn't get forgotten. If we don't do it now, you'll wind up begging me to take you to the mall an hour before your bedtime next Sunday."

Kelly glanced at the patio door to the backyard. *Sorry for making you wait. I'll save you as soon as I can.*

Mom made an odd face at her as if confused, then walked past her out the front door. Kelly followed and got in the car. On the way into the mall a short while later, she kept looking at the security people, watching them to see if any flickered. What she'd seen at the museum got her wondering how many processing facilities the aliens had set up. Could any security guard anywhere possibly be a Nolmek?

Mom checked the directory to locate an art supply store and led her upstairs to the second level. Fortunately, the place had all the indicated supplies and it didn't take too long to collect them. Mom put everything in a small hand basket and carried it over to the register.

"Hello," said a high-school-aged boy. "Welcome to ArtMax. Did you find everything you needed?"

"I did." Mom smiled at him.

He stared at her for a few seconds, his eyes glazed and a silly little smile on his face. Kelly cringed and turned away. She did *not* need to see people staring at her mother like that. The boy didn't say anything else while bagging the items and handing them over quite fast. Mom thanked him and walked out, Kelly trailing after her. The young man kept staring at Mom with an odd smile.

"Ugh. Did that kid have a crush on you?" asked Kelly. "Eww."

"Boys that age have a crush on everything."

"Eww."

Mom chuckled.

They wandered some other stores, then stopped at a coffee place where Mom got a latte and Kelly a hot chocolate. Her mother wanting to spend time with her, while totally normal, also happened to be frustrating. She needed to get home, save that guy, and finally have it out with Dad. Trying to avoid telling him the truth, allowing him to keep thinking she would be 'Ginger Snap' at his side made her feel like a liar.

Of course, she also couldn't bring herself to hurry Mom along or act uninterested in spending time with her. She *did* like spending time with her mother. So, clinging to the hope that her dad wasn't super evil—merely inconvenient evil—she kept up a smile and spent an hour or so hanging out at the mall with her mother.

After the coffee place, they stopped by a few clothing shops, each picking multiple items, then headed home. The way all the sales clerks seemed to *really* like Mom made Kelly uncomfortable. Also, her mother didn't usually splurge that much when shopping.

Of course, they had quite a bit of money in the bank now thanks to Dad… but strangely enough, Kelly didn't think any of the sales clerks had told Mom what the totals of her purchases had been. Maybe they didn't do that for people who spent a lot. They all sure had seemed distracted by her mother— every last one of them stared at her constantly with vacant, adoring smiles. Only slightly more coherent than Jaden Nieber fans at a concert.

Kelly cringed again. *Eww.*

CHAPTER THIRTY

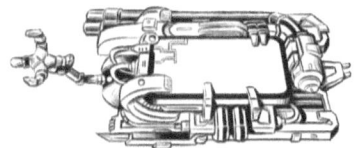

U pon arriving home, Kelly took her shopping bags containing a dress, two new tops, and her art supplies up to her room.

Mom remained downstairs, probably going to the computer den. Finally with a chance to do what she'd been waiting all day for, Kelly ZOOM-ed into her super costume and leapt out the window, gliding to a graceful landing by the tool shed. The hand-scanner chirped happily and the door opened.

Whew. He doesn't suspect anything yet. He'll probably lock me out of here once he knows we're not on the same team. She frowned, annoyed at him. Why couldn't he be a good guy, too? Even doing 'evil' things in video games to fake people made Kelly feel bad. Her father didn't have that problem. He found it funny and said something like 'we can't do that stuff in real life, so why not do it in a game?'

She would have debated if her father had really been evil all along, simply afraid of getting caught, on the elevator ride down, but the trip took a tenth of a second.

Shoomp!

At least, in her super costume, no clothing went anywhere it shouldn't on the 800-mile-an-hour elevator.

Kelly walked into the lair foyer, looking around and listening. Voices came from the left, her dad plus the two henchmen. She clenched her hands into fists. *Figures he's in the same spot the cells are.* She took a breath and tried to think about being Übergirl for a while instead of Kelly. She had to tell the truth. The time was now.

… or not.

By the time she reached the end of the corridor, she'd become too nervous. An octopus the size of a house didn't scare her anywhere near as much as the idea of hurting her father's feelings. She snuck into the room full of machinery and hid behind a monstrously large device with wires, hoses, blinking lights, and all sorts of dials that made no sense. Being tiny helped. She floated up to the top of the machine and squeezed in among the tubes to spy on Dad.

At least his chin hadn't grown any pointier.

Dad, in his big white labcoat, stood in front of another large machine of mysterious purpose. His mega-tablet hovered beside him, having advanced to the point it held itself for him. "What am I paying you two for?"

"To do stuff for you," said Zorthax.

"I wasn't expecting a literal answer." Dad pinched his nose between his eyes. "You are telling me that all the test subjects have simply disappeared?"

"Yeah, boss." Bob nodded. "We went to get them from the holding cells just like you said, and they were all gone. All but the two new ones and the doctor."

"How did they get out?" asked Dad.

Both henchmen shrugged.

Dad poked his finger at the mega-tablet's screen. "The cell doors were never opened. People don't just evaporate into thin air... well, not unless they're exposed to certain chemicals, but I'm not working on anything like that now. Where did they go?"

"Are you expecting an answer?" asked Zorthax.

"Argh!" Dad shouted. "Only if you have one."

Both henchmen hastily shook their heads.

"Go get the new ones. Leave the doctor be for now. I need him."

Bob and Zorthax hurried off.

Kelly eyed her father. Alone. This would be the perfect time to jump out and tell him. Should she say something like 'I'm here to stop your nefarious plan' or would that be too much? Maybe she should try the quiet 'Umm, Dad, can we talk?' approach? Or perhaps it would be better to simply ask him not to do it. It didn't even occur to her that she argued with herself over *how* to tell him only as a way to delay having to actually tell him anything until the henchmen returned carrying two men who both appeared to be in their mid-to-late twenties. One wore a uniform for Backgammon Pizza, the other, a polo shirt and khakis.

Bob and Zorthax walked right past the machine upon which Kelly hid to the other side of the room where they set the new test subjects on their feet next to several stacks of small metal boxes.

The two subjects stared off into space, obviously alive, but behaving as though their brains had been turned off. While typing on his mega-tablet, Dad muttered and complained to himself, having no idea how twenty-six test subjects could simply have disappeared. Both men twitched at the same time, then proceeded to pick up boxes and re-stack them in a new pile.

Kelly stared in horrified awe, watching her father control the two men with his mega-tablet like characters in a video game.

Once the men had finished relocating their piles of boxes, Dad sent the pizza guy to a whiteboard and the other to a computer. Pizza guy attempted to draw a basic picture of a house, a tree, and a sun, but it came out looking like something a three-year-old would have made. The other man simply mashed his hands into the keyboard.

Bob leaned down to look at the computer screen. "I think he forgot the password."

Zorthax sighed. "He's not even typing, Bob, just flopping around."

"Clearly, my MICE serum needs work." Dad observed the pizza man's drawing. "Tasks requiring fine motor skills or higher thought aren't possible."

Pizza guy added a series of uneven lines in an effort to put grass in front of the house, though did manage to include the word 'help'.

"Hmm. Interesting," said Dad. "Some trace of free will remains in there. Don't worry, my good man. I'm only borrowing your services for a short while. You will be returned to your boring and ordinary life soon enough."

The mega-tablet emitted a beeping chirp.

"Oh, look at the time." Dad spun to face the henchmen. "Prepare the Brain Copter."

Bob scratched his head. "The helicopter doesn't have a brain, boss."

Dad sighed. "No, I invented it. I am The Brain Trust. Consequently, it is the Brain Copter."

Pizza guy walked away from the whiteboard and began grabbing boxes that didn't exist, stacking them into another pile that didn't exist as is what tended to happen while relocating nonexistent boxes.

"Just a name," whispered Zorthax. "No brains involved."

"There are *plenty* of brains involved!" shouted Dad. "Do you two have any idea how complicated it is to invent a functional helicopter that can compact itself into an easily portable carrying case?"

The henchmen stared at Dad, their mouths open, one eye bigger than the other.

"Apparently not." Dad tapped a finger to his chin, noticed Pizza guy, and poked the mega-tablet, which caused the man to stop moving. "Then again, it rather was all a blur to me, too. Anyway. That matters not." He dismissed them with a wave. "Kindly go prepare for flight."

"You got it, boss," said Korthax.

The two huge men hurried out.

"You two, back to the holding room." Dad typed a command into his mega-tablet.

Both test subjects shambled off down the hallway.

"Ahh. Wonderful." Dad, his back to Kelly, gazed upward, admiring a giant tank of glowing yellow MICE serum. "Soon."

Kelly started to push herself up to confront him, chickened out, changed her mind, chickened out again, and changed her mind again. Finally ready to tell her father she'd gone hero, she jumped out of her hiding place—right as Dad disappeared in a flash of teleporter sparkles.

"Drat!" shouted Kelly, tapping her foot on nothing while hovering in midair. "He's probably just gone to the elevator. That teleportation thing only works inside the lair."

Shoomp! said the distant elevator.

"Yep. Ooh!" She growled and twisted around to face the hallway, knee cocked to her chest for a bullet take-off… but stopped. "Dad's leaving. I should save these people first."

The pizza guy and the man in the polo shirt continued shambling down the corridor toward the holding cells. Kelly flew past them, looking side to side until she found the cell containing the man the henchmen had brought in with a tranquilizer dart.

Honestly, Dad's prison cells looked rather comfortable. Each fifteen-foot-square space had a floor-to-ceiling transparent front wall instead of bars, carpeting, a bed, sink, and even a bathroom with a privacy door. Though, cramming a dozen people into the same room as he'd done earlier had a negative effect on comfort. Those hostages would likely give this lair bad reviews on Eep. Maybe they'd book their next abduction at a fancier supervillain lair.

She drew back her hand to punch the door open, but beeping from the left distracted her. Kelly zipped over to Pizza guy who typed 080610 into the code panel.

"Ugh." She slapped herself in the forehead. "My birthday."

Pizza guy and Office Man locked themselves in the same room. A moment later, they both jumped, snapping out of whatever trance they'd been in.

"Did we just walk down the hall and do random things?" asked Pizza guy.

"I think so. Memory is a little fuzzy." The other man rubbed his face, then froze, peering between his fingers at Kelly. "Do you see a little girl out there?"

Pizza guy pivoted to look at her. "Yeah."

"Good. I'm not seeing things." Office Man walked up to the clear barrier. "Kid, you should get out of here before that maniac comes back."

"Mark, look how that kid's dressed. She's probably that maniac's super-villain-kid or something."

She sighed. "No. I'm here to save you. I'm Übergirl!"

Pizza guy pointed at her. "Why's your belt say 'GS' on it if your name is Übergirl?"

Kelly grabbed two fistfuls of her hair and yelled, "Argh! Don't ask." Grumbling to herself, she punched in her birthdate, which opened the cell door.

"Whoa. How'd you get the code?" asked Pizza guy.

"Glen, she's a superhero. She got it somehow. Don't ask. Let's get the heck out of here." Mark—a.k.a. Office Man—rushed out of the cell.

"Wait." Kelly grabbed his arm. "Da—I mean the Brain Trust might still be outside. Let me open the other guy's cell and I'll make sure you all get out safe. And... you two have been given a mind-control serum. I need to bring you somewhere so people can cure it."

The men exchanged a glance.

"Okay, said Glen. I probably got fired already anyway."

"Fired?" asked Kelly.

"Some big guy shot me with a dart after I delivered a pizza to him." Glen pulled some money out of his pocket. "I'm still not sure how to feel about them actually paying for the pie."

"Why is that strange?" asked Mark.

"Because these guys kidnapped us but didn't want to steal a $20 pizza?" Glen scratched his head. "That doesn't make sense."

"Pizza is sacred," said Kelly, bowing her head.

"Umm, aren't we supposed to be escaping?" Mark crept down the hall.

"Yep. Hang on." Kelly ran over to the other cell and keyed in the code.

The man on the bed sat up. "What's going on? Why is there a child here? Are you doing that lunatic's bidding?"

"Weren't you listening?" asked Kelly.

"She's Übergirl and she's here to save us," deadpanned Mark.

"Don't sound so excited." Glen tapped his foot in a 'hurry the heck up' gesture.

Mark gestured at Kelly. "It's a bit weird to be rescued by a little girl."

"Do *you* have superpowers?" asked Glen.

"She's got a funny costume, not superpowers."

"Dude! She was flying before. Can you fly, Mark?"

Kelly sighed and looked at the man in the cell while the other two argued. "Come on. I'm here to get you out. Do you know why my—I mean The Brain Trust kidnapped you? I don't think you're a 'test subject.'"

"I'm not. I'm a doctor. Wilton Ainsley. Your father abducted me because he wanted my help fine-tuning his mind control substance. Only, the problem is, what he's made shouldn't possibly work. I can't advise him on how to perfect it because it defies all logic."

She ground her boot toe into the floor. "Umm..."

"Wait," said Mark. "That lunatic is your father?"

"It's a long story. Yes." She hung her head. "He went villain; I didn't. I'm gonna stop him."

"Wow, that's got to make dinner time awkward," said Glen.

Kelly puffed at her hair. "You have *no* idea. Please follow me."

She led the men back down the hall, wondering how she would get them all to the Aegis Citadel. Upon entering the outer foyer, she noticed a pile of large metal boxes. One of those would fit three adults reasonably. She'd never tried to carry much weight while flying but... hang on. She threw a massive octopus around. Three men shouldn't be a big deal at all.

"Will you please get in that box?" Kelly pointed at it.

"Now what?" asked Dr. Ainsley.

"I need to bring you to the Aegis Citadel so they can cure you from that mind control stuff. Otherwise, The Brain Trust can take you over at any time with the CAT."

Mark and Glen laughed.

"No, not a kitty. He named the machine the CAT."

"The child brings up an interesting point." Glen climbed over the side of the box and sat inside it.

Dr. Ainsley didn't appear too happy about the idea, but got in as well. Mark stood there. Kelly pushed the box with the two men to the elevator with ease. At seeing that, Mark ran up and hopped in.

The elevator did not *shoomp* on the way up, as *shoomping* would be harmful to normal humans.

Kelly dragged the box outside, lifted it up over her head, and leapt into the air, heading toward the bay. Dr. Ainsley and Mark moaned and rasped at each other about their fear of flying constantly until she set the box down by the front door of the Citadel.

Mindfreeze appeared standing next to her amid a blue flash. "Übergirl? What's going on?"

"My dad kidnapped more people. I got them out, but they've been infected with MICE."

Glen screamed and hastily checked his pockets.

"No, not mice the rodent." Kelly floated up to eye level with the adults. "MICE is his name for the mind control stuff. Mental influence control elixir."

"Oh." Mindfreeze held out her hands. "Please, all of you form a circle and take my hands."

All three men, somewhat hesitantly, obliged. Kelly grasped Dr. Ainsley's hand in her right, Mindfreeze's in her left.

The woman bowed her head, and the wooded hillside changed into a high-tech lab.

CHAPTER THIRTY-ONE

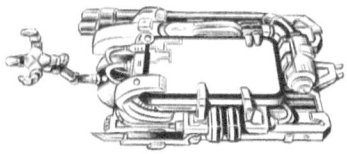

K elly stood politely out of the way while Igor the Red and Phoenix
studied the three men.

Seeing the big—possibly Russian—superhero wearing a labcoat
struck her as both funny and a little sad. The sadness came from wondering
what Dad would have been like if he hadn't gone supervillain. Despite Igor's
size and relatively brutal looks—not that she considered him ugly, but he had
the kind of intimidating face that could make traffic lights change not to slow
him down—he acted like a big, friendly teddy bear. Watching him work with
the scientific equipment started a daydream of her father being a good guy.

What did they call mad scientist types who didn't go evil?

Igor soon determined that Dr. Ainsley had not been given the MICE serum.
Evidently, Dad relied on the more old-fashioned form of controlling someone:
Zorthax and Bob standing right behind him. Mindfreeze teleported the poor
doctor home while the heroes continued taking samples from Glen and Mark.
She returned in a few minutes and helped out preparing a dose of a counter-
serum they developed from working with the first group of kidnap victims.

While Mindfreeze administered the antidote to the men, Bullet Man
appeared seemingly out of thin air, running into the room with such speed he
barely left a smear of color in the air as he passed.

"That will take a few minutes to work," said Mindfreeze. "I'll check on you in a little while then bring you home."

Both men nodded.

The four heroes collected in a group.

"The Brain Trust is a serious threat," said Phoenix.

Igor the Red held up a sample that looked tiny pinched between fingers twice as thick as the vial. "His chemical has evolved. Another few refinements, and the city will be in grave danger."

"If you ask me, it already is." Bullet Man tapped his foot rapidly enough to make a buzzing noise. "We need to deal with this guy soon."

"Agreed." Mindfreeze twisted around to look at a computer screen behind her. "The counter agent still seems to be working, but it's taking longer on these men than the other group. He's made it stronger... or gave them a larger dose."

Phoenix bowed his head. "That poor kid. I feel for her. Come on, let's deal with this."

"Right. Give me a moment to bring these two home." Mindfreeze went over to the beds where Glen and Mark relaxed, took their hands, and vanished with them in a flash of bluish light.

Igor and Phoenix turned to walk out of the lab.

Phoenix jumped at seeing Kelly. "What are you still doing here?"

"Perhaps the child is curious about the science?" Igor scratched above his eyebrow.

"I have to help do something about my dad."

Igor frowned in an approving sort of way. His face said 'not bad, this kid has nerve.'

"Oh, Kelly." Phoenix patted her on the head. "We are extremely grateful and proud of you for alerting us to this threat, but you're a little girl. You need to stay safe. Leave the crime-fighting to the professionals."

"But he's my dad. I..." She flailed her arms, breathing faster as she tried to come up with a good argument to convince them.

"Hon, you're not old enough to do dangerous things. I know it *looks* like it, but the real world isn't a comic book. People can get hurt." He took a knee in front of her. "We don't want you to get hurt."

"But I'm Übergirl!"

"When you're Über*woman*, we'll be proud to serve with you." Phoenix offered a consoling smile.

"That sounds dumb. I'm going to stay Übergirl forever."

"You do not grow up?" asked Igor, both eyebrows raising.

"No, I mean... Umm. I don't know. Pretty sure I'm still going to grow up. What I mean is, my hero name isn't going to change. Pretty sure I'm as strong as Igor, as fast as Bullet Man, and... umm. Stuff."

"That is a bold claim little one." Igor smiled. "But you are so small."

"Still wanna arm wrestle?" She raised an eyebrow.

A table appeared out of thin air, then two chairs, Bullet Man holding them both.

"Ray is fast, I will give him that." Igor took a seat.

Kelly approached, pushing the chair aside and setting her elbow on the table. "I think I need to stay on my feet for this to be a fair challenge."

Igor's hand engulfed half her arm. "Are you sure you wish to do this?"

"I trust you won't hurt me. My powers seem to only be as strong as I need so I don't hurt people."

"All right. How about I hold still and you try to push first? I do not want to, umm. What is how they say? Snap you like twig?"

"Okay."

Kelly widened her stance and pushed Igor's arm over.

"Hold on. I was not ready." Igor's mostly bald head erupted in a sheen of sweat.

Sensing a small lie, Kelly grinned. His arm had become noticeably more difficult to push, but only at the last inch. She'd been too fast for him to react to. "Okay."

"A countdown, Kevin, if you would please," said Igor.

Phoenix stood at the edge of the table between them. "Three... two... one... go!"

Kelly grunted, pushing against Igor's hand. The big man's face reddened. She poured as much effort as she could into fighting his strength. For three seconds, their hands teetered back and forth, going nowhere.

"This ain't really a fair competition," said Roy—a.k.a. Bullet Man—"Igor's arm is so low compared to hers. His forearm's longer than her entire arm. She's got the advantage of angle"

"And he has the advantage of size and mass... and leverage." Phoenix leaned closer, examining their clasped hands. (Technically, she gripped his thumb, not his hand.) "They appear to be stalemated... but that is quite impressive given how small this child is."

Mindfreeze appeared. "Are you guys read—what the heck is going on?"

Grunting, Kelly twisted at the hip, putting her whole body into it. Gradually, she pushed Igor's arm to the left about halfway down to the table.

"Unbelievable," whispered Phoenix.

"It is... angle." Igor emitted a loud groan of exertion.

"All right, all right. Both of you stop before your heads explode." Mindfreeze approached, waving in a shooing gesture. "Your faces are as red as her hair."

"Someone is going to go through several walls if they don't stop at the same time," said Phoenix. "Three... two... one... stop."

Kelly relaxed, as did Igor.

"Impressive. Though, I do not think we can call this comparison fair until you are grown up." Igor flapped his hand out to ease a cramp.

"I'm interested in this most bogus claim of her being faster than me," said Roy. "Footrace?"

"Do we have time for this?" asked Mindfreeze. "There's a guy out there dumping mind control slime into the water supply."

"It's Roy. We can spare the second and a half a footrace will take," said Phoenix.

"All right then. Main hall." Ray walked out at normal speed.

Kelly followed him down the hall away from the lab, across another room, and out to a long, straight corridor that led from the main entrance to a big chamber at the back end of the building that she wanted to call a throne room. Then again, every superhero base had one of those. A giant desk with chairs for each hero ran along the opposite wall under a big shield symbol with the word Aegis on it.

"Let's not be stupid and run toward the door." Ray approached the big, impressive desk and faced back down the corridor.

Kelly stood beside him.

Mindfreeze shook her head. "You are wasting time."

"Yes, but only one-fortieth of a second," said Roy.

"Three..." said Phoenix.

Ray smiled. "Make that three and one-fortieth of a second."

"Two... one... go!" Phoenix made a flag-drop gesture.

Kelly concentrated on accelerating herself as much as she could—the same way that made time appear to stop—and ran hard. Ray Montez sprinted along beside her, seeming pretty much exactly as fast as a normal man running at normal speed. He did, however, pull ahead of her. She stared at him, trying to run faster, but no matter how hard she pushed, he still crept gradually away—until he disappeared entirely.

Before she could wonder what happened to him, she crashed into a sheet of aluminum foil, punching a hole and skidding to a stop outside, kicking up a big cloud of dust. She peered back and cringed at a small child-shaped hole in the two-inch thick armored doors of the Citadel.

"Oops!"

Ray poked his head out to look at her. "Wow, kid. I hate to say this, but I think you actually might really be faster than me... somehow."

"But..." She hurried over to him. "You won."

"Legspan, kiddo." Ray grinned. "You've got teeny little legs. If we were the same height, you would've been the one pulling ahead of me by a little bit."

She looked down at herself. "Oh. Really?"

"I think so. But I don't understand it."

The doors opened.

"Don't understand what?" asked Mindfreeze as she and Phoenix walked outside.

Phoenix picked at the hole. "Like paper…"

"I don't understand how this kid can be so small yet she's at least as strong as Igor, probably faster than me—relatively speaking—and she can fly. All I got is being fast. All Igor has is being strong."

Igor trotted outside, having changed into his red costume. "I am not all strength. I am tough and I can do that shouting thing."

"Still. The kid's got multiple powers as good or better than people with one or two." Ray rested his hands on his hips. "How's that work?"

"I was about twenty yards away from a really big crystal when it landed. My friend Paige and I were talking, and we think being that close to the crystal might have given me a lot of power. Dad called me a Tier One hero."

"There's tiers?" asked Roy.

"Didn't you read comics?" Mindfreeze laughed. "It's a fictional thing. Tier One heroes are incredibly powerful. Only three things in that setting are more potent: Tier Zero entities, which are usually not people, then you have demigods and gods. Of course, there is still a considerable amount of power variation even within Tier One heroes."

Kelly held her chin up. "I'm Übergirl. And now that you know I'm for real, can we *please* go stop my dad from being a butthead?"

The heroes looked at each other for a long minute. Mindfreeze seemed worried. Roy's expression gave off disbelief. Igor had a 'sure why not' face.

Phoenix squatted and grasped Kelly by the shoulders. "We know you are 'for real.' The problem is that you're nine. You're a little girl. If something went wrong, we'd never forgive ourselves. You are too young to be worrying about stopping criminals. Even if it is your father. And, that's another reason you should stay out of it. No one can be asked to fight their parents or brothers or sisters."

"Or grandmothers." Igor raised a finger, then shuddered.

"Somethin' you wanna tell us?" Ray glanced up at him.

"Not now. The story is long." Igor clasped his hands in front of himself.

"But… But…" Kelly bounced on her toes. "It's my dad."

Mindfreeze brushed a hand over her hair. "You have been feeling guilty and sad for days over this. Don't do this to yourself, child. It isn't your responsibility to do anything about your father. What if you hesitate because you love your dad, and right when you let your guard down, he does something bad to someone? You should go home and let us handle this. Please."

Kelly stared down. The woman *did* have a point. She had been sick with guilt over the idea of confronting him. And she probably would be vulnerable

204 | MY DAD IS A MAD SCIENTIST

to Dad exploiting her love for him in a weak moment, just like Mr. Everything and his brother. Depending on how much of her actual father remained compared to how much Brain Trust had taken over, he might actually do something mean to her once he found out she'd gone hero. Even more so for getting in his way instead of just being heroic in general.

"All right. Please don't hurt him." She peered up at him with a pleading expression. "He's my dad and I only have one."

"Hurting people is never what we try to do." Phoenix stood. "We will do everything we can to protect the city from his plan as peacefully as possible."

"Thank you." Kelly sighed, and jumped into the air.

She flew toward home, wondering if she chickened out yet again. Asking the other heroes to stop Dad could be the smart thing to do or the coward's way out depending on how she looked at it. True, at nine, she didn't really belong running around dealing with criminals. But a few superheroes in the *Galaxy Enders* were little kids, too. And they always got involved, especially a six-year-old named Conscience. That girl had a ridiculous amount of psychic power, but to be fair, she didn't *personally* go out with the rest of the heroes. She sent psychic projections of herself which only burst into energy if they took too much damage, and that didn't really hurt her.

Once Kelly arrived home, she flew in her bedroom window, ZOOM-ed back to her normal clothes, and sat at her desk after kicking her flip-flops off. It frustrated her to be treated like a little kid and sent home, but she did have schoolwork to finish. She saved the math for last since she liked it the most and it felt like the homework version of dessert.

Not quite an hour later, Kelly finished the last problem she'd been assigned... and decided to read the next chapter in the textbook for the fun of it.

Dad's laughter echoed downstairs.

"What the...?"

She jumped out of her chair and ran to the stairs at the end of the hall, creeping down a few steps so she could peer through the railing bars at the living room television. News showed a live-action shot of an outdoor location. A big purple energy dome covered an area where several huge pipes connected to a pumping station. The field emanated from a large antenna at the middle of a shiny metal octagonal platform that did *not* look like it belonged there. Bob and Zorthax lugged huge barrels of glowing yellow gunk, lining them up in preparation to pour into a hole they'd cut in one of the water pipes.

Dad stood at the center of it all, fists on his hips, head back, laughing.

The Aegis heroes all attacked the force field, but evidently couldn't dent it. Phoenix hovered in the air above it, throwing bright orange firebeams down on top of it. Mindfreeze alternated between projecting narrow rays of blue-white light, which bounced off the shield, and staring intently at the henchmen… but that didn't do anything either.

Igor the Red, predictably, resorted to punching the shield again and again. Bullet Man appeared every so often at random spots outside, running in circles around the shield. What, exactly, he tried to do, she couldn't tell.

"People of San Francisco," said Dad in a deeper-than-normal voice. "The Brain Trust has decided that it is time to go public. Soon, I will be taking control of this city. For the short term, this should not mean any significant changes to your daily lives. However, anyone caught driving ten or more below the speed limit in the left lane will be subject to exile on a small off-world prison colony."

Mom sat on the sofa watching, her face in her hands, shaking her head the same way she did whenever Dad attempted dumb things like fixing the sink himself, or rewiring the circuit breaker without calling a real electrician, or repairing the roof without calling a contractor. She probably expected this to end with Dad in the Emergency Room as usual.

Gee, Dad. So much for you not wanting to go public or anything. Kelly cringed. Maybe that part she could take credit for. If she hadn't told the Aegis about him, they wouldn't have been assaulting his force field and he might have been able to poison the water without anyone noticing. Since he'd been caught, and ended up on television, he apparently decided to run with it.

However, it didn't look as if the Aegis would be *able* to stop him.

Bullet Man appeared by a doorway at one side of the force field, and proceeded to fiddle with a control panel. The hand scanner there looked identical to the one on the shed.

Kelly narrowed her eyes. *I have to stop Dad before he does something really bad.*

Mom picked up her phone, answering an incoming call. "Yeah, Nan. That's really him. Idiot."

Her mother always talked to her friend Nancy Westcott whenever something bad happened. She called the woman whenever good stuff happened, too. The two had been close since high school, the only one of Mom's friends who still lived in the area. That phone call should keep Mom occupied for at least an hour.

Kelly crept back up the stairs, ran to her room, and dove out the window. She hit the gem on the ZOOM bracelet to change into her super costume, then poured on speed, flying as fast as she could.

Guilt bubbled in her stomach. Her father gave her this awesome costume. He'd made the ZOOM bracelet, restored *Star Prince #17*, and even created a returning Frisbee. Okay, the Frisbee might have been like saying 'you'll never have any friends,' but he'd still invented it because he loved her. And here she flew off to break his heart. Stopping his plan felt as bad as if he'd spent weeks building a model railroad and she came over and smashed it once he finished.

Of course, model railroads didn't hurt anyone. They also didn't mind control entire towns—only the person operating the train.

She never understood how watching something go around and around in circles endlessly could be entertaining. Probably also why she fell asleep whenever Grandpa Becker put car racing on television.

I can't keep chickening out. It's time to be honest. Time to tell Dad the truth. I'm a hero. And I can't let him hurt people.

It took her only a few minutes to reach the pipe junction south of San Francisco near the lake. From the air, it became quite obvious that the Aegis hadn't been able to breach the shield. Three news helicopters orbited the area, trying to get as close as they could. Bullet Man lay unconscious a short distance from the door, smoke peeling off his body. He didn't appear dead, more likely stunned. One of the large, boxy machines inside the dome had opened in half, revealing a big gun on a post, covered in blinking lights and squiggly tubes. It swiveled and fired a pink laser beam at Mindfreeze, but she teleported away. Still, she landed on her side, holding her arm, screaming in pain.

Even teleportation couldn't outrun the speed of light.

Without even getting up, Mindfreeze teleported again before the turret could rotate after her, this time appearing in a spot with a big rock between her and the dome.

Dad! No!

Kelly dove out of the air, swinging her feet down to land by the metal arch that created a doorway in the side of the force field dome. She placed her hand on the palm-reader. A bright purple line ran down the silvery material, then a happy chirp came from the door—a section of force field—which opened by fading away.

Her father spun at the chirp, eyes wide with fear and bulging with anger. However, upon seeing *her*, he relaxed. "Ke—Ginger Snap! What are you doing here?"

A constant *thud, thud, thud* came from Igor the Red's fists hammering away at the dome.

"Grr." She stormed in, her eyes watering at the tremendously lemony scent in the air. "Ugh. Dad. Lemons?"

Phoenix raced down, trying to make it to the entrance... but the arch-shaped hole in the force field shut a half-second before he reached it. He slapped into the dome, sticking to it like a bug on a windshield... and frowned.

Dad gestured at the big drums of MICE, all glowing nuclear yellow. "I decided to add flavor. Who says mind control can't be yummy?"

"But Dad..."

"Tastes like drinking lemon meringue pie." He gripped the lapels of his lab coat, quite proud of himself.

"So, what are you doing?" She walked up to him, looking around.

Bob and Zorthax lugged a drum of MICE up a temporary metal stairway to the side of the water pipe.

"The plan is in motion. Soon, we will finish adding 2,000 gallons of my serum into the public water supply for San Francisco. I calculate that approximately fifty-five to sixty-five percent of the population will become susceptible to my CAT device within two weeks, thus allowing me to control whomever I want."

"Why?" asked Kelly.

"Why not?" Dad shrugged. "Seemed useful."

She looked up at Bob and Zorthax dumping the MICE into the water. A dozen or more empty drums already lay on the ground by the pipes. "You've already started... all those empties."

"Ahh yes. We are littering, too." Dad poked his mega-tablet, which played the thunderclap sound while he laughed maniacally. "I am a supervillain after all."

"Dad, there's something I need to confess to you."

He ceased mastermind-laughing, turned off the sound effect, and peered at her, a concerned expression on his face. "Did something happen to *Star Prince #17*?"

"No. Worse."

He raised an eyebrow. "Were you playing with matches?"

"No. Nothing that bad."

"You like Jaden Nieber's music?"

Kelly huffed. "Eek, Dad. No."

"What is wrong with the boy's music? I listen to it sometimes," said Igor the Red.

The other three Aegis members stopped in place, staring at him in horror. Even the laser turret paused firing at them to gawk at Igor.

"Hmm." Her father alternatingly raised his eyebrows, in deep thought. "You defied your mother and dug a pool in the backyard?"

She blinked. "No, Dad. You put a pool in the lair, remember?"

"Yes, but that's in the lair, not the backyard. Hmm. Let me see. You got a B on a math test?"

"No!" Kelly stomped. "Dad. Don't be ridiculous. I'm really, really, sorry."

He tilted his head. "I'm not sure I'm follow—"

She leapt into a flying punch that smashed the turret before curving around to dive bomb the force-field emitter, destroying it in a shower of flying pink crystal bits, glass, smoke, and lightning bolts that hit Bob and Zorthax, making them yell in surprise. The constant *thud, thud, thud* of Igor the Red punching the dome fell silent. As she steered back toward her father, she kicked the portable stairwell out from under the henchmen, launching it roughly a quarter-mile off into the lake. The two big guys fell straight down, the half-full drum of MICE landing on their backs.

Zorthax let out an *oof.*

Dad gasped. "Kelly Donovan, what are you doing!?"

Phoenix, Igor the Red, Mindfreeze, and Bullet Man closed in, surrounding them.

She landed in front of her father, chin high. "I'm not Ginger Snap, Dad. I'm Übergirl. I'm a good guy. I can't let you poison millions of people. I love you *so* much, but you're not yourself right now. I want my daddy back, not some Brain Trust."

"Aww," said Bob. "She's such a sweet, good little girl."

"She *is* adorable," muttered Zorthax.

"She is being incredibly disobedient and unhelpful." Dad pinched the bridge of his nose, sighing in frustration. "Do you know how long it took me to make the things you broke?"

Kelly looked up at him, trembling from emotion. There. She'd finally done it. Finally told the truth, and had no idea how he'd react. "Dad! You're being evil. I'm not a supervillain. I *can't* be a supervillain. Hurting people is bad. What happened to you? Where's my father?" Tears leaked from her eyes, but she didn't surrender to crying. Any second now, she'd probably throw up.

"What are you doing, Kelly?" whispered Dad.

"Uhh..." Zorthax propped his chin up on his hand. "Making us unemployed I think."

Bob smiled and finger-waved at her.

"I'm protecting the people of San Francisco from being mind-controlled," said Kelly in a tone of voice like she admitted to lighting a forest fire.

"You... you went *hero*?" Dad cringed. "Seriously? We were supposed to be a team."

"Dad, we could still be a team. I'd love to be a team... but I won't hurt people. If something's making you not be able to be a good guy, I will find a way to save you, Daddy."

He sank in on himself, a heartbroken stare at the floor.

Kelly cried. "Daddy, please. Whatever the aliens did to you that turned you bad, please fight it."

"I'm sorry it had to come to this... Übergirl. But everyone has choices to make." Dad started to reach for the mega-tablet.

Bullet Man disappeared and reappeared, grabbing his hand before he could push the button. "Sorry, pops. I'm gonna put the ix-nay on the explosive finale."

"I wasn't going to blow anyone up. Just knock all of you senseless and leave." Dad adjusted his labcoat.

"Oh. Well, in that case." Bullet Man let go of his wrist. "Carry on."

Dad tried to push the button, but Bullet Man's hand reappeared around his wrist again. "Psych. Just kidding."

"I can't believe I fell for that," muttered Dad.

A brief flash of light came from Mindfreeze's eyes.

Dad's eyes also flared with blue light. "What a pretty shade of—" He passed out.

Igor the Red picked Dad up as if carrying a small boy, heading away from the smashed mad-science machinery toward a shuttle waiting a little ways up the pipe. Phoenix and Bullet Man followed him.

Kelly sank to her knees, buried her face in her hands, and cried. "I'm sorry, Dad."

"He'll be fine, hon." Mindfreeze knelt and rubbed her back. "He might even get the help he needs."

She wailed, "Yeah, but I just put my daddy in jail. It's my fault he's gotta go away."

"No, sweetie." Rowena Dominguez—a.k.a. Mindfreeze—pulled Kelly into a hug. "His crimes are the reason he might have to go away for a while. Not you. You protected innocent people at great cost to yourself. That's the sign of a true hero."

"If I did something so good, why do I feel so bad?" She sniffled.

Mindfreeze relaxed the hug to look her in the eye. "Because you've learned the worst part about being a hero. Sometimes, doing the right thing hurts."

Kelly stared into the woman's eyes, pools of blue energy. "You're a psychic hero, right?"

She nodded.

"Did the aliens make him evil or is that really Dad? Can we fix him?"

Mindfreeze looked down. "I'm sorry, but I didn't see a mind in conflict. That man is who he appears to be. Though, I didn't feel any cruelty. He's sort of at the 'nice' end of evil. Maybe it's possible to help him, but it will be a difficult path."

"I understand." Kelly clung, resting her chin on the woman's shoulder. "I'm gonna do everything I can to get my dad back."

CHAPTER THIRTY-TWO

THE WORST DAUGHTER IN THE WORLD

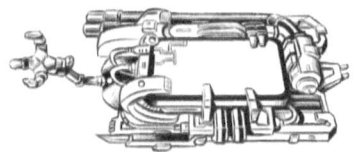

Tears fell from Kelly's eyes the whole flight back home.

The Aegis heroes apologized for dismissing her earlier, admitting that they wouldn't have been able to do anything about that force field without her. But... they still told her to go home, mostly because she needed to be with her mother. They would handle cleaning up and figure out some way to get rid of the serum that had already been added to the water.

She slipped in via her bedroom window, raised her arm, and stared at the ZOOM bracelet. It reminded her of Dad. Kelly stood there crying for several minutes before she summoned the urge to push the button and change back to her shirt and jeans. Her father hadn't been in the house much at all lately, missing several good-nights in a row. But he somehow felt *more* absent now.

Her head filled with memories of spending time with him, doing everything from playing video games to board games to going for walks or on trips to museums. Whenever they did something together, he stopped complaining about his miserable job or the other people there. No matter how upset he'd been about his life, she had always cheered him up. Even seeing him standing by the hole in the yard when he'd first started construction of the lair felt like a good, fun memory.

Head hung, Kelly trudged down the hall to the stairs.

Mom reclined on the sofa, still on the phone with Nancy talking about a trip to a technology center, and hoped it would be as fun as the jewelry store. When Kelly walked up to the sofa, her mother looked over, blinked, then whispered, "I need to go, Nance, kid issues."

"Talk later," said Nancy.

"Mom?" Kelly crawled up onto the couch, grabbed her, and burst into tears.

"Aww, sweetie. What's wrong?" Her mother held her, rocking her, kissing her on the head, patting her back. "Why are you crying? Did you and Paige have a fight?"

"No," said Kelly past tears. "It's Dad."

"Oh… you saw that story on the news, huh?"

She curled up, shaking with guilt. "Yeah. But… it's worse. It's my fault!"

"What do you mean?"

Despite frequent interruptions when crying kept her from speaking for a minute or so, Kelly explained to her mother about how Dad went supervillain, wanted to mind-control everyone in the city, kidnapped like thirty people, and… that she'd been too much of a do-gooder. "I couldn't do it. He wanted me to be his evil sidekick, Ginger Snap, but I don't like being the bad guys. Even in video games. He was gonna hurt people for real! I'm the one who told on him, but the Aegis couldn't get past his force field."

Mom brushed a hand across Kelly's hair as if petting a cat. "Yes, your father's gotten rather good at making things, hasn't he? Filled the house with robots. His creations are top of the line. Impressive if he could hold off the entire Aegis."

"He had a big laser, and he shot Mindfreeze and Bullet Man. Mom, he was going to hurt them. I had to."

"Had to what?"

She explained going there herself to help the Aegis stop Dad from poisoning the city. "I'm sorry. I know you said to support Dad. I love him, but what he did was wrong."

Her mother paused stroking her hair, appearing confused for a moment before smiling and resuming the soothing gesture. "Don't worry, hon. Everything will be fine. He's still your father no matter what he does."

"I'm so sick right now." She held her stomach.

"That's guilt, sweetie."

Kelly sniffled. "Yeah. But I felt guilty watching him hurt people and not doing anything."

"He is still your father, and you're too young to disobey him like that. Maybe you shouldn't have done anything at all. Merely stayed out of it."

"I dunno. He's my dad and I love him, but it's wrong to steal people's minds. I want Dad back, not The Brain Trust." Remembering Mindfreeze saying Dad had become The Brain Trust—not a victim of a forced character script—set off another wave of hard sobbing.

"We'll be okay, sweetie. Supervillain or not, he still gets a trial and I'm sure they will let him go."

Kelly stopped crying in an instant and sat up, blinking. "What? Let him go? Really? Why?"

"Because, sweetie." Mom patted her cheek. "Your father has an incredible amount of money. People with as much money as we have never actually go to jail for anything. Besides, the supervillains always get out of jail in time for the next issue to come out, right?"

She sighed. "This isn't a comic book... it feels like one, but it isn't. Real life got weird."

"That it did, sweetie. Don't worry. Even if there isn't some mysterious force going on deciding who's a villain and who's a hero, your father will either hire a lawyer who'll get him out in days or he'll make a helicopter out of a roll of toilet paper and two bed sheets."

Mom's joke didn't make her laugh, or even smile... but it did close the tear faucet. It happened to be funny because Kelly suspected her father actually *could* make something useful out of items like that.

They sat together for a while before her mother got up to start on dinner. Too sad and guilty to have interest in anything other than curling up on the sofa feeling like the worst daughter in the whole world, Kelly stayed put.

Eventually, Mom patted her on the shoulder. "C'mon dear. Dinner's ready."

"Dad's not gonna eat with us."

"He hasn't been eating dinner with us for a few days. If it helps, you can just pretend he's working in the lair."

"I'm not hungry."

"You need to eat."

"I'm too sad."

"You're nine. A growing girl needs nutrition."

Kelly wrapped herself around the throw pillow even tighter. "I'm too guilty."

"Do you think your father would want you to stop eating and hurt yourself? Get up off the couch and get your tail to the kitchen."

"Okay, Mom." Kelly sluggishly got to her feet and plodded after her mother into the kitchen, sitting in her usual chair.

Mom went to the counter to scoop food from pots, then took her seat, setting two plates of ravioli on the table, smothered in sauce. She dug right in.

Kelly sighed. She stabbed one of the pillows with her fork, and nibbled at the edge. The sauce had an astounding amount of garlic, but eventually, her love of cheese won her over. She ate the remainder of the pillow whole. It had a slightly odd flavor, but she'd also never had ravioli with *that* much garlic in the sauce. A second ravioli tasted even weirder. When she bit a hunk out of the third one, she noticed small green flecks in the ricotta.

What the heck is that?

She poked her finger into the cheese, and plucked out a tiny bit of broccoli. Shocked, she whirled to stare at Mom who kept her gaze down on her plate, a faint smile on her lips.

"Mom?" rasped Kelly... right as her throat began to burn. "You... put... brocco—" She gagged.

Her mother kept daintily eating, not looking up at her. Still smiling.

"Wh—"

Her voice shrank to a wheeze, then nothing as her throat swelled closed. Eyes watering, Kelly grabbed her neck, struggling to breathe. She collapsed to the floor, the room going blurry, her arms and legs no longer wanting to move. Her mouth, nose, and throat burned like she'd swallowed acid, a hot burning spike in her belly.

Mom set her fork down, stood, and stooped to pick Kelly up. "I'm sorry it had to come to this, sweetie. Your father and I both hoped you would understand. We're a *villain* family. You've been such a good girl, I'm afraid I have to punish you."

In the last second, before her vision went black, Kelly managed to look up and see her mother flashing a wicked smile.

No! Not Mom, too!

CHAPTER THIRTY-THREE

MURDERIZED

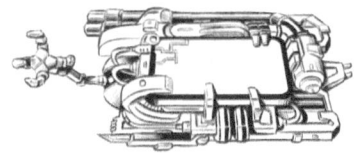

K elly found herself floating in darkness, a faint mechanical whirring coming from everywhere.

She tried to look around in search of what made the noise, but couldn't see. The only sound she'd ever heard even close to it had been at the dentist's office while the hygienist cleaned her teeth. The sudden fear she'd fallen asleep in a dental chair and dreamed the entire superhero thing shocked her awake. The sight of blue sky and trees stunned her. No dentist office ceiling, not even her bedroom.

Outside.

Her everything ached.

Dull pain filled every inch of her body down to her toes. A spiked ball of ouch had inflated inside her stomach, prickles so sharp she expected to see actual needles sticking out from inside her. When she tried to sit up and look, tightness pressed into her throat. She tried to grab her neck but couldn't move her arms. Snug metal bands holding each wrist kept them pinned at her sides. Additional metal bands gripped her ankles tight as well.

Waking up completely immobilized freaked her out enough that she screamed and struggled for a few seconds, though the cuffs holding her down didn't give an inch. Once the initial panic wore off, she realized the constant noise came from above and to either side. Two spinning saw blades as big as dinner plates attached to the ends of thin robotic arms hovered a few feet away, aimed at her face.

"Eep!" Kelly instinctively tried to jump away from them, but didn't go anywhere.

She lifted her head, grimacing at the pressure from the band around her neck squeezing. Her body lay flat upon a metal table big enough for an adult, arms beside her, legs close but not touching. A third robotic arm sprouted from the foot end of the table, supporting a laser projector that presently fired a constant bright-purple beam onto the table at the edge. A specifically *purple* laser meant one of two things: either Mom did that to be ironic since Kelly loved purple or Dad made this machine and chose purple because she liked it, never expecting she'd be the first person on it. There appeared to be enough room between her legs for the laser to creep closer without touching her—right up until it started cutting her in half in the most painfully imaginable way possible.

Growling and gasping, she struggled to break loose, but the vegetables had left her weak and listless. Whoever put her there could likely have tied her to the table with paper strips and she wouldn't have been able to get up at the moment. Well, not so much 'whoever.' Kelly had a pretty good idea who strapped her to the Murdermaster-3000: Mom.

She squirmed to get a better look at her situation. An inch-thick metal band circled her wrist, perfectly form-fitting and so tight she couldn't even rotate her arm. Mom hadn't taken the ZOOM bracelet, though it only allowed her to change outfits, so her mother likely didn't consider it an issue. Dad's super fabric would only be strong enough to resist damage if worn by a super with some sort of damage resistance power. Good chance her mother also knew her super costume wouldn't stop the laser *or* the saws if worn by an ordinary kid. And, with green vegetables in her system effectively turning her powers off, she counted as normal at the moment. No reason for Mom to take her bracelet away.

The mere thought of trying to break free set off a killer headache and cold sweat. Still, everything hurt. Kelly felt as miserable as if she had a bad flu and had fallen down ten flights of stairs. Even if she didn't have broccoli causing her throat to swell, the too-tight collar would have made it difficult to breathe. She had to guess at the metal's shininess since she couldn't see it.

A cough barked out of her with the flavor of Brussels sprouts—quite an unpleasant sensation due to having a steel ring around her neck. She gagged again at the horrible taste. Her body getting ready to vomit while she lay pinned down like a frog in biology class changed the urge to hurl from repulsive to terrifying.

"Ngh!" She squirmed, fighting the restraints as hard as she could. Alas, she had only the strength of an ordinary scrawny kid whose greatest athletic achievement thus far in life had been riding a garbage can down a hill.

Fighting made her feel even sicker, so she gave up and lay still, staring up at the sky while wallowing in pure misery. A little while later, she let out a thunderous burp that shook the nearby trees and left a cloud of green smoke in the air. She gagged on the flavor of Brussels sprouts.

A black-clad figure walked up to the base of the table. Kelly ignored them until long fingernails shot lightning bolts of squirm up her leg by tickling the bottoms of her feet.

"Stop!" Kelly squealed, screamed, and writhed, curling her toes and twisting her foot. "Please! Gah! Stop! I'm ticklish!"

"Why else do you think I'm tickling you when you can't move?" asked Mom, continuing to attack her defenseless soles for another minute or two.

Eventually, Mom laughed, stopped tickling her, and walked up to stand beside her. She wore a one-piece bodysuit, mostly black trimmed in sleek purple highlights. She, too, had a partial mask like the Übergirl costume that only covered the eyes, only hers resembled something rich people might wear at the opera, frilly and lacy. Her silver belt buckle had a large E engraved at its center.

Kelly lifted her head, gurgling at the collar pressing into her neck, and stared down her body, past her feet, at the laser. "Mom, what are you doing? Did you seriously lock me up in a deathtrap? Did Dad make this? That laser isn't gonna hurt me."

"Normally, no. I'm quite sure you'd laugh at a simple cutting laser." Mom tucked Floppet into the space between her body and left arm, then patted the plush on the head. "There. Your favorite little friend is with you for the last time you'll ever go to sleep."

Kelly looked up at her mother, horrified. Silent tears rolled out of her eyes.

"After you blacked out from the broccoli-laced ravioli, I fed you a syringe of pureed Brussels sprouts. It rather reminded me of when we had to give Mitsy her medicine. Fitting, the poor dog died soon after that. Anyway, the concentrated green vegetables should shut down your powers long enough for the laser to do its job." Her mother moved one finger in a line above Kelly's body suggesting the beam would cut her in half straight down the middle.

Oh, no. Mom reads the dark comics. "Umm. Mommy? Can we maybe not do this? My tummy hurts. I don't feel good enough to die in an elaborate deathtrap right now."

"Why aren't you hugging your favorite little rabbit?" Mom fake-gasped. "Oh, that's right, I've immobilized you with carbon-steel restraints. How unfortunate. Comfy at least?"

Kelly tugged at her arms, having about as much success as an ordinary nine-year-old at breaking them. Moving at all reminded her how sore and sick the vegetables had left her. She felt so weak she could barely lift her fingers. "Neck one's a little tight, but the other four are okay."

"Not pinching?"

"No." She limply flapped her hands. "It's kinda comfortable for a death trap, really. Still, please let me out."

"Sweetie, you know I don't like having to discipline you, but I'm afraid you've been a very, very good girl. And I can't let such good behavior like that go unpunished. You are grounded for two weeks." Mom tapped a finger to her palm while reciting, "No video games, books, or comics…"

"Aww, but Mom!" whined Kelly, squirming.

"Oh, and to make it clear how disappointed we are with your shockingly good behavior, I'm afraid I have to put you in a pointlessly elaborate and belabored deathtrap that you will no doubt wind up escaping from before it can actually hurt you. Goodnight, sweetie."

Kelly struggled at the bands holding her down, genuinely terrified that this contraption might actually be dangerous to her with the weakness in her system. "Mommy! Please don't do this. Please! You're not really a villain. I know you still love me."

Her mother stared down at her with almost guilty eyes.

"Mom. Please don't cut me in half with a laser." She strained harder, pulling at her arms and legs. The restraint bands kept her so immobile it went beyond frustrating. "I'll try to be bad from now on. Ground me for a whole month instead, just don't do this?"

Her mother turned, but didn't walk away. She took one step and hesitated again.

"C'mon. Pleeeease? Mom?"

Her mother returned, adjusted Floppet a little, and kissed her on the head. "You should have thought about what you were going to do before you behaved so well. I'm afraid it would only make me seem like a weak parent if I changed my mind now and didn't follow through with nearly killing you."

Something in her mother's eyes said part of her deep inside didn't want to do it… but the woman still walked away, leaving her strapped to the Murdermaster-3000 in the middle of the forest… probably so far away from civilization that no one would hear her screaming.

"Mom? Please don't leave me here. Please come back," yelled Kelly.

She kept begging until her mother had walked off too far to see. If she lifted her head trying to look for her, the collar pressing into her throat made it difficult to yell. Her stomach knotted up again, body shivering with fever chills caused by the evil green vegetables. Muscle cramps punched her in the legs and chest. Her stomach felt like she'd swallowed a beach ball covered in knives. Kelly spent a few minutes struggling, but couldn't move even a half inch.

The saw blades crept downward. One would probably hit her right in the face while the other aimed at her heart. It certainly seemed excessive to have saws *and* a laser. However, considering the laser would start cutting her in half from below, it would be a kindness if the saws won the race.

Sickness came in waves, fading for a moment then surging into misery and blurry periods of being so dizzy time seemed to vanish. After snapping out of one such fog, she noticed her feet had become rather warm. She lifted her head again, gawking in horror at the bright purple laser beam etching the table surface between her heels. Her mother had left *just* enough space between her legs that the cutting laser wouldn't light her jeans on fire before it advanced far enough to begin slicing her open.

"Ngh!" Kelly looked at her left arm and tried to press the ZOOM bracelet into the table to activate the purple gem, but the shackle fit her too well... almost as if it had been made specifically for her.

She blinked. *They knew. They both had to know I was a hero. Dad must've made this just in case. Wait... no. The table's way too big for me. It's gotta be like the costume, auto-adjusts for the size of the victim.* She sighed at the robotic arm holding the laser. *Mom doesn't really want to kill me, or she'd have done it right away.* That thought allowed her to start calming down. If her mother really did want to kill her, she could've done anything at all to her while she'd been passed out. Mom could've stabbed her with a knife, but what had she done? Force-fed her Brussel sprout goo from a blender. Disgusting, but not deadly. She could easily have done far worse.

"Yeah. Mom wants me to escape. She's a villain, but she still loves me."

Kelly lay still—not that she had a lot of choice—for a while, shivering from the veggie sickness, staring up at the barely-visible shape of a Nolmek mothership far above the clouds. Over almost an hour, she tried screaming randomly for help, but only succeeded in scaring a few birds out of a nearby tree. The laser crept past her ankles, reaching her calves. It didn't look like the saw blades would win the race.

The veggie sickness made her so miserable, achy, sweaty, and sick to her stomach, the idea of being murderized by this machine almost seemed like an escape rather than a bad thing. But, she wouldn't let it win. What, exactly, Mom wanted to do here, she didn't know, but killing her didn't appear to be the actual goal. As long as she remained sick and powerless, she would die. Could the dose of vegetables Mom gave her keep her sick long enough for the machine to work, or would they wear off before the laser could get her? That didn't seem right. Mom wouldn't have made it *that* easy. Kelly had to do *something* to escape. If she just waited, she wouldn't survive.

She had to make the veggies wear off faster. Had to get them out somehow.

Kelly turned her head to the right—to spare Floppet—and started thinking about the most disgusting things she could. Eating boogers. Booger-speckled ice cream sundae. Eating *someone else's* boogers. Liver and onions... with strawberries. Falling off a skateboard into dog poo—while wearing a bikini. The horror the school cafeteria called cheese steak.

Her stomach gurgled, but still, didn't quite erupt. She tried to think of something even more gross.

Kissing Jaden Nieber.

Her stomach clenched and churned. She shuddered, then projectile vomited a blast of green mess. The first breath after it stopped smelled like cat pee and dead stuff, which set off another spew. Being immobilized on her back while throwing up far exceeded the awfulness of anything else she'd ever experienced. She choked on the dreadful slime, nearly re-swallowing some barf due to being stuck on her back before sheer disgust made her spit it out and cough up a few more mouthfuls.

Out of breath, she stared straight up. A dribble of pureed Brussels sprout ran down her cheek. No matter how much she wanted to, she couldn't reach up and wipe it.

"That was the most disgusting, horrible, nasty, evil thing ever." She coughed. "I think I'd rather kiss Jaden Nieber."

She rolled her head to the side and threw up a little more.

"Bleh!'

When her body stopped convulsing from the after-puking shakes, she gasped for air and spat a few times, trying to get the taste out of her mouth.

"Okay... I got rid of the bad stuff. Please let my powers come back before the laser hits me."

Every few minutes, Kelly struggled at the bands. The sun crawled across the sky with each passing hour, moving almost as fast as the laser and saws. She alternated between freezing and overheating so bad she wanted to pass out. The laser advanced ever upward, creating a hot spot on her legs that climbed along with it. A breeze from the saw blade became noticeable at her cheek.

Still, she had no more strength than an ordinary child and couldn't break the metal restraints. Heat from the laser grew more intense at her backside, like she sat on a hot metal chair in the middle of August.

Kelly squirmed, gasping, lifting her butt an inch or two off the table to buy even a moment more time before the laser started slicing her in half. The deadly beam had come far too close for comfort. Her hands turned red from how hard she pulled at the restraining bands.

The spot the purple laser burned into the steel slipped under her, warming her backside and making her jeans smoke. If Kelly relaxed and lowered her rear end back to the table, the laser would cut her. The saw blade on the right started to tickle at her cheek. She tilted her head away.

It appeared the vegetables hadn't worn off in time. Any second now, she'd experience the worst pain of her life. She tried to push her middle even higher, but the metal around her ankles and throat wouldn't let her move any farther.

"Help!" shouted Kelly, inches from total panic. "Mooooooooom!"

CHAPTER THIRTY-FOUR

ÜBER-ORPHAN

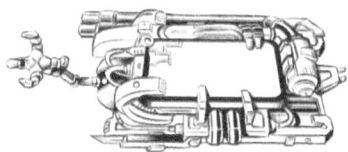

The seat of her pants increased from uncomfortably warm to painful.

"Ooh. Ooh. Hot! Hot!" She struggled to lift her butt even more to escape the purple death ray.

The stink of burning denim reached Kelly's nose. Overcome by panic, she strained even harder despite the collar nearly choking her. If she didn't do something *right this second*, she would die.

With a loud *snap*, the metal band securing her right ankle broke off the table. Kelly put her foot on the laser, then shoved it away to the side with all the strength she could force past the vegetable poison. The robotic arm snapped, falling with the laser out of sight to the ground, the beam slicing several branches off a nearby tree on the way. She swung her leg up high, knee touching her shoulder, and kicked the sawblade arm nipping at her cheek hard enough to destroy it, launching the spinning blade off into the woods. The second rotary saw had come within a half inch of her chest. Grunting, Kelly drew her leg back and stomped at the spindly robotic arm, smashing it off to the left. That saw cruised into the woods like a UFO and stuck several inches deep in a tree.

Free from immediate danger, she let her leg fall flat, her fat steel anklet clanking against the table. Kelly struggled at the other restraints, but they refused to break. Another wave of chills came on along with the mother of all stomach aches, leaving her shaking and too weak to do anything more than lay there breathing hard.

Coming that close to death evidently allowed her powers to return for a moment, but she still had veggies in her system. Since the machine could no longer hurt her, and simply provided the extremely frustrating annoyance of keeping her unable to move, she lost the will to fight... at least for a while. However, with her right leg loose, she could at least take care of her itchy nose with her knee.

For about an hour, she went from shivering to overheating to shivering, again and again, all the while as sore as if Igor the Red had punched her repeatedly in the stomach. Whoever invented vegetables needed a serious time out.

Eventually, the cold sweats and shaking stopped. She made a fist and pulled at her right arm. The cuff around her wrist bent like a fat piece of spaghetti, breaking open without much effort. Her left leg came free, also with the metal ring popping off the table. Kelly broke her left arm out, then reached up with both hands to rip the collar off her neck. After sitting up, she snapped the anklets off and tossed them aside.

She sat cross-legged atop the Murdermaster-3000, cuddling Floppet and feeling horrible. Her own mother had tried to kill her. Worse, Mom had gone supervillain, too. What the heck would Kelly do now? *Both* her parents went evil. If she returned home, would her mother try to hurt her again? Did she still even live there? Did she count as an orphan?

Overwhelming sadness lifted eventually. Kelly wiped her tears and slid off the deadly machine. Out of spite, she kicked it into a pile of unrecognizable spare parts. Despite being barefoot, the steel didn't hurt her toes. No one would ever use that particular deathtrap again. At least not to kill anyone. Maybe as a paperweight or desk curiosity.

Her stomach rumbled, pressure building. The last time she'd felt like that, she'd literally destroyed a toilet—but it had only been gas. Not wanting to blow her jeans apart into tiny scraps, she hurried over into the trees for some privacy.

The resulting gaseous side-effect of Übergirl consuming green vegetables blasted all the pine needles off the nearest tree behind her with a *bang* like a naval cannon. Two highly surprised squirrels stared at her from the bare branches. One dropped its acorn, mouth agape.

As mortifying as that had been, after letting the veggie fumes out, she felt awesome. Back to normal. Full power. Fortunately, no one saw that. People might have *heard* it, but they'd probably assume something exploded.

Time to go home... or go somewhere.

If people saw her flying without her costume, her secret identity could be in danger. She hiked her pants up and hit the purple gem on the ZOOM bracelet, half expecting to end up in her birthday suit… but the costume appeared. Her mother hadn't stolen it while she'd been unconscious. Since Dad made it for her, the clingy fabric kinda felt like he hugged her. She could do without the GS on her belt, however.

Clutching Floppet tight, she flew straight up for a look around. No sign of Mom, but San Francisco didn't seem to be too far off to the west. She swooped down by a small creek to wash the green nasty off her face and rinse out her mouth.

"Well, Flop… what am I supposed to do now?" She held the stuffed purple rabbit up and stared into its plastic eyes. "Dad's in jail. Mom tried to kill me and ran off somewhere… I'm basically an orphan. Is this what Mindfreeze meant when she said being a hero is sometimes *more* painful than being a bad guy?"

Unsurprisingly, the stuffed rabbit didn't say anything.

"Yeah, you're right. It just means I have work to do." Kelly held her chin high. "I'm Übergirl, and I won't give up! But… I'm too little to be alone."

For a while, she wandered the woods talking to Floppet, worried about being all on her own at nine, and lonely.

"What should I do? The Aegis won't take me because I'm too small. I don't wanna be adopted. New parents could take me far away and I'd never see Paige again." Kelly blinked. "Paige! She said I could stay in her room if I had to run away." She kicked a rock—that probably ended up in orbit. "I didn't run away… but I *do* need a place to stay while I figure out how to fix my parents."

Grinning, she leapt into the air, zooming toward her friend's house.

CHAPTER THIRTY-FIVE

CIVIL RIGHTS ARE A MERE TRIVIALITY

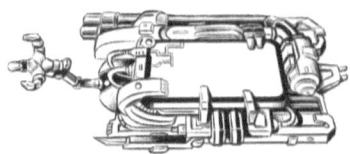

K elly floated up to Paige's bedroom window. Her friend lay on her bed in a sphinx pose, reading. A few finger-taps at the glass got her attention. Paige ran over and opened the window.

"Hey. What's up?" Paige moved aside.

"Umm. A lot." Kelly glided in, landed on her feet, and ZOOMed back to her jeans and T-shirt.

"Whoa. What happened? Did you sit on a stove or something?" asked Paige. "Your pants are burned."

"Eep." Kelly grabbed her butt in both hands. "How bad? Is there a hole?"

"No, it's just black."

"Whew." Kelly slouched, trudged over to the bed and sat on the edge. "Long story."

Paige hopped up, sitting cross-legged nearby. "So spill it."

The whole time Kelly explained about confronting her dad and what her mother did, Paige's mouth hung open.

"I thought she was a norm." Kelly raked her hair off her face. "She tricked me. I didn't figure out *both* my parents went supervillain until she tried to kill me."

"Oh, no…" Paige cringed. "Your mother is dark?"

"No. I don't think so or I really would be dead now. I mean… I guess the whole supervillain thing *forced* her to try and murderize me. She didn't want to. Not really. At least, I thought she looked guilty."

"You're still her daughter."

"But Mindfreeze said Dad isn't being controlled."

"How would she know?" Paige scoffed.

"Umm. She's a psychic. She could see into his head."

"Oh. Sorry."

Kelly squished her toes into the rug. "Can I stay here until my parents stop being evil?"

"Sure. We can tell my parents that your mom and dad went to like Europe or something for a while. I'll say I told them it was okay you stay here without asking permission first and your parents already left. I'll probably get in trouble for it, but I don't care."

Kelly hugged her. "Thanks."

"So how did your mother kidnap you? Aren't you like ridiculous?"

"Ugh. She figured out my weakness. An' when I was helpless, she strapped me onto like the Murdermaster-3000. It was gonna shred me to bits with a laser and saw blades, but I escaped."

Paige pointed at the scorch mark. "Cut that a little close, huh?"

"Yeah."

"I think you should go find your mother and confront her."

Kelly looked up. "Are you serious? After she almost killed me?"

"She didn't *defeat* you. She tricked you."

"Just like the Aegis said they would." Kelly hung her head.

"What?"

Kelly scuffed her feet back and forth over the rug. "They didn't want me helping them deal with Dad because they thought he would use being my father against me. My mom did exactly that."

"Yeah, but now you know they're both villains and she can't trick you again."

"I guess."

"You guess?" Paige jumped up to stand on her bed, waving her arms. "You're Übergirl! Are you gonna take being put in a long, complicated death trap lying down?"

"Technically, I was lying down in the deathtrap."

Paige smirked. "You're seriously not gonna do anything about what they did?"

"Heh. Nah. You're right." Kelly stood and pushed the ZOOM bracelet gem, summoning her costume. "One thing is bothering me though."

"Only one?"

Kelly smirked. "I mean one thing more than anything else. How did *both* my parents turn into supers? It's like really rare that anyone does but somehow all three of us got powers?"

"Hmm. That's a good question. Did another crystal come down in your backyard close to them?"

Kelly thought. "Hmm. Not that I saw. But... I was stuck in a book bag all day. Maybe they'd gone to the school to look for me? Of course! That night when I got home, Mom was still in her work clothes even though it was like ten at night. She and Dad had been driving, but she didn't remember why. They had to have been out looking for me. Maybe even at the school."

"Didn't you say that your parents both acted kinda weird? Maybe they got amnesia or something from the change. *You* blacked out and woke up on the ground, right? If the crystal knocked you out for a few minutes, it probably did worse to them. Or maybe since they weren't right next to it, they didn't even pass out and just went home while you were asleep."

"Maybe." Kelly sighed. "Okay. I'm going to go deal with Mom. Since she only tried to hurt *me*, I'm not gonna turn her in or anything. But if she's really evil, I won't be able to stay home."

Paige nodded. "I will happily suffer being grounded to help you."

"Thanks. This is going to sound super-sappy, but you're all I have left. You're my best friend."

"Aww. And yeah, that did sound sappy." Paige play-punched her in the shoulder. "Ow."

"Sorry."

Paige pushed her toward the window. "Don't apologize. Go confront the evil Doctor Mom."

"Oh, crap!"

"What?"

Kelly whirled and grabbed her friend by the shoulders. "My mother is Alexis Stephens."

"Uhh..." Paige blinked a few times. "Now I *know* you got hit on the head too hard."

"No, dork. Not literally. I mean, when my mother was our age, she was basically Alexis: prettiest, most popular girl in school... and the meanest." Kelly hung her head, sulking. "My whole life is a lie."

"Don't be a drama queen."

Not looking up from the rug, Kelly muttered, "My mother just tried to cut me in half with a laser. I'm allowed a little drama."

"Your mom didn't seem like a mean person at all."

"Not now." Kelly rubbed her stomach when it growled in hunger. "Dad said kids like Alexis usually 'grow out of' acting that way. I guess Mom did."

"Yeah." Paige nodded. "The bullies who never grow out of it either end up in jail or working for insurance companies."

"What?" asked Kelly.

Her friend shrugged. "I dunno. Something my mom said."

"Okay. Gonna go deal with my mom."

"Good luck. I know you'll kick her butt."

"Paige. I'm not going there to kick her butt, just… I dunno. Figure something out."

"I didn't mean kick her butt as in literally."

"Right…" She took a deep breath. "I'll be back."

FLYING HOME FROM PAIGE'S HOUSE TOOK ABOUT SIX SECONDS, SINCE THEY LIVED only a few blocks apart. Almost as soon as she went into the air, it became obvious that a massive amount of police cars had swarmed her home.

"They're investigating Dad. Grr. I can't go home looking normal or they're going to ask about Mom, and if she's not there, the cops will cart me away to like an orphanage or something. But… if I stay as Übergirl, they won't know I live there. Just a hero investigating The Brain Trust."

She swooped in and landed in the front yard.

A few cops glanced at her. She walked in the front door with all the confidence of a superhero. Police officers infested the house like fleas on a long-haired dog, examining everything. They continued to look at her, a few muttering about her being kinda small for a super. None of them bothered her for a while as she looked around the house for her mother.

It didn't surprise her that Mom had gone out somewhere, possibly to the lair, but the cops didn't appear to know about that since only one guy wandered the backyard and didn't appear interested in the tool shed. Maybe it counted as a bad lie, but Kelly didn't want to tell them about Dad's sanctuary. That felt too much like betraying her family even more. Of course, if someone needed help or her father prepared to hurt someone, she would.

Two beefy cops stepped in front of her when she came back downstairs into the living room.

"What are you doing here, kid?" asked the one on the left, Officer Miller according to his nametag.

"Investigating The Brain Trust."

The other cop, Smith, held up a family photo showing her with her parents, from about three months ago. "This looks like you."

"Umm." Kelly fidgeted. Telling little lies to her parents bugged her tons. Telling a not-so-little-lie to a cop went beyond what she could pull off with a straight face. "Yeah. Those are my parents."

Both cops nodded.

"Thought so," said Miller, while taking handcuffs from his belt. "Sorry, kid. You're under arrest for suspicion of supervillainy. Come along quietly."

"But I'm not a villain! I'm Übergirl! I helped the Aegis arrest my own dad."

"We are aware that your mother has taken on the supervillain persona, Emophage. Both parents are registered as super-powered criminals. That makes you a suspect."

"But... But..." She almost yelled that her mother tried to kill her, but if she said that, the cops would charge Mom. "You can't just arrest people because you *think* they might break the law."

Officer Miller placed her in handcuffs. "If your story checks out about helping take down The Brain Trust, the detectives will verify that and it will all be sorted out pretty quick."

"Some of you supers look cute and harmless." Officer Smith patted her cheek. "But you're really villains."

Being arrested embarrassed her even more than ending up in her birthday suit on the football field after the crystal landed. If she had to choose one, she'd much rather have kids from school catch her after a horrible costume malfunction than see her being handcuffed and escorted away by the police. One would get her laughed at. The other would forever make them wonder what she did and never trust her again.

"If you're a hero as you claim, then you won't try to resist," said Officer Smith.

Each of the two huge officers grabbed her by one hand around her biceps and escorted her outside. At least she had so much hair she could hide her face in case the neighbors were watching. When they reached a nice, new police car parked all the way at the end of the cluster of police cars, Officer Miller brought her to the back door while Smith opened the trunk to get something.

She peered up at the cop. A thin, silver device sat on top of his left ear, with a few blinking blue lights on it. It looked somewhat familiar, but she couldn't quite remember where she'd seen one of those before. One of the little boxes on his belt also had blinking lights on it. Maybe the cops got new alien-tech radios with hands-free.

A number of 'supers-trained' officers stood guard outside the house wearing exoskeleton armor that added about a foot to their height: feet on platforms, several nylon straps on their arms and legs holding the metal frame snug. Their actual hands hid inside protective armored cowls while robotic hands held strange—and large—rifles. Something about the look of the exoskeletons made her wonder if Dad made them. He seemed to have a fondness for mirror-shiny steel.

Officer Smith closed the trunk, hiding something behind his back while walking toward her. He, too, had the little thing on his ear. Kelly hung her head in shame. Smith gathered her hair up out of the way and secured a metal collar around her neck. It didn't close as tight as the one on the Murdermaster-3000, but as soon as it touched her, Officer Miller's grip on her right bicep went from barely noticeable to painfully tight.

Oh, crap! It steals powers!

The only thing that had kept her calm up until that moment had been knowing she could've ripped the handcuffs off like a spaghetti noodle and escaped whenever she wanted. If that collar took away her superpowers, she *couldn't* do anything. But… only villains *tried* to escape the police. They would take her to the station, get a detective, and she'd be cleared as not being a villain. The Aegis would definitely set it right.

She climbed into the back seat, cringing when Miller slammed the door, and kept her head down, trembling in dread. Despite not having done anything wrong, anxiety stole her appetite. The veggies Mom hit her with made her beyond sick to her stomach. She'd started to feel hungry at Paige's house… but now, she'd throw up if she even saw food.

Miller got in behind the wheel. Smith dropped into the passenger seat, the car rocking from his weight. The two massive cops could barely fit inside, their shoulders touching each other as well as the car walls. Miller started the engine, then backed away from the crowd of police cars and drove off.

Kelly kept her gaze in her lap, too ashamed to look out the window. Since when did the police carry anti-superpower collars? Why would they *arrest* her for simply being the daughter of a supervillain? That didn't sound at all American. Sure, they might have asked her to go with them because they couldn't leave a girl her age alone with both of her parents absent. But, taking a child somewhere safe wasn't supposed to involve handcuffs or power-suppressing restraints.

And they didn't read her that stuff the cops always say on Dad's TV show, right to remain silent or whatever.

Kelly looked up, peering through the metal grating, but she couldn't see out the windshield past the enormous cops since they *filled* the front of the car. She glanced to her right out the side window at passing buildings for a few minutes. Officer Miller took a right turn, then a left, driving into the parking lot of a strip mall and pulling up behind a loaf-shaped aircraft.

Her eyes widened. She stared at Smith's earpiece, then up to the shadows of the cops' heads on the grey roof: flattish, with a bunch of little nubby horns.

Crap! They're aliens! I'm not being arrested… I'm being kidnapped!

The back door of the shuttle started to open downward into a ramp.

"No!" shouted Kelly. "This isn't the police station."

'Officer Miller' laughed in a deep, inhuman voice. "Of course not. We're bringing you in for some… modifications. Your reaction to the Naazlian crystals is an anomaly. It must be studied, then you will be modified back in line with normal parameters. Permanently."

Kelly pulled at her arms, desperate to escape.

The Nolmek both turned off their holograms, no longer appearing as police officers but the big red-orange alien soldiers—and laughed at the rattle of her struggle with the handcuffs.

"Don't bother," said the alien on the right. "Those handcuffs are made from vantharium."

Metal dug into her wrists, but she only strained more, ignoring the discomfort. The cuffs warped like dense plastic despite the power-nerfing collar. Within a second of the shuttle ramp touching the ground, the chain snapped. Kelly grabbed the collar at the front of her neck, trying to rip it off. The alien metal twisted back and forth like leather, but wouldn't tear. The front tires hitting the ramp gave her the last little boost of fear she needed to break the anti-power collar in half.

Crystal bits shot off like bullets, putting holes in the police car's doors as well as breaking the windows of nearby parked cars. Both aliens yelled in alarm. The driver stomped on the gas, but Kelly launched herself out through the roof as the car zoomed into the shuttle and crashed against the interior wall. Annoyed, she landed on her feet behind the shuttle, snapped the handcuff bracelets off, then folded her arms.

What am I supposed to do with evil aliens? Everyone thinks they're awesome... I can't kill them.

"How did it disable the anomaly containment device?" asked the passenger.

"I do not have the answer for that query. Let us go inquire with the subject."

The aliens tore the doors off the car at the same time, peeling the vehicle off their bodies more than getting out of it. They stomped over the wreckage and came charging down the ramp at her. Kelly sprang up off the ground, leaping into a punch that connected with the middle of the first alien's face. He hit the inside wall so hard, the shuttle's landing gear collapsed, dumping the ship on its belly.

"Grr. Annoying flea!" shouted the other.

She turned to face him and got a great close-up view of his fist, bigger than her entire head.

The next thing she knew, she lay embedded in a car, having crushed the roof inward. Her nose hurt a little. She reached up to feel her face and discovered a small blood trickle coming out of her nostril.

Growling, Kelly leapt into the air, cruising at him. He jumped to the side, avoiding her attack by inches. Again, he tried to punch her with a hand as big as her chest. The first swing, she jumped over. The second, she dove under, then slipped between his legs before floating up behind him.

When he spun around, she kicked him in the jaw.

That Nolmek blurred nearly straight up into the sky, shrinking down to a dot. Seconds later, he fell, landing on a minivan—which exploded like a stomped-on soda can. The alien's landing also left a shallow crater in the parking lot. Neither of the two appeared dead, but both would be out of it for a while.

Kelly folded her arms, hanging in midair. She'd have to tell the Aegis that the aliens tried to grab her. Since these two 'cops' had nothing to do with her parents, that meant the Nolmek came after her for what she did to their human-processing place in the museum.

While a big problem, she had a bigger one to deal with now: Mom.

Kelly let off a scream of frustrated anguish at not being old enough to have a cell phone. Otherwise, she would've called. With so many cops at home, she didn't want to draw attention to the tool shed in the backyard. So... checking the lair would have to wait. It didn't make sense to fly randomly and look for Mom from the sky. So, she decided to go back to Paige's house and wait.

Paige's room did not contain something important: Paige.

After slipping in the window, Kelly shrugged, then changed back to her street clothes. A purple T-shirt and jeans (moderately burned in the backside), no shoes. If need be, she could borrow something or go home after the cops left. Assuming her friend went downstairs to eat, play a game, or maybe only use the bathroom, Kelly headed to the bed to sit and wait for her.

A tablet sat in the middle of the bedspread with text on its screen:

Error 404: Paige not found.

Kelly groaned, but this felt like something worse than a bad pun.
She swiped a finger at the screen.
More text appeared:

Your little friend is with me. If you want her to remain alive, you will go to the basement of the noodle restaurant downtown at the corner of Pine and Kearny. I know you are reading this because the tablet sent me a note. Paige would really like you to be here within ten minutes. – Emophage.

Kelly tossed the tablet onto the bed. "Crap! Mom! Not fair!"

CHAPTER THIRTY-SIX

GIANT BOMBS AND LIQUID SUFFERING

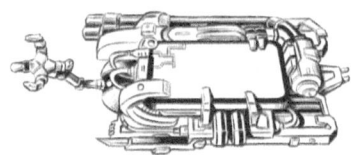

K elly's parents had never taken her to eat at the noodle restaurant in question, but the place smelled good. She made the flight in under a minute, so still had nine more before her mother did something unkind to Paige. She threw up her horrible ravioli dinner from last night and should have eaten breakfast and lunch by now—but hadn't eaten a thing.

Using super speed to eat fast tempted her, but a slightly larger problem than time got in the way of food: she didn't have any money. That meant she'd have to eat later. Stomach growling louder at the awesome aroma in the air, she trudged into the alley next to the restaurant.

A sunken stairway alongside the building led down to a red-painted door. She tried it and found it unlocked, so she stepped past it into a big basement room with dark grey cinder block walls. A giant metal sphere almost as tall as the ceiling sat in the middle of the area, made of interlocking panels. Except for one round panel about three feet across made of black material, the rest of it had a scarily familiar chrome finish. Small blinking lights flickered from the seams.

On the wall to her left hung a flat-panel television screen.

"Okay, that's either a giant alarm clock or one of those puzzle deals."

"Well, well, well…" Mom's voice came from everywhere.

"Mom?" Kelly looked around. "Where's Paige?"

"You disobedient little scamp. I told you to die, but you didn't listen." Her mother sighed. "I'm so *proud* of you for disobeying me."

Kelly blinked. "Uhh, this is getting too weird."

"However, I am heartbroken you have chosen to betray your family. I still love you, even though you are being a very good girl."

"I'm a hero, Mom. That's what heroes do! I don't like being mean to people. It makes me feel bad." She lowered her voice from yelling to a half-whisper. "I'm not a bully like you were."

Mom chuckled. "Ahh, those were the days. I forgot how much I missed that feeling of power when a few carefully chosen words to a few carefully chosen people could destroy someone. Ahh, but we all grow old and miss the days of our youth, don't we?"

"Speak for yourself. I'm not old yet."

"As punishment for your being such a respectable, moral child, you are to take this device and drop it on the Aegis Citadel. I'm sure you've guessed by now that it's a massive bomb."

"It's bigger than the doorway. How did you even get it in here? I can't take that thing anywhere."

"Cargo elevator on the other side of the room. It's a perfect fit."

Kelly slouched. "Oh."

"You will blow up the Citadel. They will see you as having turned to our side. You will join us, or... turn on the TV beside you."

"What? What kind of threat is that? Don't you mean join us or die?"

Mom's groan made the room shake. "No. I mean, turn on the TV to see what will happen if you refuse to join us."

Kelly walked over and pushed the button.

The screen powered up, showing Paige dangling over a pit of bubbling green goo from a chain wrapped around her middle, pinning her arms to her sides. Surprisingly, the girl didn't look scared at all.

"Oh, of course," shouted Paige angrily. "The normal human best friend *has* to get kidnapped." Growling, she struggled, making the chains rattle. "Seriously, Mrs. Donovan? Is this the most original idea you can come up with? Use the best friend to make Kelly do something? Let me go!"

"If you don't blow up the Citadel," said Mom, "you are going to be grounded for *three* months—and your friend gets dipped."

"Dipped?" asked Kelly. "What is that gunk? What's it gonna do to her?"

"No idea. Found it in your father's lair, but it's probably not going to be very good for her complexion. He labeled it 'liquid suffering.'"

"Dad..." Kelly shook her head. "You really need therapy."

"You're gonna leave me up here until I scream for help, aren't you?" shouted Paige from the TV.

"Hang on, Pay!" yelled Kelly. "I'm gonna get you out of there."

"She can't hear you, dear. This is a one-way feed. You have one hour to bomb the Citadel. The device will go off if it suffers a sharp impact, so all you need to do is drop it from high enough. Also, it will go off in one hour regardless of where it is. Even if you cannot get over your insufferable niceness to take your proper place with your family, leaving the device here will kill thousands of people—and ruin a really good noodle restaurant. Ta, dear. Have fun murdering the superheroes."

"Mom," muttered Kelly. "We really need to work on this whole mother-daughter activity day thing. You're doing it wrong."

Mom didn't react, perhaps having already closed her remote connection.

"Hmm." Kelly eyed the TV. "I've got an idea... and at least fifty minutes to waste before it's time to worry."

CHAPTER THIRTY-SEVEN

A MASSIVE PROBLEM

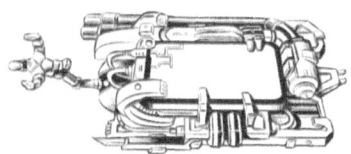

F lying faster than the speed of sound made the trip home pretty quick. Several pigeons and a hawk, however, didn't appreciate her zooming past them so fast. Kelly ran in the patio door from the back yard and raided the fridge. A plastic food-saver bin still held some of the Agitate and Incinerate chicken. She ate a whole leg herself without bothering to even heat it up as she'd become too hungry to care. Even after the full leg, she wanted to eat more. But another piece of chicken would be too much.

So, she nabbed a chocolate chip granola bar and devoured that.

Then, the reason she'd come home: she raced up to her room and grabbed her laptop. In the family computer room where her parents' computers sat on desks along with her 'gaming' system (the laptop pulled schoolwork duty more than anything else), she grabbed a spare network cable from the closet.

Mission accomplished, she ran outside and flew back to the noodle restaurant basement.

The TV that showed Paige squirming like a worm on a fishhook happened to be smart. She connected her laptop to it via the network cable. Floating cross-legged in midair, computer in her lap, she went on the attack. A sniffer program let her see the incoming video transmission and trace it back to its IP address. Plugging that IP address into a registration lookup page gave her a general location.

"Awesome."

She liked her laptop too much to leave it sitting next to a giant bomb, so she zipped home to drop it off, then flew to the northwest part of San Francisco, a residential area, and started looking around for anything suspicious. Normal people in the area probably would have seen a purple-and-lavender blur zipping back and forth. She searched as fast as she could move, peering in windows, checking backyards, and occasionally popping straight up high for an aerial view.

On one such aerial view, she spotted Mom's black car parked in front of a small house with orange-coral colored siding.

"Aha! Found you!"

The video showing Paige above a pit of 'liquid suffering' had dark stone-ish walls, which made her think basement. So, she flew over the house to the back yard, where she found a basement access hatch secured by a padlock, which didn't stand a chance against her strength. After chucking the lock aside, she pulled the doors open and glided down the stairs into a dark room full of dusty stacked boxes. A small kitchen table and some chairs stood on the left, and a workbench with old tools on the right. Directly ahead, a partition divided the second half of the basement into another room. Eerie green light glowed from the other side along with a continuous glooping noise.

Paige!

Kelly raced across the room to the partition. An instant before she went past it into the next room, a big maroon wall hit her. She sailed backward and struck the cinder blocks near the stairway out, creating a hole deep enough that she ended up sitting in it.

A man in a maroon body suit with thick armor-banded gloves a slightly darker shade of crimson squeezed through the doorway and glared at her. His costume had a metal dome that covered his head except for his mouth and nose. Two small holes in the upper part let him see.

"Ugh. *Another* giant fist? I've already been punched in the nose once today by a guy who had hands bigger than my head." She wriggled out of the wall, landing on her feet, then brushed dirt from her arms. "I'll only warn you once. I am Übergirl, and you are helping kidnap my best friend. Get out of my way."

"Massive does not work for you." The man pointed his palm at her.

A heavy, crushing force fell on Kelly, as though she had a stack of twenty or thirty cars balancing on her shoulders. She grunted, knocked to one knee by the unexpected weight. Her hands felt like giant stones at the ends of her arms. Massive slow-walked toward her, laughing.

With a growl, Kelly surged up from the ground, staggering toward him. He caught her first punch, which still knocked him back a step... but didn't put him into the wall. She kicked his right leg out from under him. He fell on his back and gave off a loud grunt. Kelly walked up onto him, fell to sit on his chest with her legs on either side of his giant head, grabbed the front of his collar, and cocked her fist back to punch him in the jaw.

"Do you surrender?"

Massive made a noise like he strained to lift a heavy object.

The arm she held up to punch him grew heavier. Figuring he did something, she pounded him in the face. His head—and the metal dome encasing it—crushed a hole in the concrete floor, but it didn't seem to bother him too much. He rolled to the right, tossing Kelly off his chest to land on all fours. Standing up took real effort fighting the tremendous weight pulling her down. She didn't quite make it all the way upright before her legs gave out and she landed on all fours again, her hands and knees denting the concrete. Her body had become so heavy that she could barely stand up.

Massive grabbed her, pinning her arms against her sides in his enormous hands. Only her head and boots stuck out of his grip. She struggled to force his gloves apart, but used up so much of her super strength fighting the crushing force pulling her down that she didn't have enough left to overpower him.

The giant oaf carried her to the small kitchen table where he set her in one of the chairs, holding her in place while wrapping a metal bar around her and the chair. Three coils pinned her arms to her sides and her upper body to the seatback, two coils held her legs to the cushion she sat on. The strange force made her body so heavy, she didn't have enough power to bend the metal.

"At least let Paige go," said Kelly.

The huge guy walked past the table to a mini kitchen setup. He opened a can, dumped the contents in a bowl, and tossed it in a microwave. Kelly squirmed, occasionally bending the thick metal tube. She tried to crush the chair, but for reasons she couldn't understand, it somehow managed to survive the forces she had to be exerting on it. Her body had to weigh significantly more than that giant octopus at the moment, since tossing that thing hadn't been anywhere near as difficult as simply lifting her arm now.

Beep.

Massive took the bowl out of the microwave and set it on the table in front of her.

Kelly leaned her head back from the rancid stench of decay.

Green beans.

"Eww."

The big guy pointed at it. "Eat."

"No. Besides, you've tied me to a chair. I can't even reach it."

Massive picked up the fork, stabbed a couple beans, and held them up to her mouth. "Eat."

A stink like dead birds and boiled dirty socks flooded her senses. "No. Ugh. That's disgusting."

He contemplated the situation, then pulled the fork back, moving it toward her again while making airplane noises. "The plane needs to go into the hangar. Open the doors."

The sight of this incredibly huge man trying to feed her like a one-year-old *almost* made her laugh. Only knowing that laughing would open her mouth let her keep a straight face.

He prodded her in the lip with the fork. Kelly struggled at the pipe wrapped around her, trying to twist her face away from the horrible green substance that watered her eyes. Despite being furious that Übergirl could be reduced to helplessness by something as common as green beans, she couldn't help but shake in fear. She had no way out of that chair with Massive's power crushing her, and it wouldn't be long before he found a way to force-feed her.

Does Mom have another Murdermaster-3000 waiting? I think I'm gonna find out.

CHAPTER THIRTY-EIGHT

MOMS CAN BE SO ANNOYING

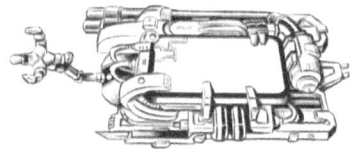

Right under her nose, the fumes wafting off the horrible green vegetables watered her eyes. Kelly gagged, trying to hold her breath. Again, Massive pretended the fork was an airplane, making noises while 'flying' it toward her mouth. When that didn't work, the huge guy attempted tickling her sides, trying to make her laugh and open her mouth.

"Mmm!" screamed Kelly, squirming in a futile attempt to evade, half scared, half furious.

Mom walked around the partition, still in her black super costume with the frilly mask. "You surprise me again, sweetie. Such a distressing level of ingenuity. How did you find this place?"

She narrowed her eyes.

"Hold off a moment, dear." Mom held up a hand at Massive. "She won't talk if you've got the beans anywhere near her."

He leaned back.

Kelly grunted, trying to wriggle free, but the steel bar only bent slightly. "You knew I'd find you here. Why else would you have set a trap?"

"Clever. Expecting you would come here doesn't mean I know *how* you'd find it."

"Traced the data feed from the webcam."

"Oh." Mom snapped her fingers. "Of course. Well, since you've chosen option three, you—"

"Option three?" Kelly wobbled side to side, squirming.

"You didn't bomb the heroes, and you didn't simply leave the bomb there to blow up in the city. You came looking for your friend. So, considering you went outside the lines, I have a new idea. Your father figured out that enough of a regular diet of vegetables will suppress your powers and keep you normal. Since you refuse to mis-behave yourself and join your father and I, you can just be an ordinary little girl. It is far too dangerous for you to play about with that hero nonsense without us to protect you. Better you are safe at home and powerless so you can't interfere in our plans."

"Mom! You and Dad can protect me just fine—if you go heroes. It's time to grow up from being bullies."

"Two choices, dear. One: a steady diet of vegetables and you go back to being normal. Two: you join us."

"Veggies make me sick! I'd constantly feel like crap! And they give me epic gas."

Massive rubbed his stomach. "Yeah. Broccoli does that to me, too. Can clear out a room."

Kelly blushed. "Umm."

"Beans or family? This should not be a difficult choice," said Mom. "And why isn't your mood changing?"

"Because, I figured you out, Mom. You could always talk to people and make them like you or get them to do what you wanted. Your superpower is changing people's emotion. No wonder I went from super sad to super happy that day Paige came over to go swimming. You *made* me feel better. But, now that I know you can do that, I can resist. It's just another attack."

Mom narrowed her eyes. "Give her the beans already."

"Sorry. They're good for you. No kid likes to eat their veggies, but you gotta." Massive picked up the fork.

"Wait. Mom, where is Paige?"

"Oh... don't worry about that now. She won't be in danger for very much longer." Her mother laughed.

"No!" A surge of protectiveness toward her only friend gave her strength. Kelly pushed her arms outward, bending the bar, but not quite enough to slip loose before the invisible force crashed down on her, pinning her to the chair. "Grr. You wanted me to finally make friends, and I did... now you're gonna take her away? Mom! Please don't! You're not really evil. The aliens are controlling you. They're controlling everyone."

Mom frowned, folding her arms. "Controlling everyone? Except for obnoxiously sweet little wanna-be heroes, apparently."

Kelly looked down at her limp arms, so heavy she could barely make her fingers twitch. Mindfreeze hadn't seen anything in Dad's head controlling him. Perhaps her mother did still love her like she always had, but she'd changed. This woman who kind of resembled Mom sounded more like a bigger version of Alexis. If Kelly had been anyone other than her daughter, she probably would have adored tormenting her and making her cry. But… Kelly refused to cry, despite worrying Paige might die.

"You want I should crush her?" asked Massive.

"No." Mom set her hands on her hips. "I didn't want to have to resort to such drastic measures, but you leave me no choice…"

Kelly shivered.

Mom pointed at Massive. "Use the *asparagus*."

Kelly sat there helpless, unable to move for a few minutes while he microwaved some asparagus spears. Mom kept her distance, watching. Kelly tried pleading with her the whole time the veggies cooked, but her mother didn't show any reaction other than an expectant raised eyebrow.

Beep.

Massive removed the plate from the microwave and set it on the table in front of her. The stench wafting from the green rods smelled worse than an abandoned nuclear reactor rinsed out with garbage truck water and rotting fish. Her stomach churned. He picked up one asparagus spear in fingers as thick as pool noodles, and stabbed her in the lips with it.

"Eat. I don't wanna be here all day. I've made your body weigh so much you can't move. I can make it weigh more so your bones crush you to death. Listen to your mother and eat your vegetables."

Kelly took a deep breath, held it, and opened her mouth a little.

"Good girl," said Massive.

"She always was an obedient little thing." Mom frowned off to the side.

Before he could shove the vegetable spear into her mouth, Kelly leaned forward to chomp off the last inch, then leaned back and spat it as hard as she could at his face. The asparagus bullet hit him in the forehead with a *clank*, denting his helmet and knocking him loopy. His concentration gone, the invisible force making her heavier ceased in an instant. Kelly tore the steel bar tying her to the chair apart, floated up, and pounded her tiny fist into the armored side of his head. Her punch launched Massive across the basement with such speed he seemed to vanish at the same instant a huge explosion of dust erupted at the far end of the room. When the cloud settled a few seconds later, it revealed a tunnel plowed a good twenty feet into the earth. Maroon patches showed in the dirt at the deep end of the tunnel. The big guy made no effort to move, likely *quite* unconscious.

Guess he's super strong but not that tough. Kelly shook her hand out, a little sore from punching him.

"Oh dear…" Mom took a step back, eyes widening.

Kelly landed and walked past her toward the wall dividing the basement in half. "Seriously? You're my mother. I can't hit you."

Upon reaching the partition, she peered around at a wide tank of glowing green slime, the 'liquid suffering,' which only came up to Kelly's knees... more a kiddie pool than a tank. A strong, somewhat familiar and not entirely unpleasant smell hung in the air. Empty chain hung from the ceiling, going straight down into the goop. The camera looking up at Paige made it seem like a huge vat. No way could her friend have disappeared in this stuff—unless it melted her.

But she knew that smell. Dad made something like it before the crystals happened, though that batch didn't glow.

Kelly leaned close, dipped a finger into the green stuff, and tasted it. In a second, her mouth went numb and tingly. Without her superpowers, she'd probably have been throwing up and crying, half-blinded, feeling as though she'd attempted to drink lava straight out of a volcano. "Hot sauce. This is Dad's habanero hot sauce... or at least tastes kinda like it. Why the heck is it glowing?"

"How should I know?" asked Mom from the other room. "This *is* your father we're talking about."

"True. He probably thought glowing would make it cooler." She turned to face her mother, hands on her hips. "Where is Paige?"

Mom held up her left wrist. "She's *un*happy and *un*safe inside that giant bomb you left sitting there. Probably screaming her head off at you for walking away, poor little dear. The chamber let her see and hear you, but kept her nice and silent. Don't worry. That bomb is pretty big so it's got plenty of air inside. It will explode long before she suffocates."

"So, umm..." Kelly walked over to her mother. "I know you didn't really want the Murdermaster-3000 to kill me, so I'm not gonna tell anyone about that. But you kidnapped my friend and put her inside a giant bomb. You also threatened to kill a lot of people in town and wanted me to blow up the Citadel. I gotta bring you in, Mom."

"I don't want you associating with those people. They're a good influence. And you betrayed your father. While betrayal is admirable, you shamefully did it for noble reasons, not for personal enrichment or power." Her mother grasped Kelly's shoulder and gave her a whack on the backside—that felt like an affectionate pat. "Ouch."

Kelly sighed, took her mother's hand, and started dragging her to the stairs.

"Sorry, dear. I need to run." Mom pressed a button on her forearm and evaporated in a cloud of teleportation sparkles.

"Ooh!" Kelly stomped, cracking the floor. "Moms can be so annoying!"

CHAPTER THIRTY-NINE
THERE REALLY IS NO GOOD PLACE FOR A GIANT BOMB

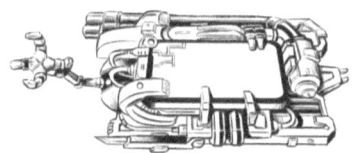

G rumbling about her mother simply disappearing, Kelly rushed out of the basement and threw herself into the sky. Flying had to be one of the most awesome superpowers ever. She adored it. However, flying when her best friend could die at any moment took much of the fun out of it.

She shot across San Francisco, annoyed that her father hadn't built any kind of communicator into her costume. He probably would have if she'd been old enough to have a cell phone. Kelly could practically hear him telling her 'oh, you'll just use it to talk to your—oh wait, you don't have any friends to call.'

"Grr."

Upon reaching the noodle place, she stopped in midair. Seconds later, the screaming of people and wailing of car alarms reached her ears. She peered back the way she'd come at dozens of people holding their ears, and a line of broken windows along the level she'd been flying.

Oops. Broke the sound barrier too low to the ground. "Umm, sorry," she whispered. "Friend's life…"

She dove into the basement stairs and landed by the giant, spherical bomb, studying the interlocking panels until she decided to focus on the only black part that resembled a hatch with no handles, windows, or hinges, definitely big enough for a person to fit through. Probably a one-way window as well.

"Who builds a huge bomb and makes a spot for someone to go inside it?" She sighed at the ceiling. "Dad."

Kelly held her hand flat and thrust her fingers into the metal, piercing it like cake. She jammed her other hand in, aiming as close as possible to the seam between panels, grabbed on, and pulled. The three-foot-wide plate popped off with a few sparks. She tossed it aside like a big metal Frisbee, and peered into the hole.

Paige occupied a small space, curled up inside a strange contraption that she would've called a cage, but it didn't have bars. Thick metal struts formed the outline of a cube with a solid metal plate at the girl's back. Shiny steel bands held her by the wrists, biceps, ankles, thighs, and waist, her hands trapped in metal boxes. A softer nylon chest harness—like something from a dangerous amusement park ride—secured her body to the back plate. She struggled, unable to move, and tried to scream past an X of silver tape over her mouth.

And she still looked *way* angry. Not at all scared.

Kelly grabbed the front of the odd cage and pulled it out of the space inside the bomb. "Sorry. I didn't know you were inside. Gimme a sec and I'll break you loose."

"Mmm!" yelled Paige.

Kelly set the cage down and reached to pull the tape off her friend's mouth.

A green gem at the middle of the chest harness lit up and shot Kelly in the face with an energy beam. She stumbled backward, more from the unexpectedness than the hit, which surprisingly hurt about as much as Alexis slapping her pre-superpowers—only hot.

"What the heck?"

"Mmm!" yelled Paige, thrashing so hard at the straps holding her to the frame that the entire cube rocked side to side.

Before Kelly could take a step, the cube opened, revealing itself to be a collapsed exoskeleton instead of a cage. Robotic hands extended from the boxes shrouding Paige's real hands. She rose upright, her feet on raised platforms that elevated her six inches taller, so she towered over Kelly. This thing looked exactly like the ones the cops had, only smaller, and all the normal nylon straps had been converted into restraints.

The exoskeleton circled to the left like a gunfighter about to draw a weapon. Paige struggled to fight it, clearly not the one controlling the machine.

"Grr. Mom! You're going to make me fight my best friend?"

"Mmmmm!" yelled Paige past the tape on her mouth.

Kelly shook her head and walked up to it. The exoskeleton went for a left hook to her head, but she ducked—right into a stomach punch from the right fist. Metal knuckles to the gut knocked the wind out of her and slammed her into the ceiling.

"Oof!" She floated down to her feet and doubled over, grabbing her belly.

The exoskeleton brought its arms together and clobbered her in the back with both hands, knocking her flat on her chest. Her cheek mushed into the concrete floor, all the air in her lungs knocked out of her.

"Mmm!" yelled Paige.

A scraping noise came from above.

Kelly flew backward, sliding over the floor away from the exoskeleton, a half-second before it stabbed a glowing red sword into the ground where she'd been. Compared to Paige's size, the weapon was about as long as Knightmare's broadsword. Even if the character from *Galaxy Enders* was real, she wouldn't have been too worried about him as normal guys with gadgets could be defeated pretty easily—take away the toys. Dr. Blaze, without his gloves, wasn't any more dangerous than an ordinary man. However, this sword gave off a scary energy that she didn't at all like. Something told her it had been made from a shard of the alien crystal.

Uh oh. Why do I think that's going to be able to cut me?

Paige screamed and squirmed, unable to stop the exoskeleton as it stomped toward Kelly.

It slashed at her, swinging sideways at neck level. Kelly ducked, but couldn't bring herself to punch her best friend. She backed off, searching for a spot to attack that would allow her to disable the suit without hurting Paige.

Unfortunately, from the front, she had little access to the metal suit except for the eight-inch leg extensions beneath her friend's sneakers. Paige's body got in the way of every possible attack. And even if she kicked or punched the mechanized arms or legs, the way Mom had strapped her friend to the machine, bending or breaking the robotic limbs would break Paige's arms or legs, too.

The exoskeleton stabbed at Kelly's chest. She leapt sideways. It pivoted and shot her with the beam again. The blast hit her in the left shoulder with a painful stinging impact that knocked her back a few steps.

Snarling, Kelly ran at it, fist raised.

Paige screamed past the tape, wide-eyed.

As if it wanted her to kill Paige, the exoskeleton stood still, not trying to defend against her attack. But instead of punching her friend, she reached in and ripped the tape off. The instant the exoskeleton realized what happened, it slashed at her. Kelly instinctively raised her left arm, blocking the blade with her bracer. A lightning bolt of pain from elbow to wrist jolted her arm as the crystal edge bounced off the mirrored metal.

"That sword can hurt you!" yelled Paige. "You gotta get out of here. Run. It won't hurt me."

Kelly yelped and jumped back, checking her arm. The bracer hadn't been damaged, not even scratched. "No way. I have to stop you—"

"It's not me!" yelled Paige. "Your mother tied me to a killer robot. I'm not controlling this thing."

"You didn't let me finish!" Kelly ducked another swing. "I have to stop you from being hurt. And don't feel bad. She tied me to a killer machine, too. At least that one isn't trying to kill *you*."

Paige snarled. "Would you be mad at me if I said I think your mother is a butt?"

"No. She's acting like one."

The exoskeleton ran at her, boosting its speed with jets in the lower legs and back. Kelly threw herself to the side, spinning in midair as the sword passed over her chest an inch above her body. It sliced off a lock of hair, which fluttered to the ground.

"Eep!" yelled Paige. "I thought so."

Kelly bounced back to her feet. The exoskeleton faked a swing at her head and caught her with a surprise sidekick to the stomach that launched her into the wall. Cinder blocks cracked behind her.

"Sorry!" yelled Paige. "I can't get out of this thing. Your mom replaced the straps and buckles with locked metal ones. She made me carry that stupid bomb like I'm a remote control toy."

Kelly leapt around in a series of cartwheels and somersaults, dodging rapid energy beams from the exoskeleton's chest harness… then felt like an idiot and stood there while it shot her a few times. "That thing is stupid. The beam doesn't really hurt that much."

"Hey, Kel?" asked Paige as the exoskeleton charged at her, raising the sword. She growled, squirming, but couldn't slow the machine down.

"Yeah?" Kelly ducked a slice from the glowing red blade, scrambling to the right.

"Why does your mom have a kid-sized exoskeleton?"

She jumped toward Paige, trying to grab the sword arm, but the exoskeleton pivoted the blade at her face, making her back off. Even as fast as she could move, the robot kept getting the sword in the way. Grumbling, she jumped a few steps back for time to think. "Umm. She probably *just* made it with the fabricators Dad built. Mom's pretty smart, so she could've figured out how to change the size. Those suits might be where Dad got some of his money from, selling them to the cops."

"Oh."

The exoskeleton ran at her despite Paige screaming at it to stop, attacking in a frenzy of slicing and stabbing that forced Kelly to run in circles and block two more strikes with her bracers. Fortunately, the crystal couldn't cut whatever metal Dad used, but she feared it would go right through the fabric parts—and her body—pretty easily.

"Sorry!" Shouted Paige.

"It's okay. Even best friends fight sometimes."

"I'm not doing it. The suit is basically wearing *me*."

"I know." Kelly grinned and leapt into a sideways tumble to avoid a lunging stab that buried nearly half the sword into the floor.

Paige growled, straining with her comparatively insignificant strength against the exoskeleton, trying to stop it from pulling the weapon out. "Did you just make a joke when we're both like really close to death?"

"Neither one of us is close to death." Kelly folded her arms. "I'm not gonna hurt you, and you're not going to kill me."

"I'm not controlling this stupid thing!"

The exoskeleton freed the sword from the floor, faced her, and raised the glowing weapon overhead in both of its metal hands before charging at her.

"I know." Kelly sidestepped, then lunged to grab the exoskeleton's back.

It spun, swiping the blade at her hand. She managed to rip something small off, but the scrap of metal didn't appear to be vital.

"Ow!" screamed Paige.

"What happened?" shouted Kelly in a worried tone.

"Let me tie you to a robot stronger than a forklift that's moving around real fast and see how comfortable it is! It's gonna rip my arms off."

Kelly snarled at the exoskeleton. She leapt at it with a punch, but it didn't stand there defenseless a second time, bringing the sword up to defend. Kelly flew up and over the blade. She could've grabbed it from behind and threw it, but her powers might adjust to the exoskeleton's toughness... which would seriously hurt Paige. So, she landed in a handstand, flipped onto her feet, and ran.

After a minute or so of running in circles dodging a giant red sword—well, giant to a nine-year-old on the small side—an idea hit her. She pretended to make an error by letting the exoskeleton trap her in the corner with nowhere to go. Back against cinder blocks, she raised her arms, poised to defend with her bracers.

"What are you doing?" shouted Paige. "No! Get out of the corner!"

The exoskeleton swung with an overhead chop. Kelly caught the blade between her crossed bracers. Another jolt of fire hit her in the arms. For a few seconds, they got into a back and forth shoving contest, sparks flying from where the crystal edge met metal. Eventually, Kelly snarled and shoved the suit back a step.

"Run!" shouted Paige, closing her eyes. "I don't wanna see this!"

The exoskeleton swung several times in rapid succession. Kelly blocked each strike with one bracer, angling her arms so the sword bounced away harmlessly. Each time the crystal blade hit metal, she gasped in genuine pain. Having that weapon anywhere near her skin—even with a quarter-inch-thick bracer in the way—hurt.

"Get out of the corner!" yelled Paige.

Evidently tired of her blocking, the exoskeleton leaned back and stabbed straight at her—exactly what she'd been waiting for. Kelly dropped straight down, the blade going over her head into the wall. Her butt hit concrete the same instant she kicked the exoskeleton's boots out from under it. The sword remained stuck in cinder blocks as Paige and the exoskeleton wearing her crashed to the floor, face down.

Kelly pounced on it and rammed her hand into the machinery on the back plate, tearing out handfuls of wires and computer parts. The exoskeleton twitched for a few seconds and went still. She climbed off it, rolled the metal suit over, and proceeded to break the bands one by one.

"Thanks." Paige unbuckled the chest harness and crawled away from the dead suit. She sat on the floor, rubbing her arm. "Can I just say that totally sucked?"

"Yeah. You can." Kelly pounded a fist into the exoskeleton, smashing it. "Because it did. But, it could have been worse."

"Easy for you to say. You weren't stuffed in that tiny little cubby for an hour. My nose itched *so* bad and I couldn't scratch it."

Kelly shivered. "That thing my mom tried to kill me with? I had to throw up while strapped to a table on my back."

"Eww."

"Yeah…" Kelly shivered at the memory of the flavor. "What I mean by worse is, the exoskeleton wasn't too bad. At least she didn't legit mind control you and actually make *you* fight me."

"Oh…" Paige's eyes widened. "Yeah, that would've been worse. But also stupid. I'm just a norm. You would have disarmed me in like half a second. That suit was moving so fast…"

"Sorry."

"What are you apologizing for?"

"Taking so long to get the idea to knock you over."

"It's okay. We still have like… ten minutes before that bomb goes off." Paige froze, mouth open.

The girls looked at each other.

"Giant bomb!" they shouted at the same time.

Kelly jumped up and ran over to the sphere, examining the opening. The cubby had nothing in it. Some wires stuck out here and there from where she ripped the panel off, but she couldn't make sense of them.

"Umm." Paige ran up beside her. "Disarm it?"

"How?"

"You're the hero. Just disarm it like they all do."

Kelly glanced at her. "I'm not a comic character. People in the real world need to like learn how to disarm bombs. It's not just something everyone with super powers knows how to do."

"Oh." Paige grabbed her. "I'm scared."

"*Now* you're scared? What about when Mom had you hanging over the liquid suffering?"

"It smelled like peppers. I wasn't worried. Liquid suffering sounds like something my dad would name a hot sauce."

Kelly laughed. "It *was* hot sauce."

"Thought so."

"Umm…" Paige tapped her foot. "You have to get it away from the city. If we can't stop it from blowing up, you can't let it blow up where it's going to hurt anyone."

"Good idea." Kelly rolled the giant sphere across the basement into the big cargo elevator, almost filling it.

"Wow, you make that look so easy. That suit barely moved it."

Kelly puffed her chest out. "I'm Übergirl!"

"Kel…" Paige made shooing motions. "Be heroic later. Bomb now."

"Right. Sorry. Be back as soon as I can."

She hit the elevator button. The lift struggled to move upward. Eventually, doors overhead opened and the platform rose up level with a small parking lot behind the restaurant… which lay strewn with all the boxes of food and supplies that should have been in the basement. Kelly ducked under the bomb, picked it up, and leapt into the air, carrying it.

Once she got a bit of altitude, she started to fly west out toward the Pacific.

"Wait… if I chuck this into the ocean, it's going to hurt fish and dolphins and stuff. I can't do that." She stopped, hanging in midair. "Umm. Where the heck can I take this thing in like five minutes that won't hurt anything? The guys from the show *Legend Breakers* always blow stuff up at Alameda bomb range, but that's too far away and this thing is *way* bigger than anything they've ever used."

She peered up at the almost ten-foot-diameter sphere. If everything but the middle hollow contained explosives, that thing could flatten most of San Francisco, and do quite a bit of damage anywhere else. Heck, even the noise of it going off would probably kill every pet bird in the city.

"Where can I… *space!*"

Grinning, Kelly flew straight up.

Not quite a minute after she began her ascent, she had the distinct experience of being a fastball abruptly changing direction from a pitch into a homerun. She mentally processed that the bomb had gone off only a second before her face made contact with the roof of a building. The next thing she knew, she lay flat on her back under a heap of concrete rubble, broken wires, and dust. A few small rocks fell on her, or landed with a clatter on wood nearby.

A stinging pain covered her entire front, as if she'd done a belly-flop from the super high diving board, hitting the water so hard it stunned her. Everything appeared to be blurry. Terrified that the bomb had somehow made her need her glasses again, she started to panic, but her vision sharpened after a few seconds. She stared up at a tunnel made of eleven small holes in the ceilings and floors that led straight to the sky. A few people's heads leaned in at varying heights, peering down at her.

She grunted and sat up out of the rubble, swatting a few bits of concrete from her hair. Twenty people in fancy business attire, all sitting around the huge oval conference table she'd landed on, gawked at her.

"Umm. Oops. Sorry for interrupting your meeting. It was an accident." She stood on the table. "My first time trying to get rid of a bomb. Wasn't sure what to do with it."

"Are you all right, kid? You're bleeding…" A woman stood from her chair, reaching up to dab at Kelly's nose with a tissue.

"Ow. Thanks. Yeah… the bomb was kinda big." Kelly scrunched her nose and poked it. "It doesn't hurt too much. "Umm, sorry again for the ceiling. I didn't mean to do that. Stupid thing exploded earlier than I thought it would and must have thrown me."

The adults all gawked at her, speechless.

"I gotta go save my friend. She's still in danger."

Kelly flew up the tunnel she made on the way in, cringing at the sight of ten stories of punctured concrete slabs. *Looking* at the path she'd plowed into the building caused more pain than making it, since she didn't remember anything between flying with the bomb and ending up on the table.

Hopefully, she'd managed to go high enough that the blast didn't hurt anyone.

CHAPTER FORTY
A PARENTAL PROBLEM OF THE LOGISTICAL KIND

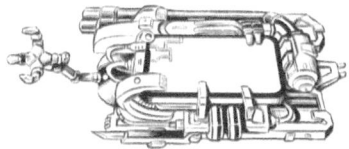

Paige waited patiently for her in the ramen restaurant's basement.

"Okay. Bomb's dealt with," said Kelly, upon gliding in via the stairs.

"What happened? I heard it explode."

"Umm. It went off in midair. No one got hurt. I carried it high enough up. Hop on my back."

Paige did. Kelly flew outside into the air. Her friend clamped on hard for the first minute or so, terrified, but eventually appeared to find flying awesome. Since she had a passenger, Kelly landed in Paige's backyard rather than try to go in via the bedroom window.

"Are you going to tell your parents my mother kidnapped you?"

"Umm."

"I'm not going to ask you not to. I just want to know what to expect."

"Well, if *both* your parents are in jail, then you'll *have* to stay with me. So maybe I will." Paige smiled playfully.

Kelly swatted at her hair, knocking away a few more bits of building. "My mom tried to kill me. I think I'm going to wind up staying with you anyway. If I go home, she'll just try to do it again."

"Umm. Okay. Well, she didn't really hurt me. We could just say she watched us today."

"Babysitters don't strap kids into combat exoskeletons."

"Most babysitters aren't supervillains. C'mon, let's go do something fun."

Kelly shook her head. "In a bit. I need to go tell the Aegis about the aliens."

"Ooh. You didn't tell them yet?"

"I did, but the aliens did something else." Kelly ground her boot into the grass. "They must think I'm a threat."

"Okay. Be careful."

"Of course." Kelly raised a fist.

Paige bumped it.

Kelly leapt into the air, flying east.

A few minutes later, she arrived at the Citadel. Someone had already fixed the hole she left in the door. However, she spotted the heroes in a third-floor lounge area with a long wall of windows separating it from an elevated patio. So, she landed on the patio and walked over to the sliding glass doors.

The four heroes stared at her in surprise. Phoenix said something, and the doors opened.

"Guys!" Kelly ran in. "The aliens tried to kidnap me."

"What?" asked all four of them almost at the same time.

Kelly hopped up on the couch and told them about the two Nolmek who disguised themselves as cops and 'arrested' her from the house, then reminded them about the museum.

"Hmm. This is no small concern." Phoenix rubbed his chin.

"Yes. I am thinking the same." Igor the Red smiled at her. "These Nolmek are far too… helpful. They are up to something."

"Kidnapping most of the population of Earth definitely counts as 'up to something.'" Bullet Man whistled.

"There are so many aliens. We will need to work with other hero groups from multiple countries." Mindfreeze paced. "All the help we can get."

Despite the scary subject, Kelly grinned at the heroes taking her seriously. "Yeah. What do you need me to do?"

Everyone looked at her. Igor appeared to be pondering, while the other three all had the same 'are you serious?' expression she hated so much.

"Kiddo." Phoenix took her hand. "This is an extremely dangerous and serious situation. You're still a little girl. You need to stay home where it's safe and—"

A door opened, allowing a young black woman with fluffy hair to run in, dressed like an ordinary office worker. "Guys, the phones are exploding!"

Kelly narrowed her eyes at the woman, who did the same. After a few seconds of sizing each other up, they appeared to both agree that they had equal levels of floof epicness and didn't need to be rivals. Kelly did, however, have much longer hair. The woman nodded to her curtly, like an Old West gunslinger acknowledging an equal. Kelly returned the nod.

"Who planted bombs in the Citadel?" demanded Igor in a near roar.

"Easy, man." Ray put a hand on his arm. "It's only a figure of speech. Means they're ringing a lot."

"Oh. I see." Igor calmed down.

"What is it, Laura?" asked Mindfreeze.

"People are reporting a large explosion high up over San Francisco. Whole bunch of different stories. Some describe a ball-shaped spacecraft, some say a missile came down from space." Laura scratched her head. "Think it's some kind of mass-confusion ability?"

"No," said Kelly. "I know exactly what happened."

"What?" asked Roy.

Mindfreeze gasped at her, then made an 'aww you poor thing' face.

"I found a giant bomb and tried to fly it away so it didn't hurt anyone. At first, I was gonna dump it in the ocean, but I didn't wanna hurt the fish. So, I tried to take it to outer space, but it went off in my face."

"How big was this bomb?" asked Phoenix. "Is that the 'thunder' we heard?"

"Umm." She flew up behind Igor, and held her hand roughly three feet above his head. "A big ball, about this high."

"Oh, and your 2:30 appointment is about due," said Lauren. "Escorting the, umm..." She checked a tablet. "Brain Trust as he's transported to the holding facility."

Kelly sank to stand on the floor, staring down. *Dad...*

"Go on home, sweetie." Mindfreeze gave her a brief hug. "Stay safe."

"Did you not hear the child? A massive bomb went off in front of her and she doesn't have a scratch." Igor the Red gestured at her. "Perhaps she could be helpful?"

"I can't be responsible for a little girl getting hurt." Phoenix stood from the sofa. "Come on guys. Suit up. We have an escort to attend. Kelly, you need to go be a kid. Have fun. Leave this stuff to the grownups."

She stood there, sulking at the floor while the Aegis walked out to get changed. Igor the Red paused at the doorway.

"Girl..."

Kelly looked up at him.

"Sometimes, people see something small and push it aside, not knowing how powerful it can be." He winked. "I am not telling you to do anything stupid, but only you can say what you *can't* do, not stuck-up flaming chickens. He thinks because you are small, you are weak." He wiggled his fingers. "I know better. That arm angle thing was just an excuse." He winked and hurried off to catch up to the others.

Kelly bit her lip, pondering. How much trouble would she get in if she followed them? It's not like she wanted to bust her Dad out of jail—well, she kind of did, but wouldn't. As much as she wanted him home, she wanted her original Dad back first. And, breaking people out of prison transports was something villains did. Even if the criminal in question happened to be her father, she wouldn't break the law or hurt people.

However, Mom absolutely would.

At the sound of jet engines overhead, Kelly ran to the patio doors and crept outside. The Aegis' shuttle glided away from the roof with Phoenix flying beside it. Unlike Kelly, his flight power left a trail of fire in his wake. It faded out pretty fast, so it had to be more of a 'looks cool' special effect than a weapon.

She flew straight up, going quite a bit higher than them to make it more difficult for anyone to notice her, then followed. A few minutes later, the shuttle stopped, hovering over downtown San Francisco. Phoenix landed in front of the police building and went inside. Kelly floated high overhead, watching, hoping no one spotted her.

Eventually, Phoenix emerged from the building and flew up to meet the shuttle. A large set of garage doors opened, from which two police vans and a high-tech tractor-trailer rolled out onto the street. Mostly dark blue with silver trim, the rig looked like an alien landing craft with wheels instead of wings. A big box about the size of a tiny car stuck out of the roof near the front of the trailer. It didn't seem to have any obvious purpose, but could've been a battery, an electric generator, even air conditioning for all she could guess.

The convoy veered left out of the police station, the Aegis shuttle and Phoenix escorting it from about a hundred feet off the ground. Kelly followed, fighting the urge to zoom down there to at least visit her father. Considering how long he'd hidden in his lair working on the MICE project, it felt as though she hadn't seen him in forever.

They took the highway south past San Mateo and San Jose, driving for over an hour before leaving civilization behind with a left turn onto a road among vast fields of brown hills dotted with sparse trees. From her perch high up, she gazed ahead along the road, which looped around a huge lake in the distance. A new-looking southerly branch of road led south from there to an enormous white building out in the middle of the desert.

Soon after the land on either side of the highway became little more than open hills and a handful of trees, the tractor-trailer abruptly died, shuddering to a stop too fast for the following police van to avoid crashing into it. The lead van drove onward for a few seconds until the driver noticed and slammed on the brakes.

The Aegis shuttle stopped to hover while Phoenix landed on the semi-trailer's roof.

A beam of black energy shrouded in dark green flew from a rut on the side of the road and nailed Phoenix in the chest. He grunted, but didn't appear to have suffered any harm from the attack.

Mom, in her super costume, and another woman, emerged from a hiding place, approaching the trailer. The other woman also wore a full bodysuit with a black-and-neon green pattern divided into four squares. Her left arm and right leg were black, right arm and left leg, white. Unlike Mom, this woman had a full-face mask that resembled a motorcycle helmet, also bright lime green.

"I cannot allow you to interfere with the police," said Phoenix. He jumped off the trailer as if to fly—and fell straight to the road on his chest with a painful sounding *whap*.

Not-Mom laughed. "Don't hurt yourself, hon."

Phoenix pushed himself up, growling, and thrust his hand at her.

"Something wrong?" asked Not-Mom.

"What on Earth?" Phoenix stared in awe at his hand.

Both police vans opened. Sixteen cops in exoskeletons jumped out, all holding rifles with barrels so fat they could've launched golf balls. Every one of them pointed their weapons at Mom and the other woman.

Kelly shivered with worry. Supervillain or not, she didn't like watching people point guns at her mother.

"This is all you, Emophage," said the other woman.

Mom held her hands out to the sides, apparently giving up.

The shuttle swooped in to land on the dirt, off the side of the road. Igor the Red, Bullet Man, and Mindfreeze rushed out, Mindfreeze teleporting to Phoenix' side.

Bullet Man appeared like a teleportation without any glowing special effects, grabbing Not-Mom from behind, pinning the woman's arms to her sides. "Got one."

She put her hand on his thigh, black light surrounded her fingers.

"Whoa... I feel... weird," said Bullet Man.

"Will all you nice officers do me a favor and get rid of these heroes?" asked Mom.

The exoskeleton-armed cops shifted their aim to Mindfreeze.

"Oh, that's not good," muttered Mindfreeze.

She teleported away an instant before a barrage of green lasers ripped up the road around Phoenix.

Kelly couldn't continue merely watching. She dove out of the sky.

The strange box on top of the trailer extended upward and rotated, its front opening to reveal a big cannon and several rocket nosecones. Two of the rockets came up to have a chat with her. Kelly dove steeper, but couldn't dodge fast enough. Fortunately, the explosion felt like a hard wallop from a pillow fight—the kind of wallop that usually *ended* a pillow fight with scream-crying and running to tell Mom how much of a butthead your brother/friend/sister was.

Kelly slapped into the dirt amid a cloud of dust and smoke. "Oof."

Igor the Red, who had still been running to the road from the shuttle, stopped beside her. "What the heck?"

She pushed herself up out of the small crater, her front covered in a layer of black char, smoke still peeling off her. "They have missiles."

"No." Igor gestured at her. "I mean, what are you doing here?"

A glint of light from the left made her look—at a car flying toward Igor the Red. She sprang into the air, catching the small sedan before it could land upside down on him. The people inside the car appeared quite grateful at not going *splat*.

"I'm helping!" she yelled, then set the car on its wheels.

Screaming, the man driving it stomped on the gas and took off.

"Oh, I like this one." Mom made a 'come here' motion at Phoenix. "Nan, give him his powers back?"

Not-Mom, who had been working on a keypad by a door into the trailer, glanced at Phoenix for a second. "Done."

Phoenix stared adoringly at Mom.

Igor the Red growled and charged at Not-Mom, running into a hail of laser beams from the exo-suited cops. The blasts left singe marks on his all-red costume, but didn't appear to hurt him.

Phoenix projected streams of fire from both hands into Igor's chest. That made the big guy grunt and slow to a determined trudge. He bellowed a brief shout at a row of four men in exoskeletons, creating a sonic wave that knocked them over backward and sent them sliding several meters. A woman officer charged him, raising her rifle to wallop him in the face. Igor picked her up and tossed her over the truck like a toy. He smashed the next cop's rifle, then also threw that man over the truck. When he reached the police van behind the big rig, he lifted it up over his head, then pivoted as if to throw it at Mom, using another brief shout to knock her over backward.

"Nan!" Yelled Mom from the ground.

Not-Mom fired a darkbeam from her left hand into Igor the Red's chest.

He blinked, made a distinct 'uh oh' face, then vanished as the police van crushed him into the road with a resounding *boom*. "Ouch. That was... not pleasant."

Not-Mom laughed. "Fools! I am Negative Nancy, and this is my sidekick Emophage."

"Nan, we talked about this." Mom stood and dusted herself off. "I'm Emophage and you're the sidekick. I never play second fiddle."

"Fine then. We're partners. No sidekicks." Negative Nancy resumed attacking the code lock.

Mindfreeze came running around the front end of the tractor-trailer, lasers scorching the pavement at her feet. "They're all in love with that woman! They'll die for her!"

Negative Nancy hit Mindfreeze with a darkbeam, catching her looking back over her shoulder at some exoskeleton cops. The attack had no visible effect other than making the woman's eyes stop glowing bright blue and appear like any other person's.

Mindfreeze skidded to a stop, her expression a perfect example of 'oh crap'.

"There is no need to kill the helpless ones," said Mom.

The exoskeleton cops all turned their attention on Kelly. She let out a yelp of startlement as fifteen men and women lit her up with lasers all at the same time, though it hurt about as much as a pelting of ping pong balls. She decided to float there and ignore them as merely annoying.

"Really, you guys can stop," said Kelly. "I've been hit by harder paper wads in class."

"Oh, crap." Mom looked up at her. "Nan. Quick. Nerf my kid before she ruins this."

Negative Nancy turned away from the panel. "Aww. She's adorable."

"Hi, Nan." Kelly waved. "If you zap me, I'm going to be mad at you."

"She'd be more adorable without her powers," said Mom.

"We're helping your father. Behave yourself." Nancy raised her hand toward Kelly.

"I *am* behaving myself. Behaving means obeying the law."

"See what I mean?" Mom sighed. "She's a lost cause. Hopelessly nice. Always does what she's told. Loves school. Reads. It's so easy to get her to go to bed at night. And... and... she loves math."

Negative Nancy gasped. "Oh, no..."

"I know, right?" asked Mom, faking a sniffle. "I really don't know where I went wrong."

"This is rather uncomfortable." Igor the Red's voice echoed from inside the van.

Kelly zoomed to the left an instant before Negative Nancy shot a darkbeam into the air at her. She flew low to the road, skimming with her chest inches from the pavement. Two more darkbeams missed due to her weaving side to side. She crashed into the van at full speed and punctured it like a bullet.

"Oops. Too fast."

Continuous laser fire swarmed after her, mostly missing, but the occasional lucky shot hit her with an irritating tap. She flew back at the van, landing behind it where Negative Nancy couldn't see her. A quick shove knocked it on its side, exposing Igor the Red, embedded in a form-fitting pothole the exact size and shape of his body.

"There is something wrong," said Igor.

"Yeah. Mom's friend turns off powers. Pretty sure it's temporary, but I don't know how long it lasts. I think I'm going to have to bonk her on the head."

Negative Nancy ran between the van and truck, raising her arm.

Kelly leapt straight up over the darkbeam, then flew toward the front of the big transport. Black energy beams chased her, missing by inches. Between her speed and tiny size, she managed to avoid them. After the twelfth straight miss, Nancy began growling—and missing by wider margins.

She's getting angry. I fail harder at video games when I get mad, too. Gotta make her even angrier.

"You're not very good at that, are you?" asked Kelly, weaving, circling, and diving.

"Sit still!" yelled Negative Nancy.

"Sweetie," said Mom. "Stand still and let Nancy zap you. I promise it won't hurt."

"Sorry, Mom. I can't do that." Kelly zipped behind the front of the truck, hiding by the grill.

The cop behind the wheel shot her in the forehead with a laser rifle, its beam passing harmlessly through the windshield.

She smirked at him. "Really?"

"Did you just defy me?" yelled Mom. "I told you to stand still!"

"Übergirl does not take orders from bad guys," shouted Kelly.

Mom gasped. "You disobedient little... I'm proud of you!"

The cop shot her in the forehead again.

"Grr." Kelly leapt up, punched her arm past the windshield, and grabbed the end of the rifle, crushing it. "Stop that! It's annoying."

Negative Nancy ran around the truck.

"Eep!" Kelly zoomed straight up, a darkbeam missing her boots by two inches.

Phoenix joined in, throwing firebeams at her as well, though he didn't try too hard to hit her. Mindfreeze stood still with her hands raised in surrender, six cops pointing rifles at her. Another three kept Ray kneeling with his hands clasped behind his head. Igor the Red hadn't bothered getting up out of the hole in the road.

Kelly flew in a corkscrew pattern, climbing, diving, and zigzagging to avoid the double-threat of darkbeams and firebeams. She stayed higher than she wanted to be so a missed firebeam didn't hit any passing cars. The momentary idea of flying in a way that made Phoenix accidentally zap Nancy with a firebeam occurred to her, but she didn't want to hurt her mother's friend.

This is ridiculous. Negative Nancy has shut down the whole Aegis. Roy, Igor, and Mindfreeze seem to be able to resist Mom's emotional manipulation, but without their powers, the cops can kill them. She looped around and came in low, sliding under the semi to ambush Negative Nancy from behind, but the woman somehow sensed her coming, firing a darkbeam out the back of her head.

Kelly rolled to the right like a fighter jet, squealing as the black energy ray passed within a finger's width of her nose. She managed to recover in time to avoid crashing into the demolished police van and took cover behind it, landing on the road with her back to the armor, breathing hard.

I gotta do something about her.

She eyed the side mirror on the prisoner transport and got an idea.

"Melinda, your kid is seriously annoying. Too fast and small," said Negative Nancy, running up behind the van. "I wanna slap the heck out of her."

"Go right ahead," said Mom. "She won't feel a thing and you'll probably break your hand. Ask me how I know."

Phoenix flew into the sky, pointing his arm down at Kelly.

Negative Nancy's footsteps went to the left, heading for the corner of the van. Kelly dashed the other way, narrowly avoiding a firebeam from Phoenix hovering directly overhead. She zipped down the road in a straight line as fast as she could fly. The weird warbly-energy-buzz of a darkbeam forming in slow motion started behind her. She crashed into the truck's side mirror, tearing it off the door, then did a midair somersault with a twist so she flew backward. A long streak of black energy crept toward her, not quite three feet away from making contact. Kelly hastily brought the mirror up, holding it in the path of the approaching negative energy.

The darkbeam deflected off the mirror, somewhat back toward Nancy but too high. Kelly adjusted her aim, putting a little more than half of the beam back into the woman, knocking her over.

Kelly dropped the mirror, zipped away from another firebeam, and landed on Nancy's chest, fist cocked. "I'm really sorry, Mrs. Westcott."

Whap.

The motorcycle helmet cracked like an eggshell under her fist. Kelly's desire to merely knock the woman out appeared to have restrained her power to do exactly that. Mrs. Westcott bled a little from the nose, but didn't appear to be seriously injured. Phoenix hovered over them, hesitating, evidently not wanting to burn Nancy as well as Übergirl.

"Ah hah! Igor the Red is baaaaack." He erupted from the road, throwing chunks of pavement and dirt everywhere merely by sitting up fast.

Mindfreeze teleported behind Mom. "Game over, ma'am."

A flash of blue light leapt from Mindfreeze's forehead into the back of Mom's skull.

Phoenix blinked, dizzy for a second. "What in the... Oh, heck no. Drat, sorry about that, kid."

Kelly gasped in worry as her mother grabbed her head and fell to one knee. All the cops swayed on their feet, shaking their heads and muttering. Mom growled, curled into a ball, then flung her arms out to either side, giving off a strong pulse of mental energy.

The intense desire to flop to the ground and sob hit Kelly, but knowing her mother tried to crush her with sadness and the emotion came from the outside let her fight it off. She clenched her jaw, her whole body shaking from the effort it took to resist. Silent tears leaked down her cheeks nonetheless.

Unfortunately... everyone else collapsed to the road, sobbing.

"Mom, please stop being a bad guy," said Kelly.

"This is what you wanted, isn't it?" snapped Mom. "Your father's going to wind up in prison until you're older than I am now. What kind of daughter are you? Who *wants* to be an orphan?"

Kelly sniffled and began crying for real. "No, Mom! You're the one who changed. Why did you and Dad have to go evil? I want you guys back."

Mom glared at her.

No matter what Kelly tried to do, it wouldn't help. She felt like a total failure. No one would ever take her seriously as a hero. Her own family didn't even want her anymore.

Mom rushed by and picked the unconscious Nancy up from the road before pushing a button on her wristband, and they both disappeared in a flicker of teleportation sparkles.

"I'm just gonna stand here and let them go because I'm such a failure," whispered Kelly. She sniffled and wiped her eyes, but couldn't stop crying. "Wait. No. I'm not. Mom's making me feel like this. I let her get into my head."

Apathy faded.

Mom—and an unconscious Nancy—burst out of the ditch at the side of the road on a sleek black-and-purple motorcycle, skidding onto the highway. In a hail of dust and shrieking tires, her mother drove off across the dirt to the other lanes that led back toward civilization. Kelly couldn't bring herself to chase them, partly out of guilt, partly out of worry that Mom plus Negative Nancy taking on her alone could go bad. She doubted her mother would seriously kill her, but Negative Nancy could keep her powerless for who knows how long. Mom *definitely* would do something mean like lock her in a dungeon, safe, alive, but helpless to interfere with her plans.

To beat Mom, she'd have to do something that hurt too much to think about. She'd have to hit her... and that just felt wrong. Phoenix had a good point. She would leave arresting her parents to someone else. She'd *stop* their schemes, but she couldn't get physical with them. Punching Nancy once already felt like she'd done something super bad. If they ran away, they ran away.

Hearing Igor the Red sobbing sounded so far beyond wrong that it cheered her up enough to stop sulking. All four heroes and the cops cried like characters in movies when someone died. Several of the exoskeleton-boosted officers hugged each other for comfort, metal hands clanking on metal back-plates.

"Ugh, Mom. What did you do?"

She trudged around to the side of the trailer, and found the door open.

"Oh, crap."

Kelly ran to the door and pulled it open. A narrow hallway led to the left past four small holding cells with clear front walls. Three empties, and one with Dad sitting on a bed inside. The sight of him in an orange jumpsuit hurt more than the missile hitting her.

"Hey, sweetie," said Dad. "Having fun?"

"No, not really." She walked down the row to stand outside his cell.

"Did you decide to come to your senses and get me out of here?"

She stared down at her purple boots. "Dad, you kidnapped people and tried to mind control San Francisco."

"So? What's wrong with mind controlling San Francisco? People do that all the time. Haven't you ever heard of yoga? Vegans? Crystal healing?"

"Everything, Dad. Everything." Kelly sniffled and wiped at her cheeks. "I thought the aliens made you into a bad guy because they turned the planet into a comic book. But, Mindfreeze looked into your head. You really *did* decide to go supervillain."

"Of course. I'm a mad scientist. See, hon, the problem with inventing stuff is that society has these pesky rules and ethics. Progress has to break a few eggs on the way to greatness."

"No it doesn't, Dad. You used to tell me that the bad guy stuff was just 'blowing off steam' when we played games."

"Sure it was. Same thing now, only the game has become the world." He laughed. "All of this is a game to me."

She pressed her hands to the clear wall. "It's not a game to me. I love you. You and Mom both went evil. I can't do that. You've made me an orphan."

"Aww, sweetie." Dad stood and walked closer. "Don't be like that. Just because we play on different sides doesn't mean we don't love you. As soon as I deal with this legal mess, we'll figure it out. If you're not going to break me out of here, go on home. I've made arrangements. You don't have to go anywhere. The authorities won't come looking for you or anything."

"What? How… that doesn't make any sense. The cops aren't gonna let me live alone at nine." She stared up through her gawking reflection at him.

"Does a kid your size playing handball with a giant octopus make sense?"

"Before the aliens, I would have said no."

"There you go. If you can throw an octopus the size of a private Bermuda vacation bungalow around like a tennis ball, I can arrange things so you can live at home even if both your mother and I are otherwise occupied."

She bonked her head on the glass. "I'm gonna save you."

"Great. Door's right there." He pointed. "Smash away."

"Not that way, Dad. I mean get *you* back. Not The Brain Trust. I'm not gonna stop looking for a way to fix you."

Phoenix and Mindfreeze climbed into the trailer. The leader of the Aegis appeared worried for a second until Mindfreeze patted his shoulder, then he relaxed.

"I am simultaneously proud of and disappointed in you, Kelly," said Dad. "It's a strange feeling."

"Gonna save you, Dad," whispered Kelly, sliding her hand up to be opposite his on the glass.

"Relax," whispered Mindfreeze. "She means mentally."

"Don't worry, sweetie. You are smart and determined... and powerful as heck. I have no doubt you will succeed sooner or later. Also, don't worry about me. The Brain Trust cannot be stopped or contained for long." A loud thunderclap came out of nowhere while he laughed maniacally.

"Where on Earth did that noise come from?" asked Phoenix.

Dad held up a tiny silver box. "It's a harmless sound emitter. Made it from the toilet paper in here plus a few screws."

Kelly laughed. Of course her father could make a gadget out of something like toilet paper.

"Sorry," said Phoenix, "But we have to confiscate that."

"Of course." Dad offered the device on a raised palm.

Phoenix glanced at Mindfreeze.

"Surprising... it's not a trick." She blinked.

Phoenix typed in a code, opening the cell door.

Kelly ran in and hugged her father.

He handed the sound emitter to Phoenix, picked Kelly up, and held her tight. "It is a real change having my kid trying to ruin all of my plans instead of being excited about doing stuff together, but I still love you."

She squeezed him. In that moment, her face mushed against his chest, she would've given anything to have her parents back... even her superpowers.

Phoenix, reluctantly, tapped her on the shoulder after a few minutes.

She released the hug. "I have to go."

"Me too, kiddo. But, I'll see you soon." He winked.

It bothered her to see him not at all upset about going to jail. That made her wonder if he had a plan to escape already. She hung her head and stepped out of the cell. Phoenix shut the door. Dad resumed sitting on the bed, as calm as could be.

Kelly followed the others back to the road. Phoenix slid the transport trailer door closed. A beep indicated it locked. The cops dragged the ruined van off the side of the road, leaving it to pick up later. The transport truck had no problem starting, which got the Aegis heroes talking about Negative Nancy likely having a power to make machines stop working, too. Eventually, the eight cops plus the driver from the destroyed van got on the Aegis shuttle, since it had plenty of room.

Phoenix and Kelly flew close together above the transport, escorting it down the road. The convoy drove in a circle most of the way around the giant lake, which signs called the San Luis Reservoir, and headed south to the new prison facility about two miles south of the water.

The square buildings inside the complex all glimmered bright white, apparently made from metal. A double-layer of energy fences surrounded the place. Police guards in exoskeletons patrolled on top of a third wall made of concrete and steel. As far as she could see in all directions lay open desert.

Merely looking at the place frightened Kelly. It seemed like the sort of facility no one ever came back from.

"Whoa. That place is scary."

"It's only been there a couple days." Phoenix glided closer to her as they flew. "Alien technology built it ridiculously fast. It's a specialized corrections facility for super-powered offenders. Only three of them exist in the whole country."

"Aliens?" She gawked at him. "We are not giving Dad to aliens. I *will* break him out of that truck before I let the aliens have him. They're evil!"

"No… they only gave us the tech to build the prison. It's all operated by humans."

"Are they going to be nice to him? This one comic I read had a supers prison and it was really, really cruel."

"That's fiction, hon. The same people who run normal prisons are in charge here, too. Just more technology to deal with super powers."

The convoy stopped at the outer gate. Phoenix took Kelly's hand and glided to land nearby on the road while their shuttle set down at a safe distance. Cops in exoskeletons, Igor the Red, Bullet Man, and Mindfreeze walked down the shuttle's rear ramp. The cops followed the transport truck into the prison facility while the Aegis heroes collected outside on the road by Phoenix.

"Hanging outside?" asked Bullet Man. "Kinda got a bad feeling going into that place?"

"No." Phoenix shook his head. "There's just no reason for us to."

Kelly cringed each time the force field fence closed or reactivated with a loud buzz. When the transport truck carrying her father vanished behind the steel gate, she bowed her head. Guilt at betraying her father got into a war with not wanting to cry in front of the Aegis.

A soft hand squeezed her shoulder. "Are you okay, hon?" asked Mindfreeze.

"No. My dad's in jail and it's my fault."

"No, dear. It's his fault. You are an amazing child. Don't give up. We'll find a way to help him."

Kelly looked up at the woman. White hair framed a face of deep brown, two glowing blue energy pool eyes stared at her, radiating kindness. "But you said he really was a supervillain. The aliens aren't *making* him be bad."

"That is true. But, that doesn't mean we can't help him change." Mindfreeze squeezed her hand. "If the doctors in there determine *why* he wants to be a supervillain, it's possible they can convince him to use his inventions for the greater good rather than his personal schemes."

Men shouted random commands from inside the walls. A heavy electric motor whirred, laboring as if moving something heavy. The sound cut off a minute later with a thud that shook the ground under her boots.

"I'm not gonna give up on him." She clenched her hands into fists.

"Say it." Igor the Red slapped Phoenix on the shoulder.

The Aegis leader set his hands on his hips, shaking his head and chuckling. "Übergirl, that's twice now you've made the difference between us experiencing total failure and completing our mission. Maybe I was too quick to dismiss you for being a little kid, but I want you to know that we don't think you're weak. Only young. If something happened to you…"

"I understand." She held her chin high. "If you tell me to sit out because something really is too dangerous, I will. But I'm a lot tougher than I look."

He smiled. "We will take that into consideration. Now… about your situation. Both of your parents are absent."

"Dad said I should go home and it would be okay."

"He's a supervillain." Bullet Man shrugged. "Should anything he says be trusted?"

"Probably not." Kelly smirked. "But he might have done something bad. I need to at least go look at it. If I can't stay there, I'm going to live with my friend and her parents."

"I'll take you," said Mindfreeze.

Kelly managed a weak smile, still too sad about Dad to feel happy. "I can handle this. You guys have evil aliens to stop, remember?"

"At least call us and let us know what's going on." Igor glanced at the others. "We can share with her the number, yes?"

"I don't have a cell phone. My parents won't get me one until I'm twelve, and we don't have a house phone because… who has house phones? Wait… there's probably a phone in the lair. Every secret lair has some kind of ability to call people."

Bullet Man appeared to teleport from a few feet away right in front of her with a business card held out, a phone number already handwritten on the back. "Here, kiddo. This is our special number. Do *not* give that to anyone who isn't part of the Aegis."

Her eyes bulged in shock. That card became as valuable as *Star Prince #17*. Perhaps more so. She accepted the card, then looked up at them, mouth agape. "Does that mean I'm... you're..."

"Every group needs a mascot," said Phoenix.

Igor swatted him on the arm.

"All right. You're provisionally on the team." Phoenix offered a handshake.

"Provisionally?" Kelly shook his hand.

"That means because you're still so young, you're not *required* to do anything. You can help if you want—and it's outside school hours."

She closed her eyes to withstand the crash of happiness and guilt. Becoming a 'real' hero would have been the single most awesome moment of her life—if it didn't feel like she had to trade away her family to get it. But, her parents wouldn't be gone forever.

No matter what, Übergirl would get them back.

CHAPTER FORTY-ONE

WEAKNESS, WEAKNESS, EVERYWHERE

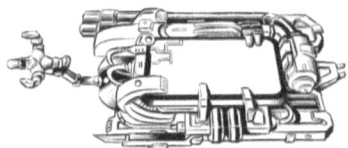

S upersonic flight did strange things.

If she rolled over on her back, she couldn't hear herself shout. Chest down, she could. It took her a moment to guess that when she faced down in the standard superhero flying pose, air coming out of her mouth went past her ears. If she flew on her back, the sound never made it to her ears because she flew forward faster than the speed of sound.

She slowed down enough not to smash every window in her neighborhood and cruised in low over her home. Except for her parents' absence, it appeared normal. Seeing the place reminded her that her mother and father wouldn't be there, which made her heartsick. But, she drowned that emotion in hope before landing and going inside. As expected, it remained empty of people. Only the various robots her father had made to do the cleaning and cooking remained. The flying spheres rotated to 'watch' her, but none did anything or spoke, likely waiting for her to ask them something.

Her bedroom looked as expected, everything where it should be: no damage, no fires, no kidnapped friends tied to bombs. If she tried to pretend real hard, she could almost make believe she *didn't* have superpowers and her parents were downstairs getting dinner ready while Dad complained about his job and Mom patted herself on the back for making a big sale.

I'd let Alexis Stephens throw me in the garbage every day for the rest of my life if I could get my parents back.

Sadly, despite superpowers having become reality, wish-making still didn't work.

Sorrow, anger, excitement, worry, and grief mixed, leaving her feeling not much of anything but blah. Kelly headed downstairs and went to the backyard, approaching the tool shed. Despite expecting an error buzz, she tried the palm reader anyway. It chirped happily.

"Wow. Mom didn't lock me out? No 'supervillain lair is for supervillains' thing?"

She stepped inside.

Shoomp!

After a quick look around among the various corridors, chambers, and rooms, she didn't find anything dangerous or scary. No kidnapped people, no half-made doomsday device, or even the hint that he had started some other project. The place felt... dormant. As if Dad knew he'd be gone for a while and made everything nice and neat.

She sighed.

In the command and control room, she flopped in Dad's big chair. His mega-tablet had somehow made it back here, sitting on the desk. The computer let her log in with a hand-scan, so she spent a while searching among his files, looking for anything that might explain why he'd chosen to go supervillain.

She found folders with test data. One for her, one for Mom, and one for Nancy Westcott. Nancy's folder didn't contain any information.

The machines probably didn't work on her.

Mom's folder had information about her powers, largely based on emotional manipulation, though she had become modestly tougher than a normal person, able to shrug off small bullets. Her mother could know whatever emotion people around her experienced at any given moment, and change their mood if she wanted. Dad's tests recorded that the effects appeared to last only a few minutes after she left the area; however, she also had the ability to make permanent changes on norms who had no superpowers. Apparently, Mom and Dad used Alexis Stephens' parents as test subjects. Mom permanently altered their emotional reaction to their daughter, turning them from horrible parents to being completely overwhelmed with love at the mere sight of her.

Apparently, Mom did this because she'd been angry at how Alexis had treated Kelly for so long. She had planned to attack the girl directly, making her constantly terrified of everything, but when Kelly told her about what she'd seen at their house, Mom shifted the blame for Alexis being a bully onto the parents as much as the girl. The file didn't say anything about Mom doing anything to Alexis, though the girl *did* seem much more timid lately. But that could have come from being confused at the drastic change in her parents.

According to Dad's notes, Mom chose the name Emophage because the ending –phage meant devourer. Mom called herself the 'devourer of emotions,' more or less.

The story of her mother being a high school bully and ruining like five people's lives made Kelly sick to her stomach. Well, perhaps she didn't ruin their *whole* lives, but made the rest of high school horrible and destroyed what could have been lifelong friendships. Being dumped in a giant sloppy garbage can and thrown down a hill a few times a week was nothing compared to having all your friends start hating you and everyone thinking you did something super bad.

Dad didn't self-analyze much, but he did have some notes that admitted to his having no clue at all how he made stuff or where the materials to make them even came from. He had apparently also gained a small amount of superhuman toughness, as well as near immunity to poisons and acid. As far as making stuff went, whenever he got an idea, he would somehow manage to find whatever parts he needed. Complex or rare things took much longer. The MICE serum, for example, required a specific chemical he couldn't simply pull out of… wherever. So, he made another machine to open holes in walls, allowing Bob and Zorthax to physically steal the chemical. Dad even had a note 'Why would Kelly think it's weird that we have an 800-gallon tank of nitric acid?'

"Kelly," said Mom—right behind her.

She shrieked at being surprised, and spun.

Mom stood beside the chair, barefoot, wearing sweat pants and a dark blue T-shirt. Only, she didn't look *quite* right. Thin lines marked her face by her mouth, her eyes gave off a faint amount of amber light, and her skin looked too pale.

"Umm… You're not my mother."

"That's right, sweetie," said the woman. "I am an android made to look like her that your father created in the event you needed someone to take care of you while your parents were away or if anything more permanently bad happened to them. Until further notice, you are to regard me as your parent. I have been informed that you have a difference of opinion with your biological parents regarding good and evil."

"Yeah…" Kelly took a step back, expecting a trap.

"I suffer from no such attraction to good or evil. My only desire is to be your guardian and caretaker. I expect you to follow rules, do as you're told, and behave yourself."

"Wait… you *don't* want me to break rules?"

"Of course not. What kind of mother wants their child to be disobedient?"

Kelly whistled. "One who has issues. So... you're Robo-Mom?"

"It would make me feel better if you just called me 'Mom,' but I would understand your need to separate your biological mother from me. Perhaps you could refer to me as 'Mom' and the other woman as 'bio-mom' until such time as her mental state returns to being a proper caregiver."

"That could work. I still think she loves me."

"She does, but, for example, I would never put you in a deathtrap."

"Okay. That's a big plus. How do I know this isn't a trick?"

Robo-Mom scratched her head. "I suppose you don't. You will have to trust your father really loves you."

"I do. He's just... going through a hard time right now."

"That's true."

"Can I try something?" asked Kelly.

"Will I ground you for it?"

"No."

"Then okay."

Kelly walked around the chair and hugged the robot. Surprisingly, she felt warm, also squishy like actual Mom. "Guess you're why Dad says I can stay home. People will think you're Mom."

"Correct." Robo-Mom patted her back. "I am glad you're safe, sweetie. I will be here for you all day, by the way. Your father made sure we have enough money to survive for a long time."

"He stole it, didn't he?"

"Perhaps some... he did sell a few inventions to the government. I don't know the particulars of where it all came from."

"Isn't it wrong to steal money? We shouldn't use it."

"The money he acquired through suspicious means came from wealthy corporations who won't miss it and are arguably more evil than your father has become. Besides, you can't return it since you don't know where it came from. And, you're only nine years old and have no access to the bank accounts."

Kelly stuck out her tongue.

"Speaking of your being nine, it's bedtime."

"It's only 8:35 p.m. Bio-mom let me stay up until nine if I wasn't too tired. And I haven't eaten much today. Can I have dinner please?"

"All right. Go get changed and wash your hands."

"Okay."

She ran down the hall to the elevator, *shoomped* to the surface, and flew into the house via her bedroom window. A gem tap on the ZOOM bracelet shifted her costume back to her T-shirt and scorched jeans, which she traded for her nightgown. After washing her hands, she went downstairs.

Bob and Zorthax sat on the couch watching television.

"Whoa." Kelly stopped short at the bottom of the stairs, one hand on the railing, one foot still on the step behind her. "What are you guys doing here?"

"The boss said we can stay here while he's away." Zorthax smiled at her.

"We're going to help protect you. That's our job now." Bob appeared thrilled.

Kelly smiled. "Cool."

She padded down the hall to the kitchen where a sphere-bot set a plate of chicken nuggets and fries on the table. Kelly squinted, pulling a nugget open to check for suspicious veggie particles, but the food appeared to be legit. Smelled good, too.

Robo-Mom walked in via the patio glass and sat at the table with her. "I know this might take some getting used to, but I'm probably the most advanced AI on Earth right now. You can talk to me like you spoke to your mother before she changed."

"Okay. I'm worried about Dad."

"I am, too."

"Do you think I did the right thing or should I have helped him instead?"

Robo-Mom patted her on the hand. "It's a difficult situation with no easy answers. As your mother, I want you to do the right thing. Act with empathy and kindness. If you ask me, you did the right thing even though it was extremely difficult, and certainly not a choice a child your age should ever have to make."

"Well... superheroes. How many kids my age have to worry about an alien invasion and can fly as fast as a fighter jet?"

Mom gazed into space. "Probability suggests there are approximately 154 million people on the planet with superpowers. That is roughly two percent of the population. Assuming an even distribution of powers with no relationship to age, that would be around ten to thirteen million children nine or younger with powers. There isn't enough information to predict how many of that group can fly at all, or fly as fast as a supersonic aircraft. Your second condition, worrying about an alien invasion would apply to everyone on the planet so it's meaningless."

"Mom?" asked Kelly.

"Yes?"

"Did you mean to sound like a robot?"

"Oh... sorry." She leaned her elbows on the table, smiling. "I don't imagine there are too many kids in your position."

Kelly grinned.

After she ate, Kelly went upstairs to her bedroom. Given that she *just* ate, Robo-Mom let her stay up a little longer so the food settled. She passed the time reading the newest *Waif* series novel. Eventually, her replacement mom walked in.

"All right, sweetie. Lights out. Go brush your teeth and get ready for bed."

"I'm not really tired. I have stuff to do, like saving my parents."

Robo-Mom approached the bed, half-smirking. "Don't make me use the salad-shooter."

"The what?" Kelly blinked.

The robot pointed at her with an index finger that split open to reveal a small barrel resembling a handgun. "This fires a vegetable based goop that will render you powerless for a short time. While you are temporarily a normal child, you will be subject to discipline."

Kelly gasped. "You're not gonna strap me to the Murdermaster-3000 again are you?"

"Of course not!" Robo-Mom looked horrified. Her finger-gun closed. "I meant being grounded, time outs, that sort of thing. But I would much prefer that you don't. My memories—even though they are artificial—suggest you are abnormally well-behaved for a child your age. Occasional small white lies are to be expected from any kid."

"Oh, whew." Kelly wiped the sweat off her forehead. "And that's really super lame."

"What is?" asked Robo-Mom.

"Why did I have to get stuck with a superhero weakness on something *so* common? Vegetables are *everywhere*. Why couldn't it be something like fragments of a destroyed alien planet from ten thousand light years away?"

Mom raised an eyebrow. "You mean the supposedly rare alien rocks that every villain seems to have no problem whatsoever finding tons of?"

Kelly grumbled. "Yeah."

"C'mon. You need to go to sleep. Go brush and get ready. How were the chicken nuggets?"

She closed her book and jumped off the bed. "Pretty good... but you didn't make them, the ball-bot did."

Robo-Mom tapped her head. "Wireless. I can take control of any robot in the house. You bet your little behind *I* made them."

"Cool." Kelly smiled.

Okay... maybe this won't suck.

"Umm. Can I make a call real quick? I forgot to tell the Aegis everything is okay here."

"Sure." Robo-Mom handed over a cell phone. "And after this, you *will* stop stalling. It's already twenty minutes past your bedtime."

"Okay, Mom."

CHAPTER FORTY-TWO

NOT WORTH IT

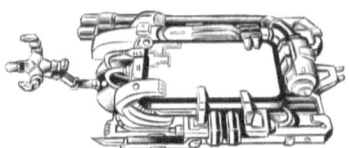

Glowing star stickers covered Kelly's purple ceiling, emitting faint greenish light.

Staring at them made her feel like the worst daughter in the world, remembering the Saturday that she and Dad put them up two years ago. A ladder would have made too much sense for that man, so he'd boosted her up to stand on his shoulders. At least until Mom saw this and sent him to the store to buy a ladder.

She wondered what kind of ceiling her father would be staring at. Would he be in a painfully bright cell with a glass wall instead of bars and concrete everywhere else? Or would it all be shiny steel? He'd probably like that. Everything Dad made, from the house robots to the Murdermaster-3000 had been chromed to a mirror finish.

"I'm sorry, Dad. But you hurt people." Kelly sighed. "The world's gone nuts. How long is it going to take before someone realizes I'm nine and basically living alone?" She didn't expect Zorthax or Bob would do much more than provide physical protection. "I don't care if I'm small. I'm gonna do something about the aliens. Gonna help you guys."

Kelly closed her eyes and daydreamed about flying to the school, tearing that enormous crystal from the ground, and tossing it out into space. Maybe if she got rid of all the crystals, the planet would go back to normal. Even if it meant she lost her superpowers and went back to being a normal geeky kid who bullies tossed headfirst into giant trashcans, she'd do it to get her parents back. That stuff about the Earth's magnetic field collapsing had to be a lie.

Being Übergirl exceeded all expectations of awesome, but not if she had to lose her parents in order to have powers.

Even more than flying or being so strong and tough, she wanted to curl up on the sofa with her not-a-supervillain parents and watch a movie, hear Dad laugh, have Mom fussing with her hair. She used to like Dad's laugh, but he hadn't done it often enough... always in a bad mood over his job. Now, he laughed way too often, and not in a good way either. Especially with that stupid thunder sound effect.

Robo-Mom walked in. "Hi, Sweetie."

Kelly peered up at the near-perfect copy of her mother. Dad even gave the robot her mother's warm, caring expression. Seeing that made her realize how scheming and cold her real mother had gradually become since the crystals. If the two Moms stood next to each other, she could've told them apart simply by the look in their eyes even without the mild robotic features of the duplicate. It hurt to think that the kinder looking woman had a literal heart of steel—or whatever he'd made it from.

"Your little buddy misses you." Robo-Mom set Floppet under Kelly's left arm, then tucked her in.

Kelly stared into the machine's faintly-glowing amber eyes with the oddest sense that her real mother might be watching her. "I love you, Mom. And I miss you. If you guys can't stop being evil on your own, I'll save you."

Robo-Mom put a hand over her heart, her expression sad. After a moment, she brushed at Kelly's hair. "Don't do anything foolish, sweetie. I want you to stay safe. You're still a kid. Now go to sleep."

"Night, Mom." Kelly smiled. "Oh, and I might still be a kid... but I am Übergirl."

fin

ACKNOWLEDGMENTS

A few years ago, James Wymore asked me to write a short story for an anthology he was curating for his *Actuator* world. The first story I wrote for this anthology fit my wheelhouse of being a cyberpunk tale. By the time his second *Actuator* anthology was ready for submissions, things had changed. The setting had exploded into a genre free-for-all and the new short story had to be a genre-mix up.

Up to that point, I hadn't cared much for mixing stuff around, but for whatever reason, I allowed James to talk me into writing the short *The Ruin of Man*. It remains the strangest thing I have yet written, a story where a high elf ranger picks up six guns in the Old West and teams up with a steampunk tinker, a vampire, and… Übergirl.

A character that started as part of a genre clash short story stuck with me. For years, I'd had the idea to spin her off into a series of her own gnawing at me and it took me a while to figure out how to make her story stand by itself without the background of the *Actuator* universe. When I finally got the idea (that you just read), I bounced it off him and he seemed excited to see where it went.

So, with much excitement, thank you to James Wymore for ultimately inspiring the Ubergirl character.

Also, thank you for reading this book!

Additional thanks to Ricky Gunawan for the cover art and interior art.

Many thanks to Lee Sheridan for editing.

The Story will continue in *Aliens Ate My Homework*

ABOUT THE AUTHOR

Originally from South Amboy NJ, Matthew has been creating science fiction and fantasy worlds for most of his reasoning life. Since 1996, he has developed the "Divergent Fates" world, in which *Division Zero, Virtual Immortality, The Awakened Series, The Harmony Paradox, and the Daughter of Mars series* take place. Along with being an editor at Curiosity Quills press, he has worked in IT and technical support.

Matthew is an avid gamer, a recovered WoW addict, Gamemaster for two custom RPG systems, and a fan of anime, British humour, and intellectual science fiction that questions the nature of reality, life, and what happens after it.

He is also fond of cats.

Visit me online at:

Facebook: https://www.facebook.com/MatthewSCoxAuthor
Amazon: https://www.amazon.com/author/mscox
Pinterest: https://www.pinterest.com/matthewcox10420/
Goodreads: https://www.goodreads.com/author/show/7712730.Matthew_S_Cox
Email: mcox2112@gmail.com

OTHER BOOKS BY MATTHEW S. COX

Divergent Fates Universe Novels

Division Zero series

- Division Zero
- Lex De Mortuis
- Thrall
- Guardian
- Harbinger

The Awakened series

- Prophet of the Badlands
- Archon's Queen
- Grey Ronin
- Daughter of Ash
- Zero Rogue
- Angel Descended

Daughter of Mars series

- The Hand of Raziel
- Araphel
- Ghost Black

Virtual Immortality series

- Virtual Immortality
- The Harmony Paradox

Prophet of the Badlands Series

- Prophet's Journey

Divergent Fates Anthology

- Of Myth and Shadow
- The Girl Who Found the Sun

Winter Solstice series (with J.R. Rain)

- Convergence
- Containment
- Catalyst

Alexis Silver series (with J.R. Rain)

- Silver Light
- Deep Silver
- Silver Quarrel

Samantha Moon Origins series (with J.R. Rain)

- New Moon Rising
- Moon Mourning

Vampire For Hire series (with J.R. Rain)

- Moon Master
- Dead Moon
- Lost Moon

Maddy Wimsey series (with J.R. Rain)

- The Devil's Eye
- The Drifting Gloom
- Dark Mercy

Samantha Moon Case Files series (with J.R. Rain)

- Blood Moon

Immortal Operative series (with J.R. Rain)

- Broken Ice

Four Elements series (with J.R. Rain)

- The Elementalist

- The Black Rose
- The Wakefield Curse

Young Adult Novels

The Eldritch Heart Series

- The Eldritch Heart
- The Cursed Crown

Evergreen Series

- Evergreen
- The World That Remains
- The Lucky Ones
- Nuclear Summer

Standalones

- Caller 107
- The Summer the World Ended
- Nine Candles of Deepest Black
- The Forest Beyond the Earth
- Out of Sight

Middle Grade Novels

The Adventures of Ubergirl series

- My Dad is a Mad Scientist
- Aliens Ate My Homework
- The End of all Halloweens

Tales of Widowswood series

- Emma and the Banderwigh
- Emma and the Silk Thieves
- Emma and the Silverbell Faeries
- Emma and the Elixir of Madness

- Emma and the Weeping Spirit

Standalones

- Citadel: The Concordant Sequence
- The Cursed Codex
- The Menagerie of Jenkins Bailey